IN VITAM MORTEM

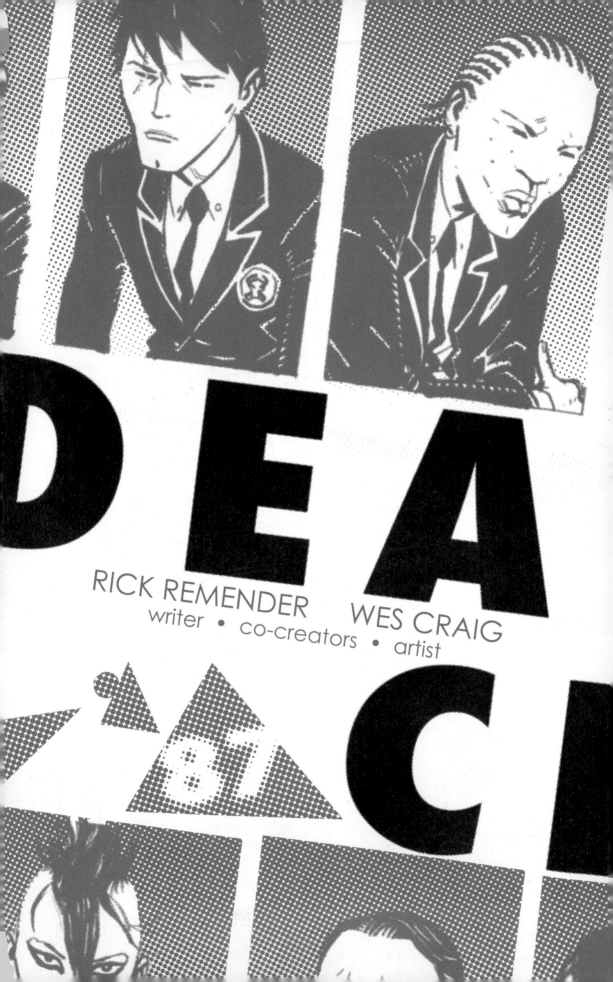

RICK REMENDER   WES CRAIG
writer   •   co-creators   •   artist

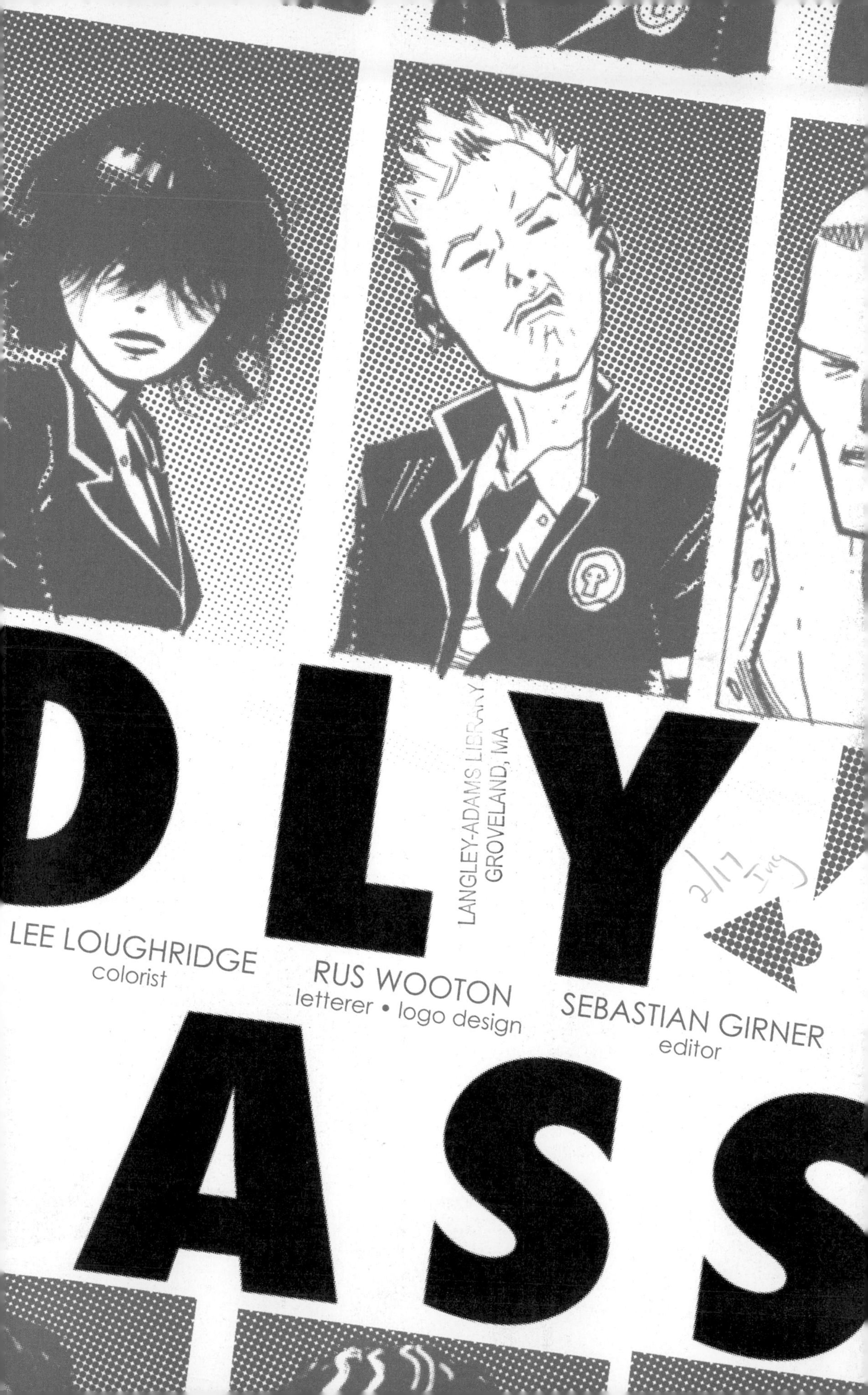
D LY
A S S

LEE LOUGHRIDGE
colorist

RUS WOOTON
letterer • logo design

SEBASTIAN GIRNER
editor

INTRODUCTION

In order for you to have hated high school so much there have to be others out there who loved it. I mean, right? Somebody was having a grand time at this place that you're forced to go to, can't leave, and no one of authority takes you seriously, all while a rigid social order is being established so that the cream of the crop can crush everyone beneath them. What's that sound like? Life? No... In real life, you can leave. You can call a cop...or a lawyer. No one comes to your cubicle at work and rams your head into your computer screen. So, what's that sound like? Like prison, right? Yeah...and they hold reunions for this place, so people can gather from all over to remember the best time of their lives. Well, at least it wasn't boring, I guess...

To be fair, I met my wife in high school. I was a definite bottom-of-the-totem-pole kind of guy, and she was definitely not. It was social suicide for her to be with me. Luckily, I was on the verge of graduation and my wife, though a couple grades younger, is a genius and managed to get out of the concrete nut house and start going to college early. Neither of us is racing to our reunions.

So Rick Remender has dug into his personal bag of horrors, which, if you've read his editorials, sound pretty damn horrible, and brought us this *Deadly Class*—A high school for assassins which, except for a little killing here and there, is just like regular school. In fact, if you just read all the killing as a physical expression of a mental and emotional state of mind, it really is high school, which is enough.

Being a memoir of sorts wrapped in the guise of a crime thriller (or vice versa), the story is set in the 1980s. It's steeped in the music and pop culture of that decade. For myself, who also grew up at that time, it's another layer of reality that sucks me back into my own nightmares. It's also a reminder of how alone and desperate it feels to be a kid. The fact that teens being taught to kill would care so much to love or hate a particular band or movie director just tells us how much we're all searching to connect to each other, even as we act out with harsh words, social humiliation, idiotic behavior...or by simply bashing someone's head in with a lead pipe.

Our main boy is Marcus—an outcast even among outcasts. I don't know Mr. Remender well enough to tell you if he's the author's stand-in, but I can tell you he's the perfect, absolute bottom-of -the-totem-pole character. Marcus has no parents, which, of course, is the single biggest factor in determining the pecking order of high school. He also has a distinct inability to conform to the rules of etiquette within the social structure of school and even within his own clique of bottom-of-the-barrel outcasts. He wants friends, he needs them but listens more to the voice in his head than to his friends. This may be because an element of the story is that Marcus might be a psychopath, but as one who spent a lot of time in his own head, I can tell you it's probably just another layer of self-sabotage.

Like many at the bottom of the shit pile, though, Marcus has two things going for him: an instinct for survival and a big dream. For Marcus that big dream is revenge. Not just any revenge though. Marcus wants to kill Ronald Reagan—our puppet-headed President during the 1980s—whose best day came as an actor in 1942's *King's Row* but as President, became a symbol for many as where it all went wrong. As hysterical as his declaring ketchup to be a school-worthy vegetable was, his equally head-scratching policies that led to mental institutions dumping the deranged on the street resulted in tragedy, especially for Marcus.

Remender has enlisted an impressive team for this sideways trip down memory lane. Artist Wes Craig makes each character distinctive and youthful, and he delivers the action with amazing fluidity. He also draws a hell of an acid trip. While wholly his own artist, there are nods in his style to the great eighties period cartoonists like Frank Miller and Steve Rude among others. Letterer Rus Wooton chose a style that takes a page from John Workman's brilliant work on Simonson's *Thor*, again from that era.

I've worked with colorist Lee Loughridge on countless projects because Lee is one of the best. His work here on *Deadly Class* is stellar. Like a great film score he carries the mood, and again we have the period. Don't think we don't notice he's using an old school, flat color approach (personally, my favorite) like a Glynis Oliver or Klaus Janson, where the brilliance lies in choosing the right colors to lie next to each other to create mood and effect rather than just rendering everything to mud.

I think it's clear that this band of outcasts has a plan.

It's an evil plan, but it's also a damn good one.

David Lapham
Carefree, AZ
June 2014

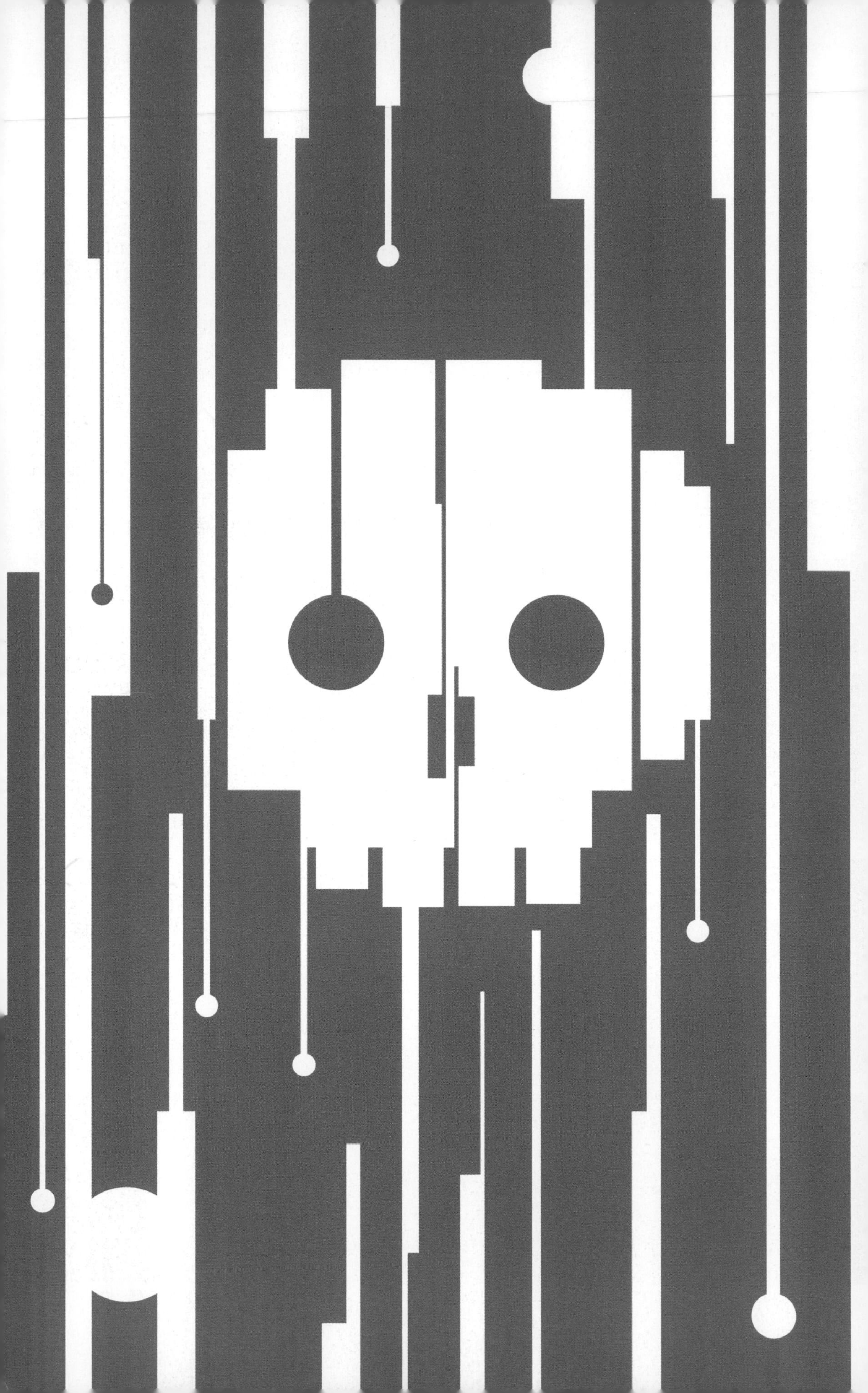

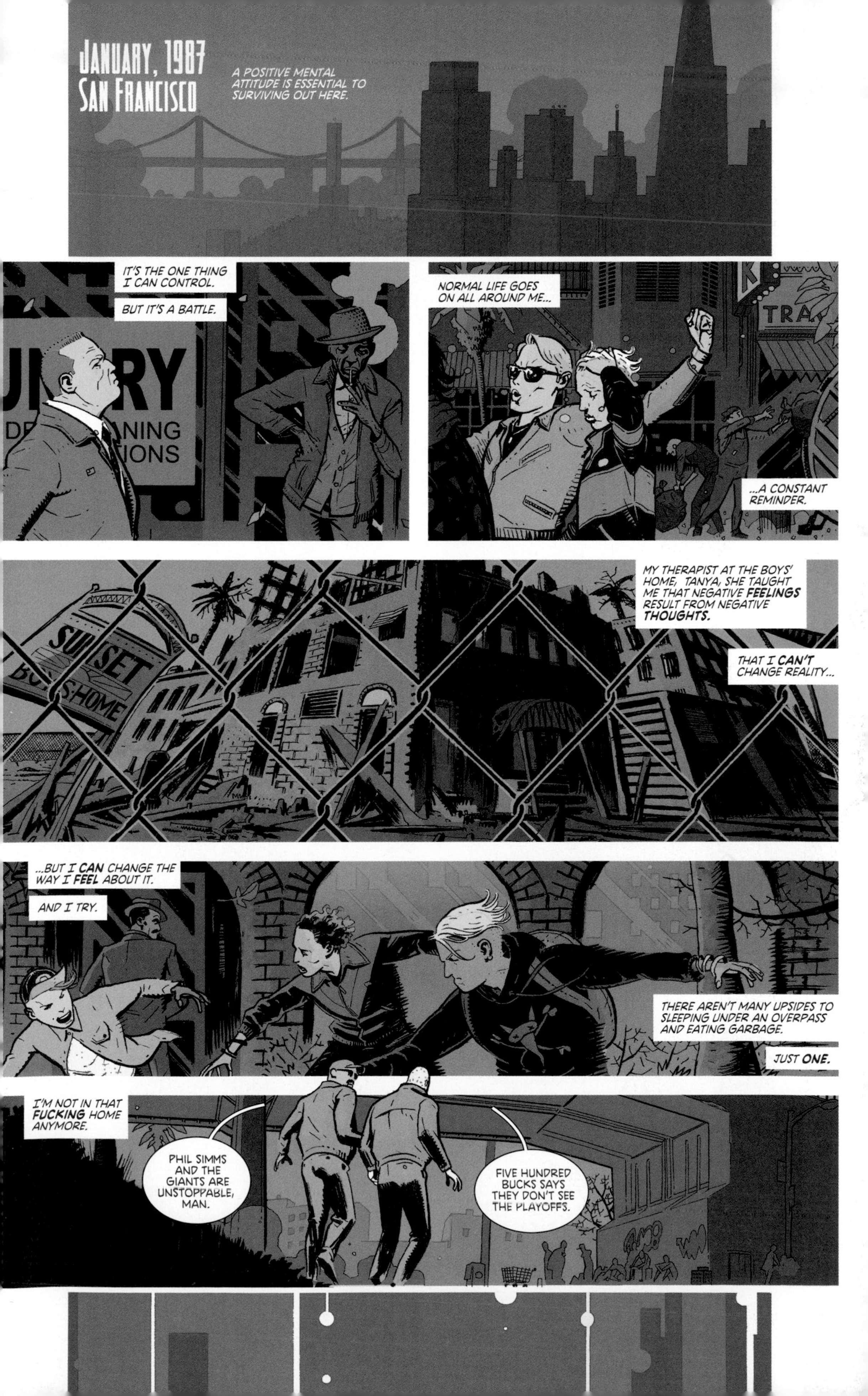

JANUARY, 1987
SAN FRANCISCO
A POSITIVE MENTAL ATTITUDE IS ESSENTIAL TO SURVIVING OUT HERE.
IT'S THE ONE THING I CAN CONTROL.
BUT IT'S A BATTLE.
NORMAL LIFE GOES ON ALL AROUND ME...
...A CONSTANT REMINDER.
MY THERAPIST AT THE BOYS' HOME, TANYA, SHE TAUGHT ME THAT NEGATIVE FEELINGS RESULT FROM NEGATIVE THOUGHTS.
THAT I CAN'T CHANGE REALITY...
SUNSET BOYS HOME
...BUT I CAN CHANGE THE WAY I FEEL ABOUT IT.
AND I TRY.
THERE AREN'T MANY UPSIDES TO SLEEPING UNDER AN OVERPASS AND EATING GARBAGE.
JUST ONE.
I'M NOT IN THAT FUCKING HOME ANYMORE.
PHIL SIMMS AND THE GIANTS ARE UNSTOPPABLE, MAN.
FIVE HUNDRED BUCKS SAYS THEY DON'T SEE THE PLAYOFFS.

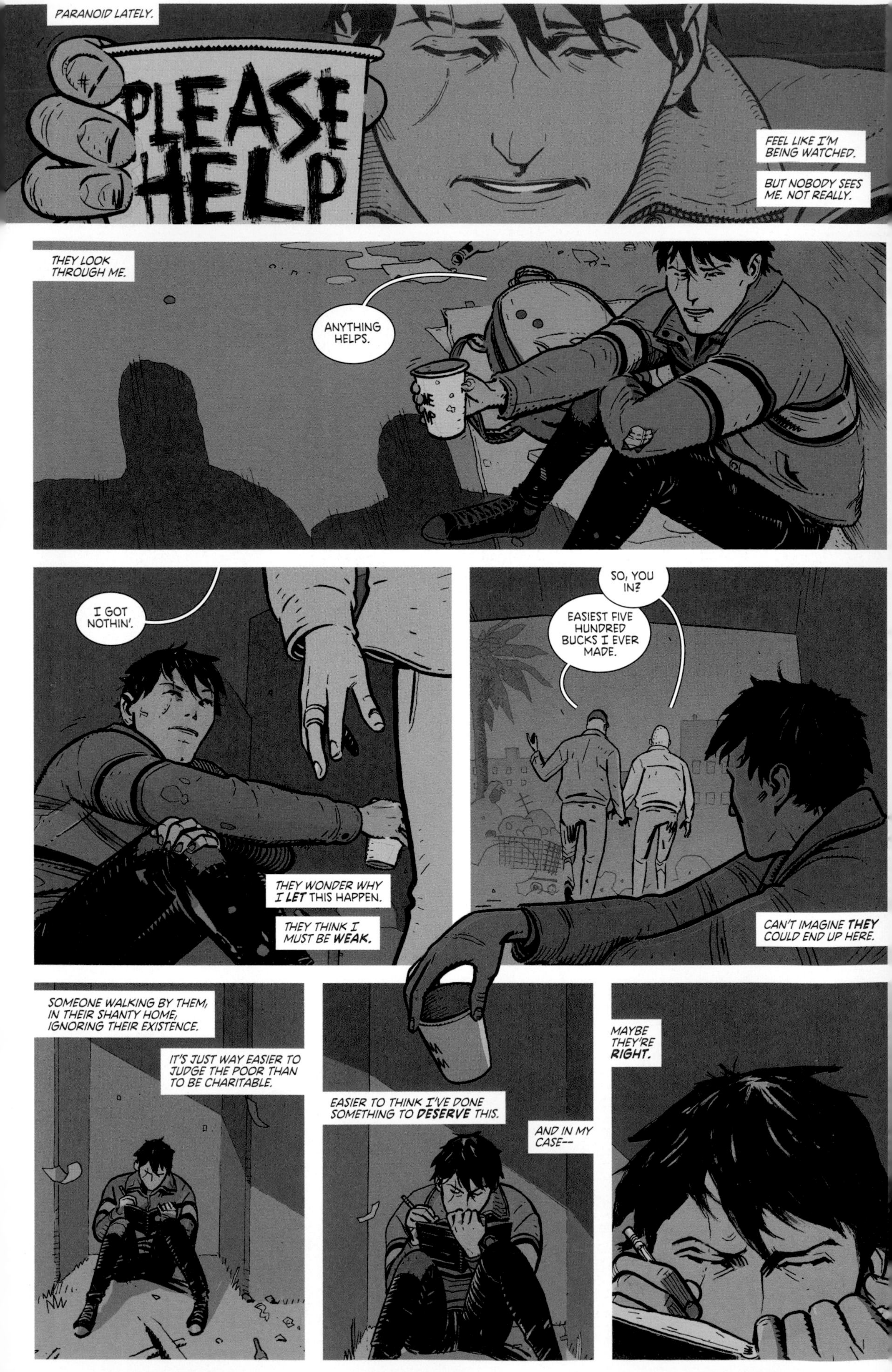
PARANOID LATELY.
PLEASE HELP
FEEL LIKE I'M BEING WATCHED.
BUT NOBODY SEES ME. NOT REALLY.
THEY LOOK THROUGH ME.
ANYTHING HELPS.
I GOT NOTHIN'.
THEY WONDER WHY I LET THIS HAPPEN.
THEY THINK I MUST BE WEAK.
SO, YOU IN?
EASIEST FIVE HUNDRED BUCKS I EVER MADE.
CAN'T IMAGINE THEY COULD END UP HERE.
SOMEONE WALKING BY THEM, IN THEIR SHANTY HOME, IGNORING THEIR EXISTENCE.
IT'S JUST WAY EASIER TO JUDGE THE POOR THAN TO BE CHARITABLE.
EASIER TO THINK I'VE DONE SOMETHING TO DESERVE THIS.
AND IN MY CASE--
MAYBE THEY'RE RIGHT.

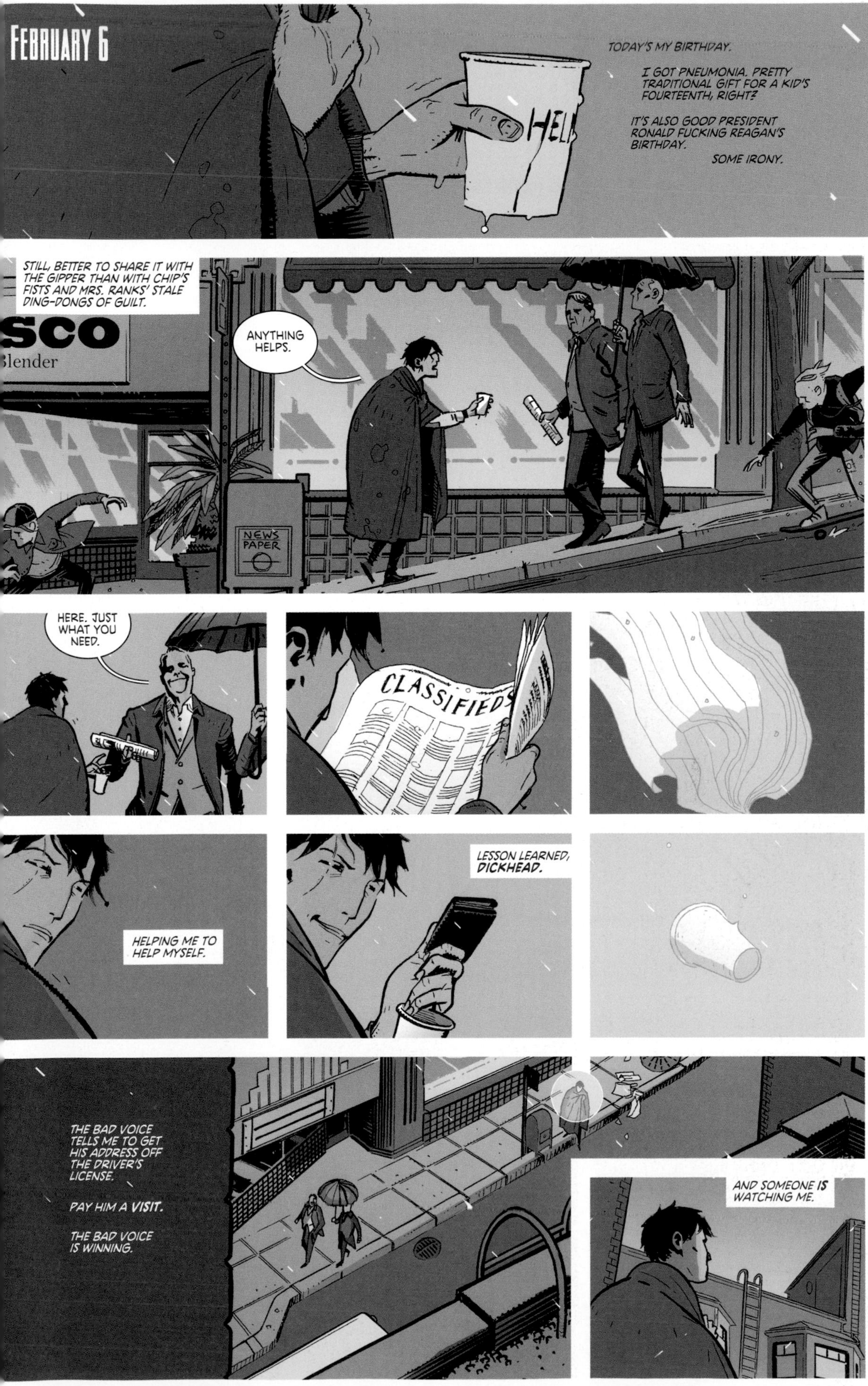
FEBRUARY 6
HELP
TODAY'S MY BIRTHDAY.
I GOT PNEUMONIA. PRETTY TRADITIONAL GIFT FOR A KID'S FOURTEENTH, RIGHT?
IT'S ALSO GOOD PRESIDENT RONALD FUCKING REAGAN'S BIRTHDAY.
SOME IRONY.
STILL, BETTER TO SHARE IT WITH THE GIPPER THAN WITH CHIP'S FISTS AND MRS. RANKS' STALE DING-DONGS OF GUILT.
SCO
Blender
ANYTHING HELPS.
NEWS PAPER
HERE. JUST WHAT YOU NEED.
CLASSIFIEDS
HELPING ME TO HELP MYSELF.
LESSON LEARNED, **DICKHEAD.**
THE BAD VOICE TELLS ME TO GET HIS ADDRESS OFF THE DRIVER'S LICENSE.
PAY HIM A **VISIT.**
THE BAD VOICE IS WINNING.
AND SOMEONE **IS** WATCHING ME.

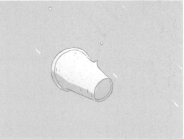

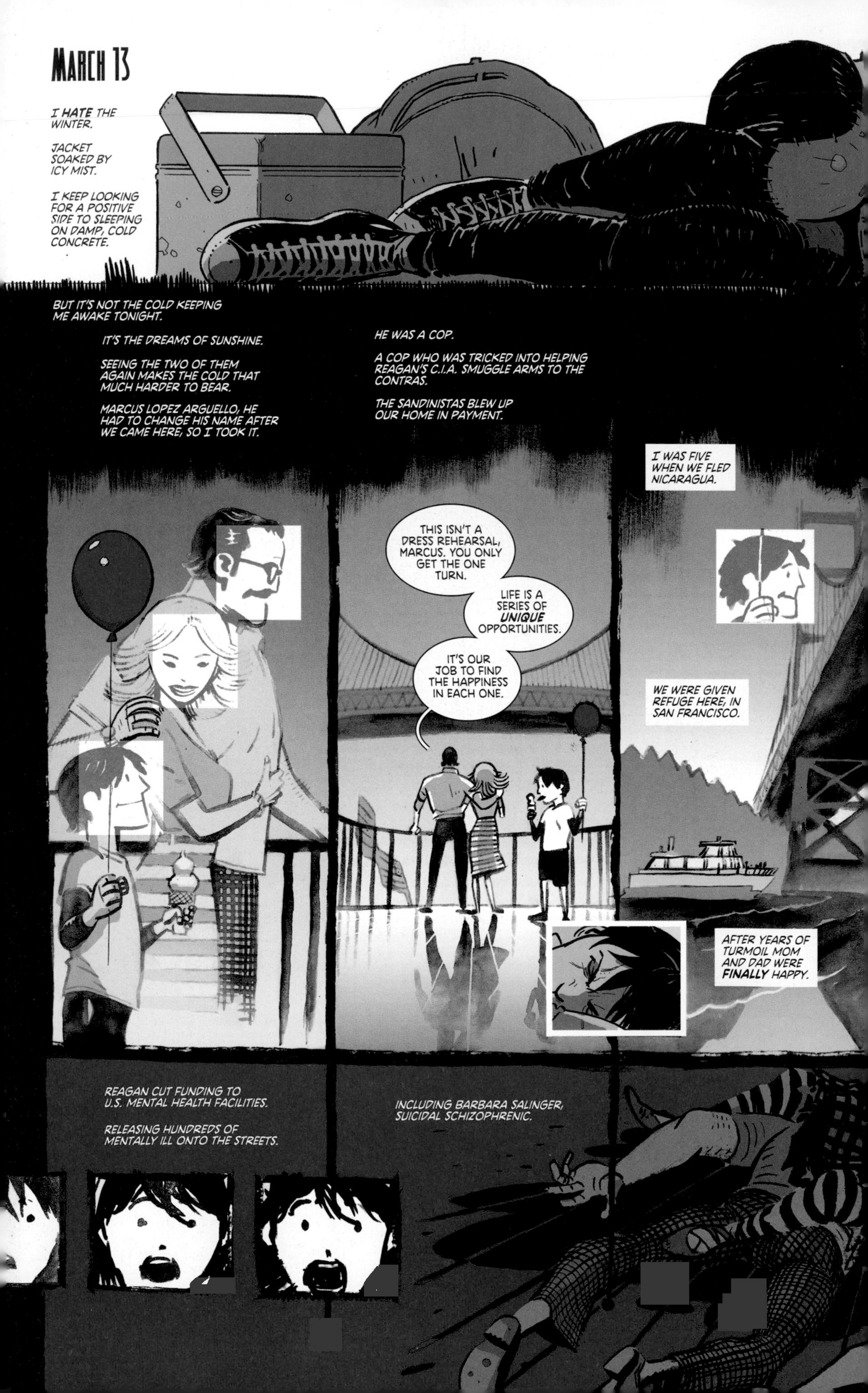
MARCH 13
I HATE THE WINTER.
JACKET SOAKED BY ICY MIST.
I KEEP LOOKING FOR A POSITIVE SIDE TO SLEEPING ON DAMP, COLD CONCRETE.
BUT IT'S NOT THE COLD KEEPING ME AWAKE TONIGHT.
IT'S THE DREAMS OF SUNSHINE.
SEEING THE TWO OF THEM AGAIN MAKES THE COLD THAT MUCH HARDER TO BEAR.
MARCUS LOPEZ ARGUELLO, HE HAD TO CHANGE HIS NAME AFTER WE CAME HERE, SO I TOOK IT.
HE WAS A COP.
A COP WHO WAS TRICKED INTO HELPING REAGAN'S C.I.A. SMUGGLE ARMS TO THE CONTRAS.
THE SANDINISTAS BLEW UP OUR HOME IN PAYMENT.
I WAS FIVE WHEN WE FLED NICARAGUA.
THIS ISN'T A DRESS REHEARSAL, MARCUS. YOU ONLY GET THE ONE TURN.
LIFE IS A SERIES OF UNIQUE OPPORTUNITIES.
IT'S OUR JOB TO FIND THE HAPPINESS IN EACH ONE.
WE WERE GIVEN REFUGE HERE, IN SAN FRANCISCO.
AFTER YEARS OF TURMOIL MOM AND DAD WERE FINALLY HAPPY.
REAGAN CUT FUNDING TO U.S. MENTAL HEALTH FACILITIES.
RELEASING HUNDREDS OF MENTALLY ILL ONTO THE STREETS.
INCLUDING BARBARA SALINGER, SUICIDAL SCHIZOPHRENIC.

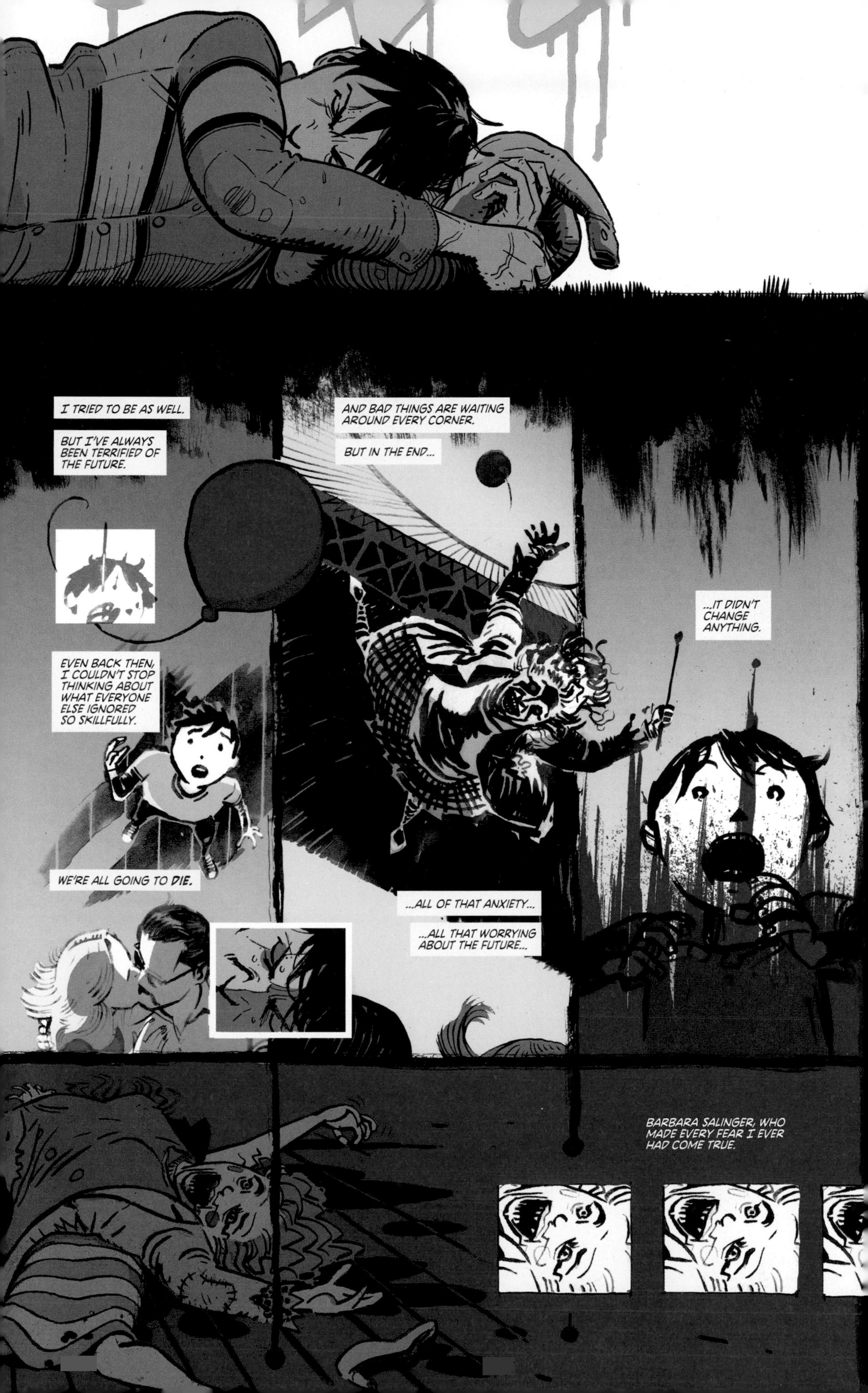
I TRIED TO BE AS WELL.
BUT I'VE ALWAYS BEEN TERRIFIED OF THE FUTURE.
EVEN BACK THEN, I COULDN'T STOP THINKING ABOUT WHAT EVERYONE ELSE IGNORED SO SKILLFULLY.
WE'RE ALL GOING TO DIE.
AND BAD THINGS ARE WAITING AROUND EVERY CORNER.
BUT IN THE END...
...ALL OF THAT ANXIETY...
...ALL THAT WORRYING ABOUT THE FUTURE...
...IT DIDN'T CHANGE ANYTHING.
BARBARA SALINGER, WHO MADE EVERY FEAR I EVER HAD COME TRUE.

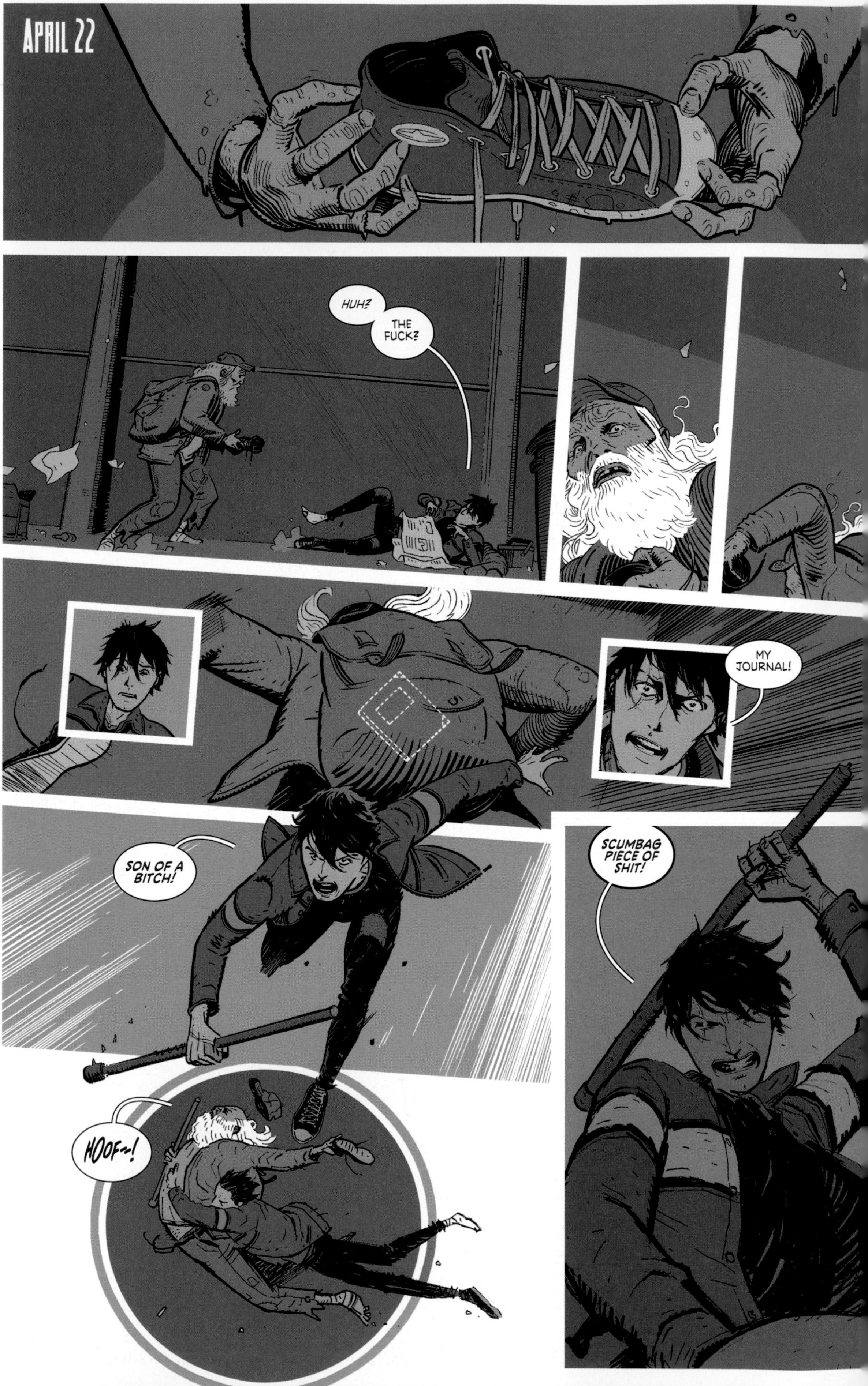
April 22
HUH?
THE FUCK?
MY JOURNAL!
SON OF A BITCH!
SCUMBAG PIECE OF SHIT!
HOOF--!

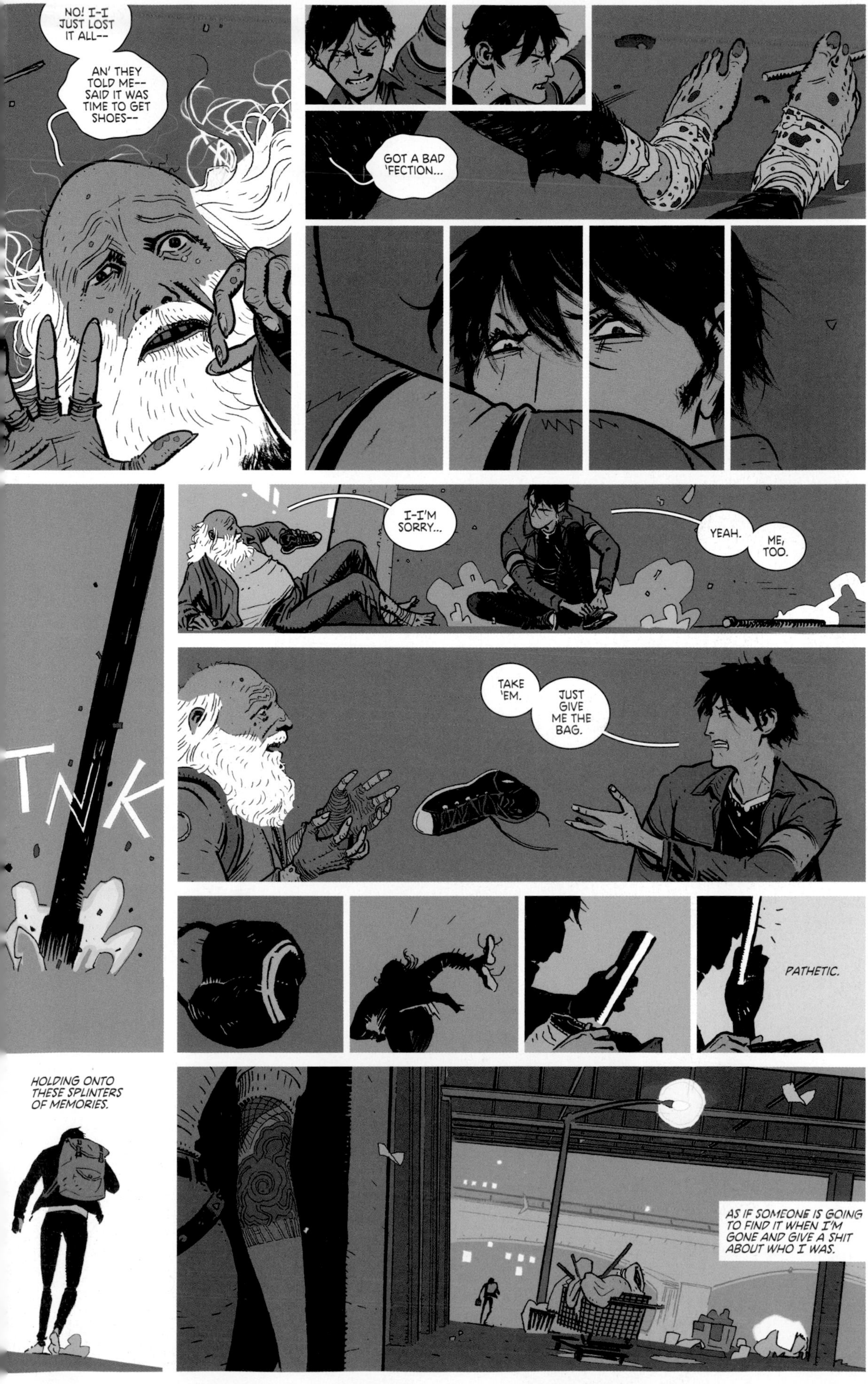
NO! I-I JUST LOST IT ALL--
AN' THEY TOLD ME-- SAID IT WAS TIME TO GET SHOES--
GOT A BAD 'FECTION...
I-I'M SORRY...
YEAH.
ME, TOO.
TNK
TAKE 'EM.
JUST GIVE ME THE BAG.
PATHETIC.
HOLDING ONTO THESE SPLINTERS OF MEMORIES.
AS IF SOMEONE IS GOING TO FIND IT WHEN I'M GONE AND GIVE A SHIT ABOUT WHO I WAS.

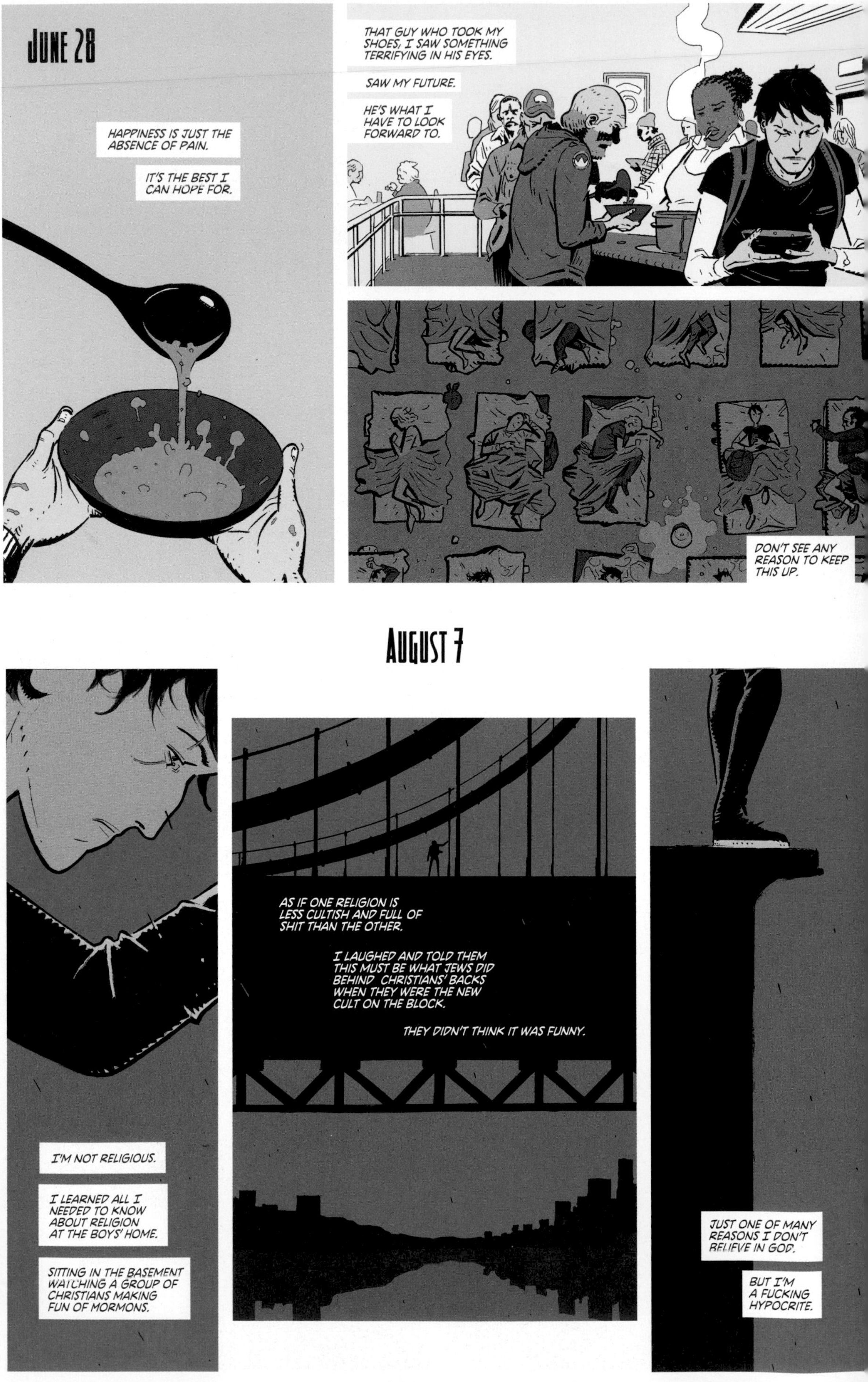
JUNE 28
HAPPINESS IS JUST THE ABSENCE OF PAIN.
IT'S THE BEST I CAN HOPE FOR.
THAT GUY WHO TOOK MY SHOES, I SAW SOMETHING TERRIFYING IN HIS EYES.
SAW MY FUTURE.
HE'S WHAT I HAVE TO LOOK FORWARD TO.
DON'T SEE ANY REASON TO KEEP THIS UP.
AUGUST 7
I'M NOT RELIGIOUS.
I LEARNED ALL I NEEDED TO KNOW ABOUT RELIGION AT THE BOYS' HOME.
SITTING IN THE BASEMENT WATCHING A GROUP OF CHRISTIANS MAKING FUN OF MORMONS.
AS IF ONE RELIGION IS LESS CULTISH AND FULL OF SHIT THAN THE OTHER.
I LAUGHED AND TOLD THEM THIS MUST BE WHAT JEWS DID BEHIND CHRISTIANS' BACKS WHEN THEY WERE THE NEW CULT ON THE BLOCK.
THEY DIDN'T THINK IT WAS FUNNY.
JUST ONE OF MANY REASONS I DON'T BELIEVE IN GOD.
BUT I'M A FUCKING HYPOCRITE.

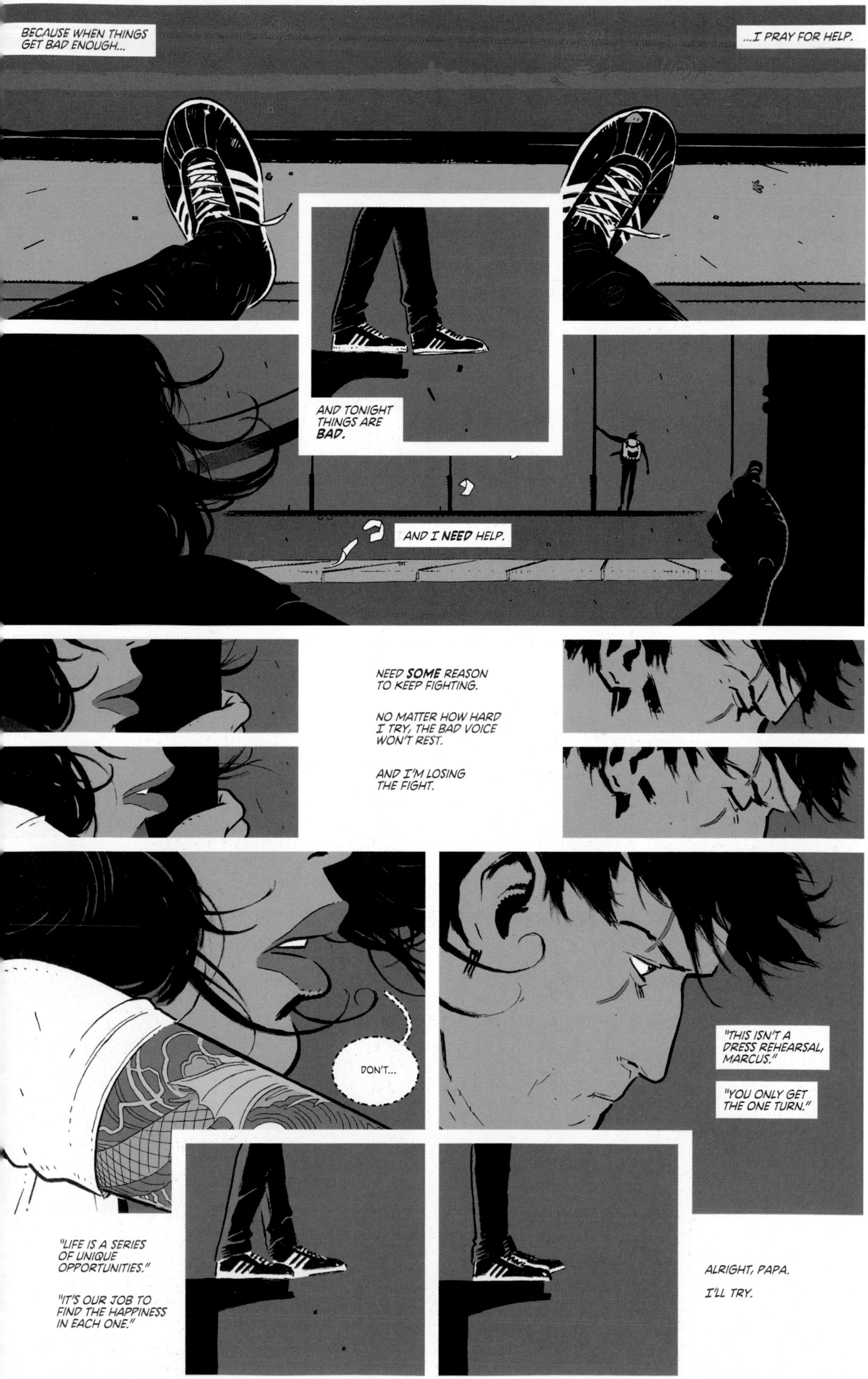
BECAUSE WHEN THINGS GET BAD ENOUGH...
...I PRAY FOR HELP.
AND TONIGHT THINGS ARE **BAD.**
AND I **NEED** HELP.
NEED **SOME** REASON TO KEEP FIGHTING.
NO MATTER HOW HARD I TRY, THE BAD VOICE WON'T REST.
AND I'M LOSING THE FIGHT.
DON'T...
"THIS ISN'T A DRESS REHEARSAL, MARCUS."
"YOU ONLY GET THE ONE TURN."
"LIFE IS A SERIES OF UNIQUE OPPORTUNITIES."
"IT'S OUR JOB TO FIND THE HAPPINESS IN EACH ONE."
ALRIGHT, PAPA.
I'LL TRY.

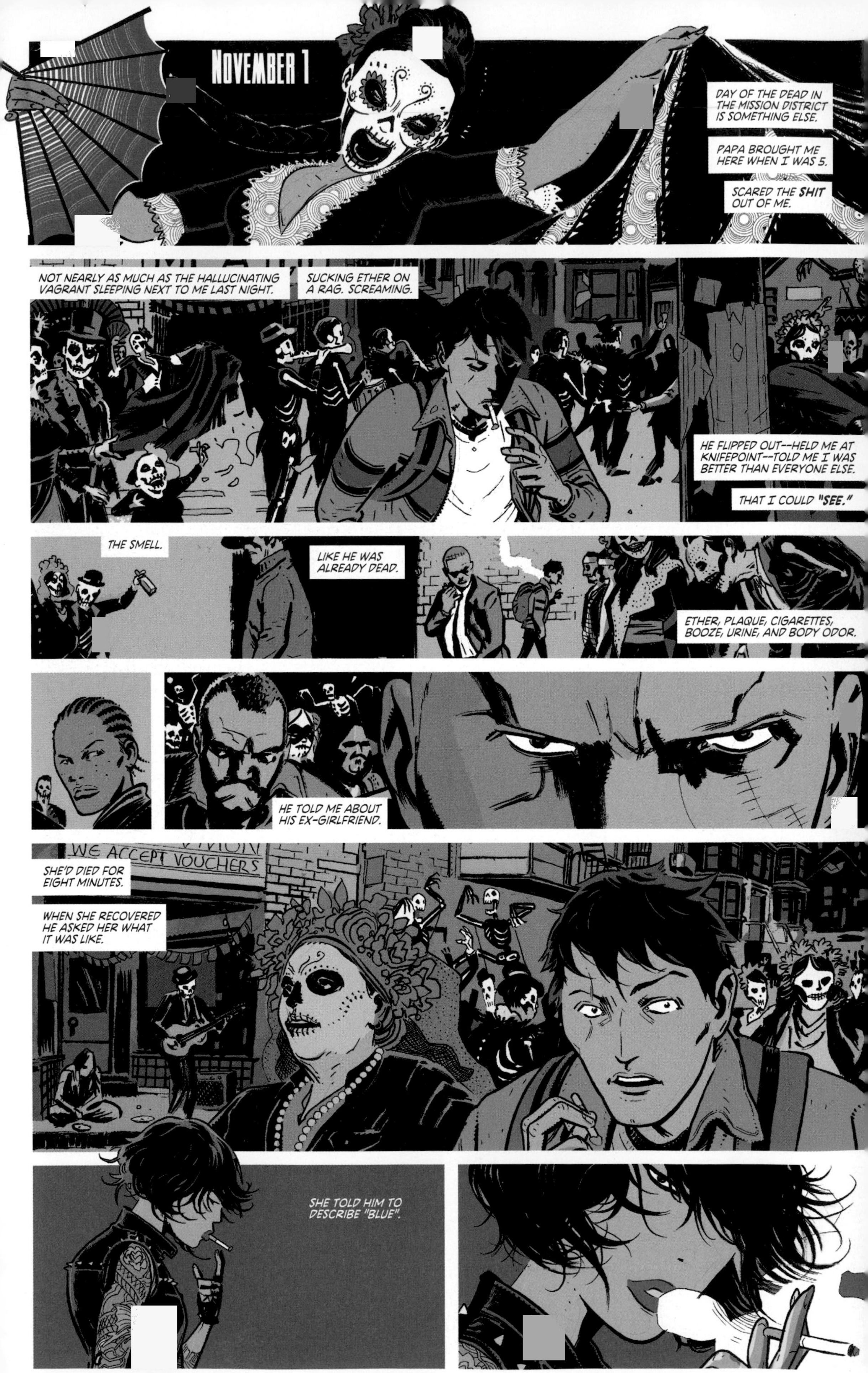
November 1
DAY OF THE DEAD IN THE MISSION DISTRICT IS SOMETHING ELSE.
PAPA BROUGHT ME HERE WHEN I WAS 5.
SCARED THE SHIT OUT OF ME.
NOT NEARLY AS MUCH AS THE HALLUCINATING VAGRANT SLEEPING NEXT TO ME LAST NIGHT.
SUCKING ETHER ON A RAG. SCREAMING.
HE FLIPPED OUT--HELD ME AT KNIFEPOINT--TOLD ME I WAS BETTER THAN EVERYONE ELSE.
THAT I COULD "SEE."
THE SMELL.
LIKE HE WAS ALREADY DEAD.
ETHER, PLAQUE, CIGARETTES, BOOZE, URINE, AND BODY ODOR.
HE TOLD ME ABOUT HIS EX-GIRLFRIEND.
WE ACCEPT VOUCHERS
SHE'D DIED FOR EIGHT MINUTES.
WHEN SHE RECOVERED HE ASKED HER WHAT IT WAS LIKE.
SHE TOLD HIM TO DESCRIBE "BLUE".

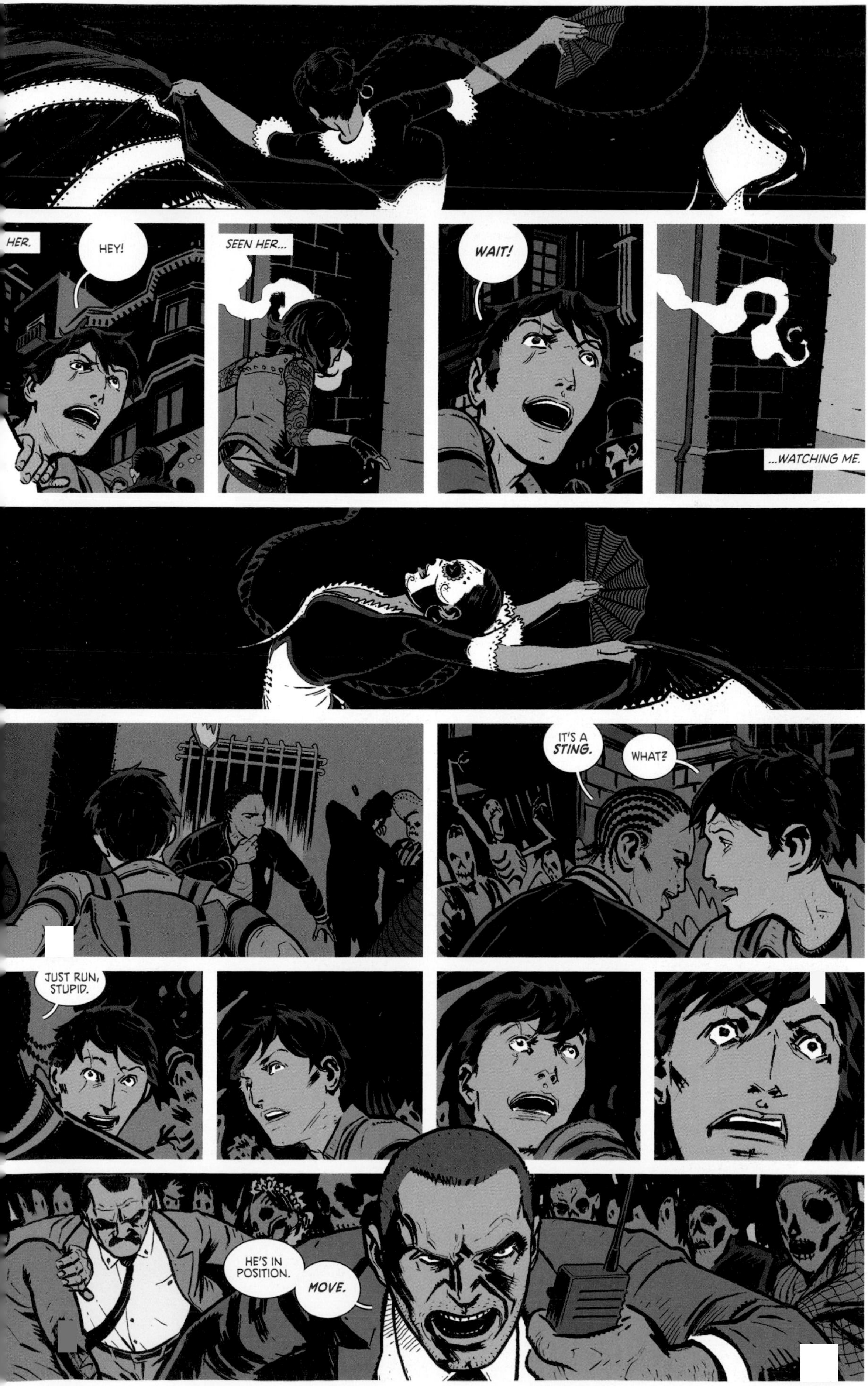
HER.
HEY!
SEEN HER...
WAIT!
...WATCHING ME.
IT'S A STING.
WHAT?
JUST RUN, STUPID.
HE'S IN POSITION.
MOVE.

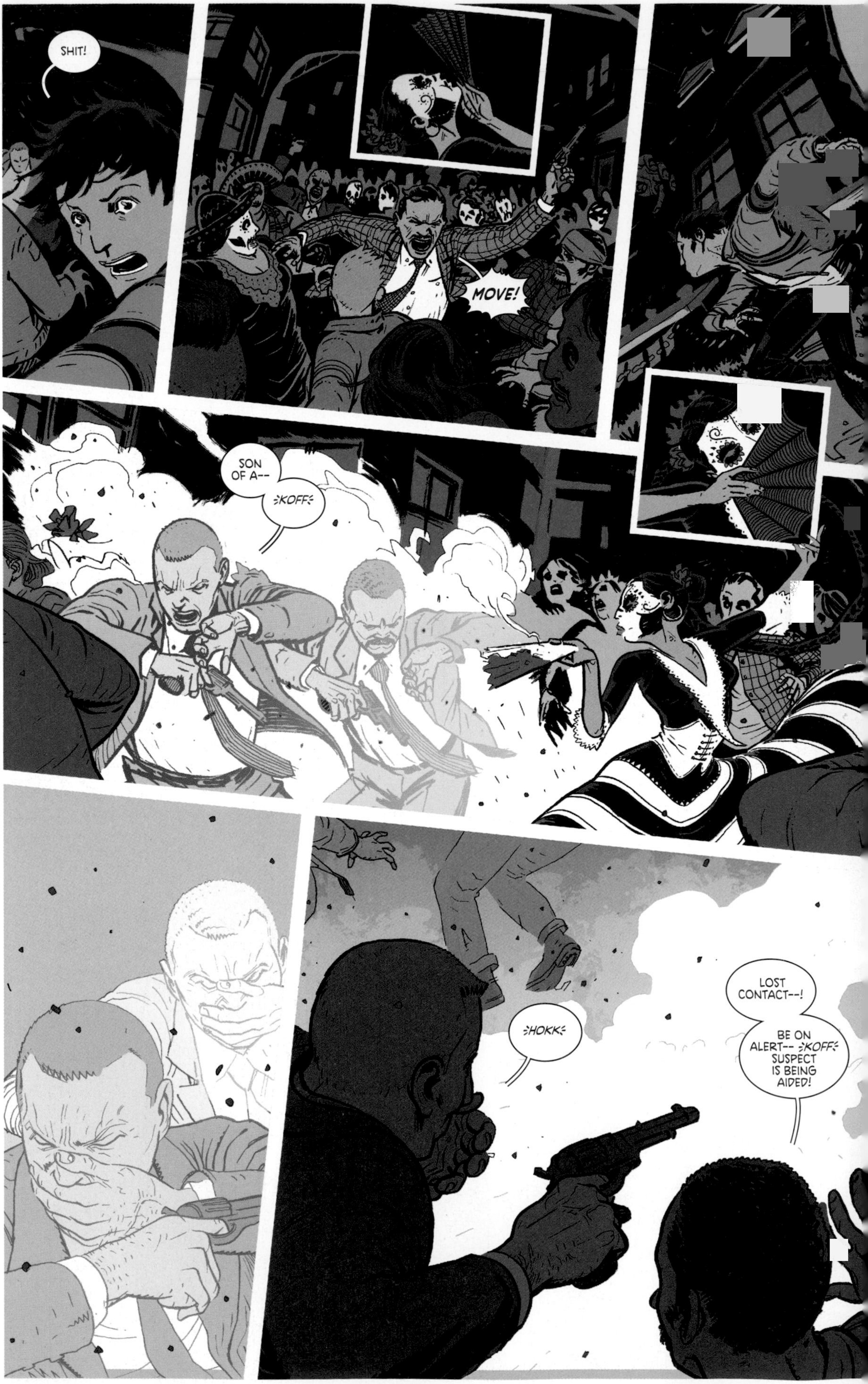
SHIT!
MOVE!
SON OF A--
KOFF
HOKK
LOST CONTACT--!
BE ON ALERT-- KOFF SUSPECT IS BEING AIDED!

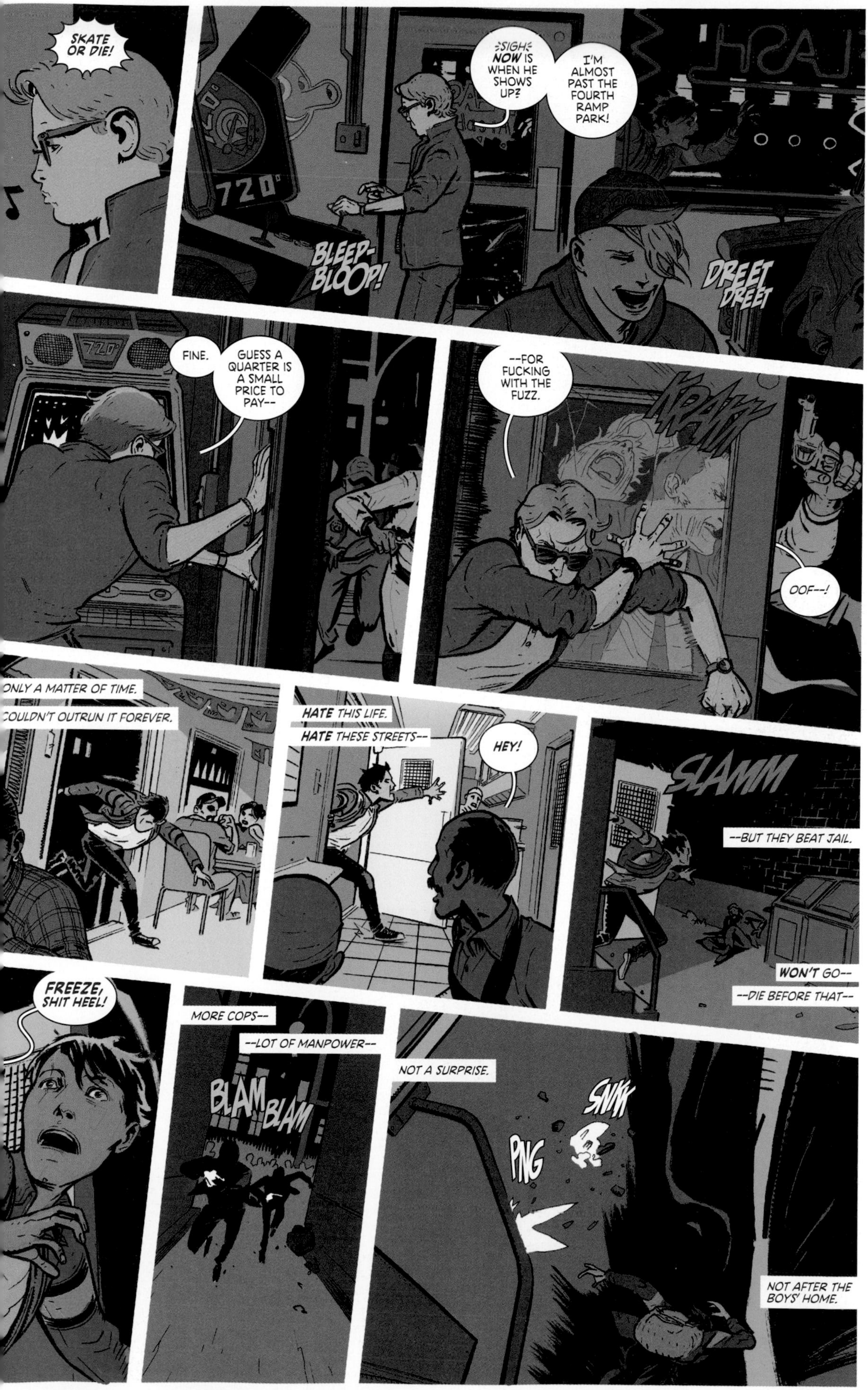
SKATE OR DIE!
SIGH NOW IS WHEN HE SHOWS UP?
I'M ALMOST PAST THE FOURTH RAMP PARK!
720°
BLEEP-BLOOP!
DREET DREET
FINE.
GUESS A QUARTER IS A SMALL PRICE TO PAY--
--FOR FUCKING WITH THE FUZZ.
KRAKK
OOF--!
ONLY A MATTER OF TIME.
COULDN'T OUTRUN IT FOREVER.
HATE THIS LIFE.
HATE THESE STREETS--
HEY!
SLAMM
--BUT THEY BEAT JAIL.
WON'T GO--
--DIE BEFORE THAT--
FREEZE, SHIT HEEL!
MORE COPS--
--LOT OF MANPOWER--
BLAM BLAM
NOT A SURPRISE.
SNIKK
PNG
NOT AFTER THE BOYS' HOME.

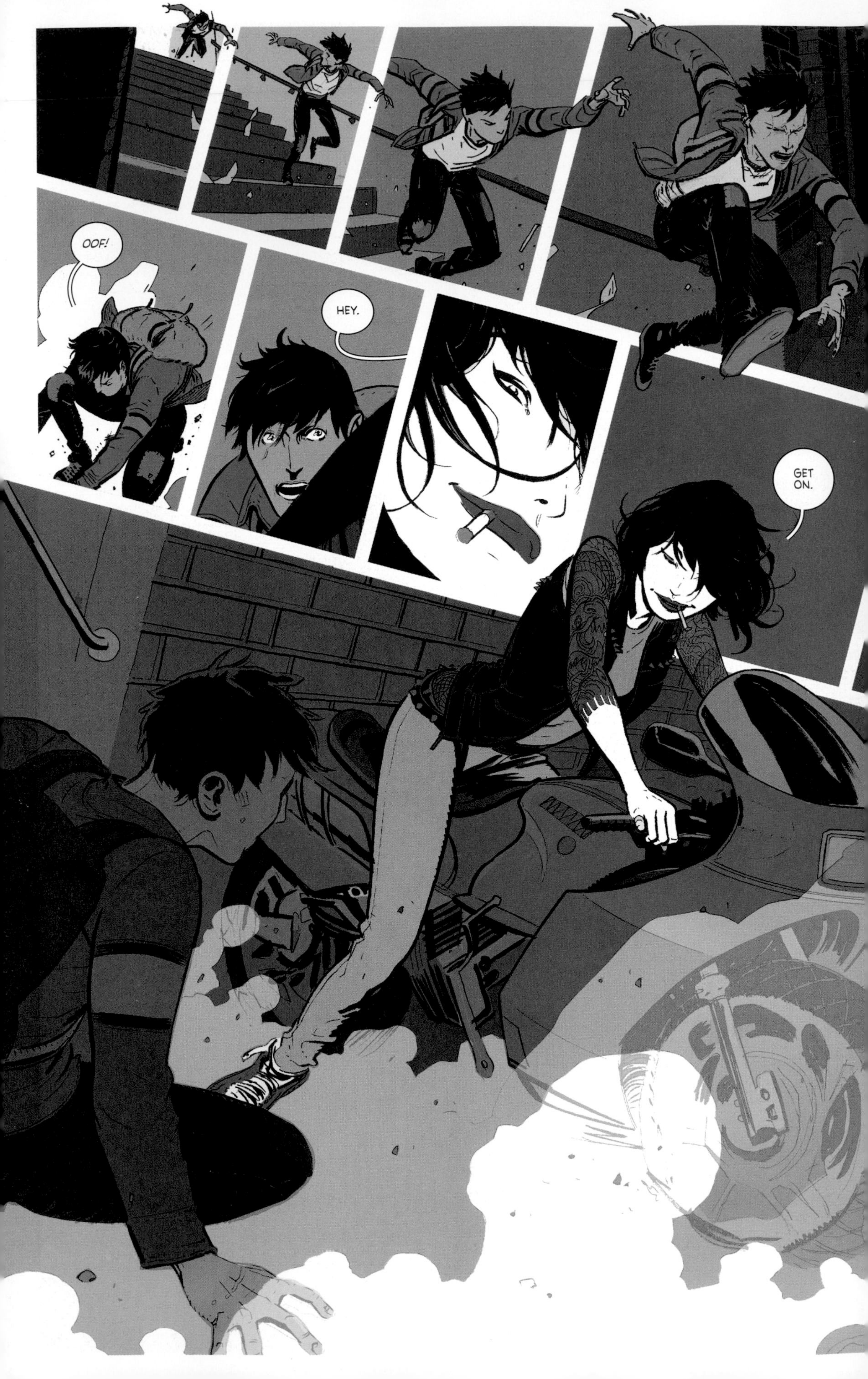
OOF!
HEY.
GET ON.

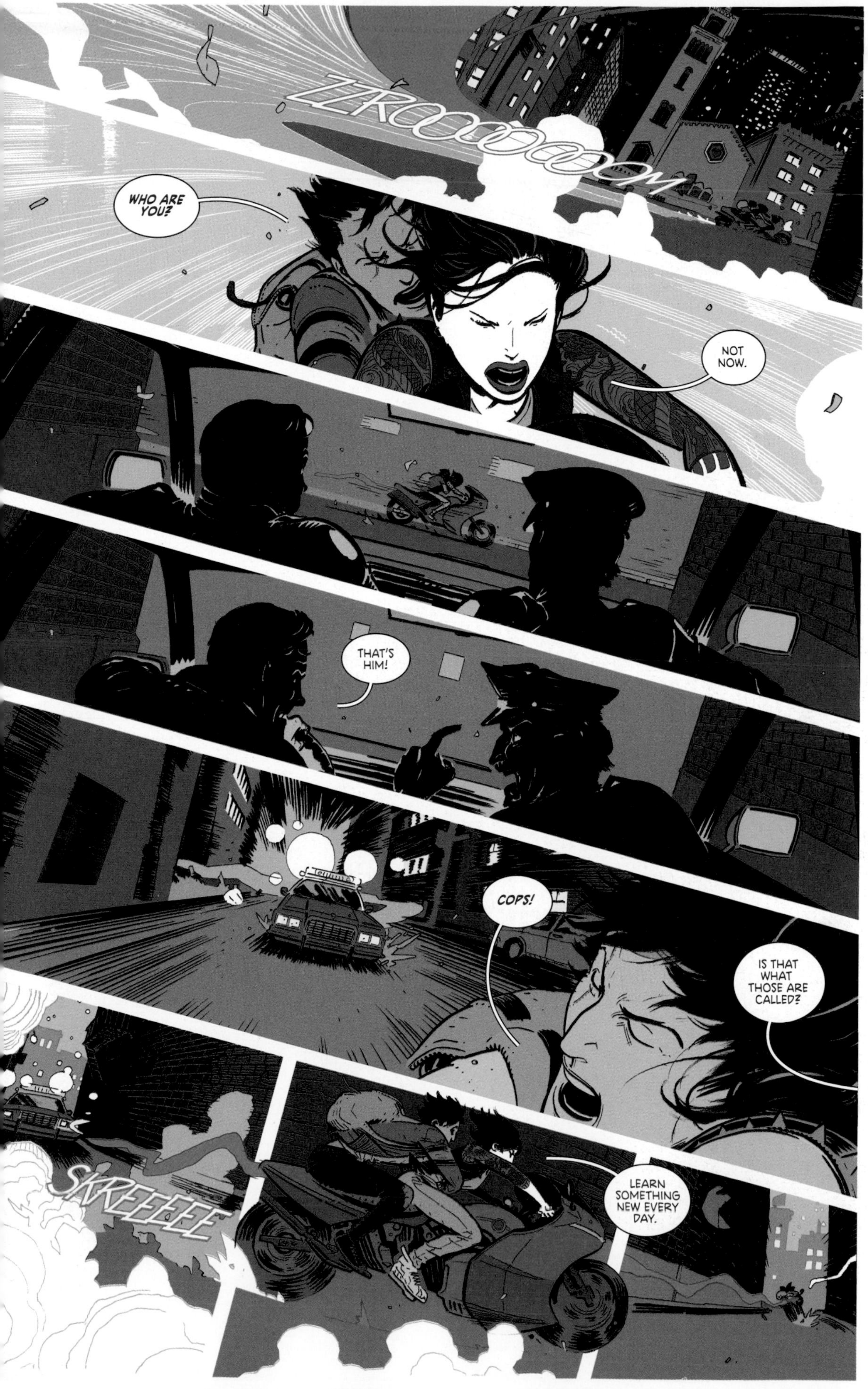
ZZROOOOOOOOM
WHO ARE YOU?
NOT NOW.
THAT'S HIM!
COPS!
IS THAT WHAT THOSE ARE CALLED?
SKREEEEEE
LEARN SOMETHING NEW EVERY DAY.

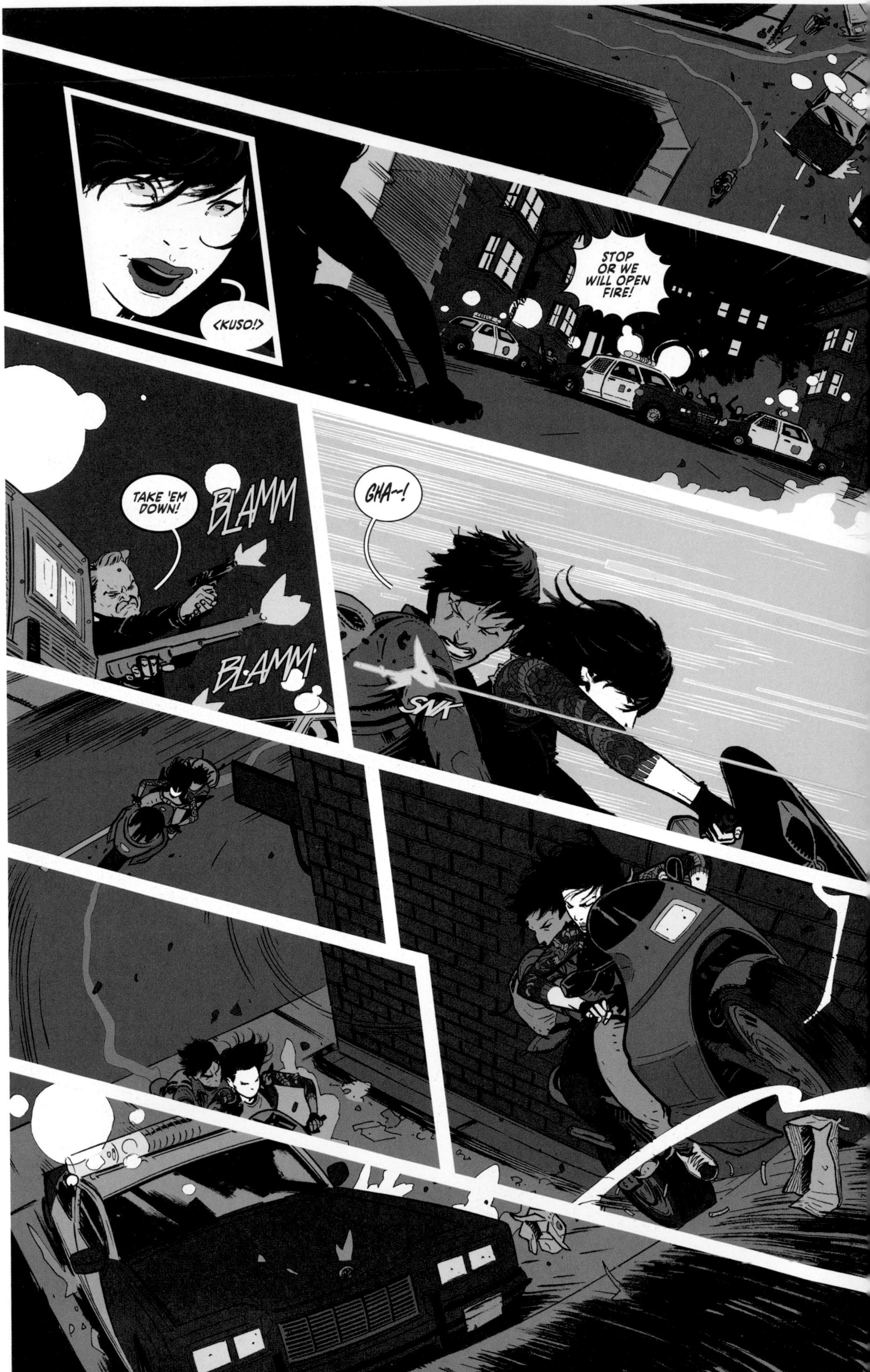

STOP OR WE WILL OPEN FIRE!
<KUSO!>
TAKE 'EM DOWN!
BLAMM
BLAMM
GHA--!
SNK

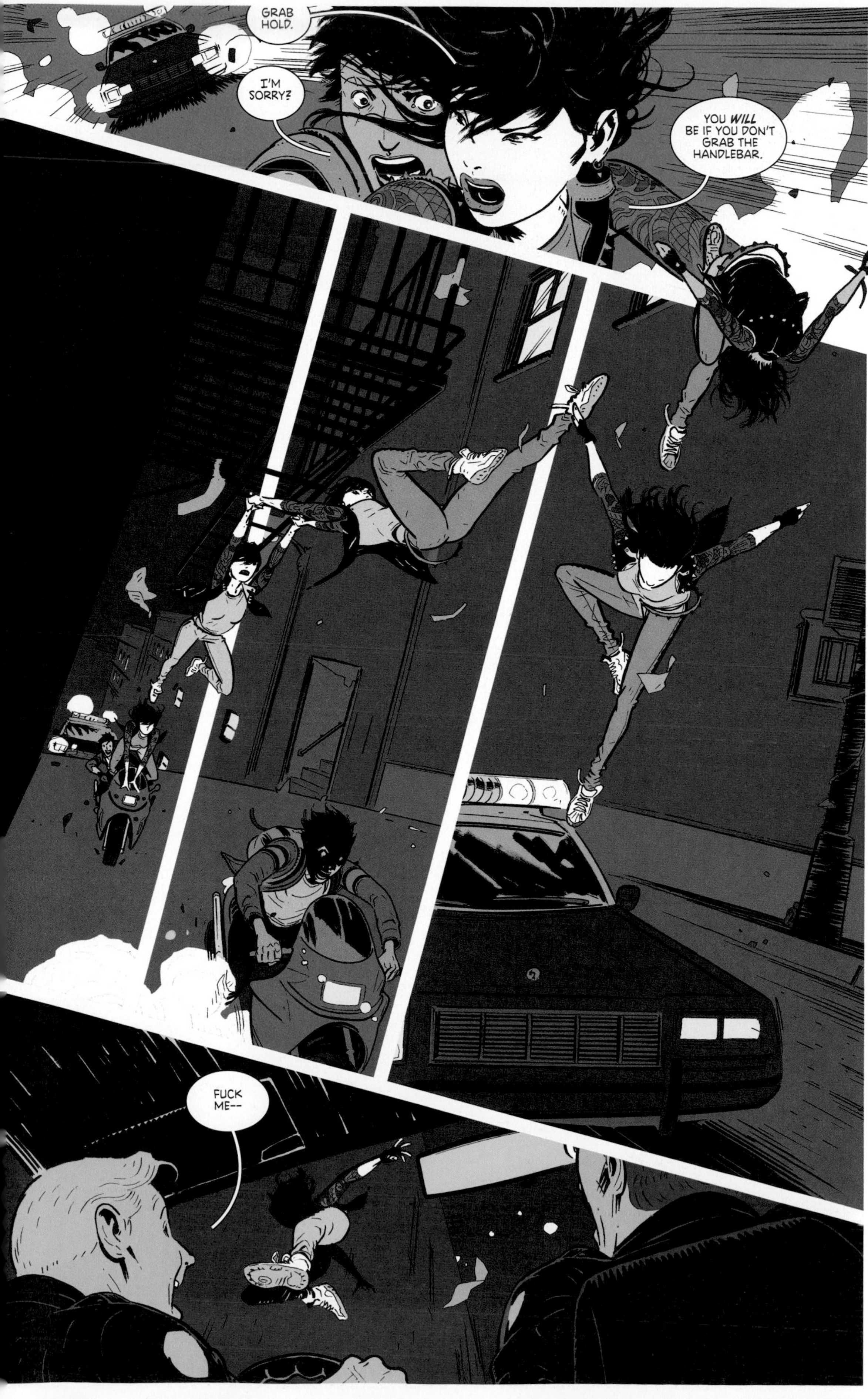
GRAB HOLD.
I'M SORRY?
YOU WILL BE IF YOU DON'T GRAB THE HANDLEBAR.
FUCK ME--

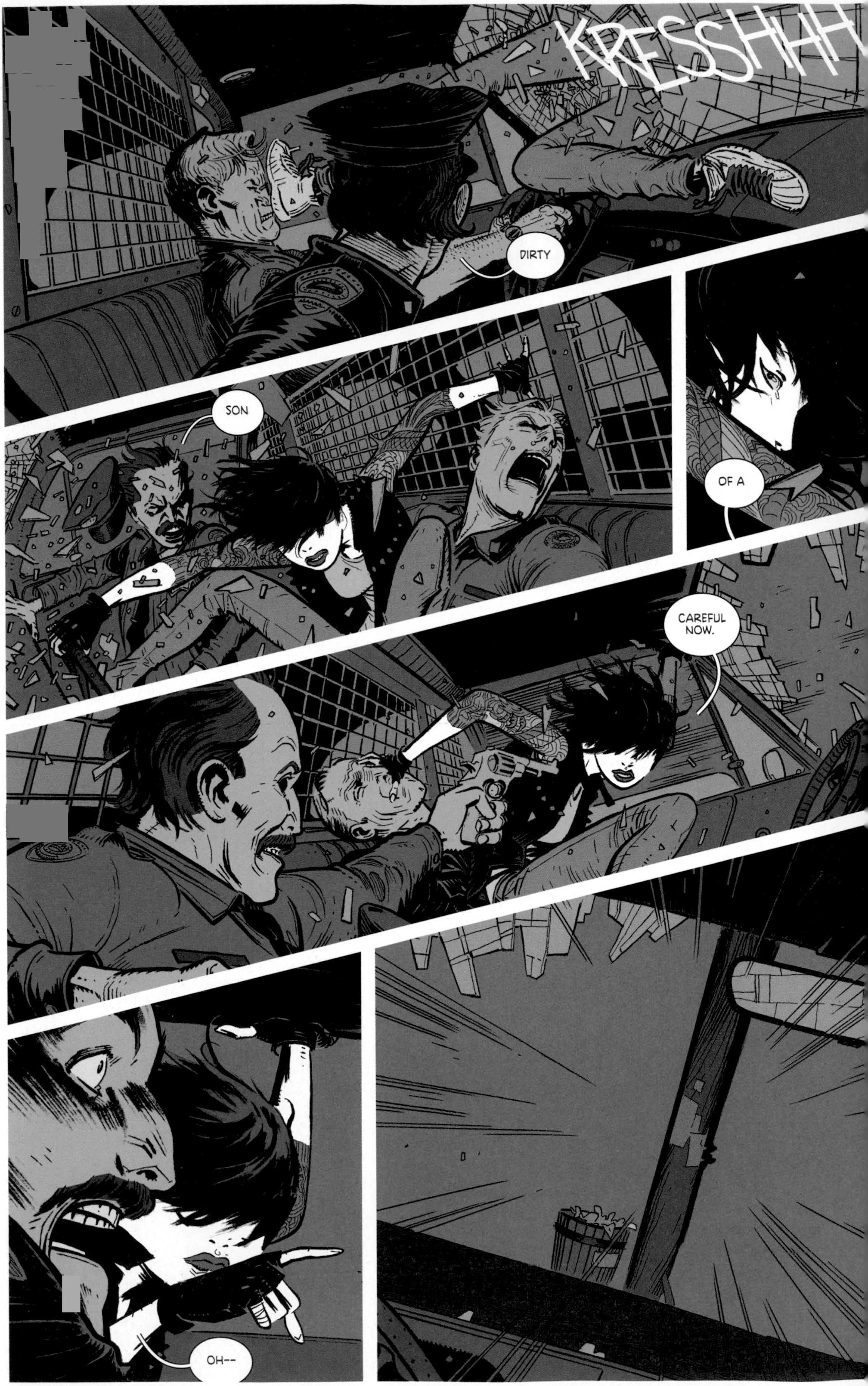
KRESSHHH
DIRTY
SON
OF A
CAREFUL NOW.
OH--

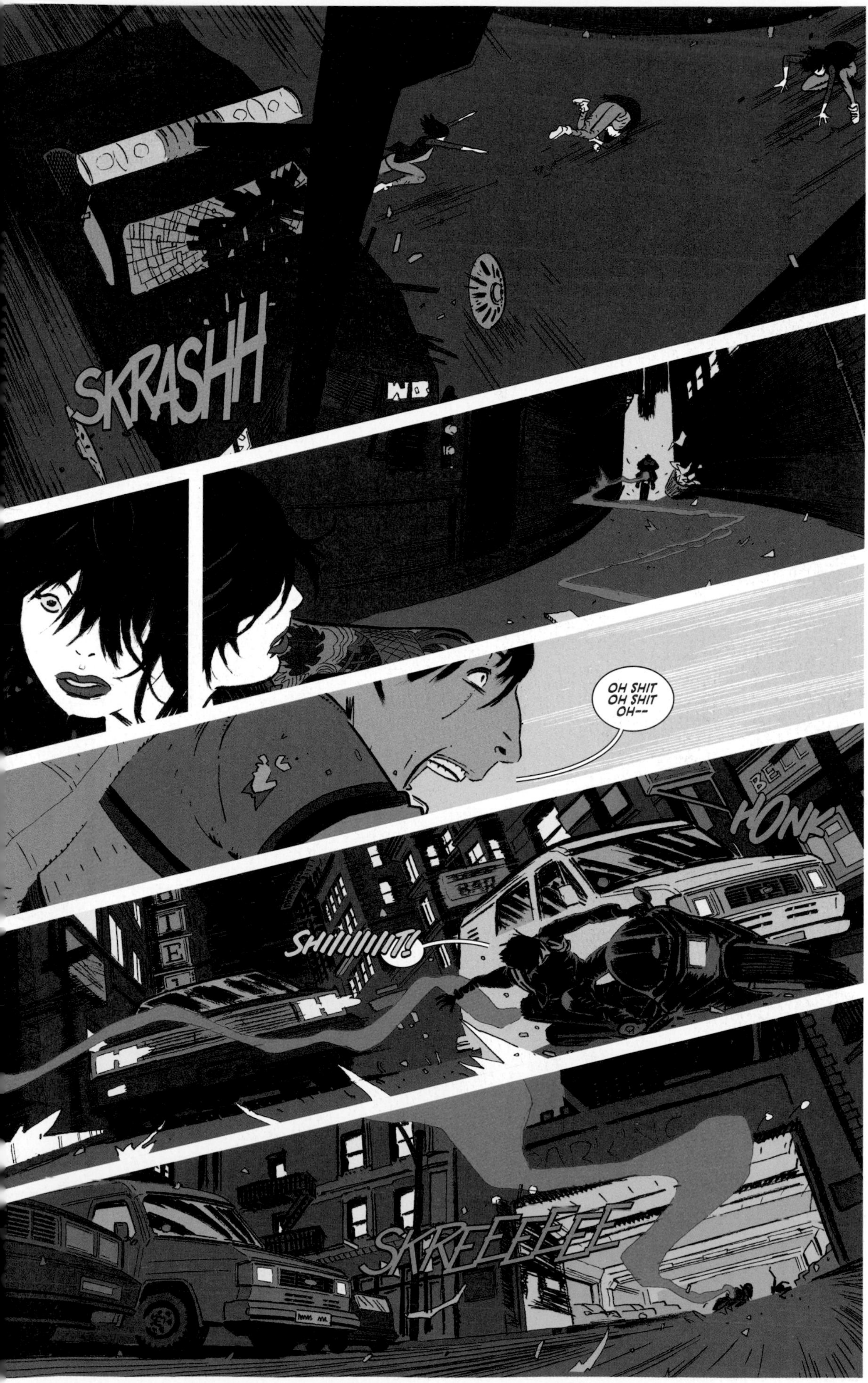
SKRASHH
OH SHIT OH SHIT OH--
HONK
SHIIIIIIIIT!
SKREEEEEEE

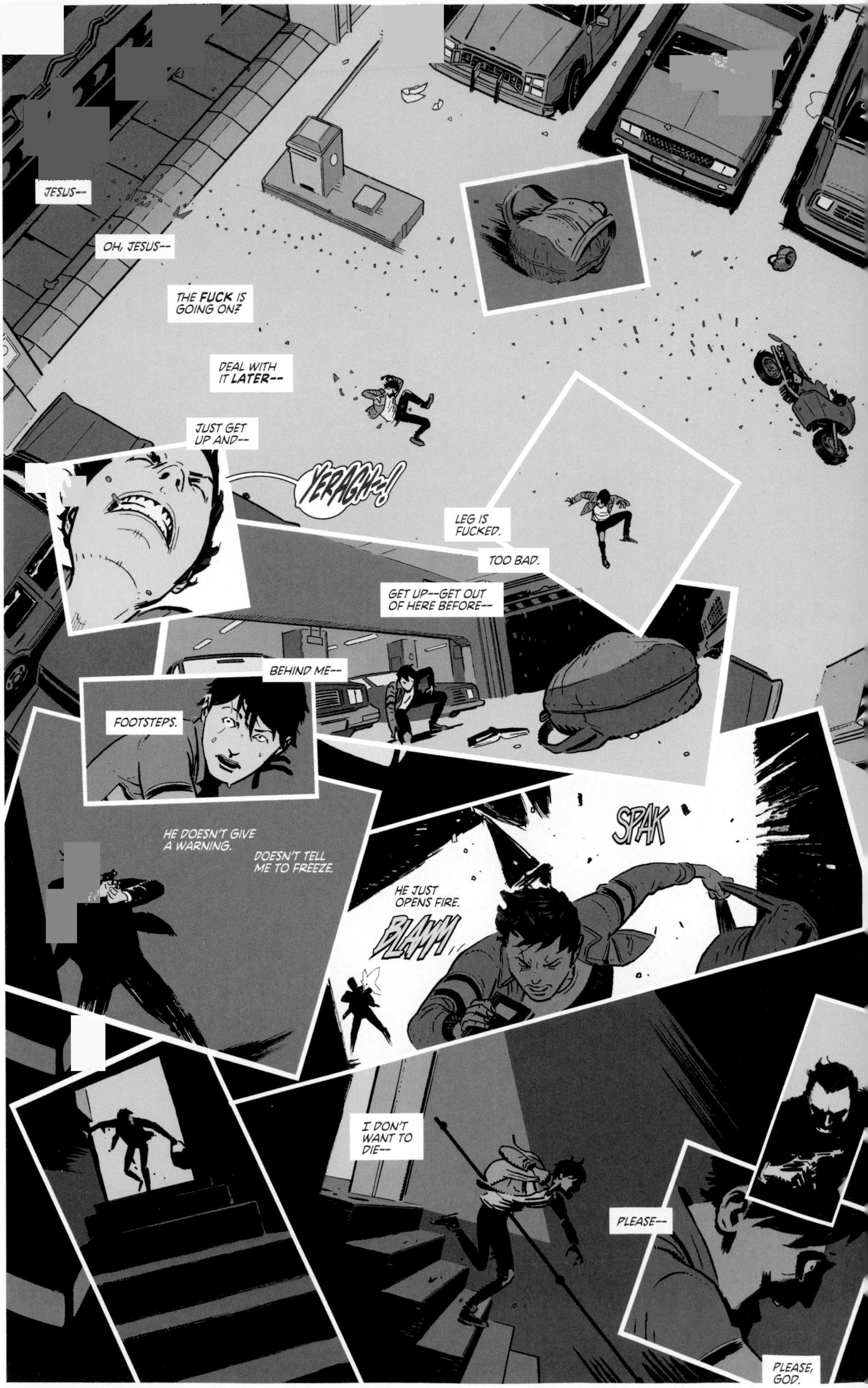
JESUS--
OH, JESUS--
THE FUCK IS GOING ON?
DEAL WITH IT LATER--
JUST GET UP AND--
YERAGH--!
LEG IS FUCKED.
TOO BAD.
GET UP--GET OUT OF HERE BEFORE--
BEHIND ME--
FOOTSTEPS.
HE DOESN'T GIVE A WARNING.
DOESN'T TELL ME TO FREEZE.
SPAK
HE JUST OPENS FIRE.
BLAMM
I DON'T WANT TO DIE--
PLEASE--
PLEASE, GOD.

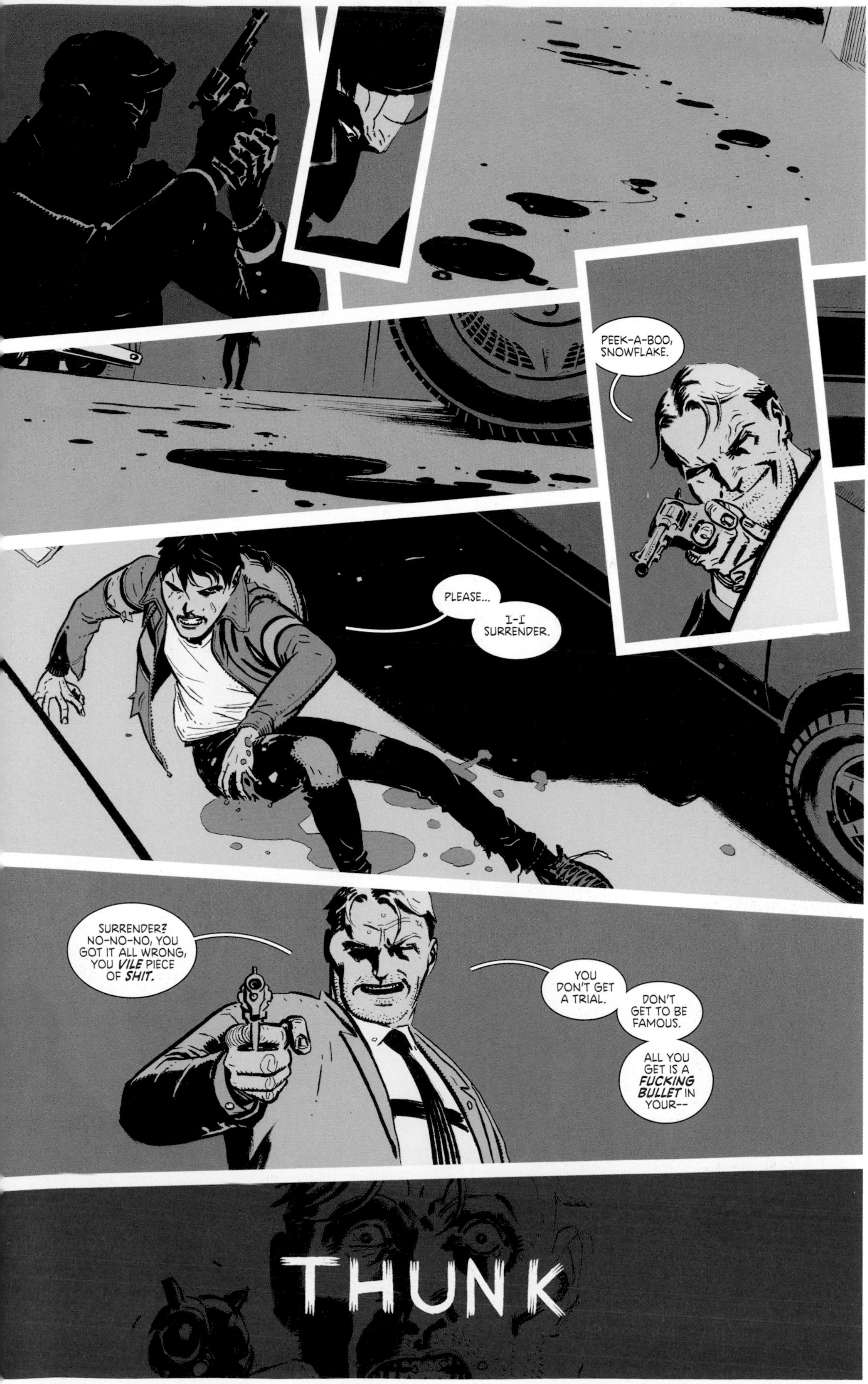
PEEK-A-BOO, SNOWFLAKE.
PLEASE...
I-I SURRENDER.
SURRENDER? NO-NO-NO, YOU GOT IT ALL WRONG, YOU *VILE* PIECE OF *SHIT.*
YOU DON'T GET A TRIAL.
DON'T GET TO BE FAMOUS.
ALL YOU GET IS A *FUCKING BULLET* IN YOUR--
THUNK

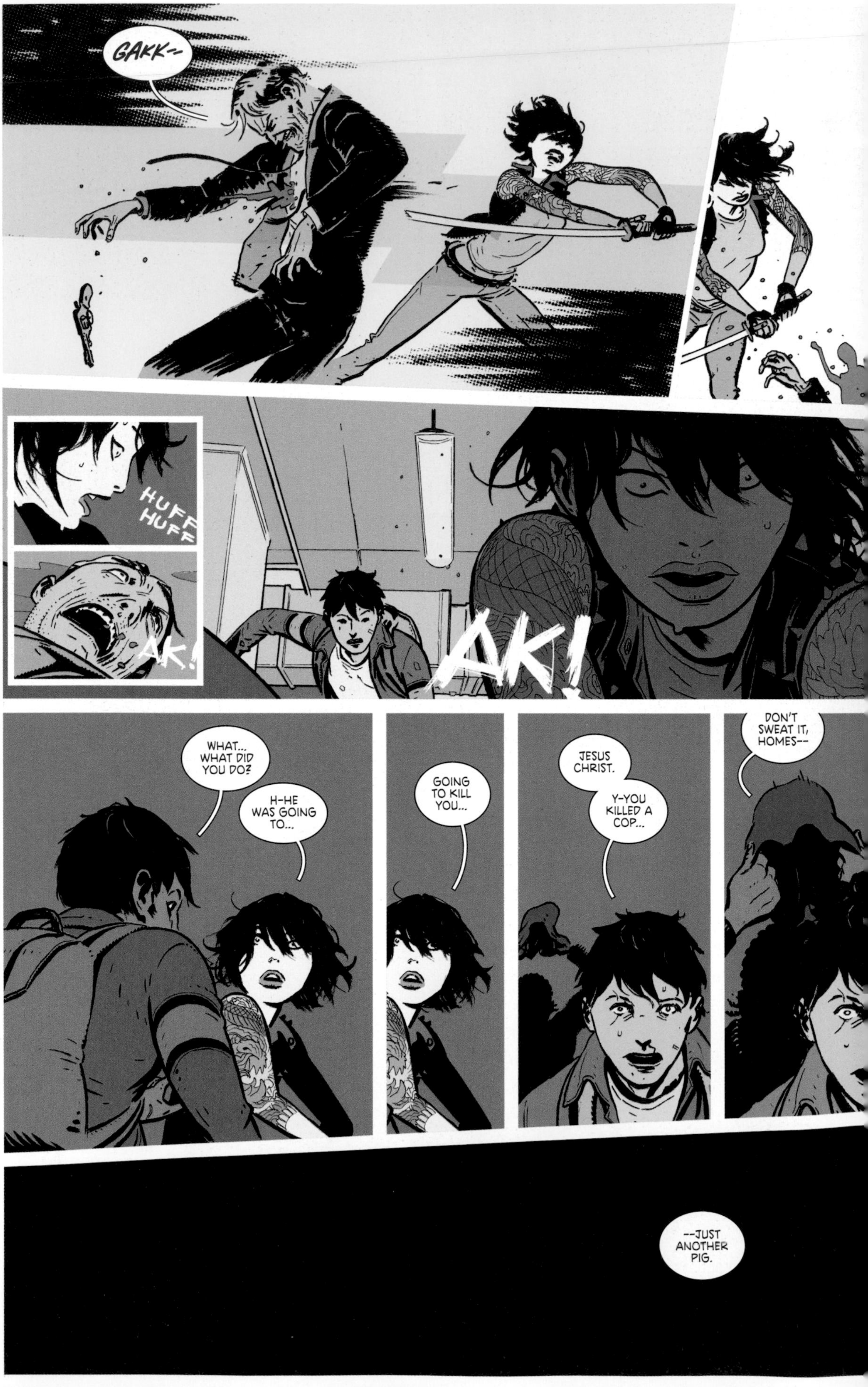
GAKK--
HUFF HUFF
AK!
AK!
WHAT... WHAT DID YOU DO?
H-HE WAS GOING TO...
GOING TO KILL YOU...
JESUS CHRIST.
Y-YOU KILLED A COP...
DON'T SWEAT IT, HOMES--
--JUST ANOTHER PIG.

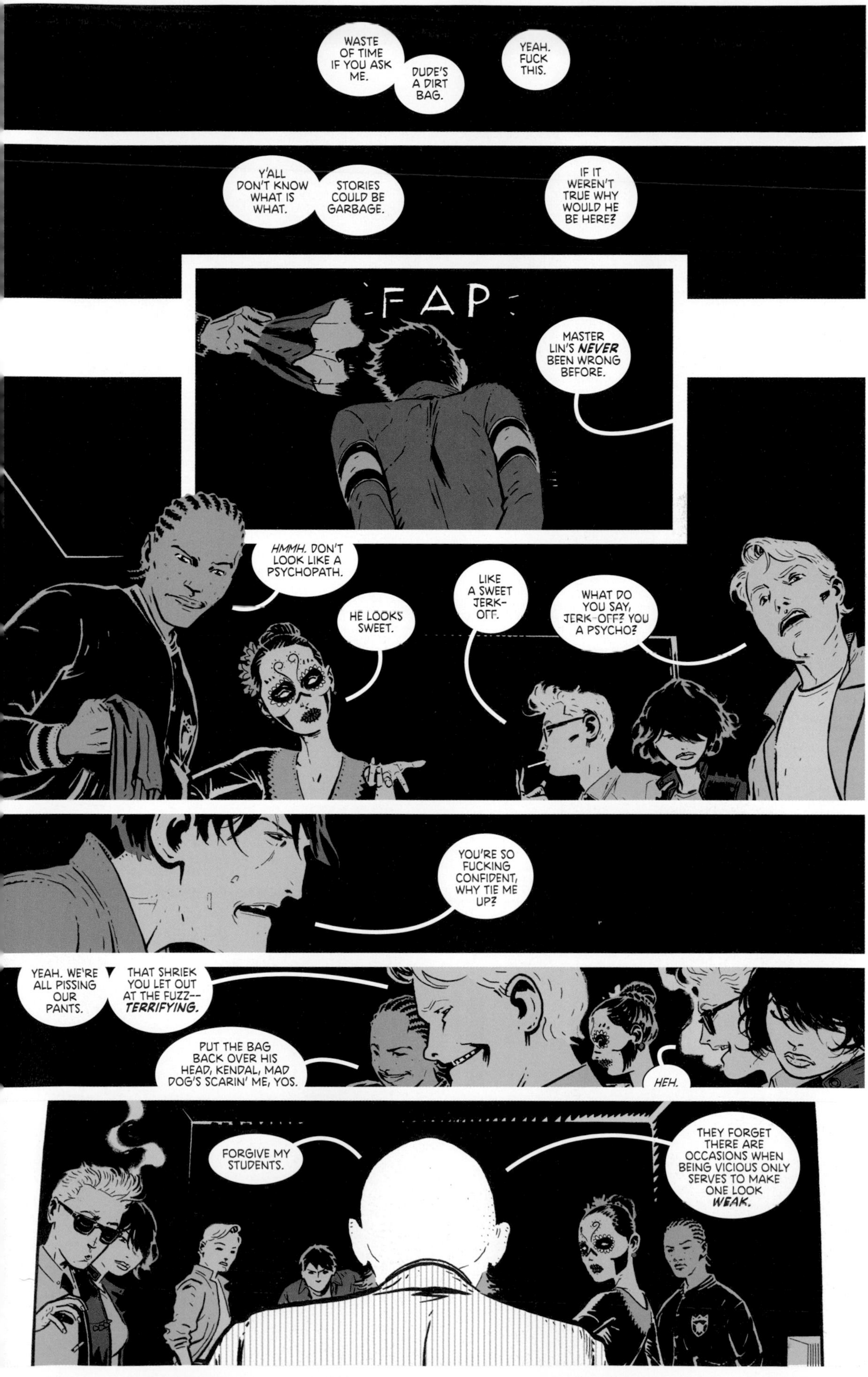
WASTE OF TIME IF YOU ASK ME.
DUDE'S A DIRT BAG.
YEAH. FUCK THIS.
Y'ALL DON'T KNOW WHAT IS WHAT.
STORIES COULD BE GARBAGE.
IF IT WEREN'T TRUE WHY WOULD HE BE HERE?
FAP
MASTER LIN'S NEVER BEEN WRONG BEFORE.
HMMH. DON'T LOOK LIKE A PSYCHOPATH.
HE LOOKS SWEET.
LIKE A SWEET JERK-OFF.
WHAT DO YOU SAY, JERK-OFF? YOU A PSYCHO?
YOU'RE SO FUCKING CONFIDENT, WHY TIE ME UP?
YEAH. WE'RE ALL PISSING OUR PANTS.
THAT SHRIEK YOU LET OUT AT THE FUZZ-- TERRIFYING.
PUT THE BAG BACK OVER HIS HEAD, KENDAL, MAD DOG'S SCARIN' ME, YOS.
HEH.
FORGIVE MY STUDENTS.
THEY FORGET THERE ARE OCCASIONS WHEN BEING VICIOUS ONLY SERVES TO MAKE ONE LOOK WEAK.

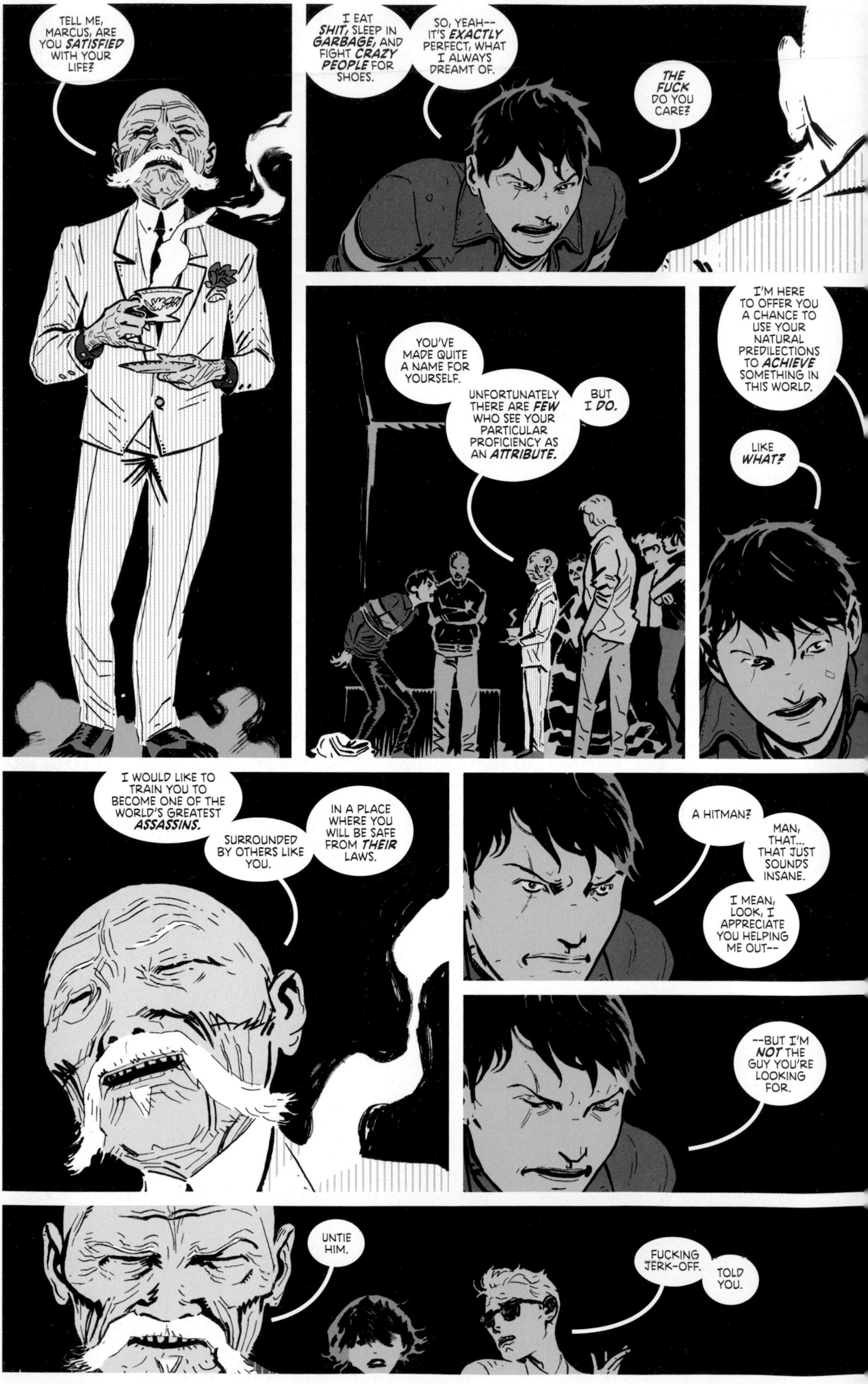
TELL ME, MARCUS, ARE YOU SATISFIED WITH YOUR LIFE?
I EAT SHIT, SLEEP IN GARBAGE, AND FIGHT CRAZY PEOPLE FOR SHOES.
SO, YEAH-- IT'S EXACTLY PERFECT, WHAT I ALWAYS DREAMT OF.
THE FUCK DO YOU CARE?
YOU'VE MADE QUITE A NAME FOR YOURSELF.
UNFORTUNATELY THERE ARE FEW WHO SEE YOUR PARTICULAR PROFICIENCY AS AN ATTRIBUTE.
BUT I DO.
I'M HERE TO OFFER YOU A CHANCE TO USE YOUR NATURAL PREDILECTIONS TO ACHIEVE SOMETHING IN THIS WORLD.
LIKE WHAT?
I WOULD LIKE TO TRAIN YOU TO BECOME ONE OF THE WORLD'S GREATEST ASSASSINS.
SURROUNDED BY OTHERS LIKE YOU.
IN A PLACE WHERE YOU WILL BE SAFE FROM THEIR LAWS.
A HITMAN?
MAN, THAT... THAT JUST SOUNDS INSANE.
I MEAN, LOOK, I APPRECIATE YOU HELPING ME OUT--
--BUT I'M NOT THE GUY YOU'RE LOOKING FOR.
UNTIE HIM.
FUCKING JERK-OFF.
TOLD YOU.

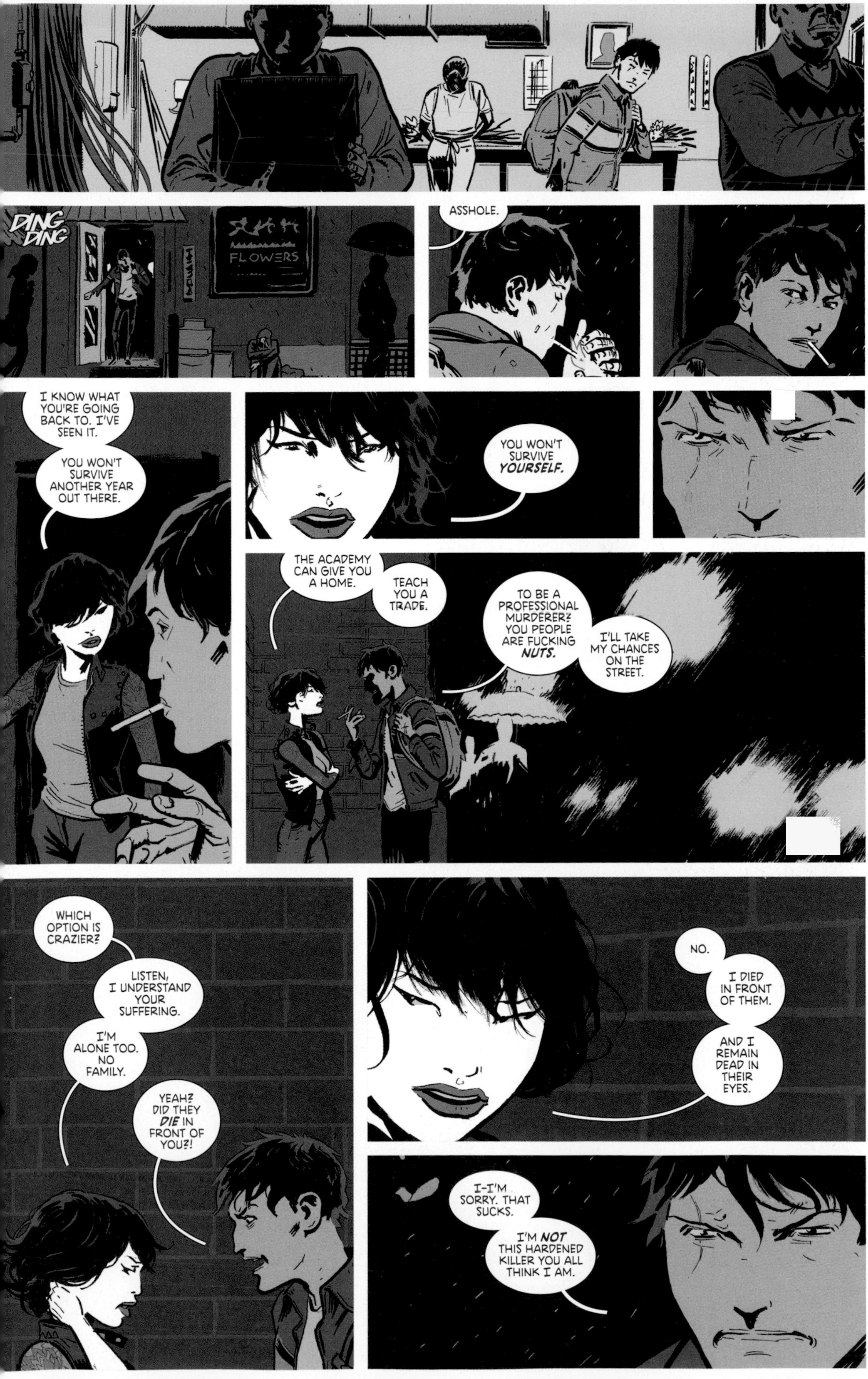
DING DING
FLOWERS
ASSHOLE.
I KNOW WHAT YOU'RE GOING BACK TO. I'VE SEEN IT.
YOU WON'T SURVIVE ANOTHER YEAR OUT THERE.
YOU WON'T SURVIVE *YOURSELF.*
THE ACADEMY CAN GIVE YOU A HOME.
TEACH YOU A TRADE.
TO BE A PROFESSIONAL MURDERER? YOU PEOPLE ARE FUCKING *NUTS.*
I'LL TAKE MY CHANCES ON THE STREET.
WHICH OPTION IS CRAZIER?
LISTEN, I UNDERSTAND YOUR SUFFERING.
I'M ALONE TOO. NO FAMILY.
YEAH? DID THEY *DIE* IN FRONT OF YOU?!
NO.
I DIED IN FRONT OF THEM.
AND I REMAIN DEAD IN THEIR EYES.
I-I'M SORRY. THAT SUCKS.
I'M *NOT* THIS HARDENED KILLER YOU ALL THINK I AM.

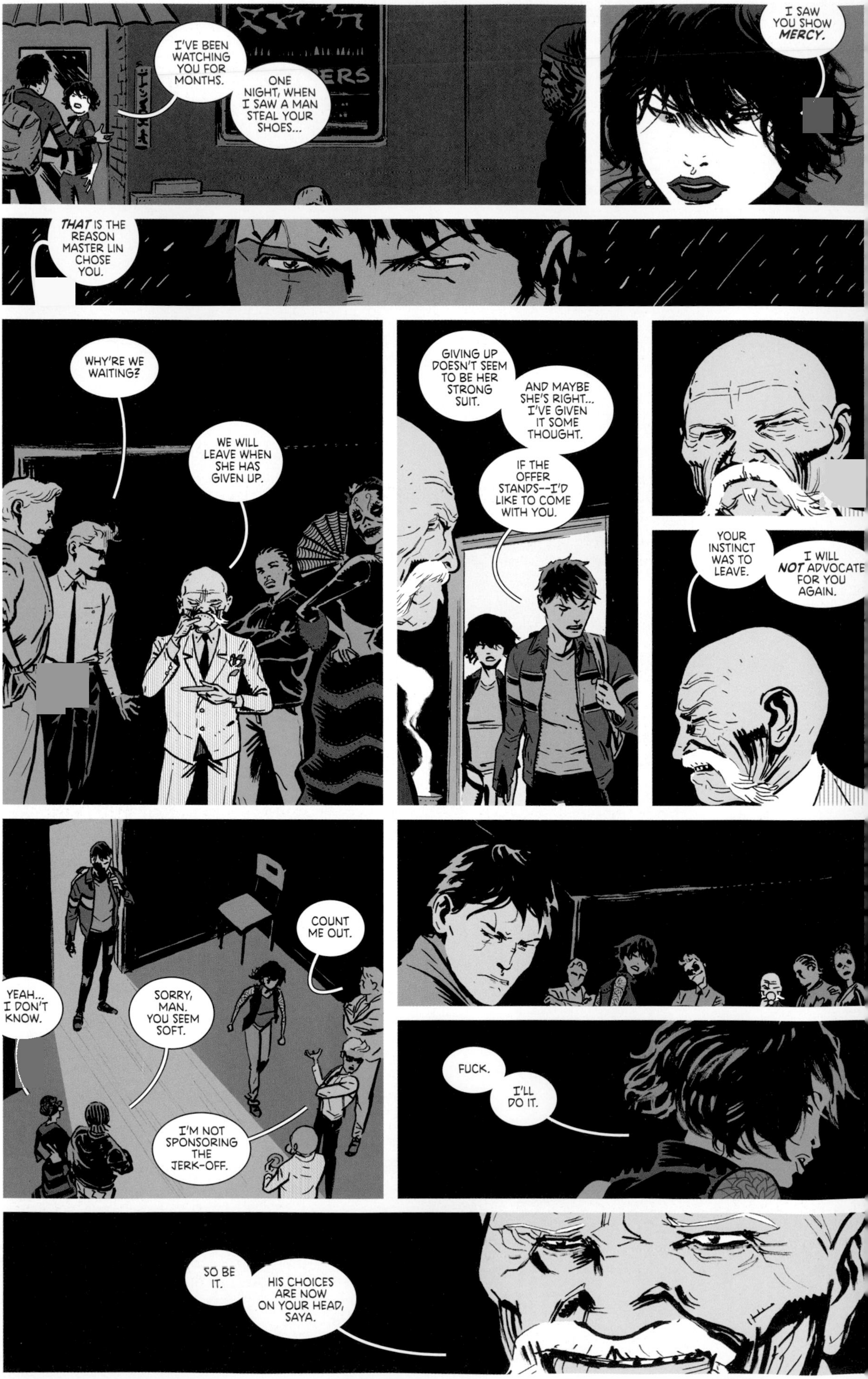
I'VE BEEN WATCHING YOU FOR MONTHS.
ONE NIGHT, WHEN I SAW A MAN STEAL YOUR SHOES...
I SAW YOU SHOW *MERCY.*
THAT IS THE REASON MASTER LIN CHOSE YOU.
WHY'RE WE WAITING?
WE WILL LEAVE WHEN SHE HAS GIVEN UP.
GIVING UP DOESN'T SEEM TO BE HER STRONG SUIT.
AND MAYBE SHE'S RIGHT... I'VE GIVEN IT SOME THOUGHT.
IF THE OFFER STANDS--I'D LIKE TO COME WITH YOU.
YOUR INSTINCT WAS TO LEAVE.
I WILL *NOT* ADVOCATE FOR YOU AGAIN.
YEAH... I DON'T KNOW.
SORRY, MAN. YOU SEEM SOFT.
COUNT ME OUT.
I'M NOT SPONSORING THE JERK-OFF.
FUCK.
I'LL DO IT.
SO BE IT.
HIS CHOICES ARE NOW ON YOUR HEAD, SAYA.

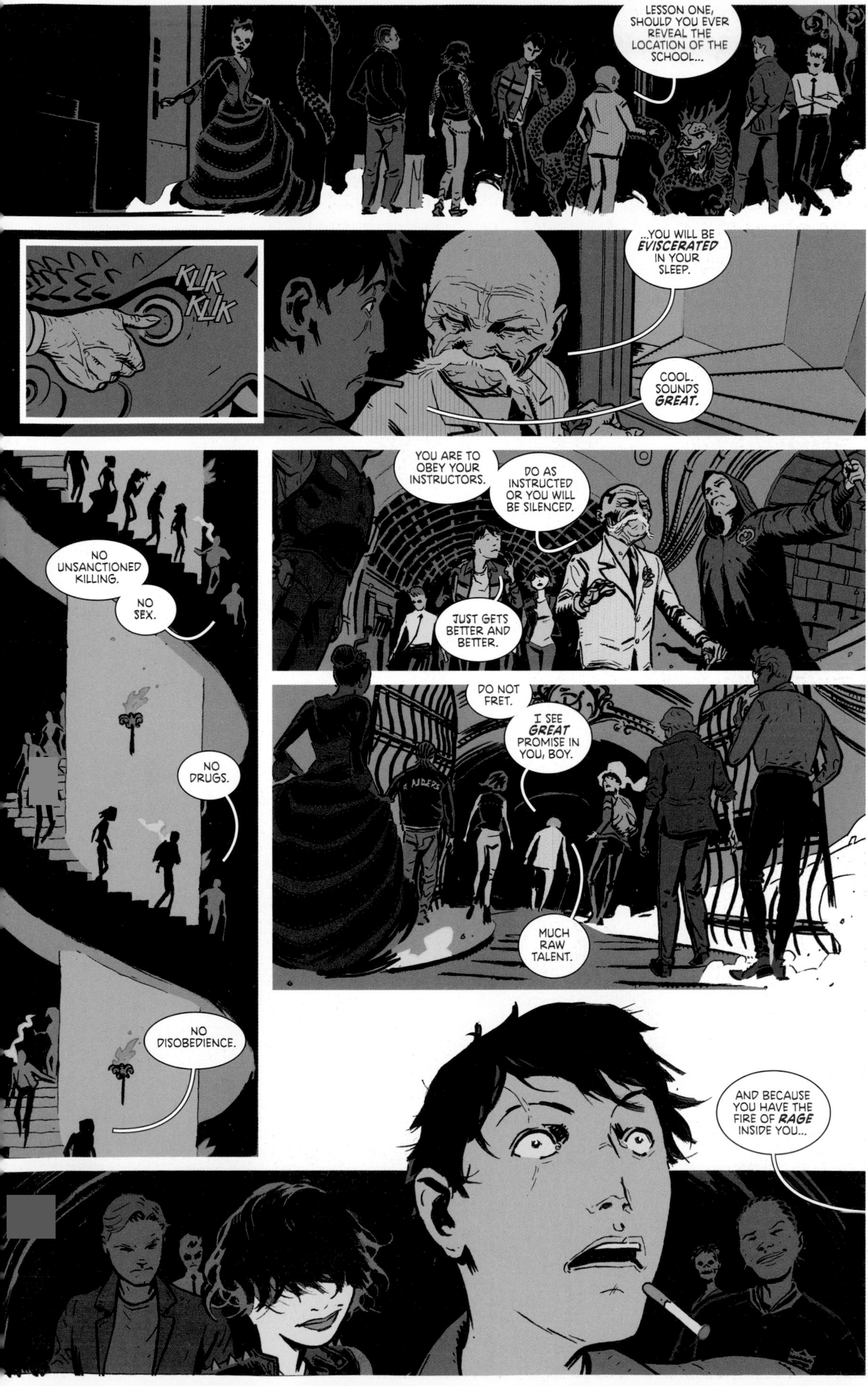
LESSON ONE, SHOULD YOU EVER REVEAL THE LOCATION OF THE SCHOOL...
KLIK KLIK
...YOU WILL BE EVISCERATED IN YOUR SLEEP.
COOL. SOUND'S GREAT.
NO UNSANCTIONED KILLING.
NO SEX.
NO DRUGS.
NO DISOBEDIENCE.
YOU ARE TO OBEY YOUR INSTRUCTORS.
DO AS INSTRUCTED OR YOU WILL BE SILENCED.
JUST GETS BETTER AND BETTER.
DO NOT FRET.
I SEE GREAT PROMISE IN YOU, BOY.
MUCH RAW TALENT.
AND BECAUSE YOU HAVE THE FIRE OF RAGE INSIDE YOU...

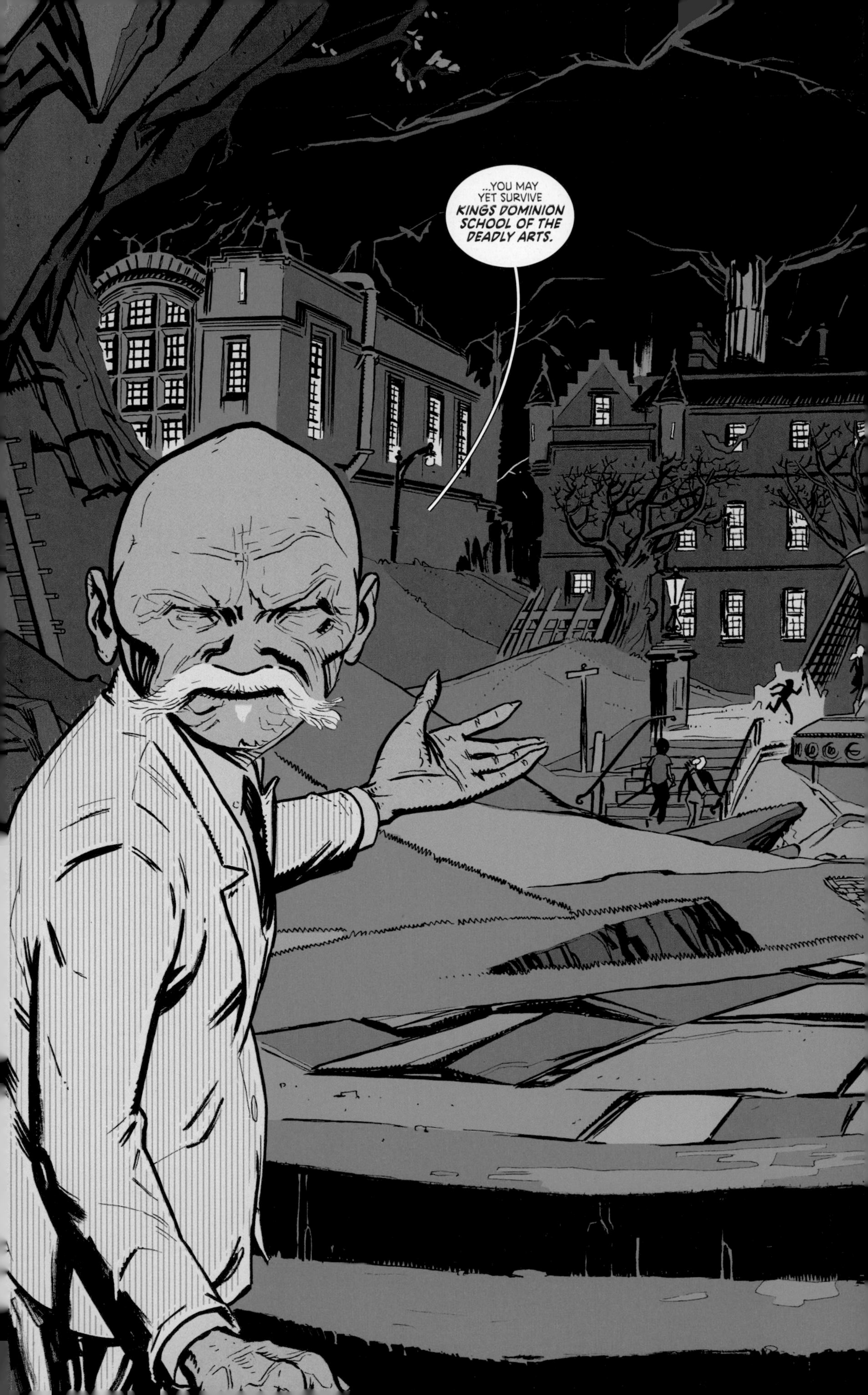
...YOU MAY YET SURVIVE KINGS DOMINION SCHOOL OF THE DEADLY ARTS.

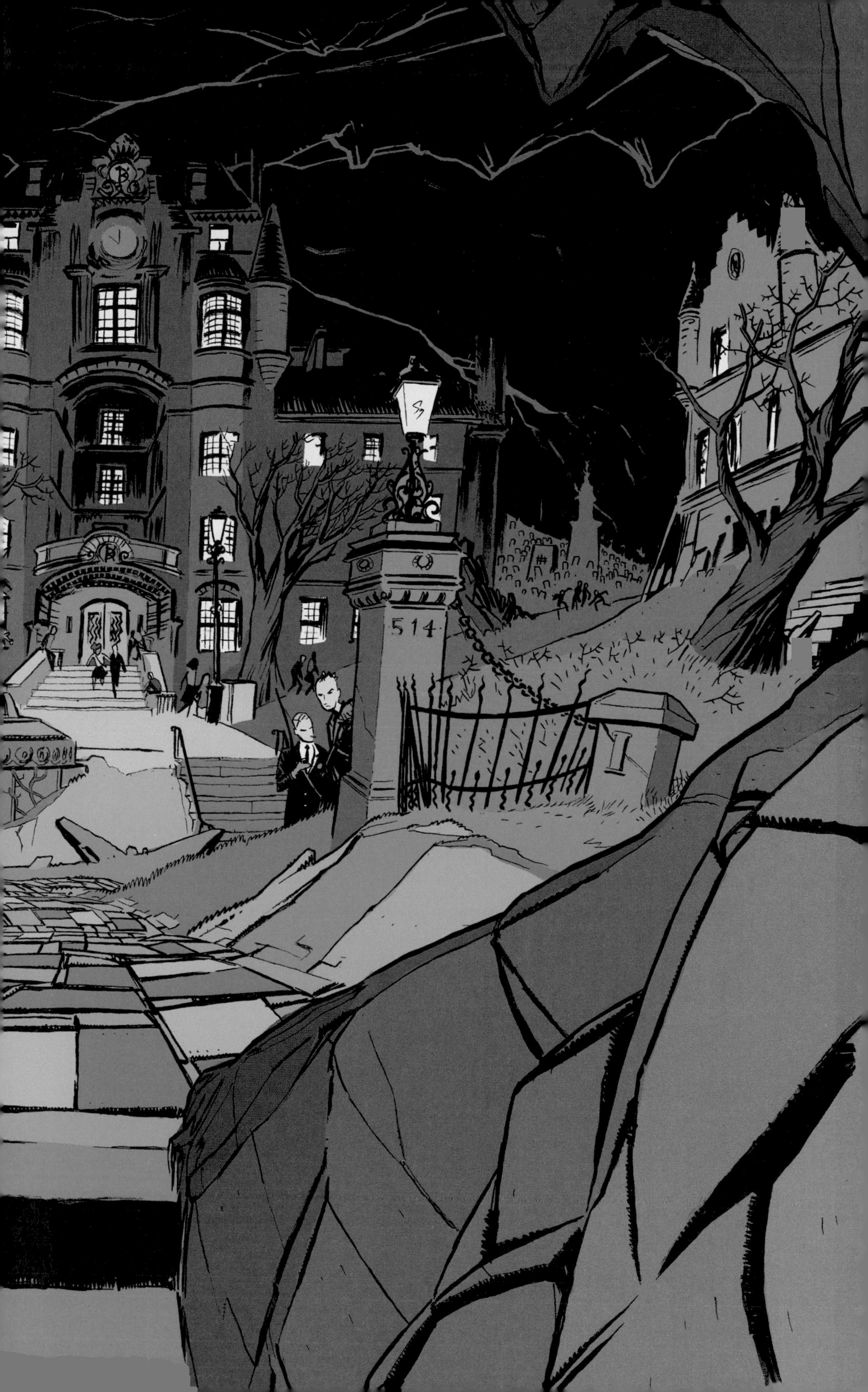
514

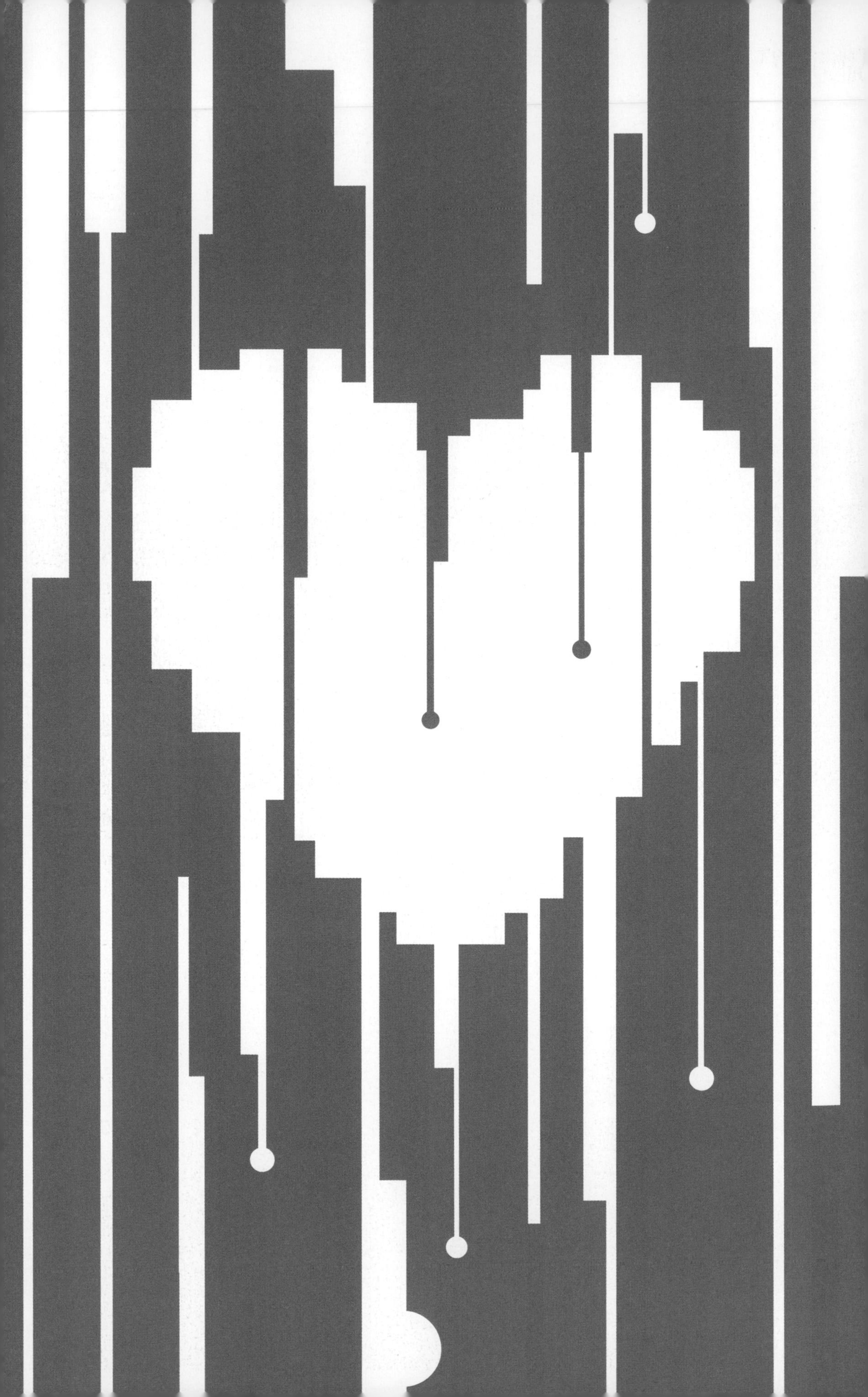

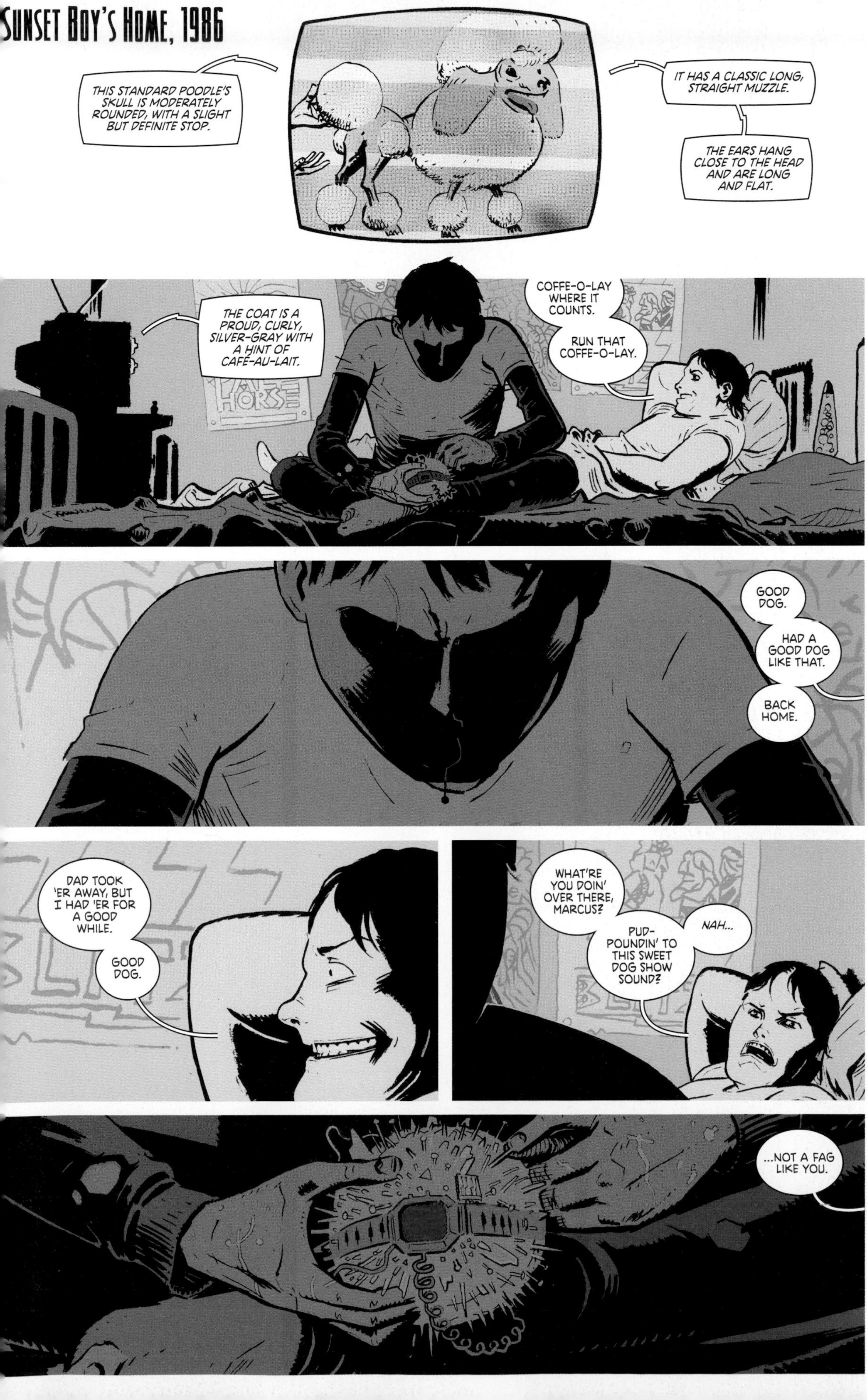
SUNSET BOY'S HOME, 1986
THIS STANDARD POODLE'S SKULL IS MODERATELY ROUNDED, WITH A SLIGHT BUT DEFINITE STOP.
IT HAS A CLASSIC LONG, STRAIGHT MUZZLE.
THE EARS HANG CLOSE TO THE HEAD AND ARE LONG AND FLAT.
THE COAT IS A PROUD, CURLY, SILVER-GRAY WITH A HINT OF CAFÉ-AU-LAIT.
COFFE-O-LAY WHERE IT COUNTS.
RUN THAT COFFE-O-LAY.
GOOD DOG.
HAD A GOOD DOG LIKE THAT.
BACK HOME.
DAD TOOK 'ER AWAY, BUT I HAD 'ER FOR A GOOD WHILE.
GOOD DOG.
WHAT'RE YOU DOIN' OVER THERE, MARCUS?
PUD-POUNDIN' TO THIS SWEET DOG SHOW SOUND?
NAH...
...NOT A FAG LIKE YOU.

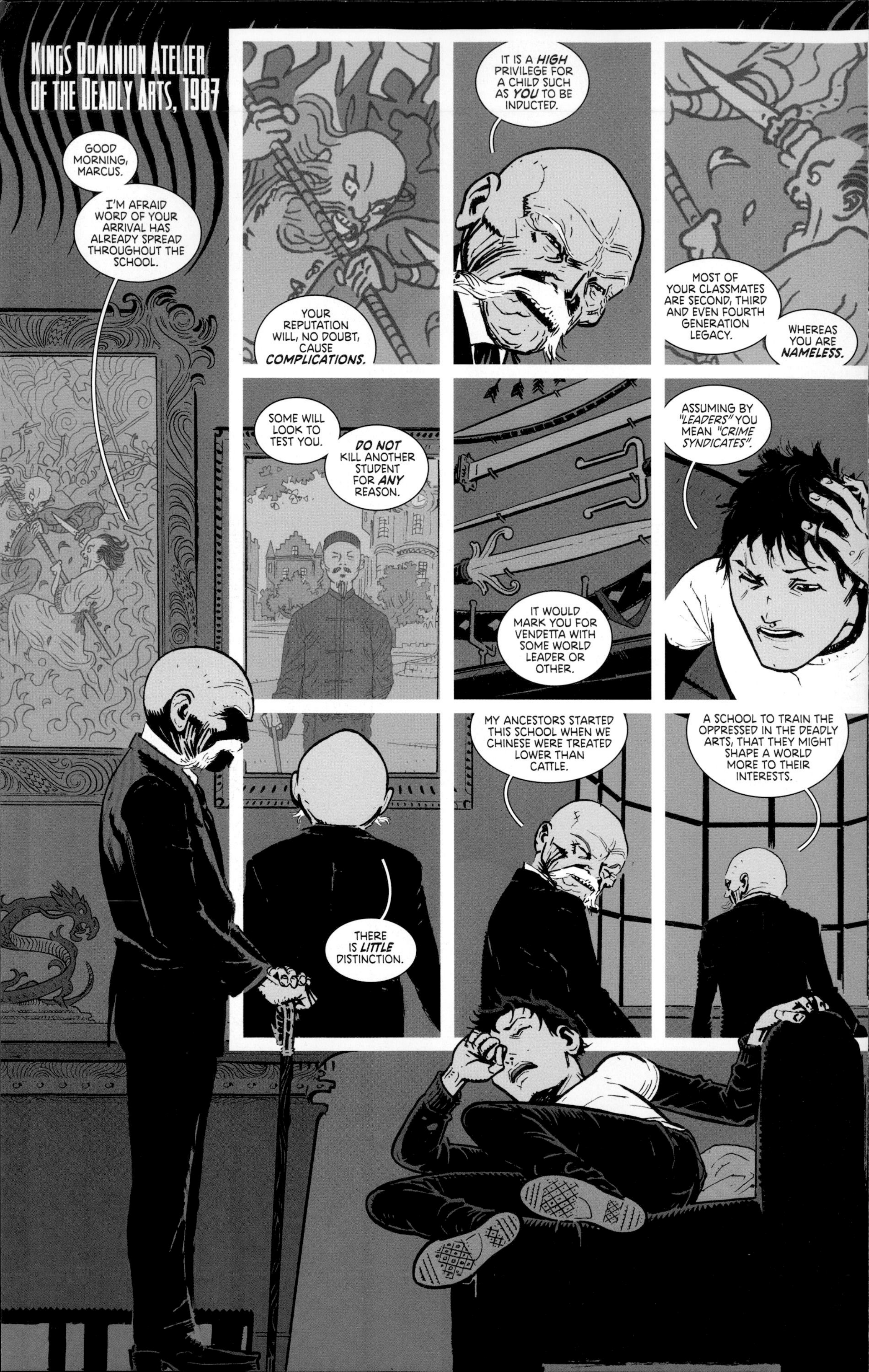
KINGS DOMINION ATELIER OF THE DEADLY ARTS, 1987
GOOD MORNING, MARCUS.
I'M AFRAID WORD OF YOUR ARRIVAL HAS ALREADY SPREAD THROUGHOUT THE SCHOOL.
YOUR REPUTATION WILL, NO DOUBT, CAUSE COMPLICATIONS.
IT IS A HIGH PRIVILEGE FOR A CHILD SUCH AS YOU TO BE INDUCTED.
MOST OF YOUR CLASSMATES ARE SECOND, THIRD AND EVEN FOURTH GENERATION LEGACY.
WHEREAS YOU ARE NAMELESS.
SOME WILL LOOK TO TEST YOU.
DO NOT KILL ANOTHER STUDENT FOR ANY REASON.
IT WOULD MARK YOU FOR VENDETTA WITH SOME WORLD LEADER OR OTHER.
ASSUMING BY "LEADERS" YOU MEAN "CRIME SYNDICATES".
THERE IS LITTLE DISTINCTION.
MY ANCESTORS STARTED THIS SCHOOL WHEN WE CHINESE WERE TREATED LOWER THAN CATTLE.
A SCHOOL TO TRAIN THE OPPRESSED IN THE DEADLY ARTS, THAT THEY MIGHT SHAPE A WORLD MORE TO THEIR INTERESTS.

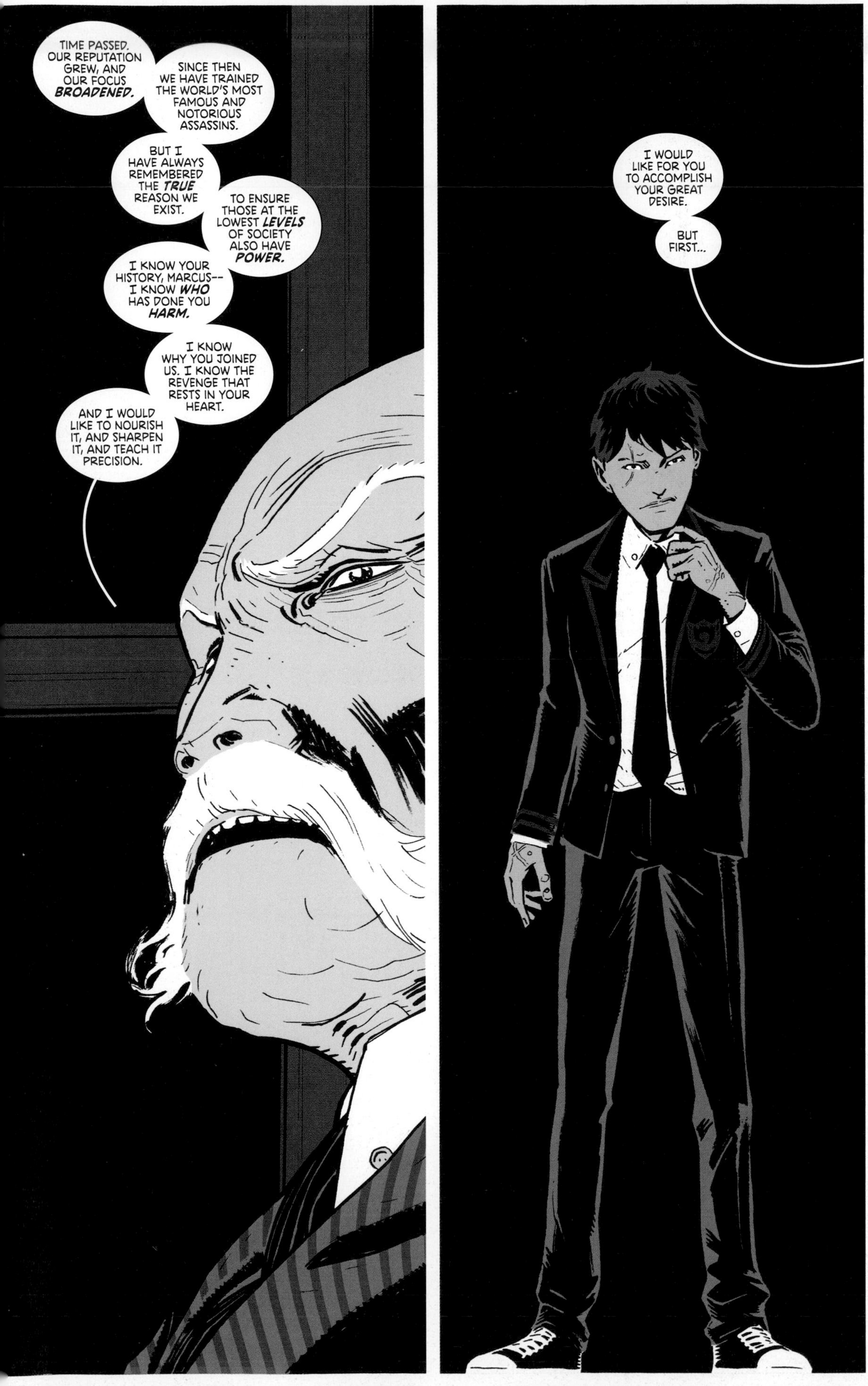
TIME PASSED. OUR REPUTATION GREW, AND OUR FOCUS BROADENED.
SINCE THEN WE HAVE TRAINED THE WORLD'S MOST FAMOUS AND NOTORIOUS ASSASSINS.
BUT I HAVE ALWAYS REMEMBERED THE TRUE REASON WE EXIST.
TO ENSURE THOSE AT THE LOWEST LEVELS OF SOCIETY ALSO HAVE POWER.
I KNOW YOUR HISTORY, MARCUS-- I KNOW WHO HAS DONE YOU HARM.
I KNOW WHY YOU JOINED US. I KNOW THE REVENGE THAT RESTS IN YOUR HEART.
AND I WOULD LIKE TO NOURISH IT, AND SHARPEN IT, AND TEACH IT PRECISION.
I WOULD LIKE FOR YOU TO ACCOMPLISH YOUR GREAT DESIRE.
BUT FIRST...

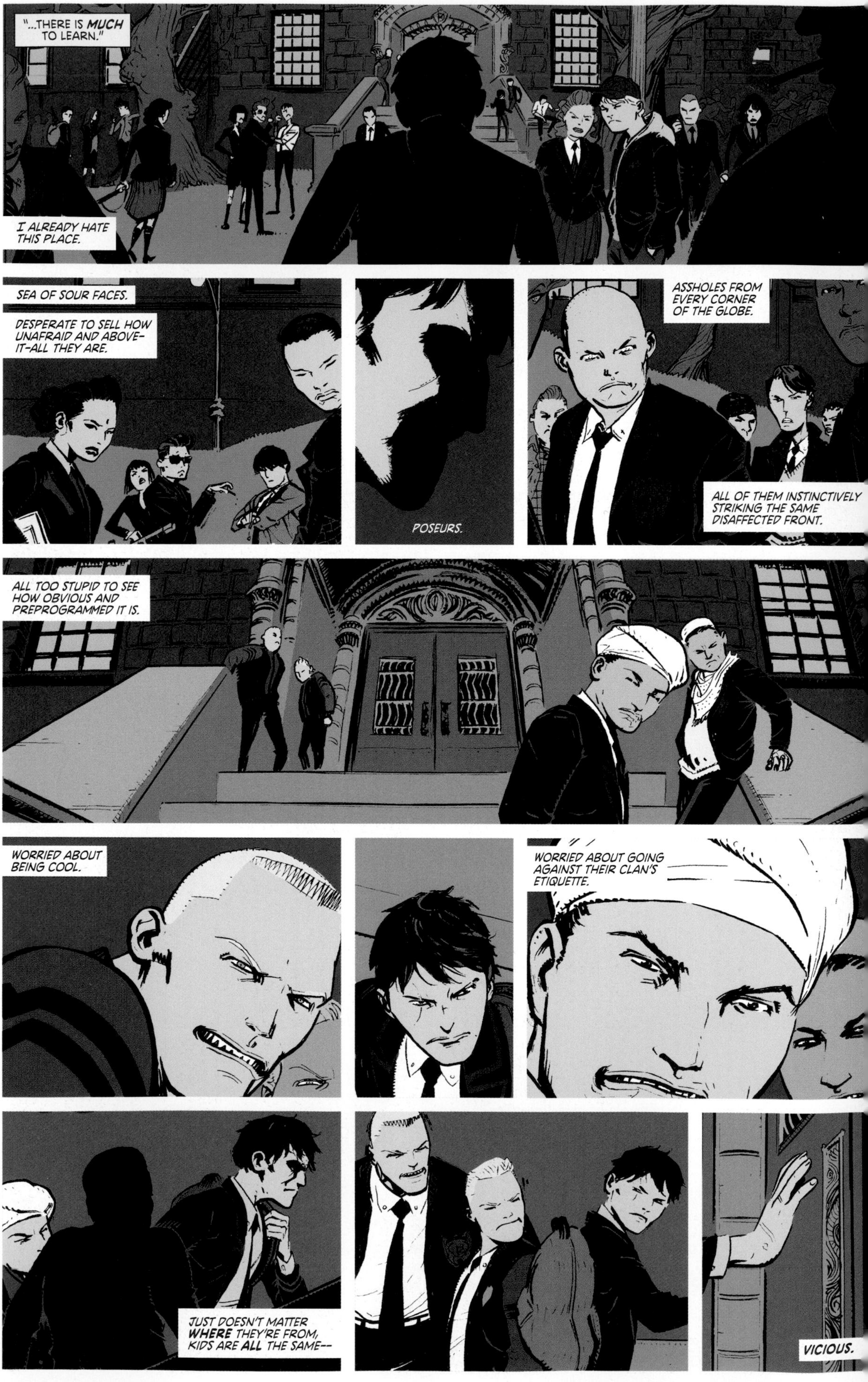
"...THERE IS MUCH TO LEARN."
I ALREADY HATE THIS PLACE.
SEA OF SOUR FACES.
DESPERATE TO SELL HOW UNAFRAID AND ABOVE-IT-ALL THEY ARE.
POSEURS.
ASSHOLES FROM EVERY CORNER OF THE GLOBE.
ALL OF THEM INSTINCTIVELY STRIKING THE SAME DISAFFECTED FRONT.
ALL TOO STUPID TO SEE HOW OBVIOUS AND PREPROGRAMMED IT IS.
WORRIED ABOUT BEING COOL.
WORRIED ABOUT GOING AGAINST THEIR CLAN'S ETIQUETTE.
JUST DOESN'T MATTER WHERE THEY'RE FROM, KIDS ARE ALL THE SAME--
VICIOUS.

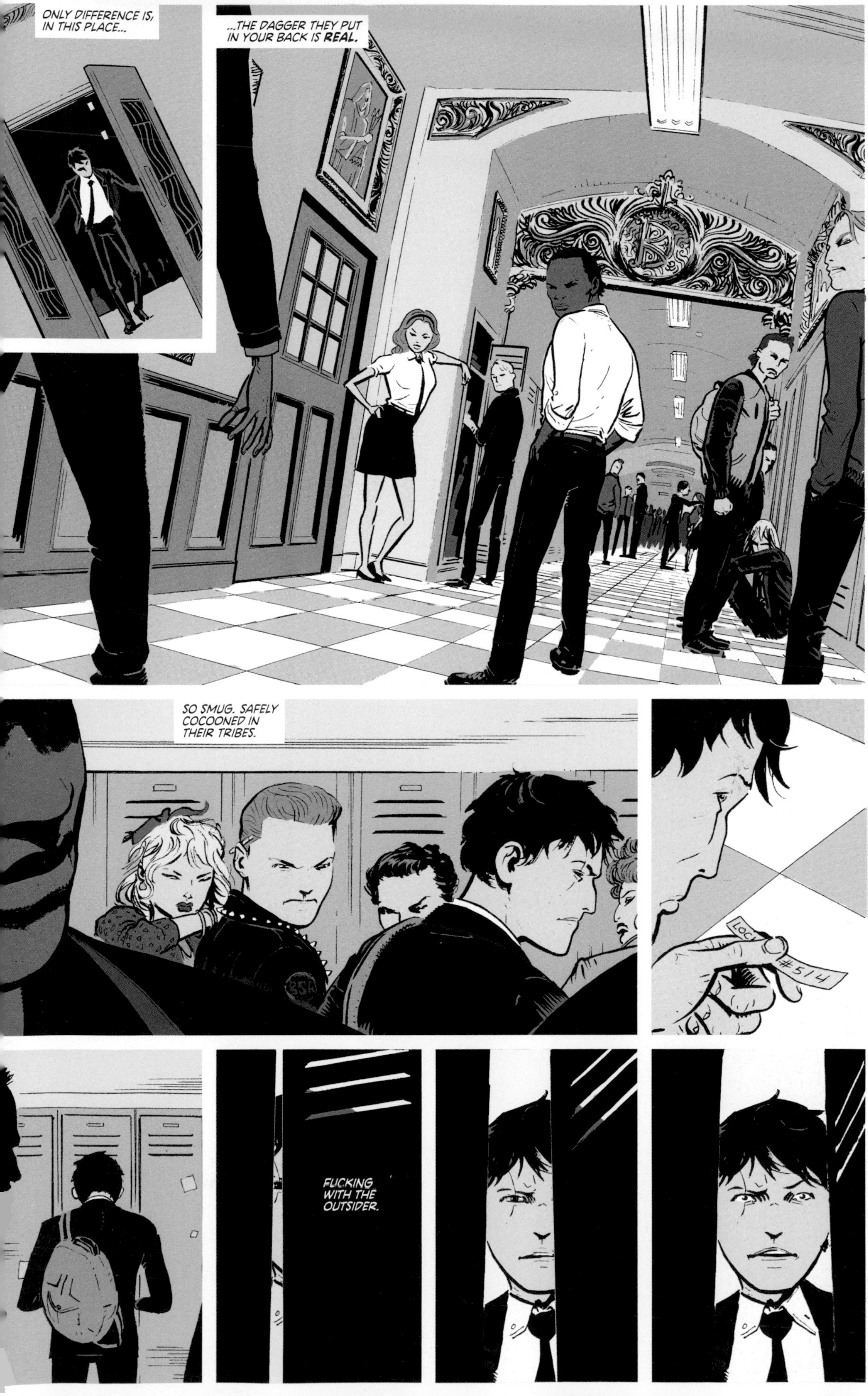
ONLY DIFFERENCE IS, IN THIS PLACE...
...THE DAGGER THEY PUT IN YOUR BACK IS **REAL.**
SO SMUG. SAFELY COCOONED IN THEIR TRIBES.
LOCK #514
FUCKING WITH THE OUTSIDER.

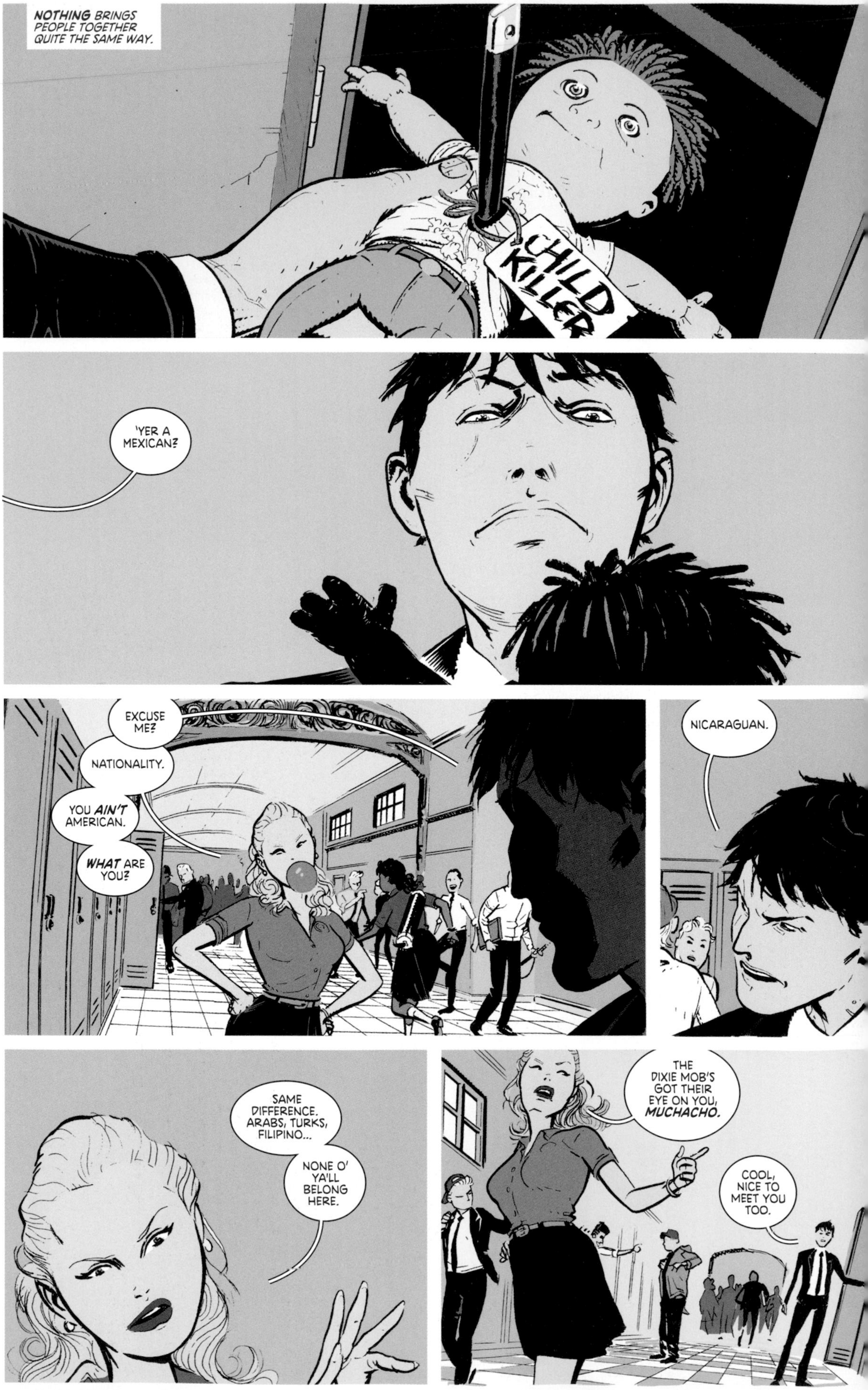
NOTHING BRINGS PEOPLE TOGETHER QUITE THE SAME WAY.
CHILD KILLER
'YER A MEXICAN?
EXCUSE ME?
NATIONALITY.
YOU AIN'T AMERICAN.
WHAT ARE YOU?
NICARAGUAN.
SAME DIFFERENCE. ARABS, TURKS, FILIPINO...
NONE O' YA'LL BELONG HERE.
THE DIXIE MOB'S GOT THEIR EYE ON YOU, MUCHACHO.
COOL, NICE TO MEET YOU TOO.

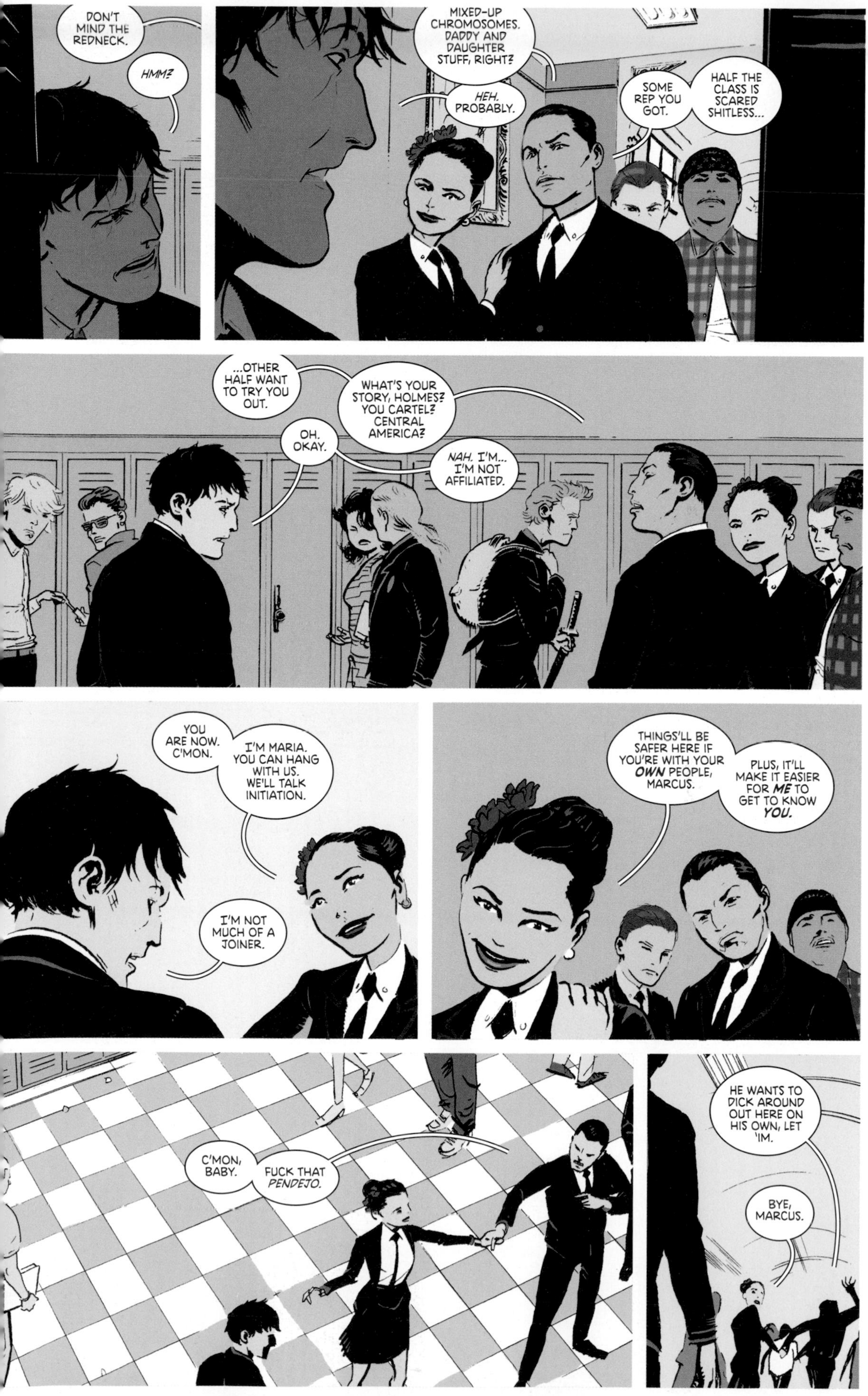
DON'T MIND THE REDNECK.
HMM?
MIXED-UP CHROMOSOMES. DADDY AND DAUGHTER STUFF, RIGHT?
HEH. PROBABLY.
SOME REP YOU GOT.
HALF THE CLASS IS SCARED SHITLESS...
...OTHER HALF WANT TO TRY YOU OUT.
WHAT'S YOUR STORY, HOLMES? YOU CARTEL? CENTRAL AMERICA?
OH. OKAY.
NAH. I'M... I'M NOT AFFILIATED.
YOU ARE NOW. C'MON.
I'M MARIA. YOU CAN HANG WITH US. WE'LL TALK INITIATION.
I'M NOT MUCH OF A JOINER.
THINGS'LL BE SAFER HERE IF YOU'RE WITH YOUR OWN PEOPLE, MARCUS.
PLUS, IT'LL MAKE IT EASIER FOR ME TO GET TO KNOW YOU.
C'MON, BABY.
FUCK THAT PENDEJO.
HE WANTS TO DICK AROUND OUT HERE ON HIS OWN, LET 'IM.
BYE, MARCUS.

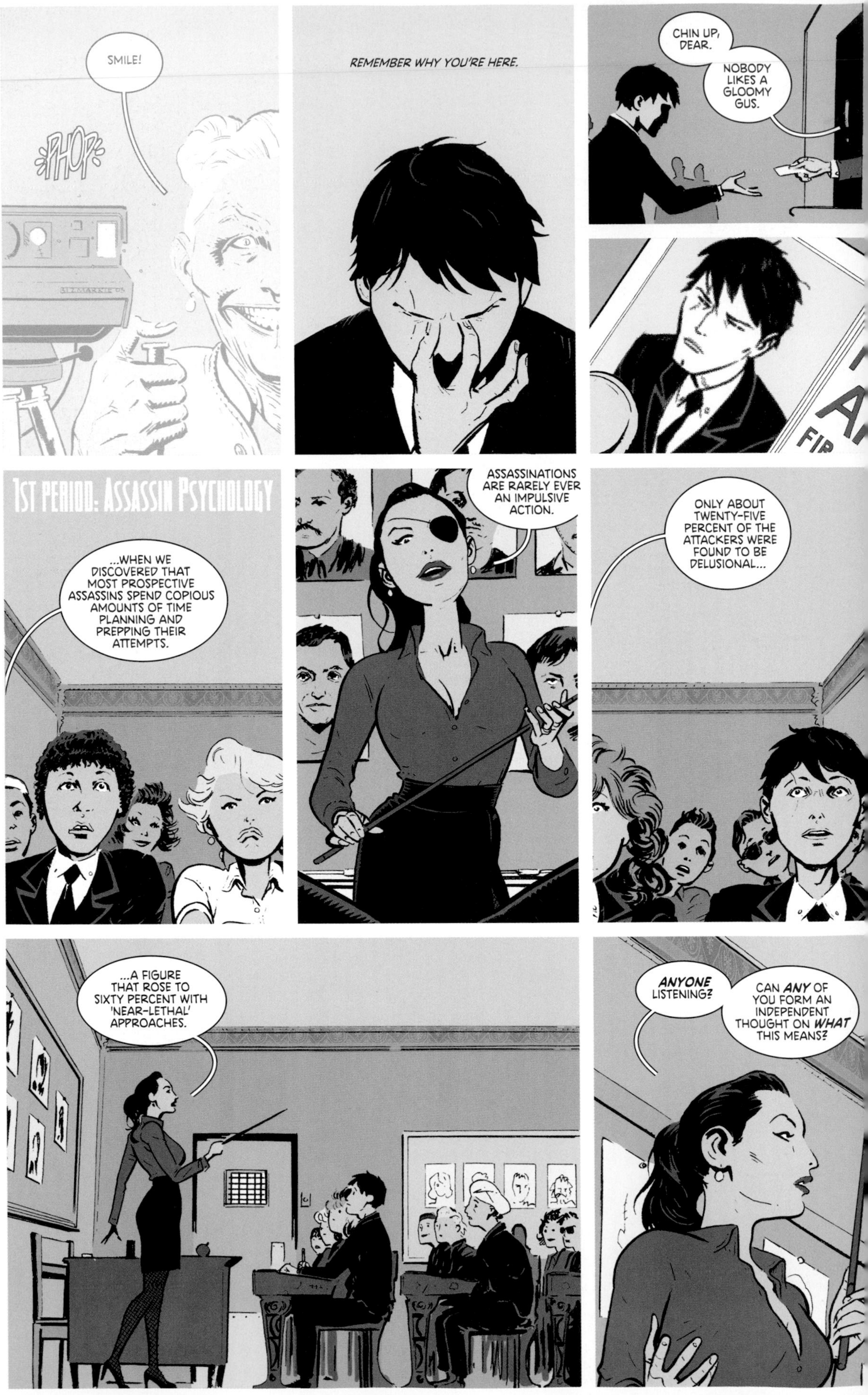
SMILE!
PHOP
REMEMBER WHY YOU'RE HERE.
CHIN UP, DEAR.
NOBODY LIKES A GLOOMY GUS.
1ST PERIOD: ASSASSIN PSYCHOLOGY
...WHEN WE DISCOVERED THAT MOST PROSPECTIVE ASSASSINS SPEND COPIOUS AMOUNTS OF TIME PLANNING AND PREPPING THEIR ATTEMPTS.
ASSASSINATIONS ARE RARELY EVER AN IMPULSIVE ACTION.
ONLY ABOUT TWENTY-FIVE PERCENT OF THE ATTACKERS WERE FOUND TO BE DELUSIONAL...
...A FIGURE THAT ROSE TO SIXTY PERCENT WITH 'NEAR-LETHAL' APPROACHES.
ANYONE LISTENING?
CAN ANY OF YOU FORM AN INDEPENDENT THOUGHT ON WHAT THIS MEANS?

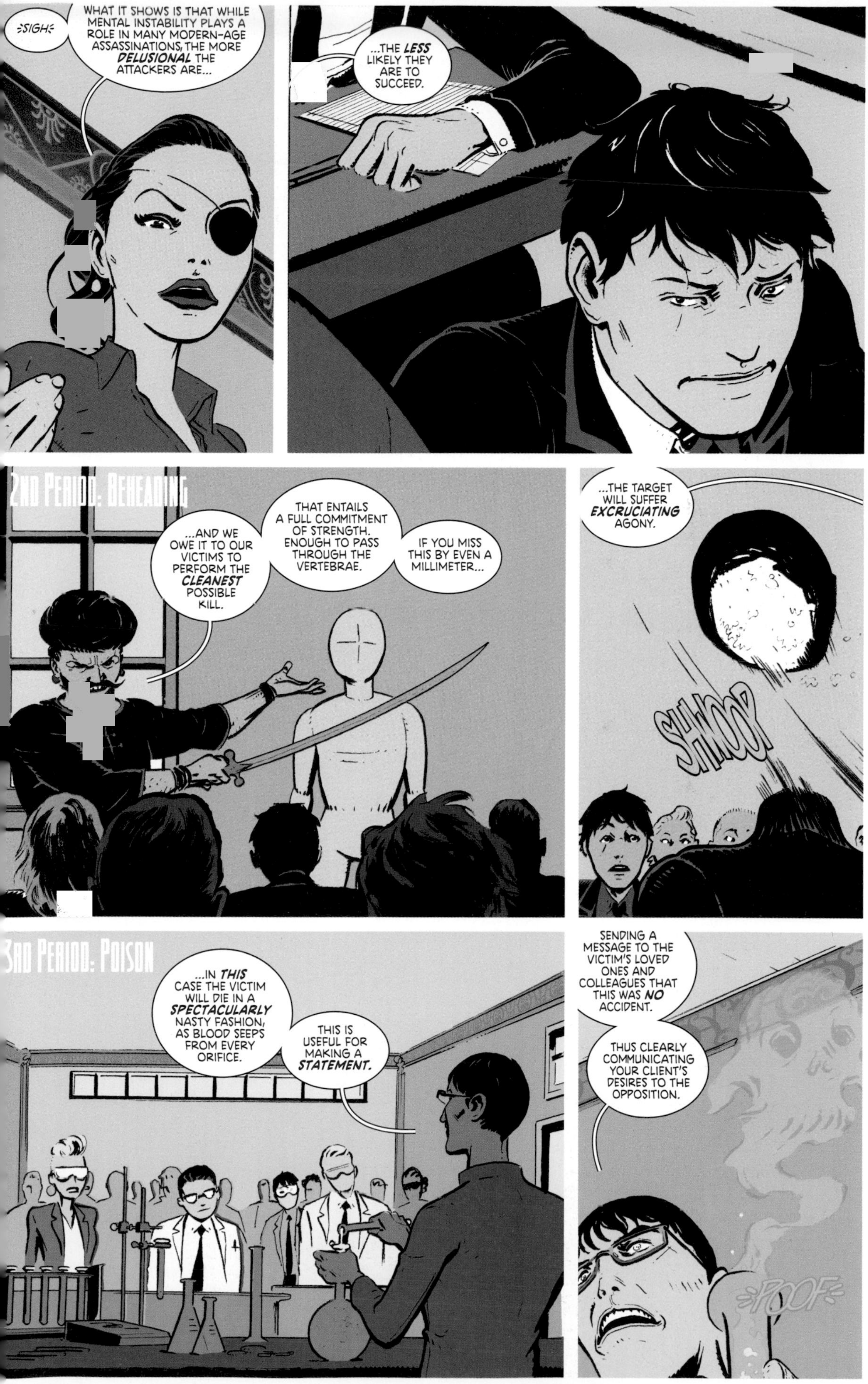

SIGH
WHAT IT SHOWS IS THAT WHILE MENTAL INSTABILITY PLAYS A ROLE IN MANY MODERN-AGE ASSASSINATIONS, THE MORE DELUSIONAL THE ATTACKERS ARE...
...THE LESS LIKELY THEY ARE TO SUCCEED.
2ND PERIOD: BEHEADING
...AND WE OWE IT TO OUR VICTIMS TO PERFORM THE CLEANEST POSSIBLE KILL.
THAT ENTAILS A FULL COMMITMENT OF STRENGTH. ENOUGH TO PASS THROUGH THE VERTEBRAE.
IF YOU MISS THIS BY EVEN A MILLIMETER...
...THE TARGET WILL SUFFER EXCRUCIATING AGONY.
SHOOP
3RD PERIOD: POISON
...IN THIS CASE THE VICTIM WILL DIE IN A SPECTACULARLY NASTY FASHION, AS BLOOD SEEPS FROM EVERY ORIFICE.
THIS IS USEFUL FOR MAKING A STATEMENT.
SENDING A MESSAGE TO THE VICTIM'S LOVED ONES AND COLLEAGUES THAT THIS WAS NO ACCIDENT.
THUS CLEARLY COMMUNICATING YOUR CLIENT'S DESIRES TO THE OPPOSITION.
POOF

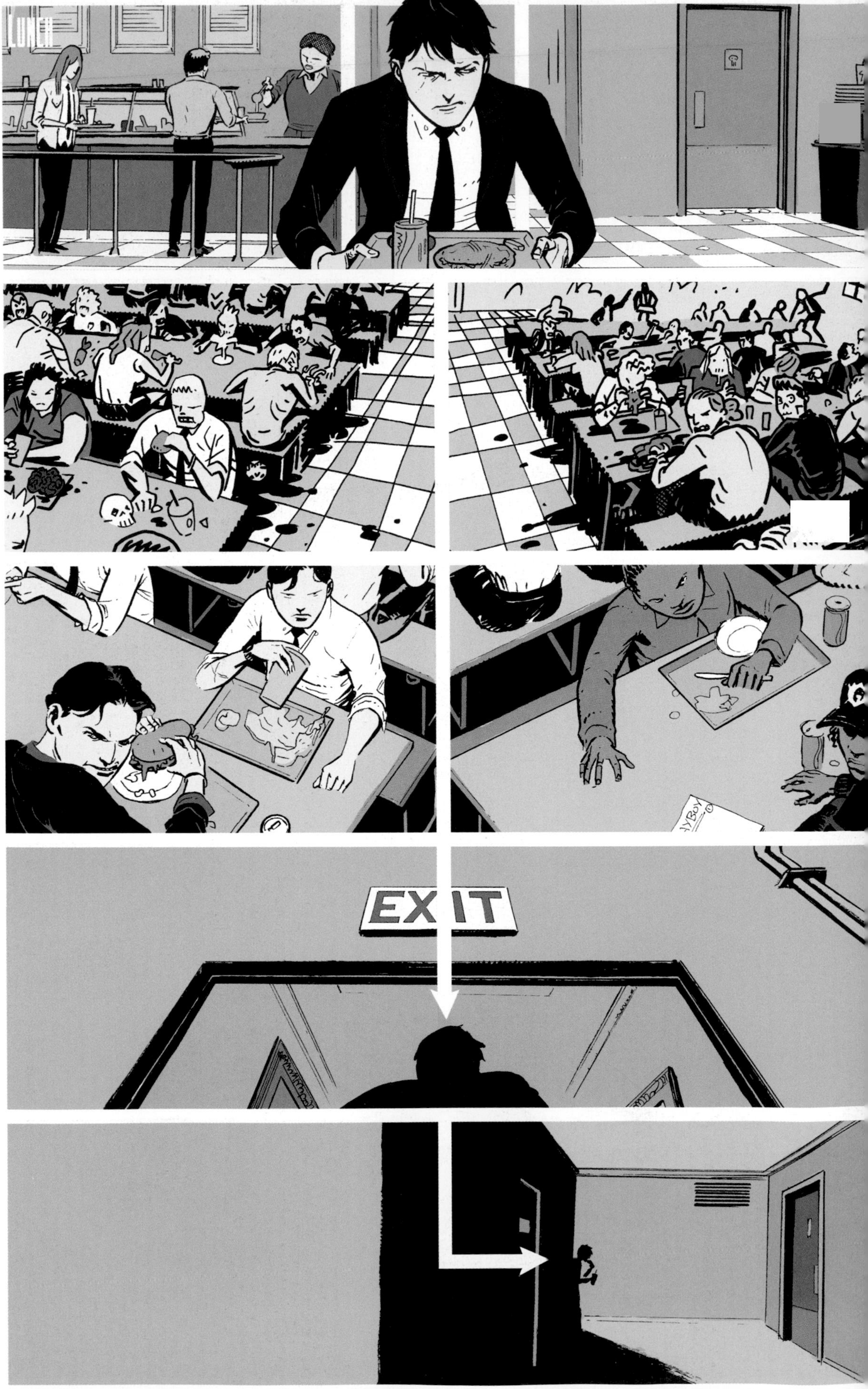
LUNCH
EXIT

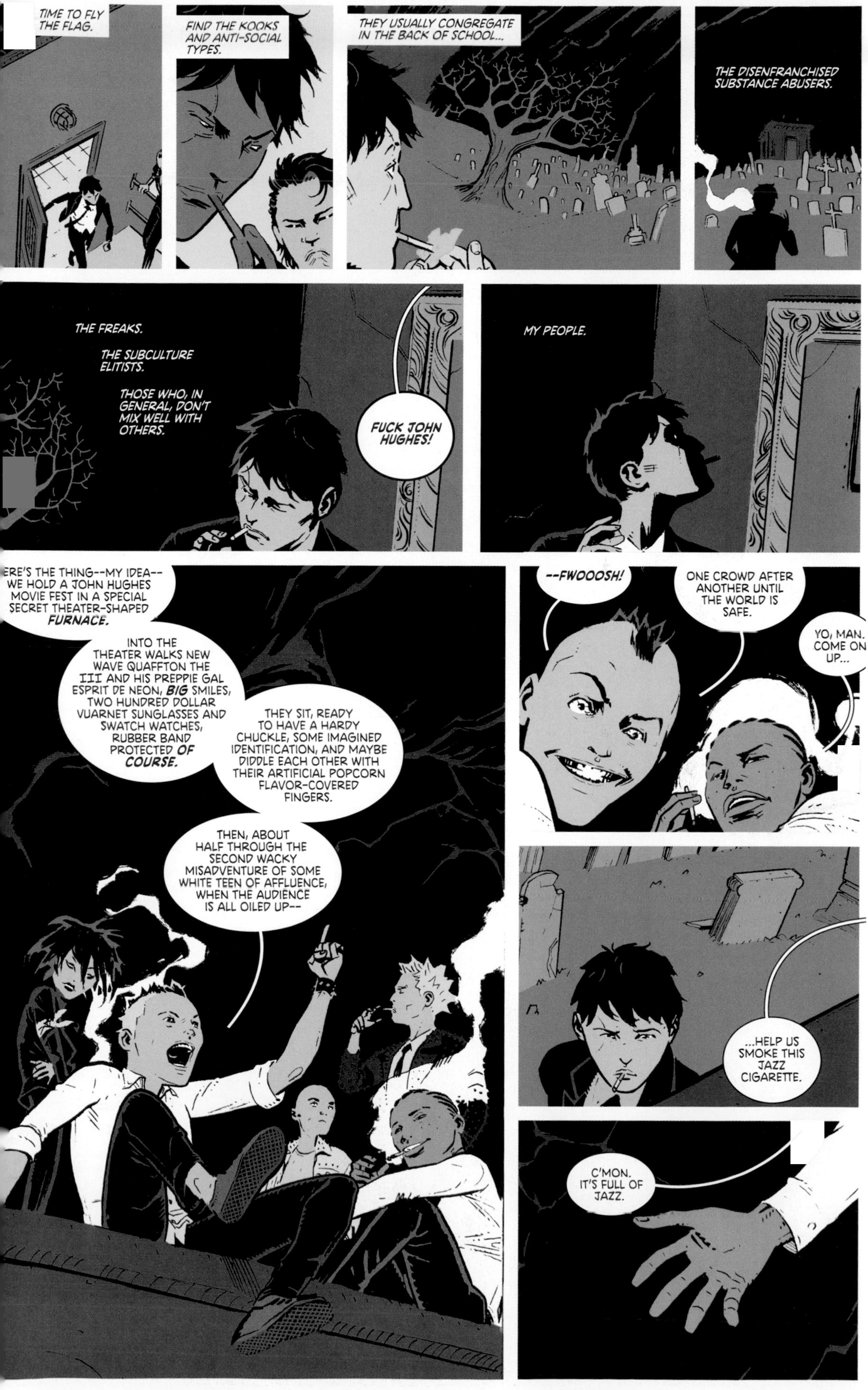
TIME TO FLY THE FLAG.
FIND THE KOOKS AND ANTI-SOCIAL TYPES.
THEY USUALLY CONGREGATE IN THE BACK OF SCHOOL...
THE DISENFRANCHISED SUBSTANCE ABUSERS.
THE FREAKS.
THE SUBCULTURE ELITISTS.
THOSE WHO, IN GENERAL, DON'T MIX WELL WITH OTHERS.
FUCK JOHN HUGHES!
MY PEOPLE.
ERE'S THE THING--MY IDEA--WE HOLD A JOHN HUGHES MOVIE FEST IN A SPECIAL SECRET THEATER-SHAPED FURNACE.
INTO THE THEATER WALKS NEW WAVE QUAFFTON THE III AND HIS PREPPIE GAL ESPRIT DE NEON, BIG SMILES, TWO HUNDRED DOLLAR VUARNET SUNGLASSES AND SWATCH WATCHES, RUBBER BAND PROTECTED OF COURSE.
THEY SIT, READY TO HAVE A HARDY CHUCKLE, SOME IMAGINED IDENTIFICATION, AND MAYBE DIDDLE EACH OTHER WITH THEIR ARTIFICIAL POPCORN FLAVOR-COVERED FINGERS.
THEN, ABOUT HALF THROUGH THE SECOND WACKY MISADVENTURE OF SOME WHITE TEEN OF AFFLUENCE, WHEN THE AUDIENCE IS ALL OILED UP--
--FWOOOSH!
ONE CROWD AFTER ANOTHER UNTIL THE WORLD IS SAFE.
YO, MAN. COME ON UP...
...HELP US SMOKE THIS JAZZ CIGARETTE.
C'MON. IT'S FULL OF JAZZ.

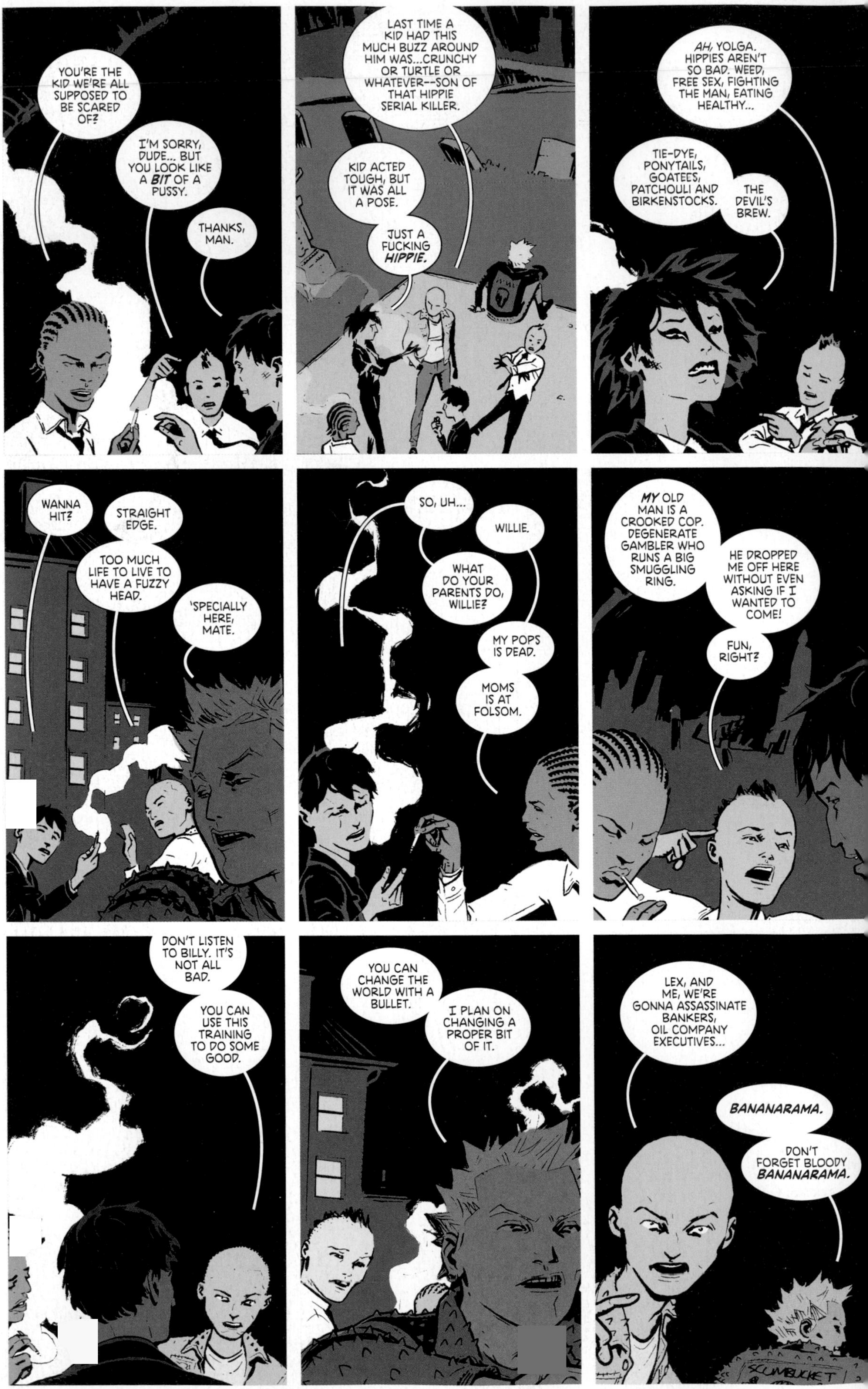
YOU'RE THE KID WE'RE ALL SUPPOSED TO BE SCARED OF?
I'M SORRY, DUDE... BUT YOU LOOK LIKE A *BIT* OF A PUSSY.
THANKS, MAN.
LAST TIME A KID HAD THIS MUCH BUZZ AROUND HIM WAS...CRUNCHY OR TURTLE OR WHATEVER--SON OF THAT HIPPIE SERIAL KILLER.
KID ACTED TOUGH, BUT IT WAS ALL A POSE.
JUST A FUCKING *HIPPIE.*
AH, YOLGA. HIPPIES AREN'T SO BAD. WEED, FREE SEX, FIGHTING THE MAN, EATING HEALTHY...
TIE-DYE, PONYTAILS, GOATEES, PATCHOULI AND BIRKENSTOCKS.
THE DEVIL'S BREW.
WANNA HIT?
STRAIGHT EDGE.
TOO MUCH LIFE TO LIVE TO HAVE A FUZZY HEAD.
'SPECIALLY HERE, MATE.
SO, UH...
WILLIE.
WHAT DO YOUR PARENTS DO, WILLIE?
MY POPS IS DEAD.
MOMS IS AT FOLSOM.
MY OLD MAN IS A CROOKED COP. DEGENERATE GAMBLER WHO RUNS A BIG SMUGGLING RING.
HE DROPPED ME OFF HERE WITHOUT EVEN ASKING IF I WANTED TO COME!
FUN, RIGHT?
DON'T LISTEN TO BILLY. IT'S NOT ALL BAD.
YOU CAN USE THIS TRAINING TO DO SOME GOOD.
YOU CAN CHANGE THE WORLD WITH A BULLET.
I PLAN ON CHANGING A PROPER BIT OF IT.
LEX, AND ME, WE'RE GONNA ASSASSINATE BANKERS, OIL COMPANY EXECUTIVES...
BANANARAMA.
DON'T FORGET BLOODY *BANANARAMA.*
SCUMBUCKET

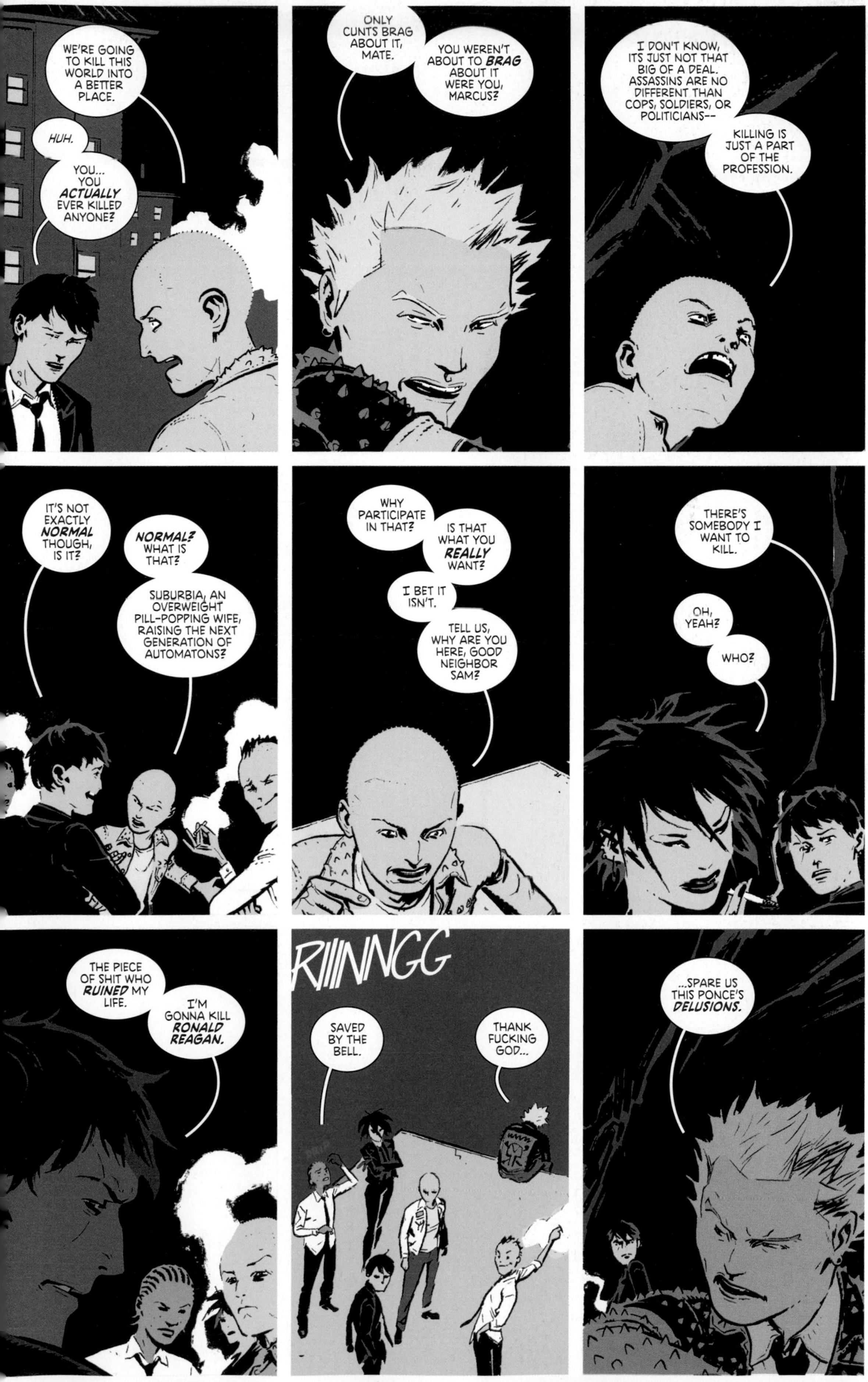
WE'RE GOING TO KILL THIS WORLD INTO A BETTER PLACE.
HUH.
YOU... YOU ACTUALLY EVER KILLED ANYONE?
ONLY CUNTS BRAG ABOUT IT, MATE.
YOU WEREN'T ABOUT TO BRAG ABOUT IT WERE YOU, MARCUS?
I DON'T KNOW, ITS JUST NOT THAT BIG OF A DEAL. ASSASSINS ARE NO DIFFERENT THAN COPS, SOLDIERS, OR POLITICIANS--
KILLING IS JUST A PART OF THE PROFESSION.
IT'S NOT EXACTLY NORMAL THOUGH, IS IT?
NORMAL? WHAT IS THAT?
SUBURBIA, AN OVERWEIGHT PILL-POPPING WIFE, RAISING THE NEXT GENERATION OF AUTOMATONS?
WHY PARTICIPATE IN THAT?
IS THAT WHAT YOU REALLY WANT?
I BET IT ISN'T.
TELL US, WHY ARE YOU HERE, GOOD NEIGHBOR SAM?
THERE'S SOMEBODY I WANT TO KILL.
OH, YEAH?
WHO?
THE PIECE OF SHIT WHO RUINED MY LIFE.
I'M GONNA KILL RONALD REAGAN.
RIIINNGG
SAVED BY THE BELL.
THANK FUCKING GOD...
...SPARE US THIS PONCE'S DELUSIONS.

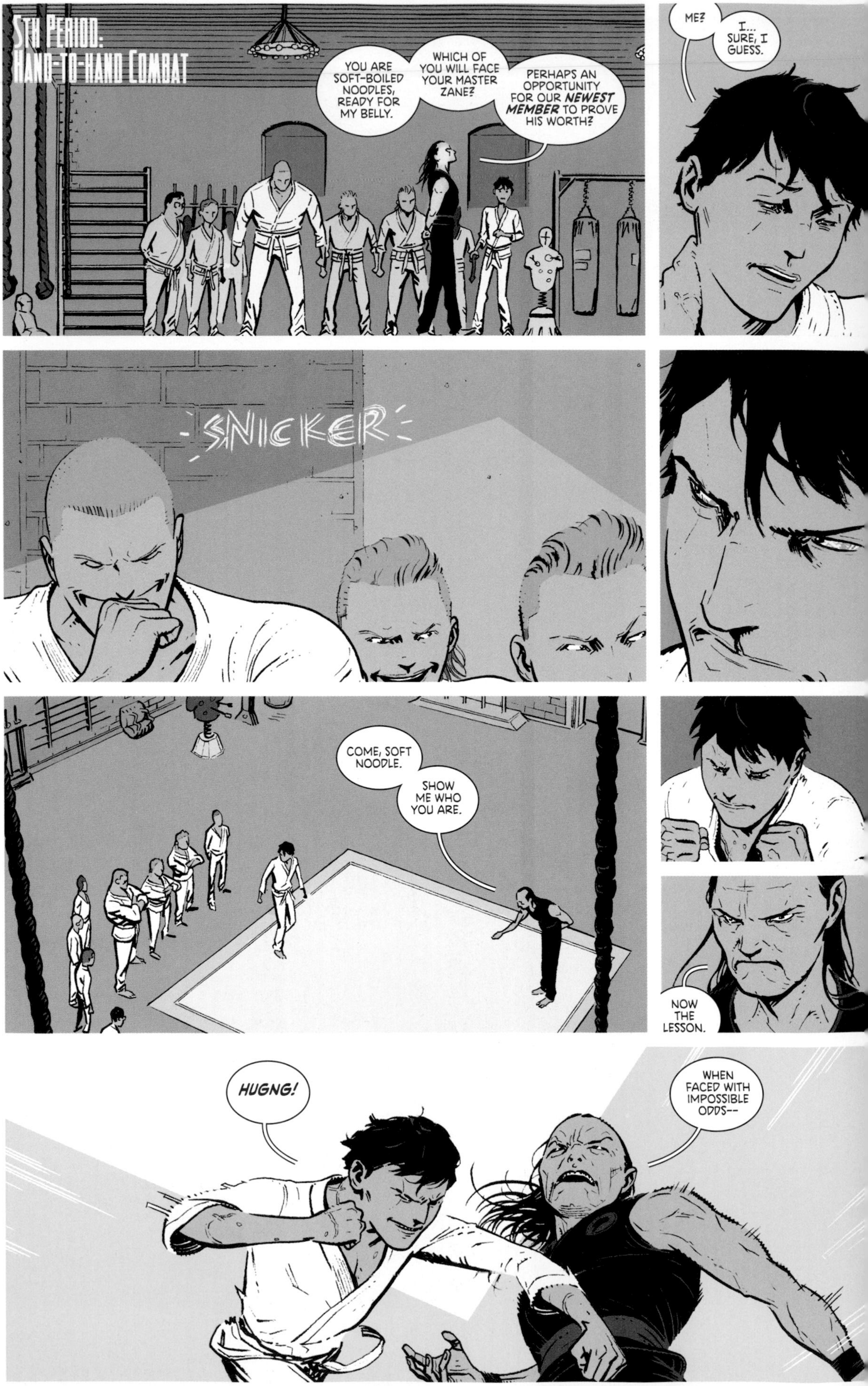
5TH PERIOD: HAND-TO-HAND COMBAT
YOU ARE SOFT-BOILED NOODLES, READY FOR MY BELLY.
WHICH OF YOU WILL FACE YOUR MASTER ZANE?
PERHAPS AN OPPORTUNITY FOR OUR NEWEST MEMBER TO PROVE HIS WORTH?
ME?
I... SURE, I GUESS.
SNICKER
COME, SOFT NOODLE.
SHOW ME WHO YOU ARE.
NOW THE LESSON.
HUGNG!
WHEN FACED WITH IMPOSSIBLE ODDS--

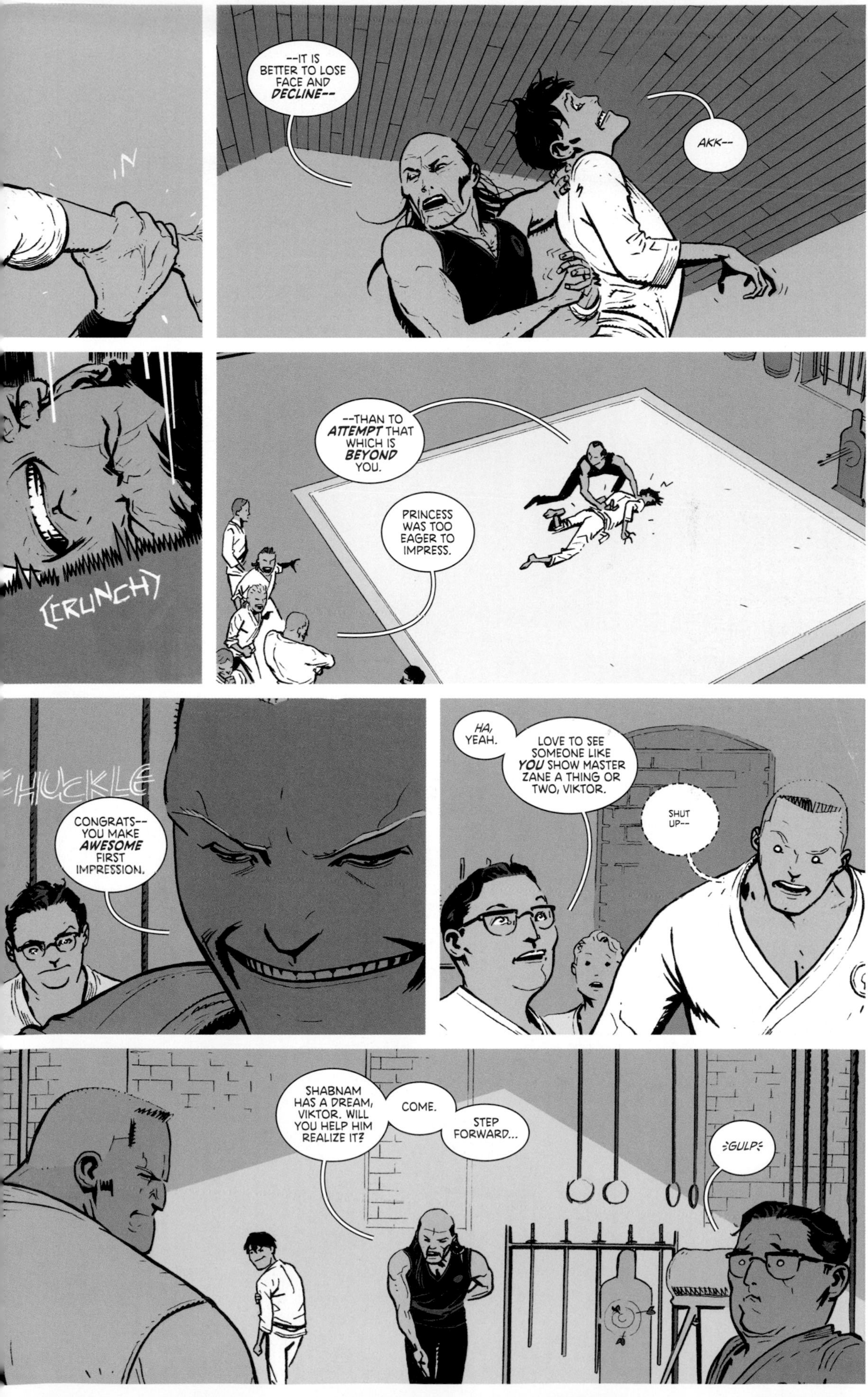
--IT IS BETTER TO LOSE FACE AND DECLINE--
AKK--
CRUNCH
--THAN TO ATTEMPT THAT WHICH IS BEYOND YOU.
PRINCESS WAS TOO EAGER TO IMPRESS.
CHUCKLE
CONGRATS-- YOU MAKE AWESOME FIRST IMPRESSION.
HA, YEAH.
LOVE TO SEE SOMEONE LIKE YOU SHOW MASTER ZANE A THING OR TWO, VIKTOR.
SHUT UP--
SHABNAM HAS A DREAM, VIKTOR. WILL YOU HELP HIM REALIZE IT?
COME.
STEP FORWARD...
GULP

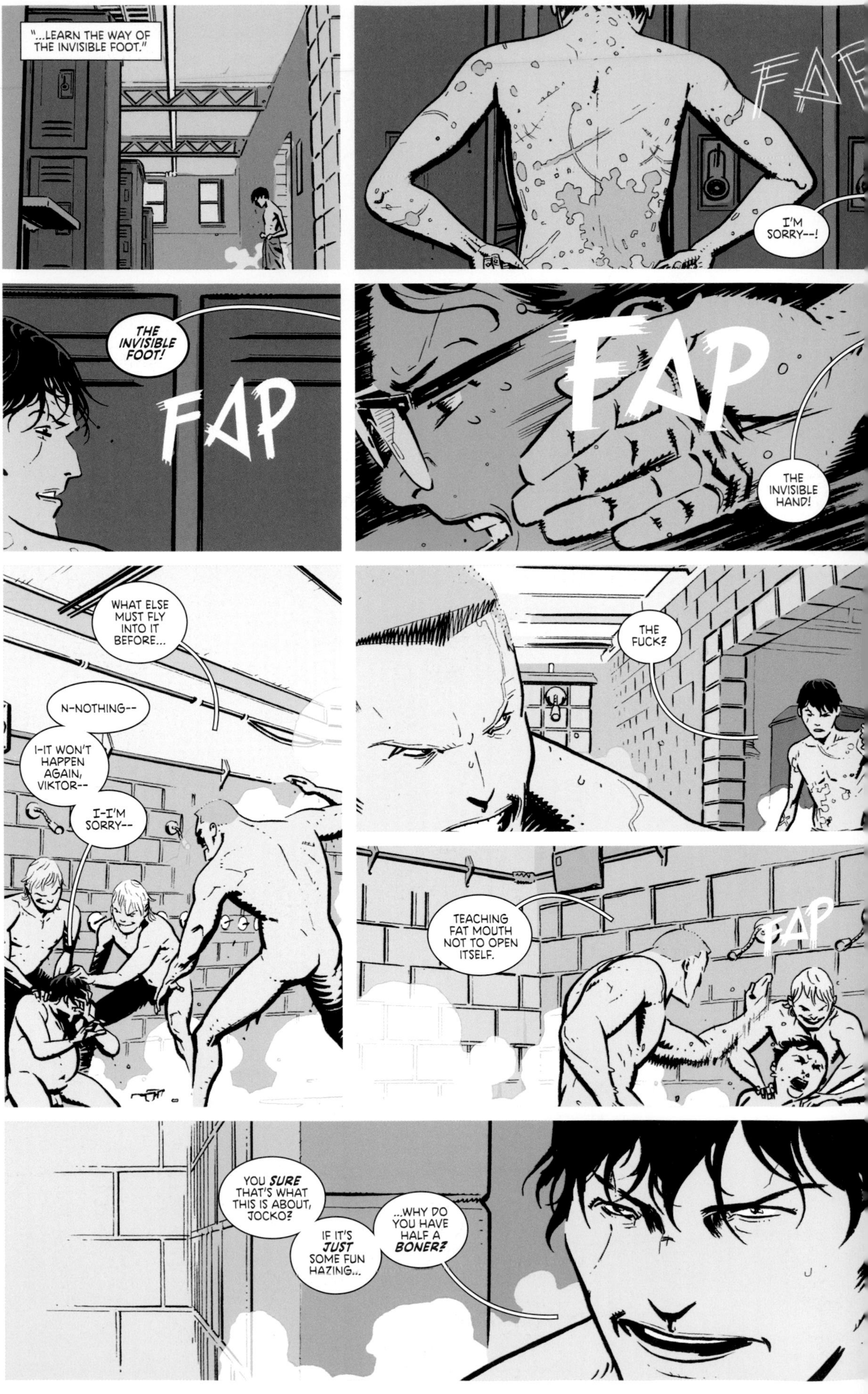
"...LEARN THE WAY OF THE INVISIBLE FOOT."
FAP
I'M SORRY--!
THE INVISIBLE FOOT!
FAP
FAP
THE INVISIBLE HAND!
WHAT ELSE MUST FLY INTO IT BEFORE...
N-NOTHING--
I-IT WON'T HAPPEN AGAIN, VIKTOR--
I-I'M SORRY--
THE FUCK?
TEACHING FAT MOUTH NOT TO OPEN ITSELF.
FAP
YOU SURE THAT'S WHAT THIS IS ABOUT, JOCKO?
IF IT'S JUST SOME FUN HAZING...
...WHY DO YOU HAVE HALF A BONER?

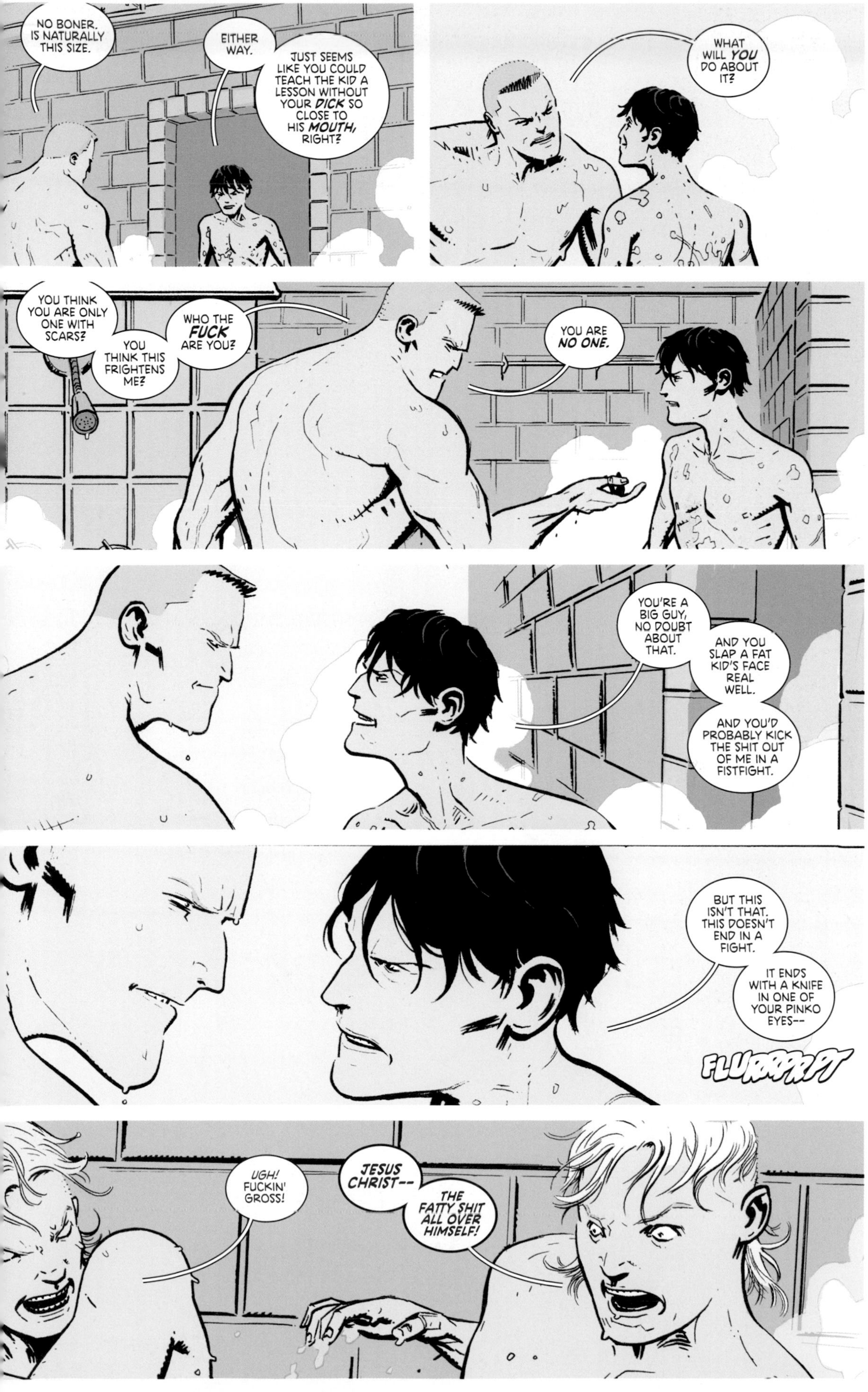
NO BONER. IS NATURALLY THIS SIZE.
EITHER WAY.
JUST SEEMS LIKE YOU COULD TEACH THE KID A LESSON WITHOUT YOUR *DICK* SO CLOSE TO HIS *MOUTH,* RIGHT?
WHAT WILL *YOU* DO ABOUT IT?
YOU THINK YOU ARE ONLY ONE WITH SCARS?
YOU THINK THIS FRIGHTENS ME?
WHO THE *FUCK* ARE YOU?
YOU ARE *NO ONE.*
YOU'RE A BIG GUY, NO DOUBT ABOUT THAT.
AND YOU SLAP A FAT KID'S FACE REAL WELL.
AND YOU'D PROBABLY KICK THE SHIT OUT OF ME IN A FISTFIGHT.
BUT THIS ISN'T THAT. THIS DOESN'T END IN A FIGHT.
IT ENDS WITH A KNIFE IN ONE OF YOUR PINKO EYES--
FLURRRRPT
UGH! FUCKIN' GROSS!
JESUS CHRIST--
THE FATTY SHIT ALL OVER HIMSELF!

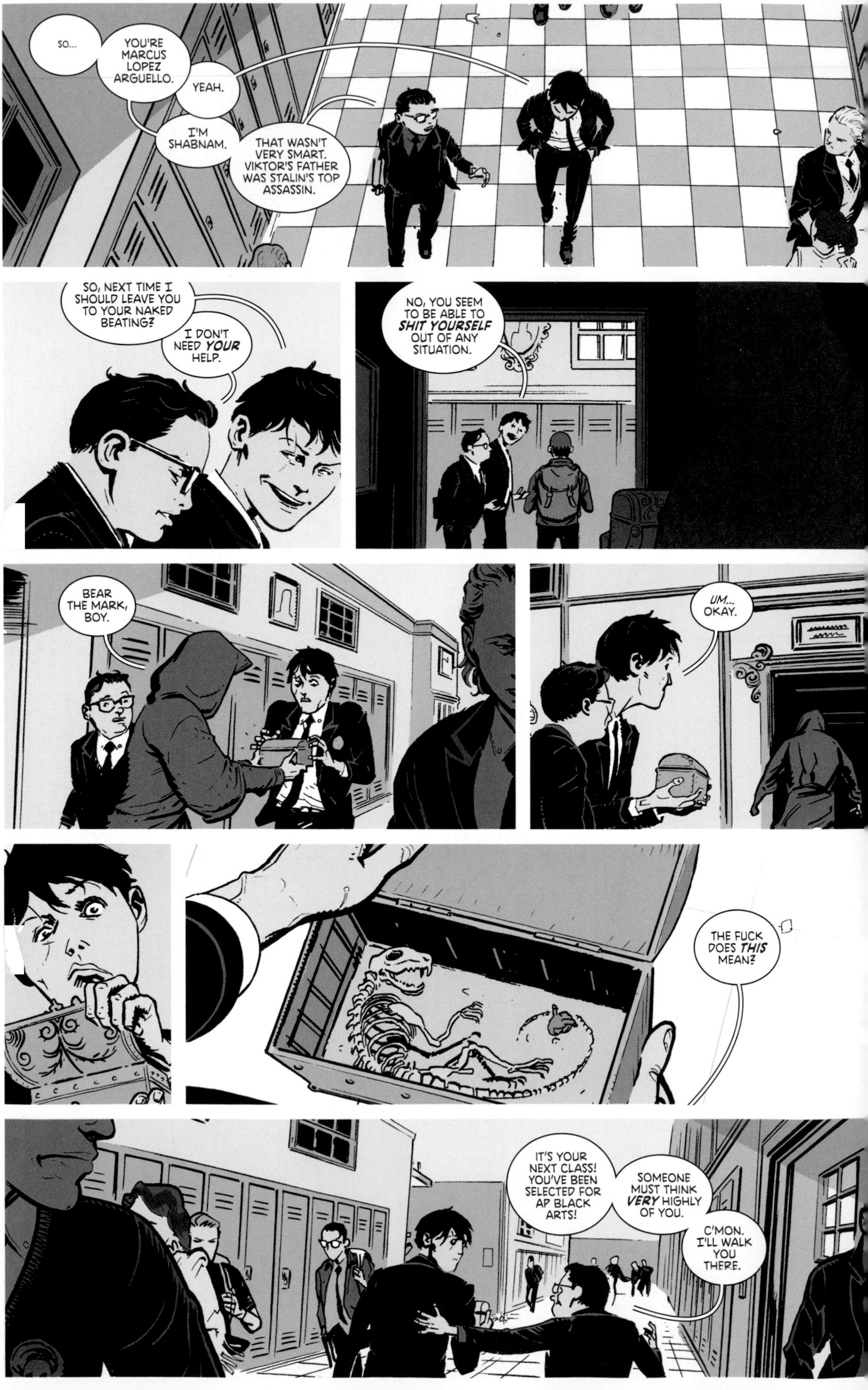
SO...
YOU'RE MARCUS LOPEZ ARGUELLO.
YEAH.
I'M SHABNAM.
THAT WASN'T VERY SMART. VIKTOR'S FATHER WAS STALIN'S TOP ASSASSIN.
SO, NEXT TIME I SHOULD LEAVE YOU TO YOUR NAKED BEATING?
I DON'T NEED YOUR HELP.
NO, YOU SEEM TO BE ABLE TO SHIT YOURSELF OUT OF ANY SITUATION.
BEAR THE MARK, BOY.
UM... OKAY.
THE FUCK DOES THIS MEAN?
IT'S YOUR NEXT CLASS! YOU'VE BEEN SELECTED FOR AP BLACK ARTS!
SOMEONE MUST THINK VERY HIGHLY OF YOU.
C'MON. I'LL WALK YOU THERE.

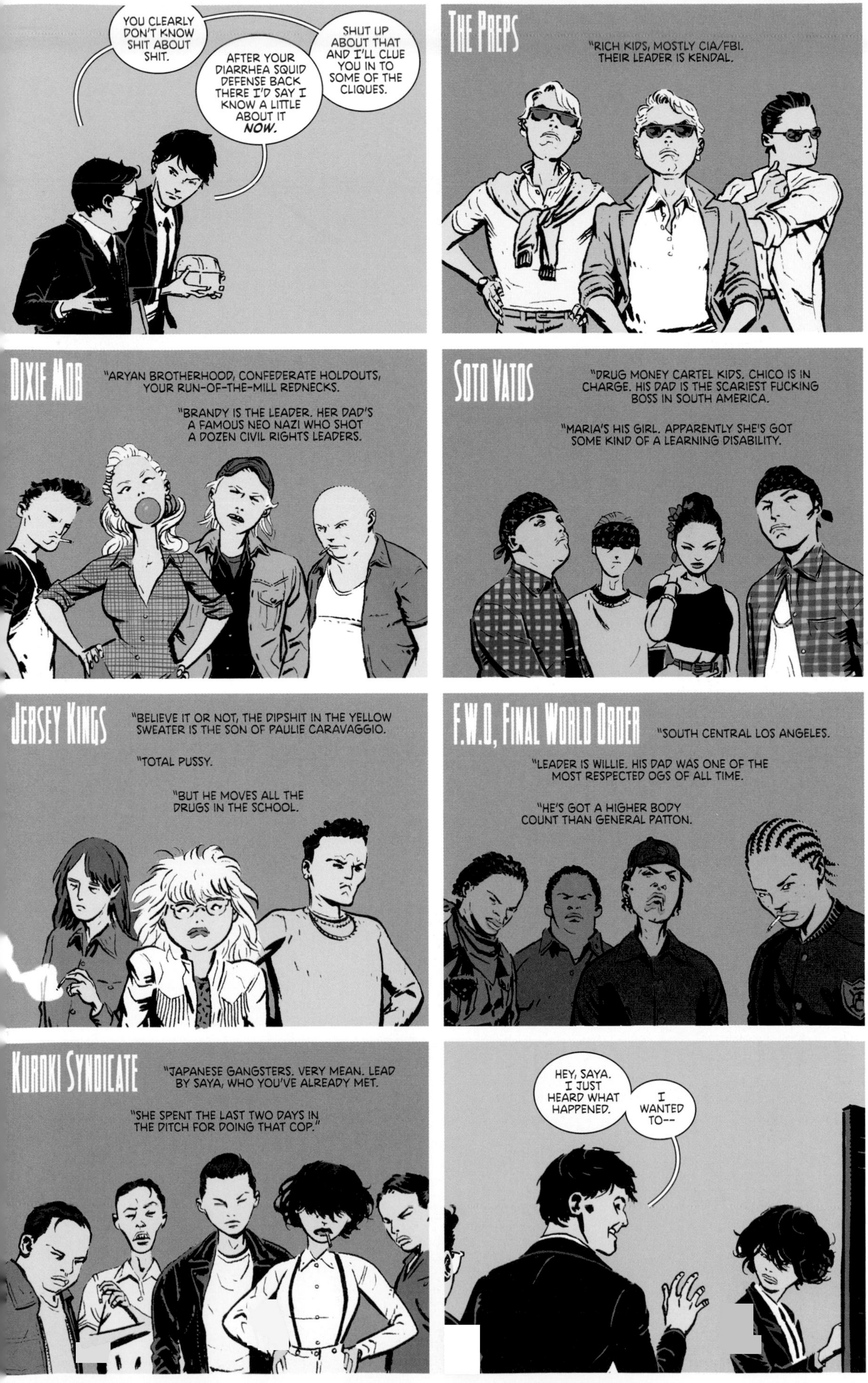

YOU CLEARLY DON'T KNOW SHIT ABOUT SHIT.
AFTER YOUR DIARRHEA SQUID DEFENSE BACK THERE I'D SAY I KNOW A LITTLE ABOUT IT NOW.
SHUT UP ABOUT THAT AND I'LL CLUE YOU IN TO SOME OF THE CLIQUES.
THE PREPS
"RICH KIDS, MOSTLY CIA/FBI. THEIR LEADER IS KENDAL.
DIXIE MOB
"ARYAN BROTHERHOOD, CONFEDERATE HOLDOUTS, YOUR RUN-OF-THE-MILL REDNECKS.
"BRANDY IS THE LEADER. HER DAD'S A FAMOUS NEO NAZI WHO SHOT A DOZEN CIVIL RIGHTS LEADERS.
SOTO VATOS
"DRUG MONEY CARTEL KIDS. CHICO IS IN CHARGE. HIS DAD IS THE SCARIEST FUCKING BOSS IN SOUTH AMERICA.
"MARIA'S HIS GIRL. APPARENTLY SHE'S GOT SOME KIND OF A LEARNING DISABILITY.
JERSEY KINGS
"BELIEVE IT OR NOT, THE DIPSHIT IN THE YELLOW SWEATER IS THE SON OF PAULIE CARAVAGGIO.
"TOTAL PUSSY.
"BUT HE MOVES ALL THE DRUGS IN THE SCHOOL.
F.W.O, FINAL WORLD ORDER
"SOUTH CENTRAL LOS ANGELES.
"LEADER IS WILLIE. HIS DAD WAS ONE OF THE MOST RESPECTED OGS OF ALL TIME.
"HE'S GOT A HIGHER BODY COUNT THAN GENERAL PATTON.
KUROKI SYNDICATE
"JAPANESE GANGSTERS. VERY MEAN. LEAD BY SAYA, WHO YOU'VE ALREADY MET.
"SHE SPENT THE LAST TWO DAYS IN THE DITCH FOR DOING THAT COP."
HEY, SAYA. I JUST HEARD WHAT HAPPENED.
I WANTED TO--

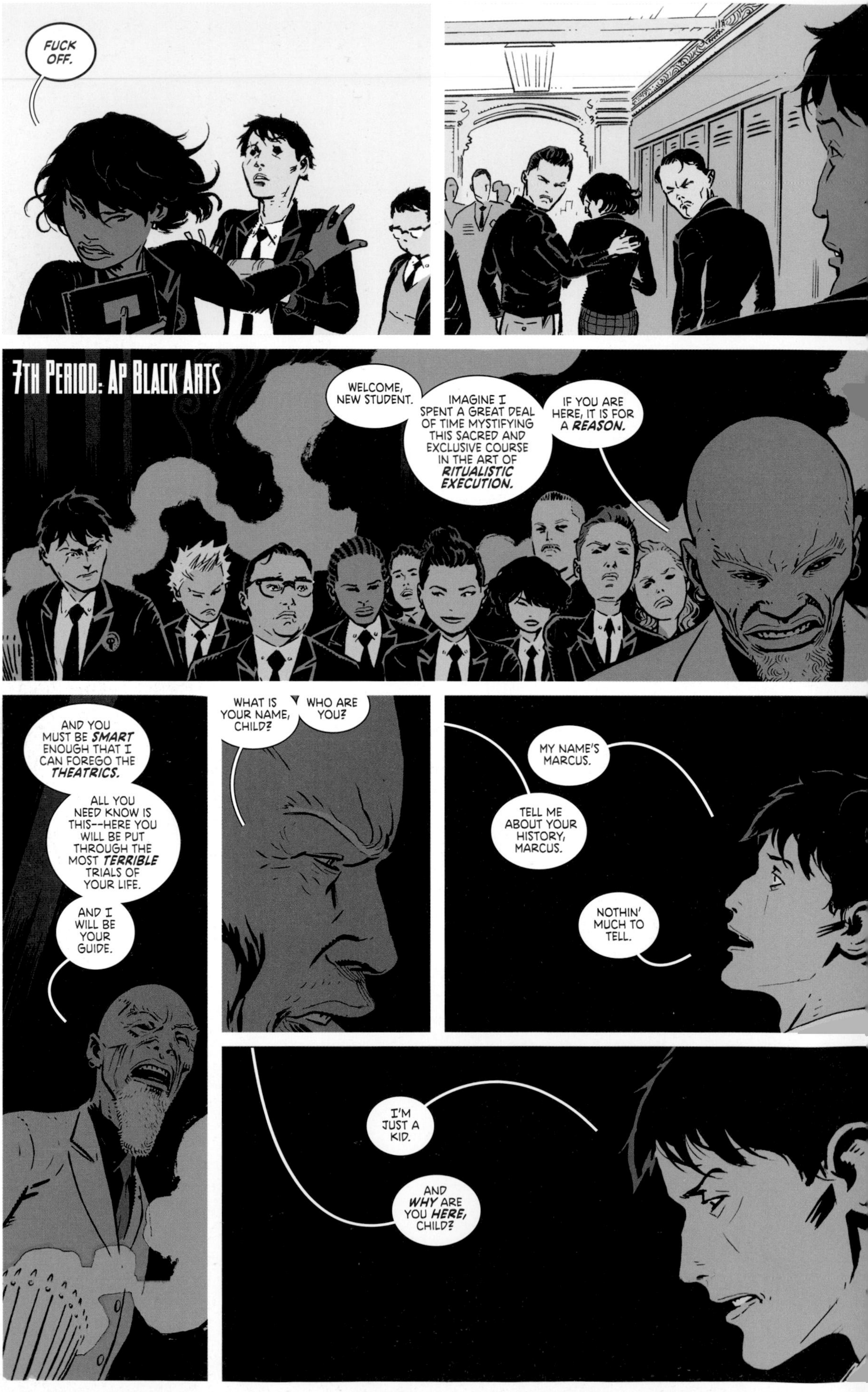
FUCK OFF.
7TH PERIOD: AP BLACK ARTS
WELCOME, NEW STUDENT.
IMAGINE I SPENT A GREAT DEAL OF TIME MYSTIFYING THIS SACRED AND EXCLUSIVE COURSE IN THE ART OF RITUALISTIC EXECUTION.
IF YOU ARE HERE, IT IS FOR A REASON.
AND YOU MUST BE SMART ENOUGH THAT I CAN FOREGO THE THEATRICS.
ALL YOU NEED KNOW IS THIS--HERE YOU WILL BE PUT THROUGH THE MOST TERRIBLE TRIALS OF YOUR LIFE.
AND I WILL BE YOUR GUIDE.
WHAT IS YOUR NAME, CHILD?
WHO ARE YOU?
MY NAME'S MARCUS.
TELL ME ABOUT YOUR HISTORY, MARCUS.
NOTHIN' MUCH TO TELL.
I'M JUST A KID.
AND WHY ARE YOU HERE, CHILD?

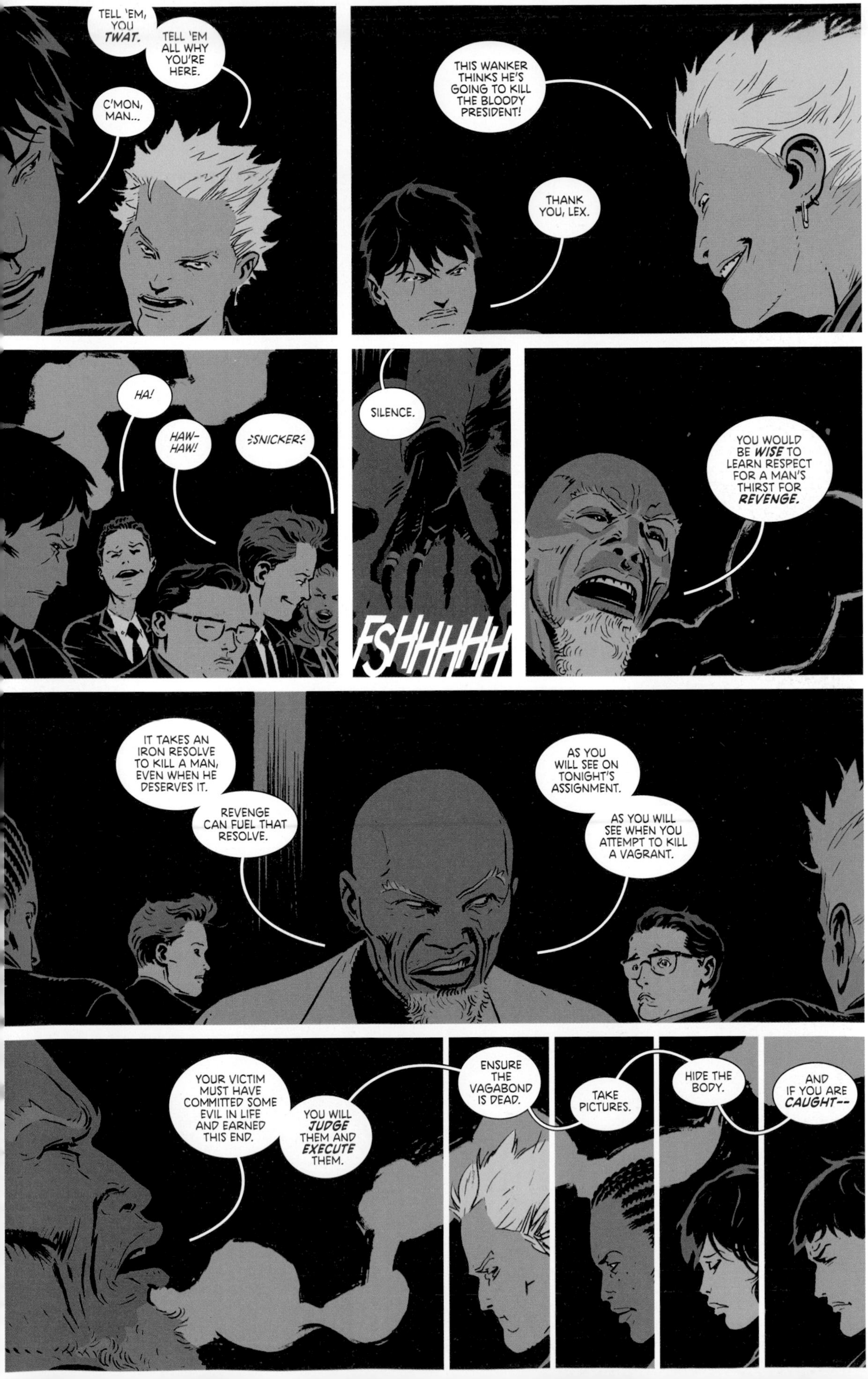
TELL 'EM, YOU TWAT.
TELL 'EM ALL WHY YOU'RE HERE.
C'MON, MAN...
THIS WANKER THINKS HE'S GOING TO KILL THE BLOODY PRESIDENT!
THANK YOU, LEX.
HA!
HAW-HAW!
:SNICKER:
SILENCE.
FSHHHHH
YOU WOULD BE WISE TO LEARN RESPECT FOR A MAN'S THIRST FOR REVENGE.
IT TAKES AN IRON RESOLVE TO KILL A MAN, EVEN WHEN HE DESERVES IT.
REVENGE CAN FUEL THAT RESOLVE.
AS YOU WILL SEE ON TONIGHT'S ASSIGNMENT.
AS YOU WILL SEE WHEN YOU ATTEMPT TO KILL A VAGRANT.
YOUR VICTIM MUST HAVE COMMITTED SOME EVIL IN LIFE AND EARNED THIS END.
YOU WILL JUDGE THEM AND EXECUTE THEM.
ENSURE THE VAGABOND IS DEAD.
TAKE PICTURES.
HIDE THE BODY.
AND IF YOU ARE CAUGHT--

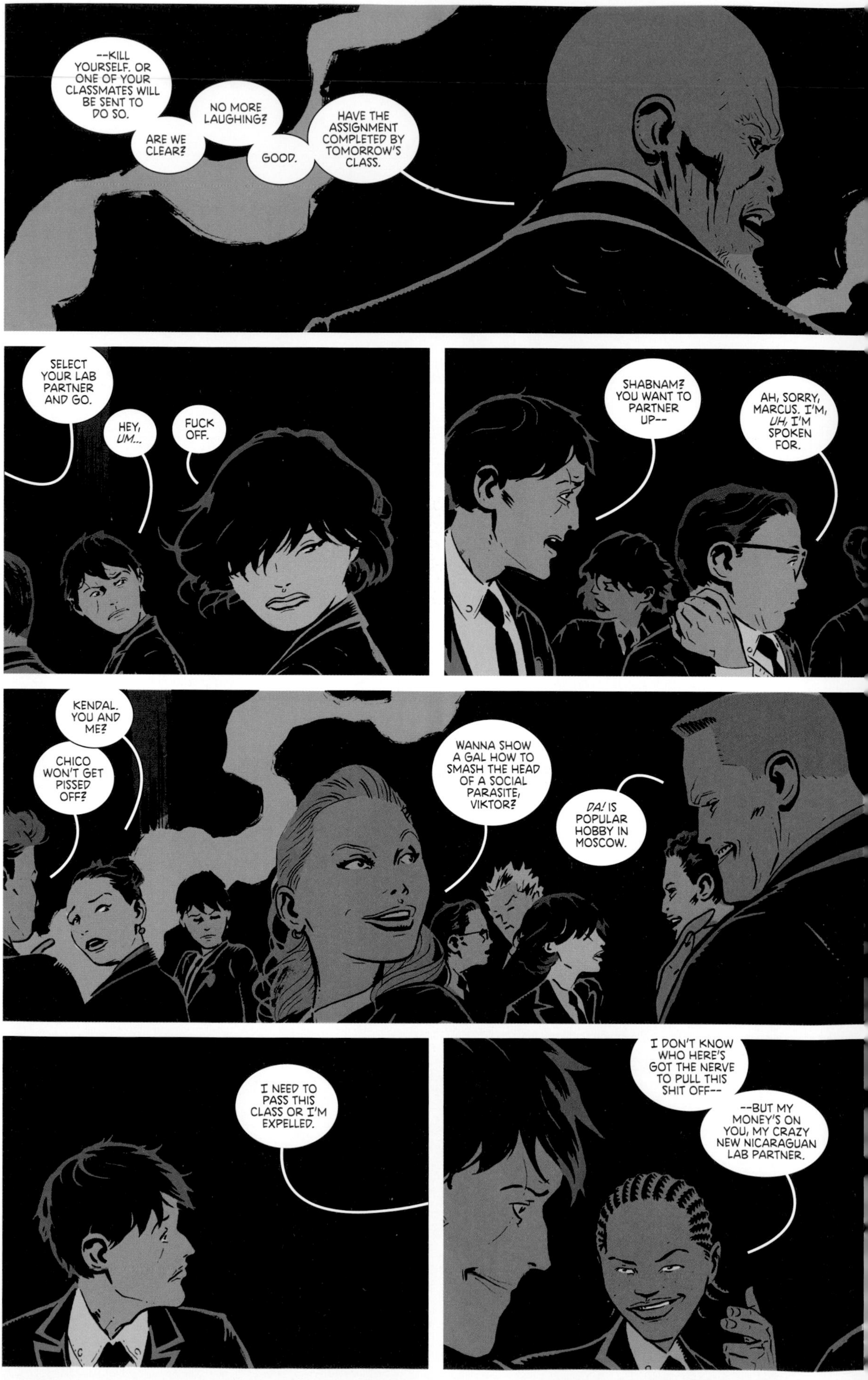
--KILL YOURSELF. OR ONE OF YOUR CLASSMATES WILL BE SENT TO DO SO.
ARE WE CLEAR?
NO MORE LAUGHING?
GOOD.
HAVE THE ASSIGNMENT COMPLETED BY TOMORROW'S CLASS.
SELECT YOUR LAB PARTNER AND GO.
HEY, *UM...*
FUCK OFF.
SHABNAM? YOU WANT TO PARTNER UP--
AH, SORRY, MARCUS. I'M, *UH,* I'M SPOKEN FOR.
KENDAL. YOU AND ME?
CHICO WON'T GET PISSED OFF?
WANNA SHOW A GAL HOW TO SMASH THE HEAD OF A SOCIAL PARASITE, VIKTOR?
DA! IS POPULAR HOBBY IN MOSCOW.
I NEED TO PASS THIS CLASS OR I'M EXPELLED.
I DON'T KNOW WHO HERE'S GOT THE NERVE TO PULL THIS SHIT OFF--
--BUT MY MONEY'S ON YOU, MY CRAZY NEW NICARAGUAN LAB PARTNER.

EST. 1637

IN VITAM MORTEM

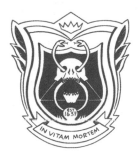

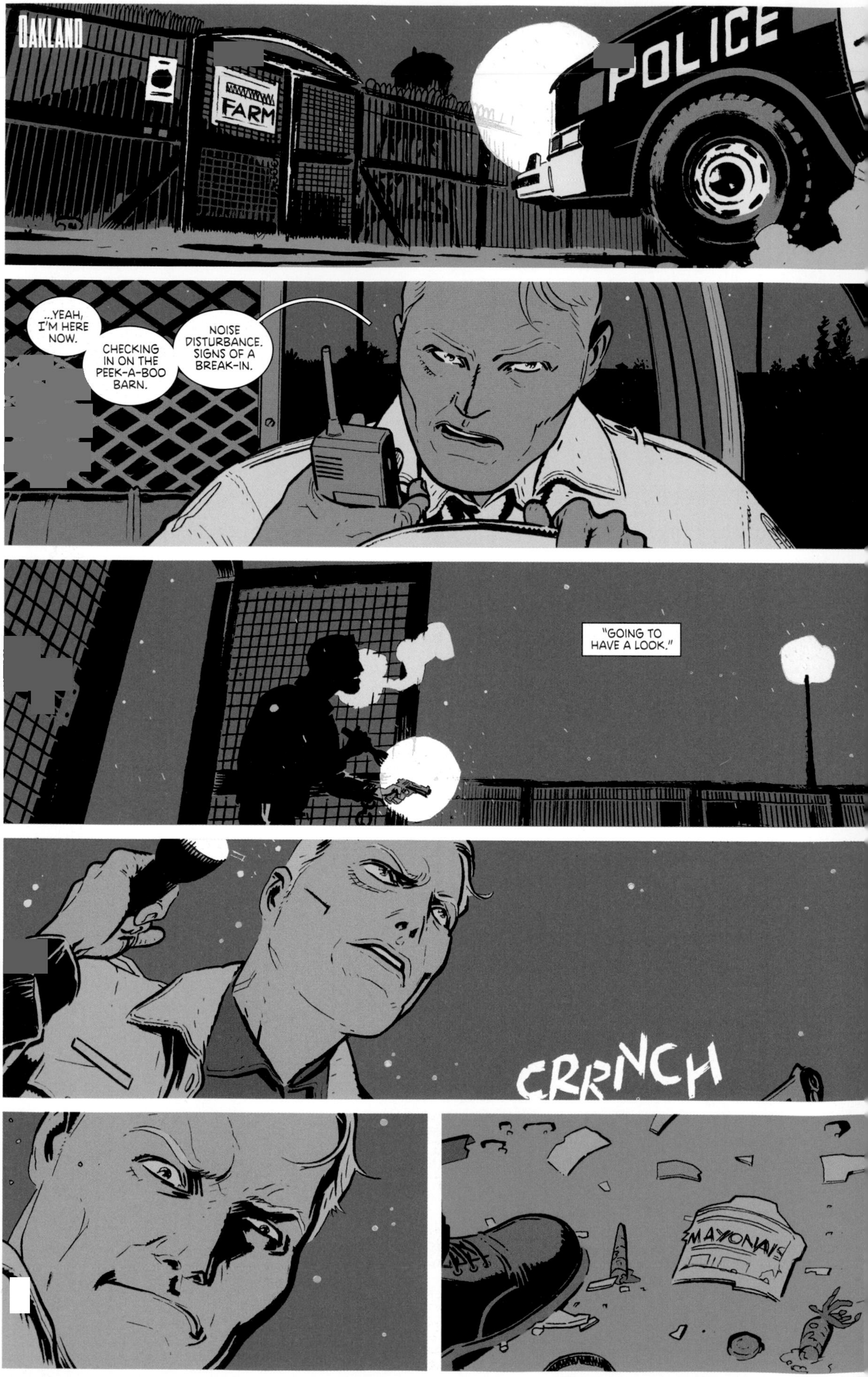
OAKLAND
FARM
POLICE
...YEAH, I'M HERE NOW.
CHECKING IN ON THE PEEK-A-BOO BARN.
NOISE DISTURBANCE. SIGNS OF A BREAK-IN.
"GOING TO HAVE A LOOK."
CRRNCH
MAYONAIS

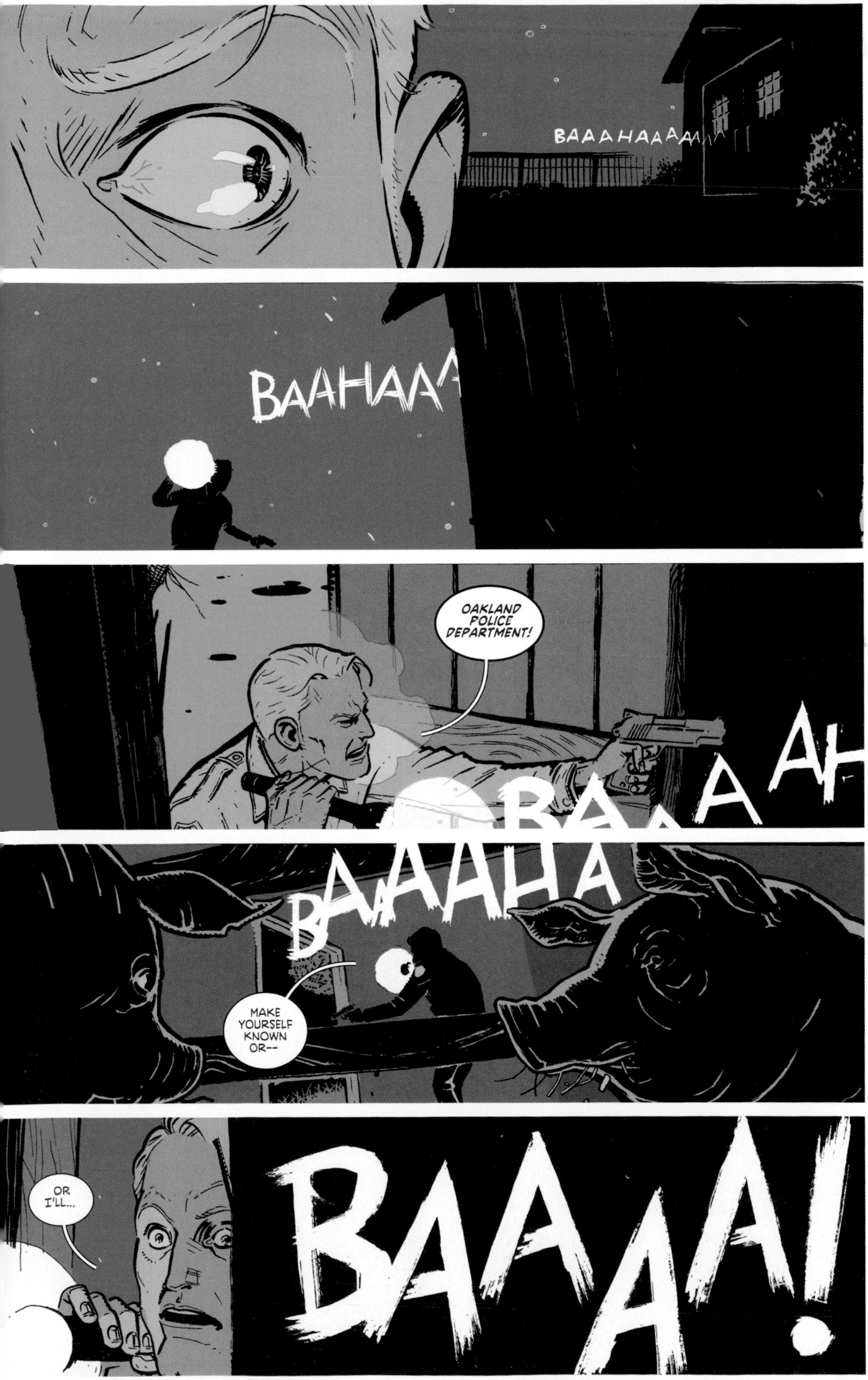
BAAAHAAAA
BAAHAAA
OAKLAND POLICE DEPARTMENT!
BAA A AH
BAAAHA
MAKE YOURSELF KNOWN OR--
OR I'LL...
BAAA!

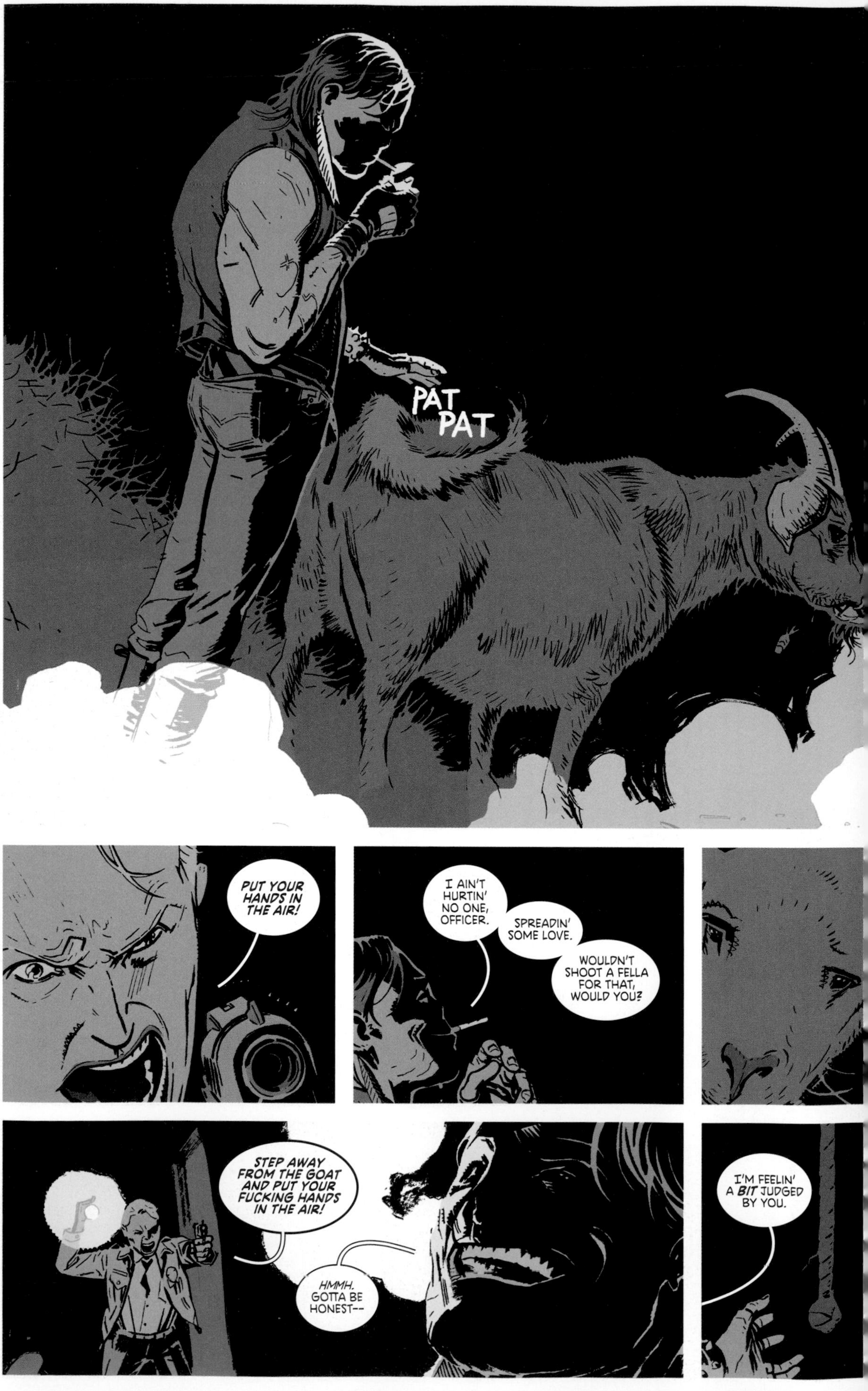

PAT PAT
PUT YOUR HANDS IN THE AIR!
I AIN'T HURTIN' NO ONE, OFFICER.
SPREADIN' SOME LOVE.
WOULDN'T SHOOT A FELLA FOR THAT, WOULD YOU?
STEP AWAY FROM THE GOAT AND PUT YOUR FUCKING HANDS IN THE AIR!
HMMH. GOTTA BE HONEST--
I'M FEELIN' A BIT JUDGED BY YOU.

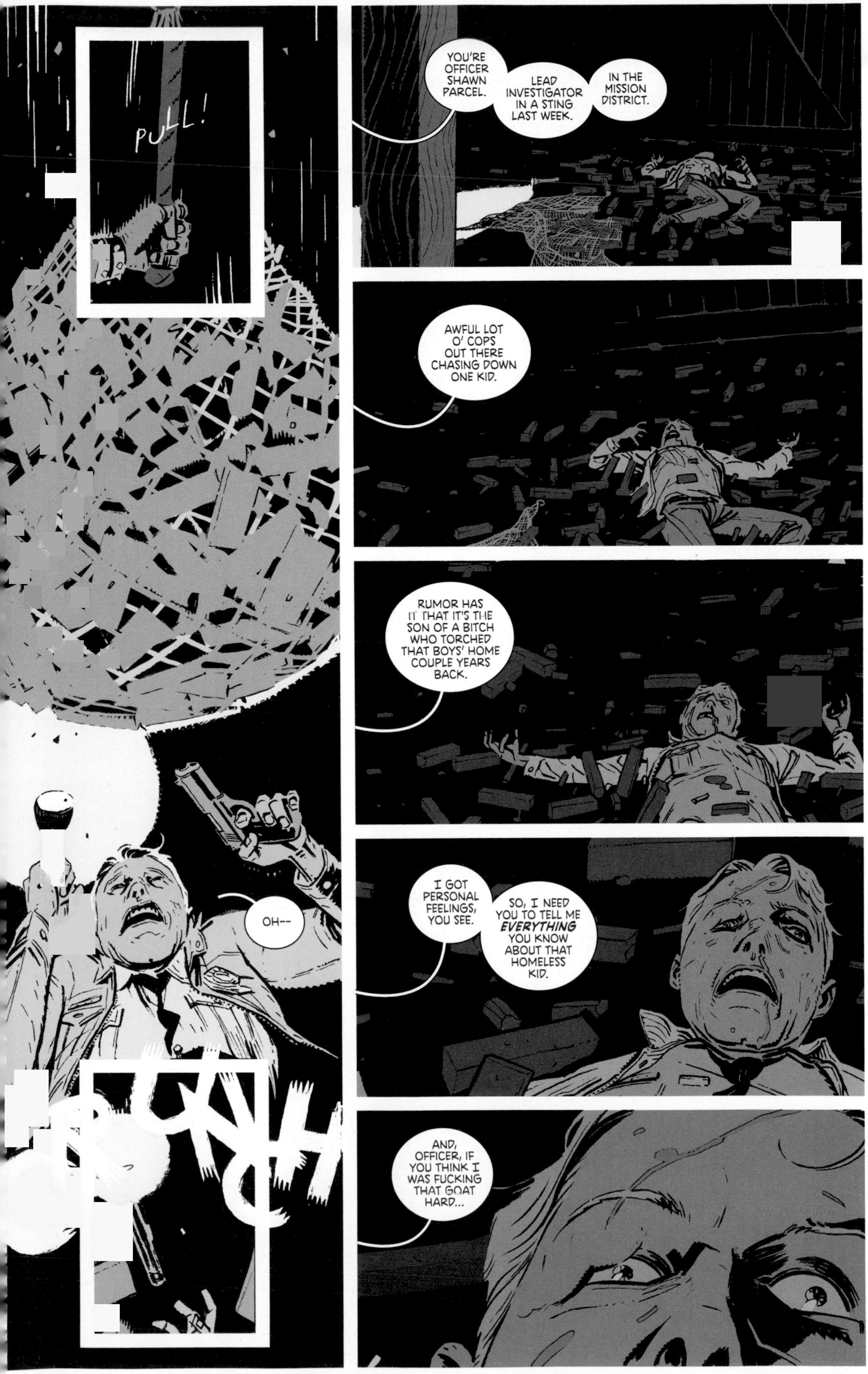
PULL!
OH--
YOU'RE OFFICER SHAWN PARCEL.
LEAD INVESTIGATOR IN A STING LAST WEEK.
IN THE MISSION DISTRICT.
AWFUL LOT O' COPS OUT THERE CHASING DOWN ONE KID.
RUMOR HAS IT THAT IT'S THE SON OF A BITCH WHO TORCHED THAT BOYS' HOME COUPLE YEARS BACK.
I GOT PERSONAL FEELINGS, YOU SEE.
SO, I NEED YOU TO TELL ME *EVERYTHING* YOU KNOW ABOUT THAT HOMELESS KID.
AND, OFFICER, IF YOU THINK I WAS FUCKING THAT GOAT HARD...

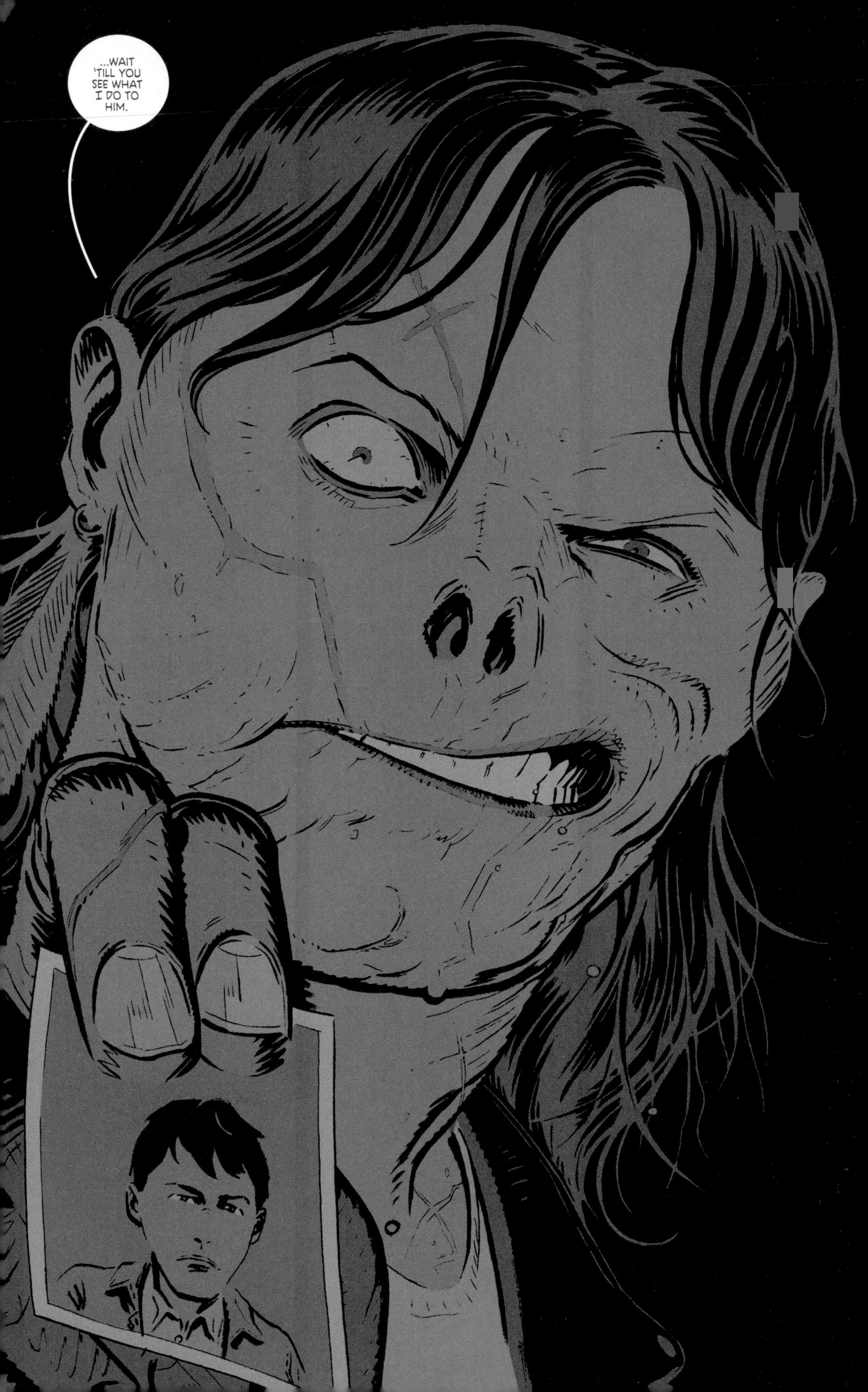
...WAIT 'TILL YOU SEE WHAT I DO TO HIM.

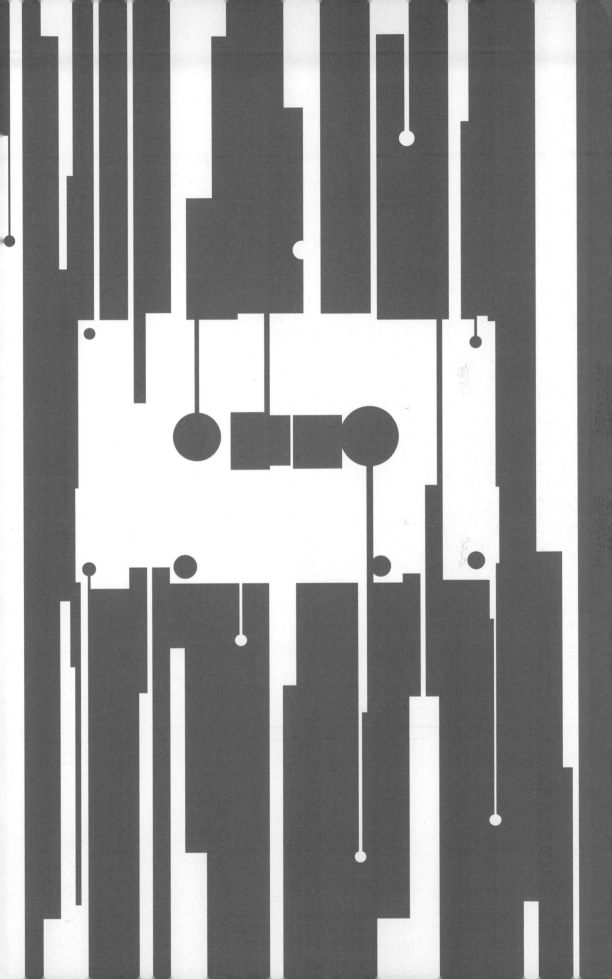

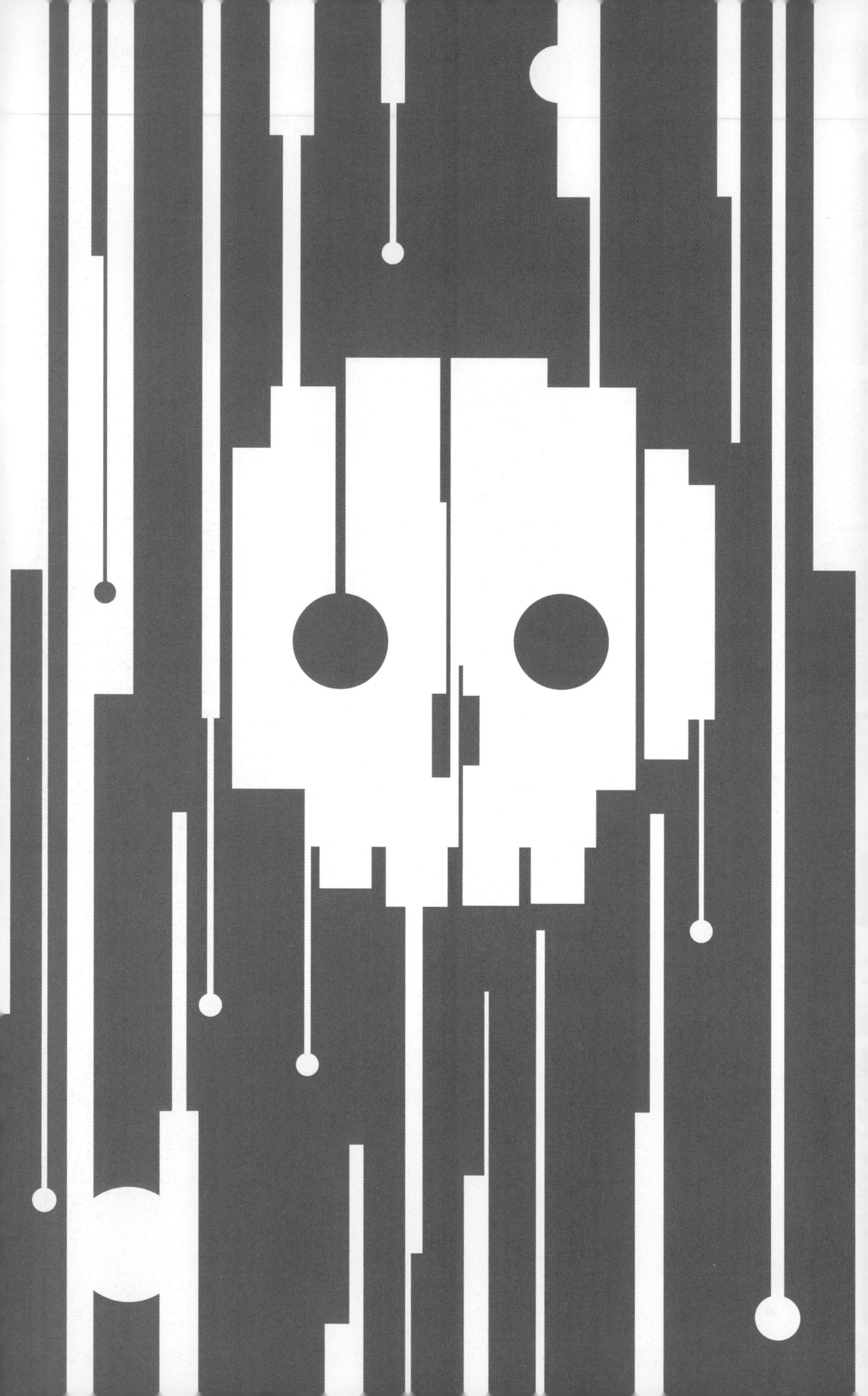

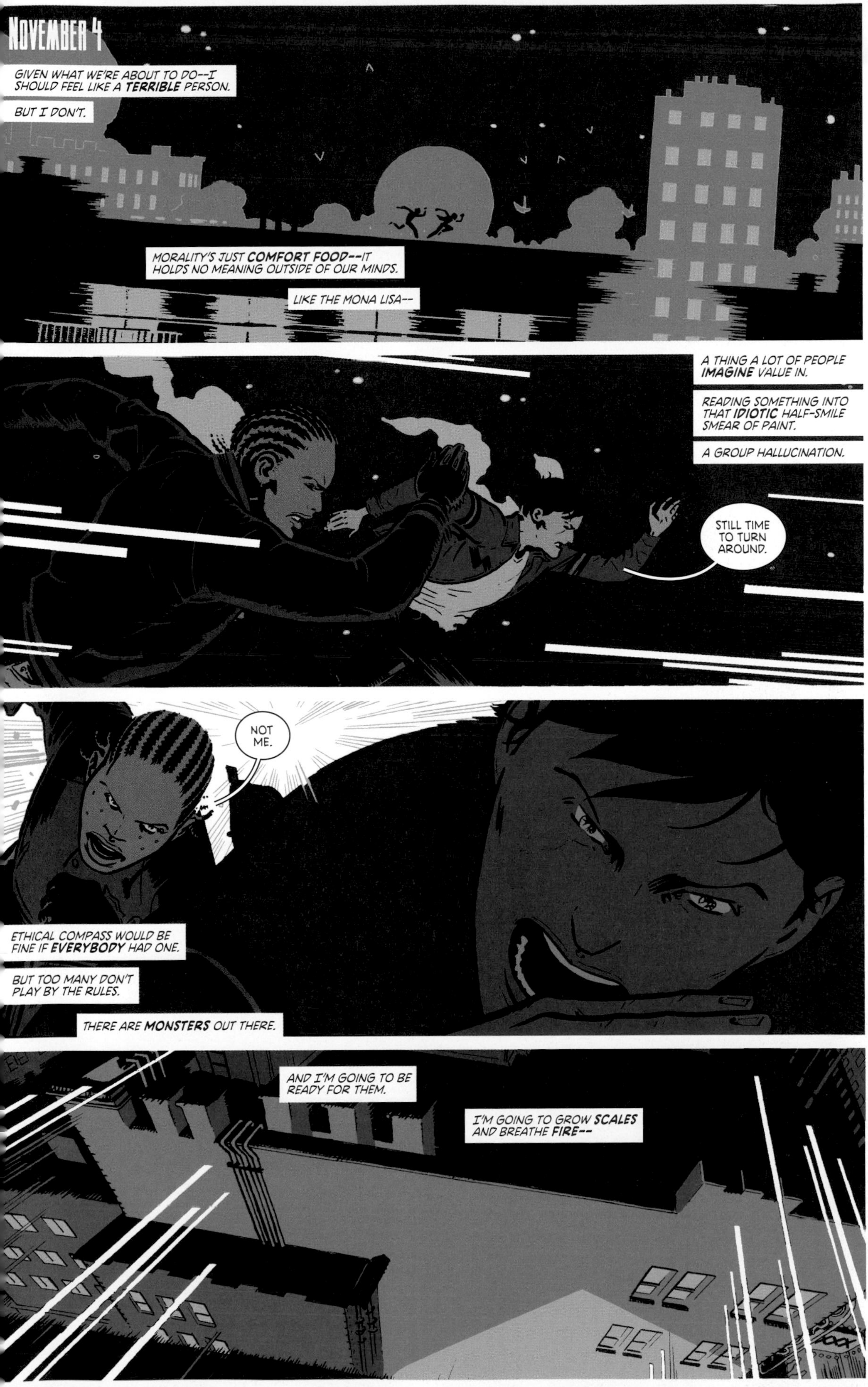
NOVEMBER 4
GIVEN WHAT WE'RE ABOUT TO DO--I SHOULD FEEL LIKE A TERRIBLE PERSON.
BUT I DON'T.
MORALITY'S JUST COMFORT FOOD--IT HOLDS NO MEANING OUTSIDE OF OUR MINDS.
LIKE THE MONA LISA--
A THING A LOT OF PEOPLE IMAGINE VALUE IN.
READING SOMETHING INTO THAT IDIOTIC HALF-SMILE SMEAR OF PAINT.
A GROUP HALLUCINATION.
STILL TIME TO TURN AROUND.
NOT ME.
ETHICAL COMPASS WOULD BE FINE IF EVERYBODY HAD ONE.
BUT TOO MANY DON'T PLAY BY THE RULES.
THERE ARE MONSTERS OUT THERE.
AND I'M GOING TO BE READY FOR THEM.
I'M GOING TO GROW SCALES AND BREATHE FIRE--

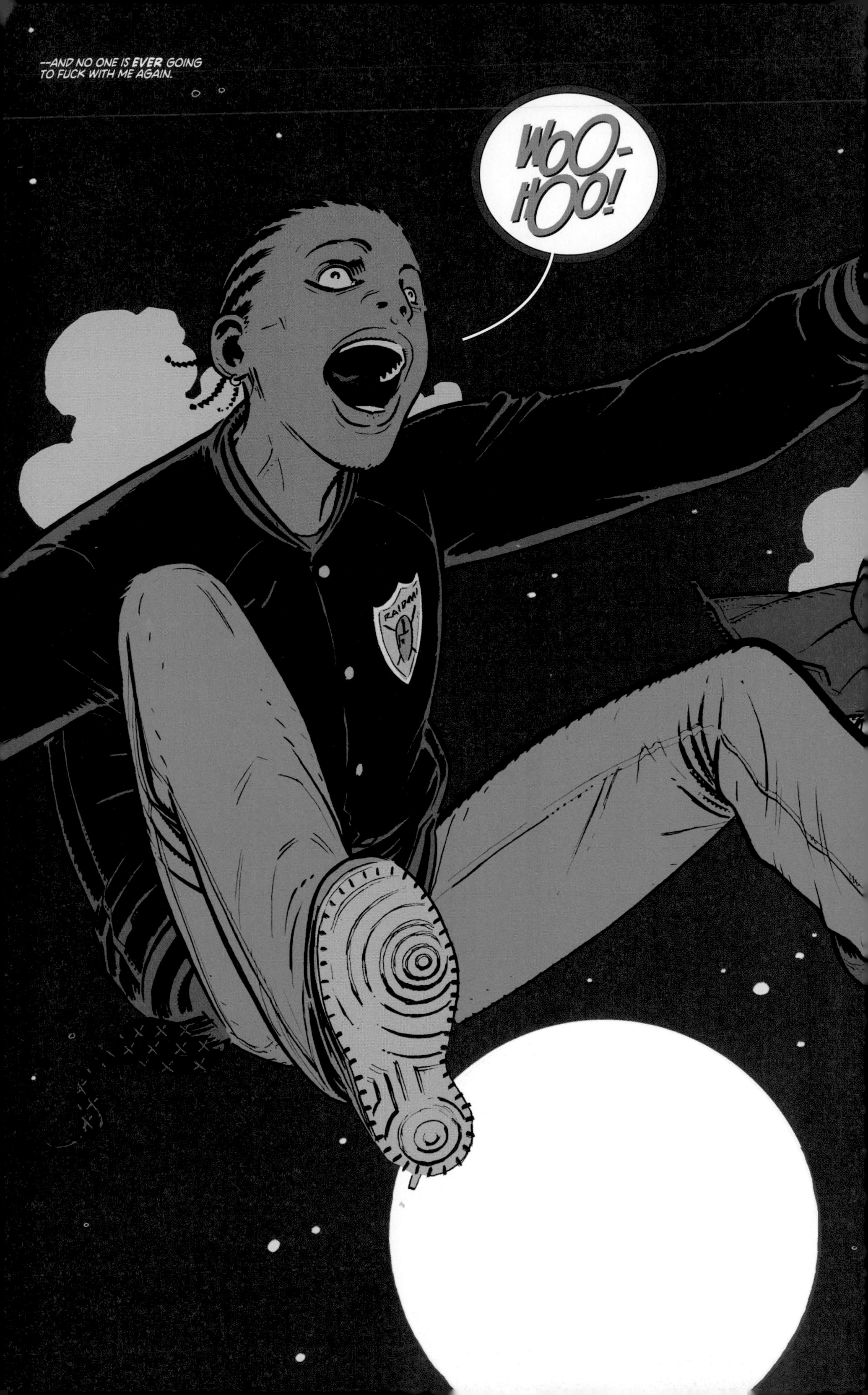
--AND NO ONE IS **EVER** GOING TO FUCK WITH ME AGAIN.
WOO-HOO!

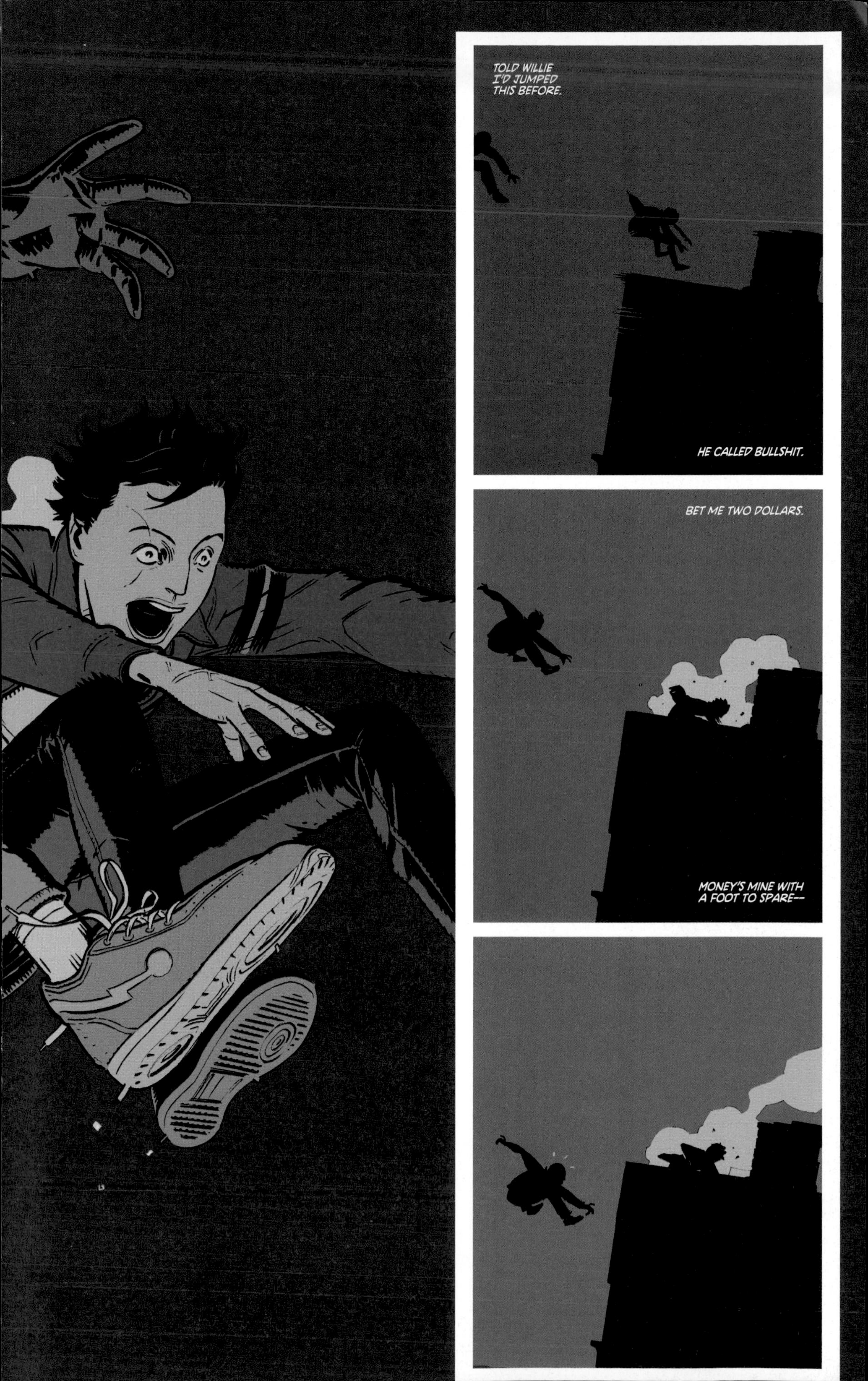
TOLD WILLIE I'D JUMPED THIS BEFORE.
HE CALLED BULLSHIT.
BET ME TWO DOLLARS.
MONEY'S MINE WITH A FOOT TO SPARE--

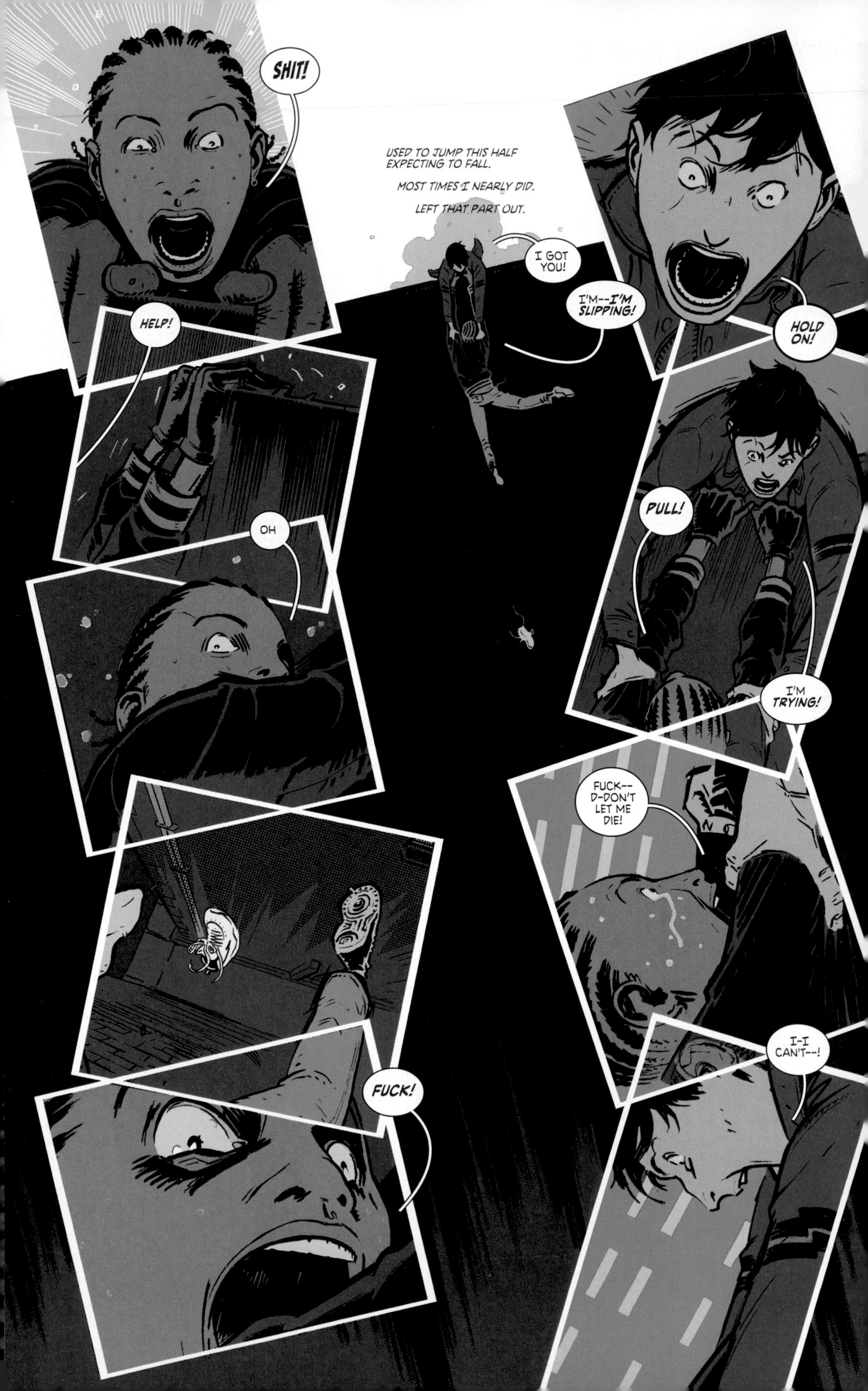
SHIT!
HELP!
OH
USED TO JUMP THIS HALF EXPECTING TO FALL.
MOST TIMES I NEARLY DID.
LEFT THAT PART OUT.
I GOT YOU!
I'M--I'M SLIPPING!
HOLD ON!
PULL!
I'M TRYING!
FUCK--D-DON'T LET ME DIE!
FUCK!
I-I CAN'T--!

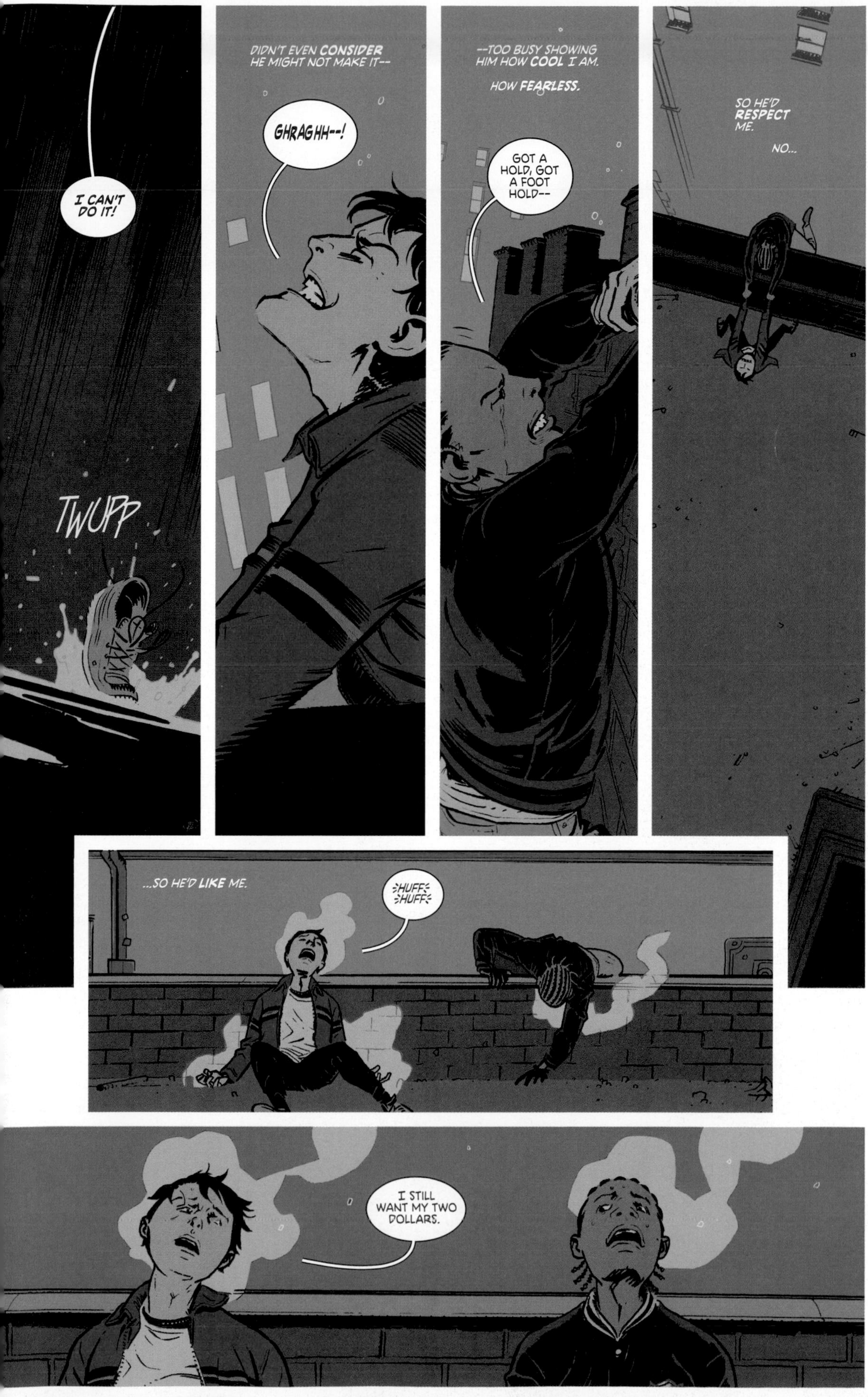
I CAN'T DO IT!
TWUPP
DIDN'T EVEN CONSIDER HE MIGHT NOT MAKE IT--
GHRAGHH--!
--TOO BUSY SHOWING HIM HOW COOL I AM.
HOW FEARLESS.
GOT A HOLD, GOT A FOOT HOLD--
SO HE'D RESPECT ME.
NO...
...SO HE'D LIKE ME.
HUFF HUFF
I STILL WANT MY TWO DOLLARS.

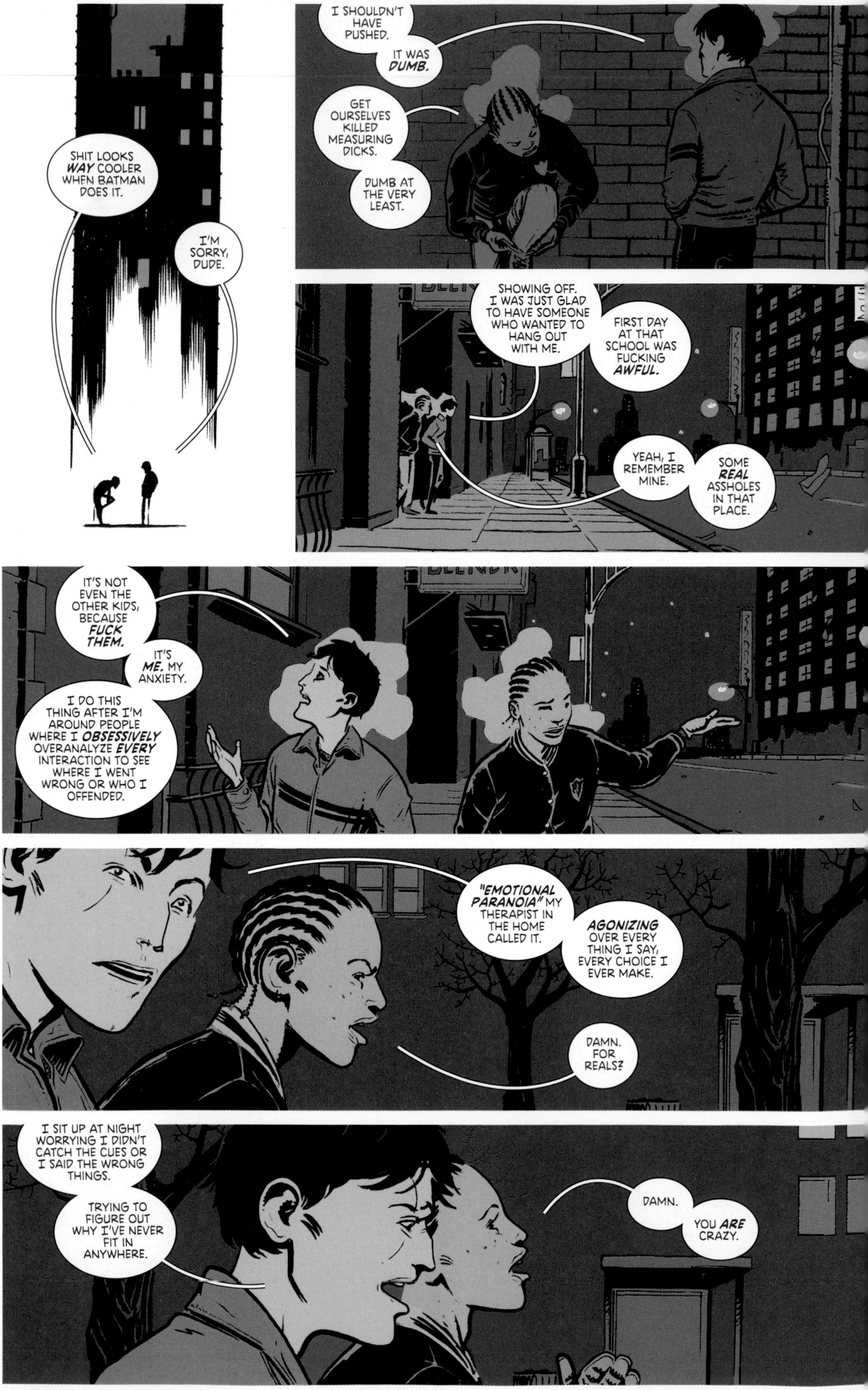
SHIT LOOKS WAY COOLER WHEN BATMAN DOES IT.
I'M SORRY, DUDE.
I SHOULDN'T HAVE PUSHED.
IT WAS DUMB.
GET OURSELVES KILLED MEASURING DICKS.
DUMB AT THE VERY LEAST.
SHOWING OFF. I WAS JUST GLAD TO HAVE SOMEONE WHO WANTED TO HANG OUT WITH ME.
FIRST DAY AT THAT SCHOOL WAS FUCKING AWFUL.
YEAH, I REMEMBER MINE.
SOME REAL ASSHOLES IN THAT PLACE.
IT'S NOT EVEN THE OTHER KIDS, BECAUSE FUCK THEM.
IT'S ME. MY ANXIETY.
I DO THIS THING AFTER I'M AROUND PEOPLE WHERE I OBSESSIVELY OVERANALYZE EVERY INTERACTION TO SEE WHERE I WENT WRONG OR WHO I OFFENDED.
"EMOTIONAL PARANOIA" MY THERAPIST IN THE HOME CALLED IT.
AGONIZING OVER EVERY THING I SAY, EVERY CHOICE I EVER MAKE.
DAMN. FOR REALS?
I SIT UP AT NIGHT WORRYING I DIDN'T CATCH THE CUES OR I SAID THE WRONG THINGS.
TRYING TO FIGURE OUT WHY I'VE NEVER FIT IN ANYWHERE.
DAMN.
YOU ARE CRAZY.

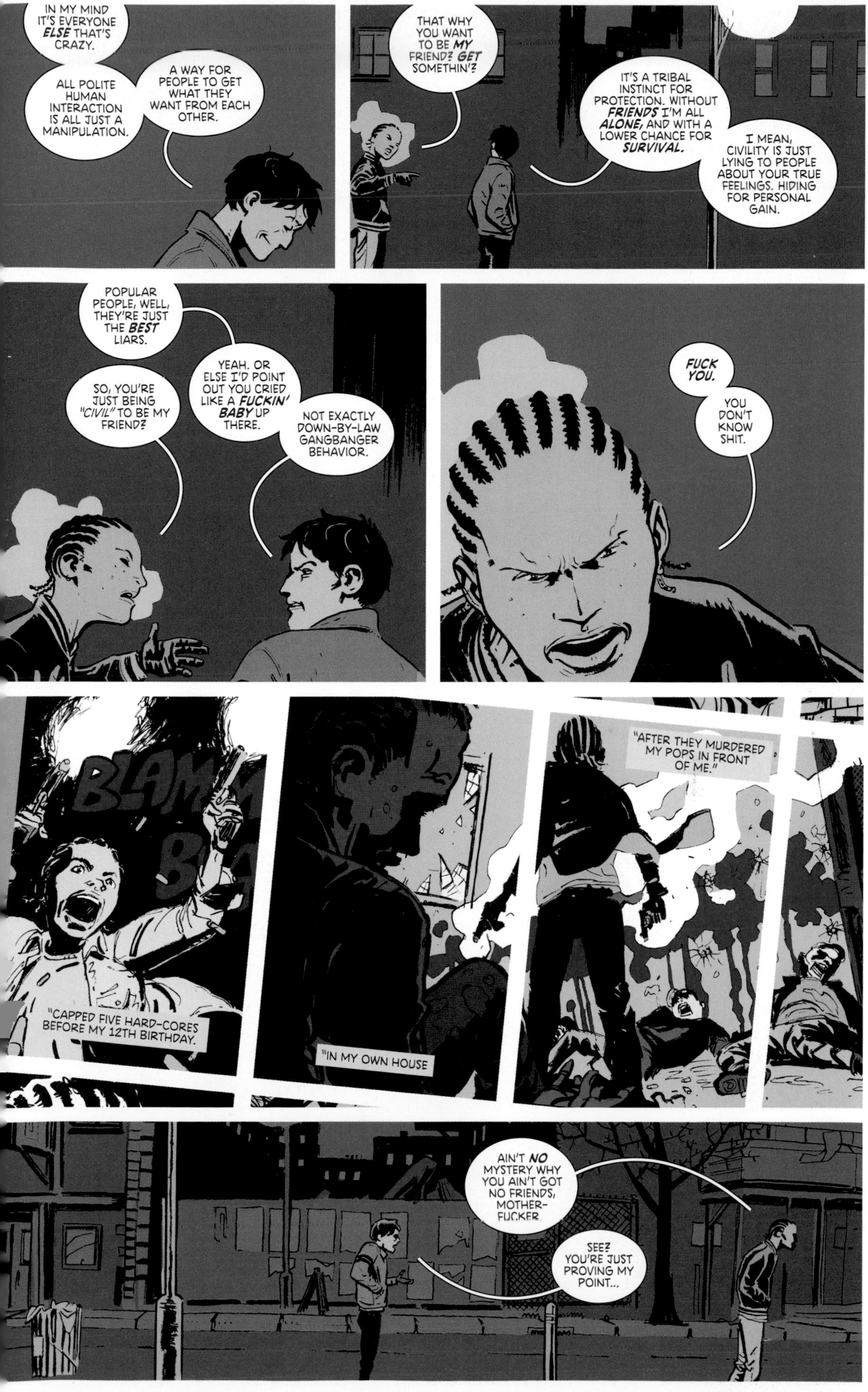
IN MY MIND IT'S EVERYONE ELSE THAT'S CRAZY.
ALL POLITE HUMAN INTERACTION IS ALL JUST A MANIPULATION.
A WAY FOR PEOPLE TO GET WHAT THEY WANT FROM EACH OTHER.
THAT WHY YOU WANT TO BE MY FRIEND? GET SOMETHIN'?
IT'S A TRIBAL INSTINCT FOR PROTECTION. WITHOUT FRIENDS I'M ALL ALONE, AND WITH A LOWER CHANCE FOR SURVIVAL.
I MEAN, CIVILITY IS JUST LYING TO PEOPLE ABOUT YOUR TRUE FEELINGS. HIDING FOR PERSONAL GAIN.
POPULAR PEOPLE, WELL, THEY'RE JUST THE BEST LIARS.
SO, YOU'RE JUST BEING "CIVIL" TO BE MY FRIEND?
YEAH. OR ELSE I'D POINT OUT YOU CRIED LIKE A FUCKIN' BABY UP THERE.
NOT EXACTLY DOWN-BY-LAW GANGBANGER BEHAVIOR.
FUCK YOU.
YOU DON'T KNOW SHIT.
BLAMM
"CAPPED FIVE HARD-CORES BEFORE MY 12TH BIRTHDAY.
"IN MY OWN HOUSE
"AFTER THEY MURDERED MY POPS IN FRONT OF ME."
AIN'T NO MYSTERY WHY YOU AIN'T GOT NO FRIENDS, MOTHER-FUCKER.
SEE? YOU'RE JUST PROVING MY POINT...

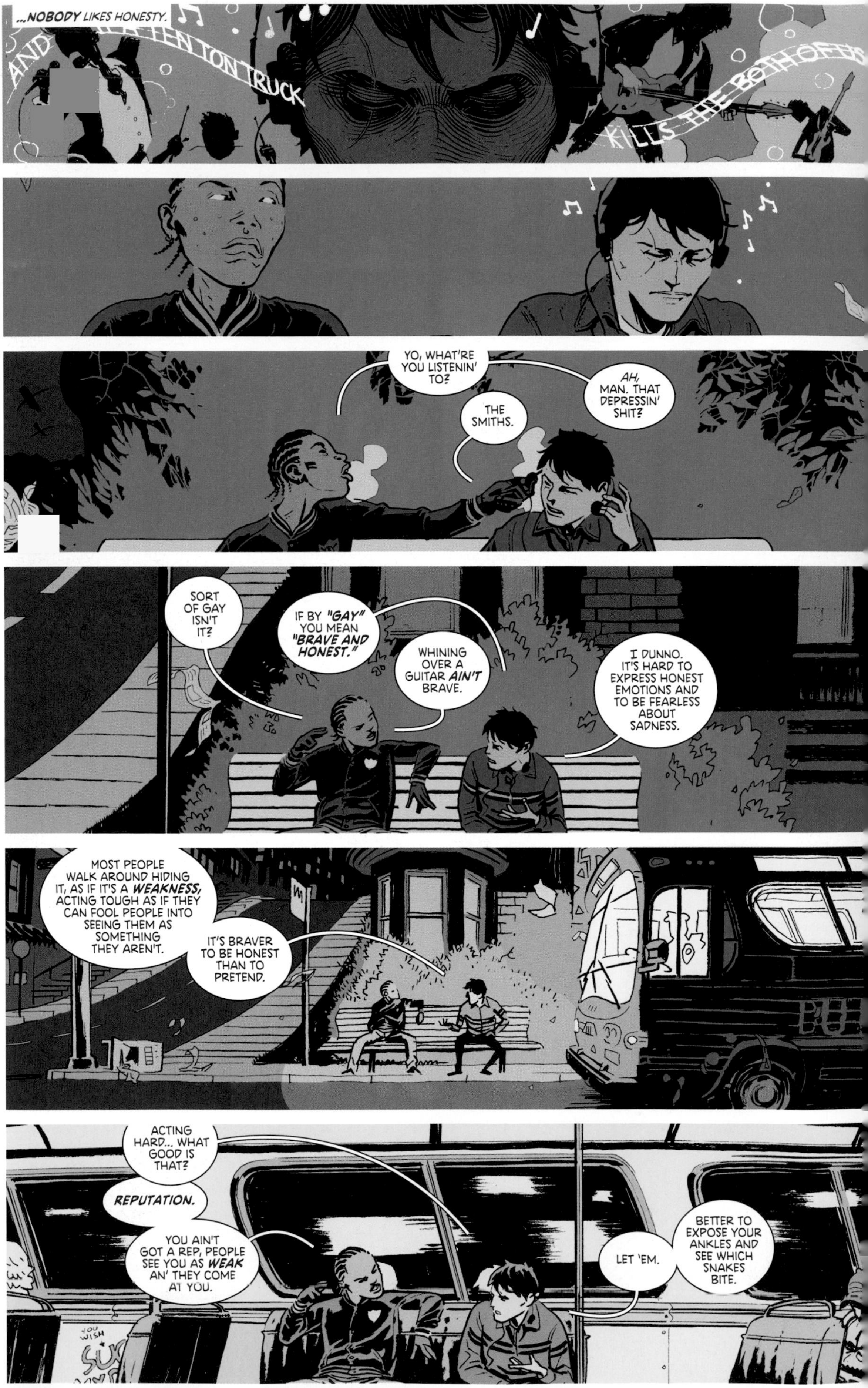

...NOBODY LIKES HONESTY.
AND IF A TEN TON TRUCK KILLS THE BOTH OF US
YO, WHAT'RE YOU LISTENIN' TO?
THE SMITHS.
AH, MAN. THAT DEPRESSIN' SHIT?
SORT OF GAY ISN'T IT?
IF BY "GAY" YOU MEAN "BRAVE AND HONEST."
WHINING OVER A GUITAR AIN'T BRAVE.
I DUNNO. IT'S HARD TO EXPRESS HONEST EMOTIONS AND TO BE FEARLESS ABOUT SADNESS.
MOST PEOPLE WALK AROUND HIDING IT, AS IF IT'S A WEAKNESS, ACTING TOUGH AS IF THEY CAN FOOL PEOPLE INTO SEEING THEM AS SOMETHING THEY AREN'T.
IT'S BRAVER TO BE HONEST THAN TO PRETEND.
ACTING HARD... WHAT GOOD IS THAT?
REPUTATION.
YOU AIN'T GOT A REP, PEOPLE SEE YOU AS WEAK AN' THEY COME AT YOU.
LET 'EM.
BETTER TO EXPOSE YOUR ANKLES AND SEE WHICH SNAKES BITE.
YOU WISH

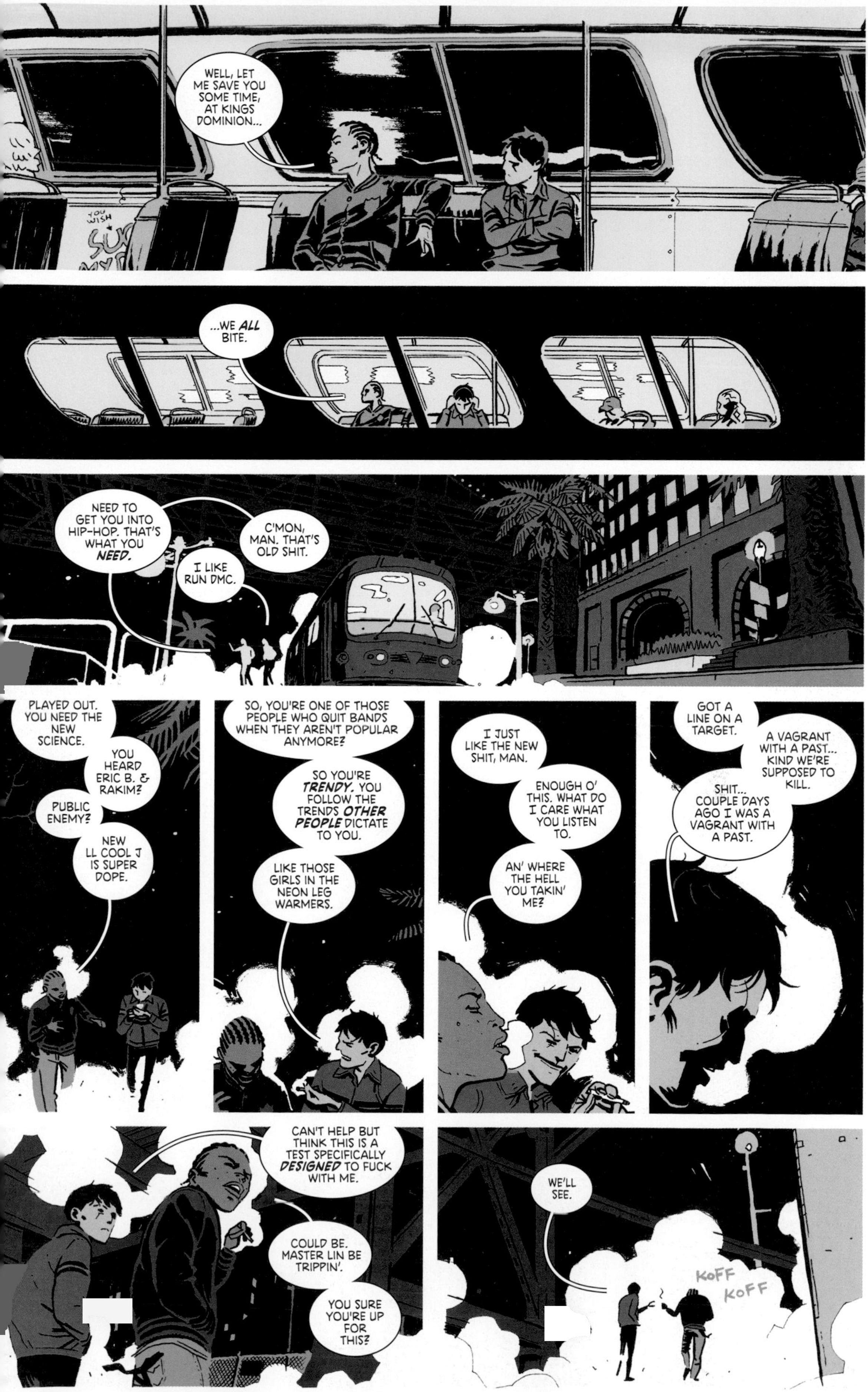
WELL, LET ME SAVE YOU SOME TIME, AT KINGS DOMINION...
YOU WISH
...WE ALL BITE.
NEED TO GET YOU INTO HIP-HOP. THAT'S WHAT YOU NEED.
I LIKE RUN DMC.
C'MON, MAN. THAT'S OLD SHIT.
PLAYED OUT. YOU NEED THE NEW SCIENCE.
YOU HEARD ERIC B. & RAKIM?
PUBLIC ENEMY?
NEW LL COOL J IS SUPER DOPE.
SO, YOU'RE ONE OF THOSE PEOPLE WHO QUIT BANDS WHEN THEY AREN'T POPULAR ANYMORE?
SO YOU'RE TRENDY. YOU FOLLOW THE TRENDS OTHER PEOPLE DICTATE TO YOU.
LIKE THOSE GIRLS IN THE NEON LEG WARMERS.
I JUST LIKE THE NEW SHIT, MAN.
ENOUGH O' THIS. WHAT DO I CARE WHAT YOU LISTEN TO.
AN' WHERE THE HELL YOU TAKIN' ME?
GOT A LINE ON A TARGET.
A VAGRANT WITH A PAST... KIND WE'RE SUPPOSED TO KILL.
SHIT... COUPLE DAYS AGO I WAS A VAGRANT WITH A PAST.
CAN'T HELP BUT THINK THIS IS A TEST SPECIFICALLY DESIGNED TO FUCK WITH ME.
COULD BE. MASTER LIN BE TRIPPIN'.
YOU SURE YOU'RE UP FOR THIS?
WE'LL SEE.
KOFF
KOFF

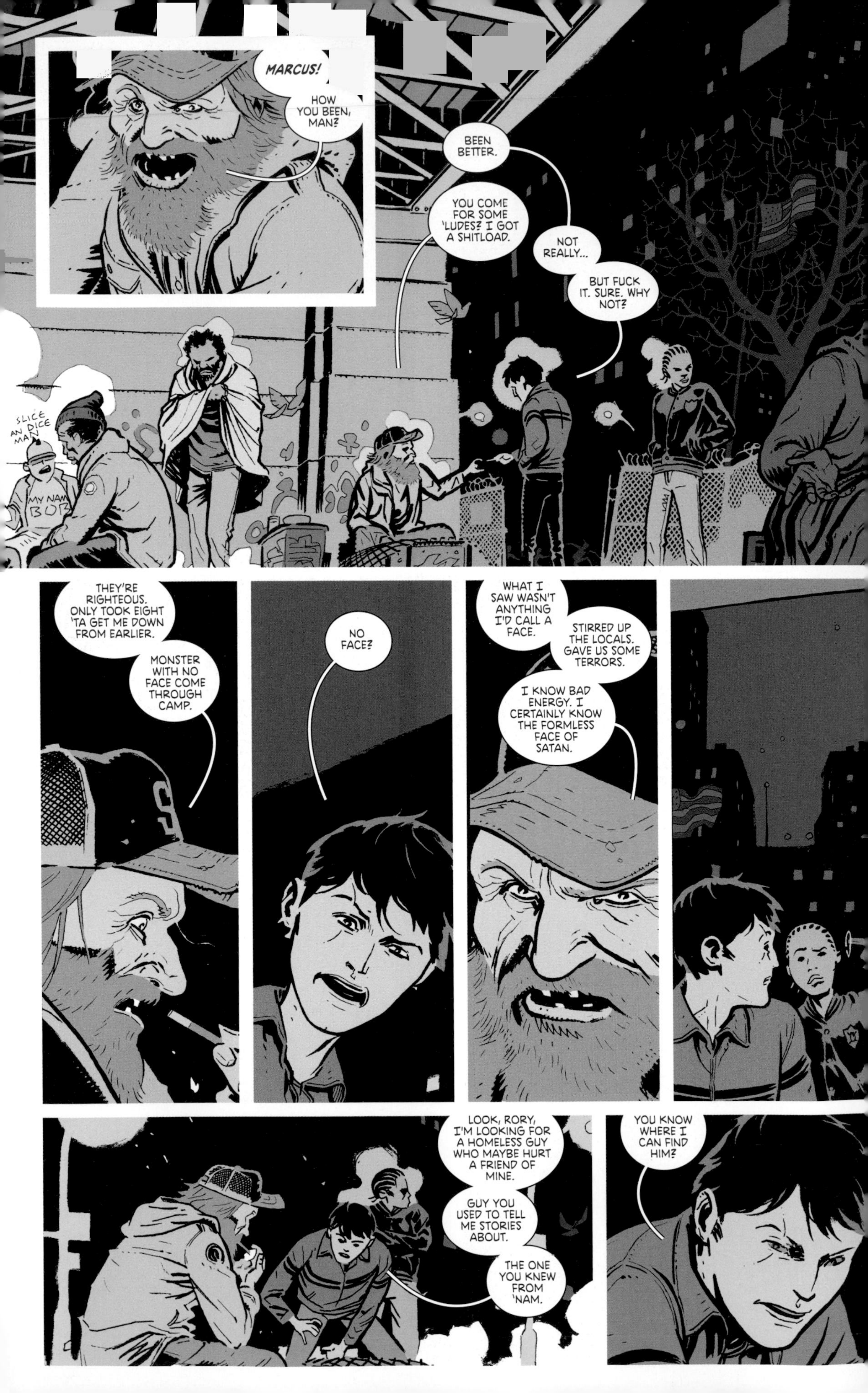
MARCUS!
HOW YOU BEEN, MAN?
BEEN BETTER.
YOU COME FOR SOME 'LUDES? I GOT A SHITLOAD.
NOT REALLY...
BUT FUCK IT. SURE. WHY NOT?
SLICE AN DICE MAN
MY NAM
THEY'RE RIGHTEOUS. ONLY TOOK EIGHT 'TA GET ME DOWN FROM EARLIER.
MONSTER WITH NO FACE COME THROUGH CAMP.
NO FACE?
WHAT I SAW WASN'T ANYTHING I'D CALL A FACE.
STIRRED UP THE LOCALS. GAVE US SOME TERRORS.
I KNOW BAD ENERGY. I CERTAINLY KNOW THE FORMLESS FACE OF SATAN.
LOOK, RORY, I'M LOOKING FOR A HOMELESS GUY WHO MAYBE HURT A FRIEND OF MINE.
GUY YOU USED TO TELL ME STORIES ABOUT.
THE ONE YOU KNEW FROM 'NAM.
YOU KNOW WHERE I CAN FIND HIM?

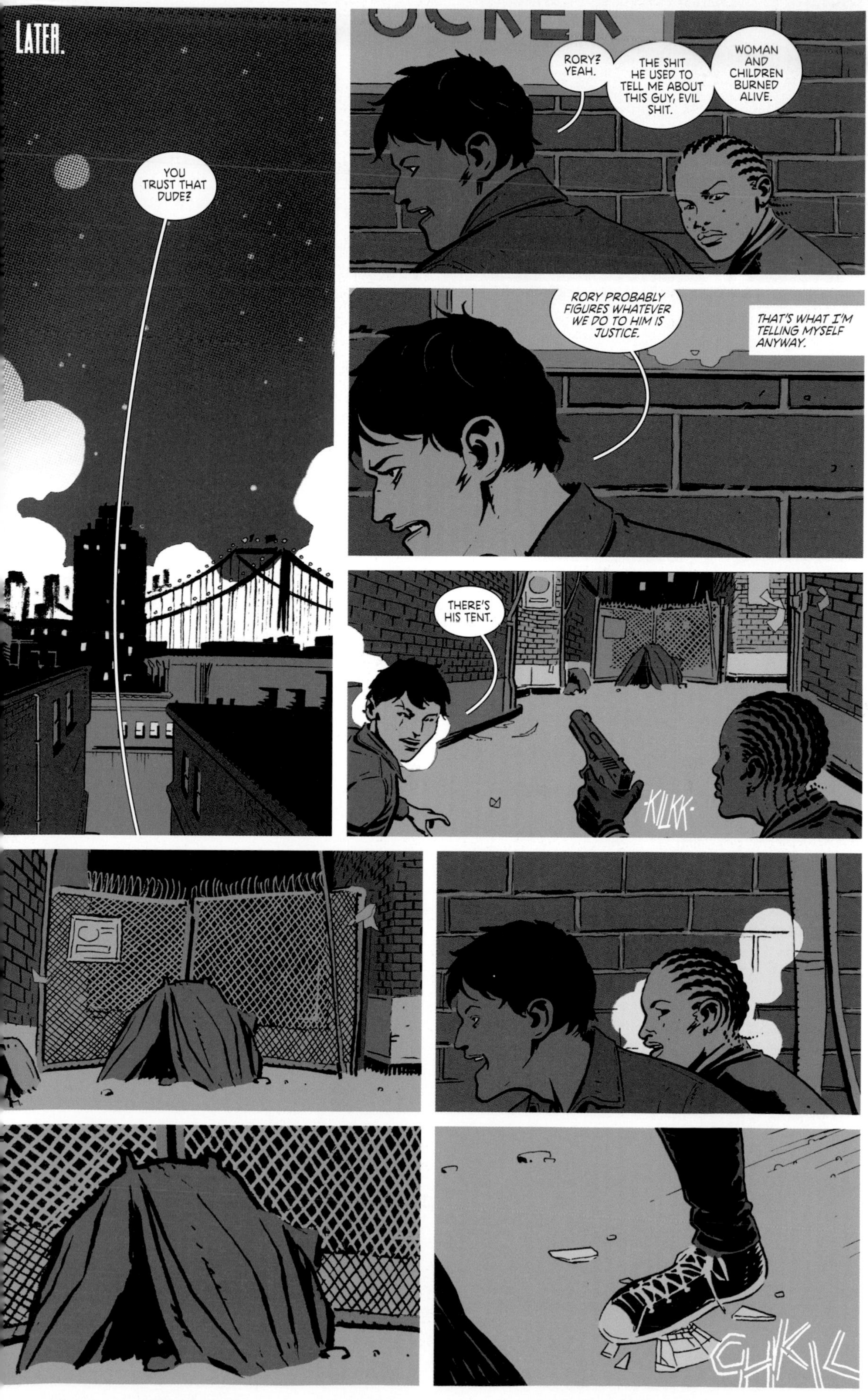
LATER.
YOU TRUST THAT DUDE?
RORY? YEAH.
THE SHIT HE USED TO TELL ME ABOUT THIS GUY, EVIL SHIT.
WOMAN AND CHILDREN BURNED ALIVE.
RORY PROBABLY FIGURES WHATEVER WE DO TO HIM IS JUSTICE.
THAT'S WHAT I'M TELLING MYSELF ANYWAY.
THERE'S HIS TENT.
KILKK
CHKLL

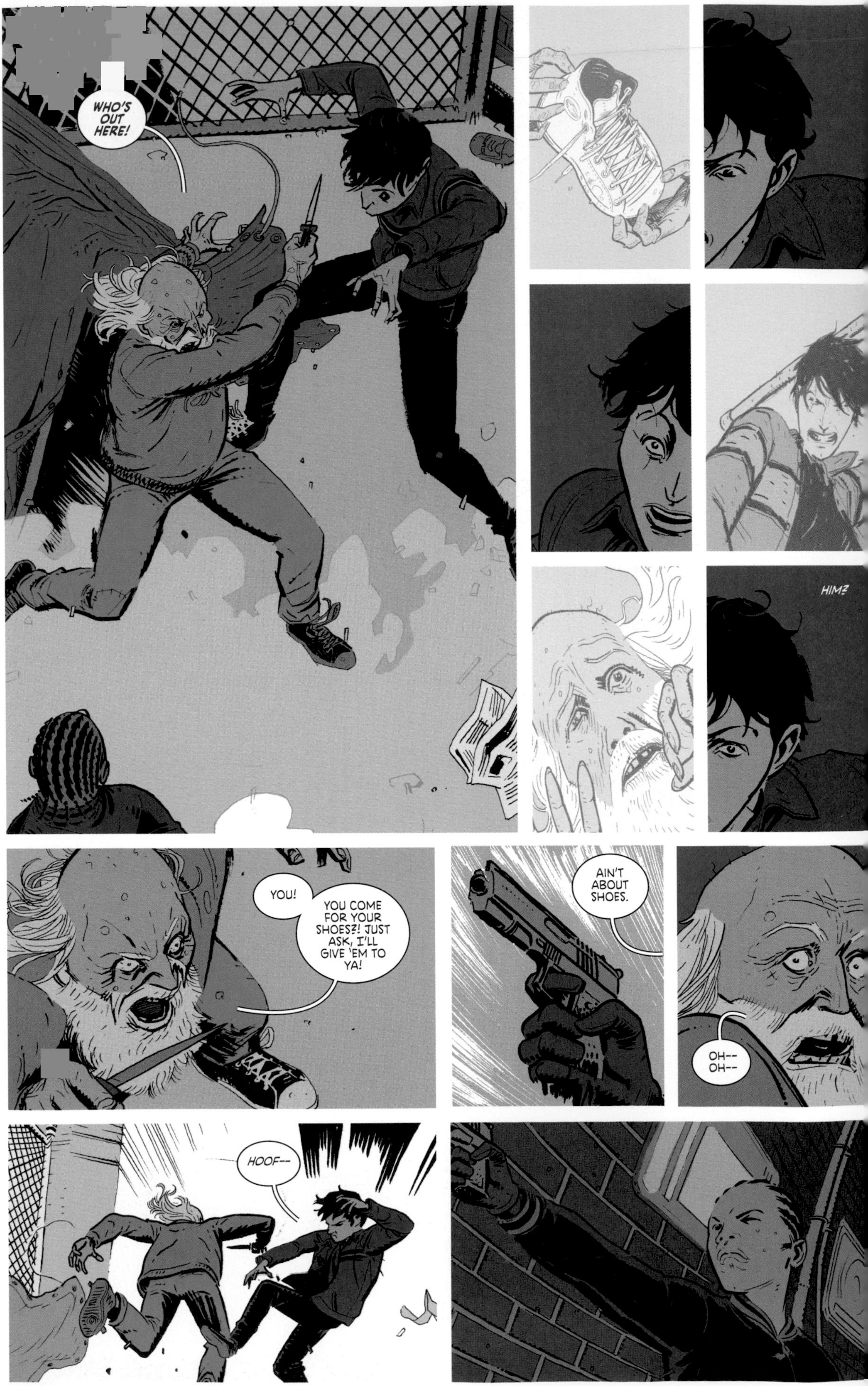
WHO'S OUT HERE!
HIM?
YOU!
YOU COME FOR YOUR SHOES?! JUST ASK, I'LL GIVE 'EM TO YA!
AIN'T ABOUT SHOES.
OH-- OH--
HOOF--

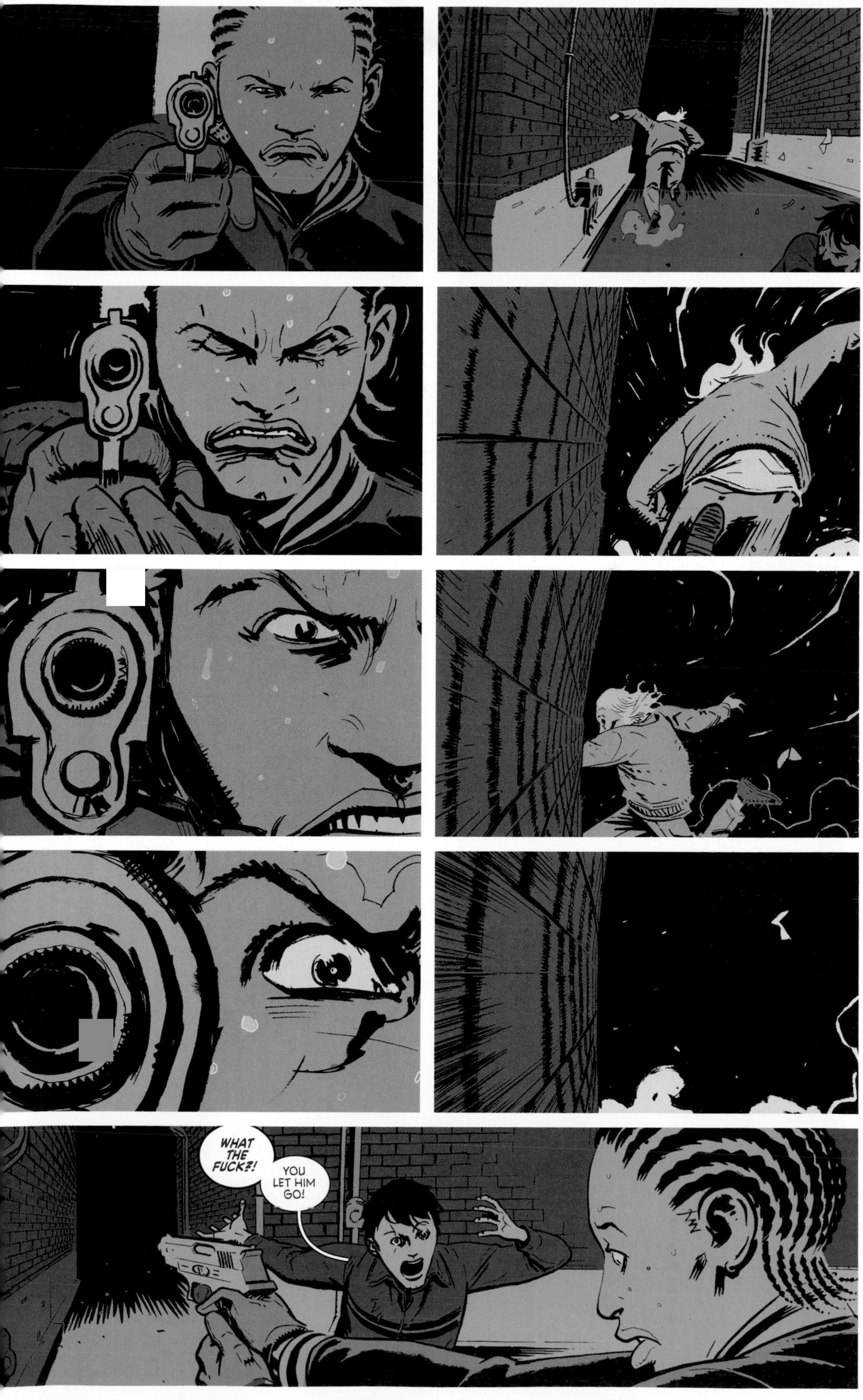
WHAT THE FUCK?!
YOU LET HIM GO!

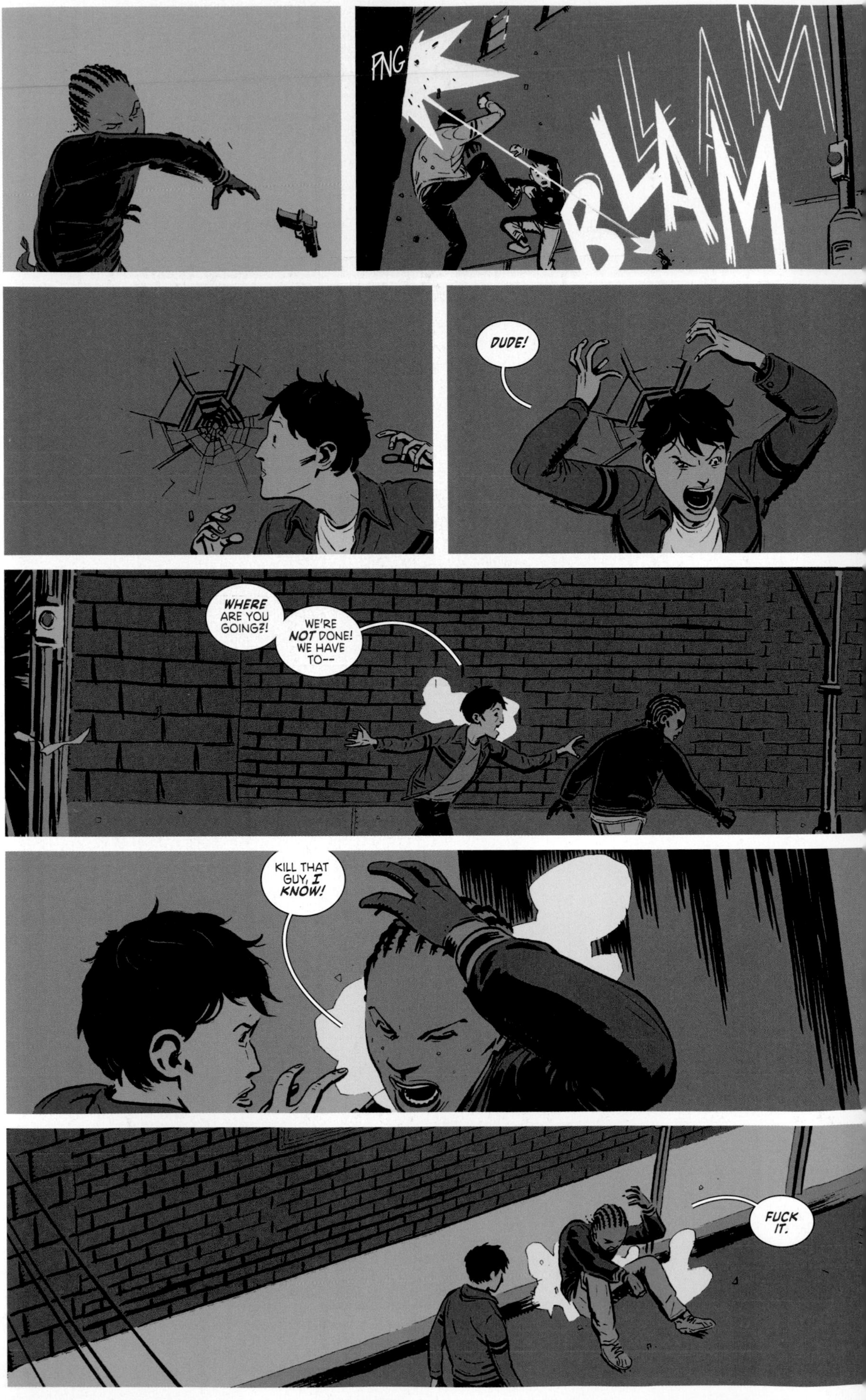
PNG
BLAM
BLAM
DUDE!
WHERE ARE YOU GOING?!
WE'RE NOT DONE! WE HAVE TO--
KILL THAT GUY, I KNOW!
FUCK IT.

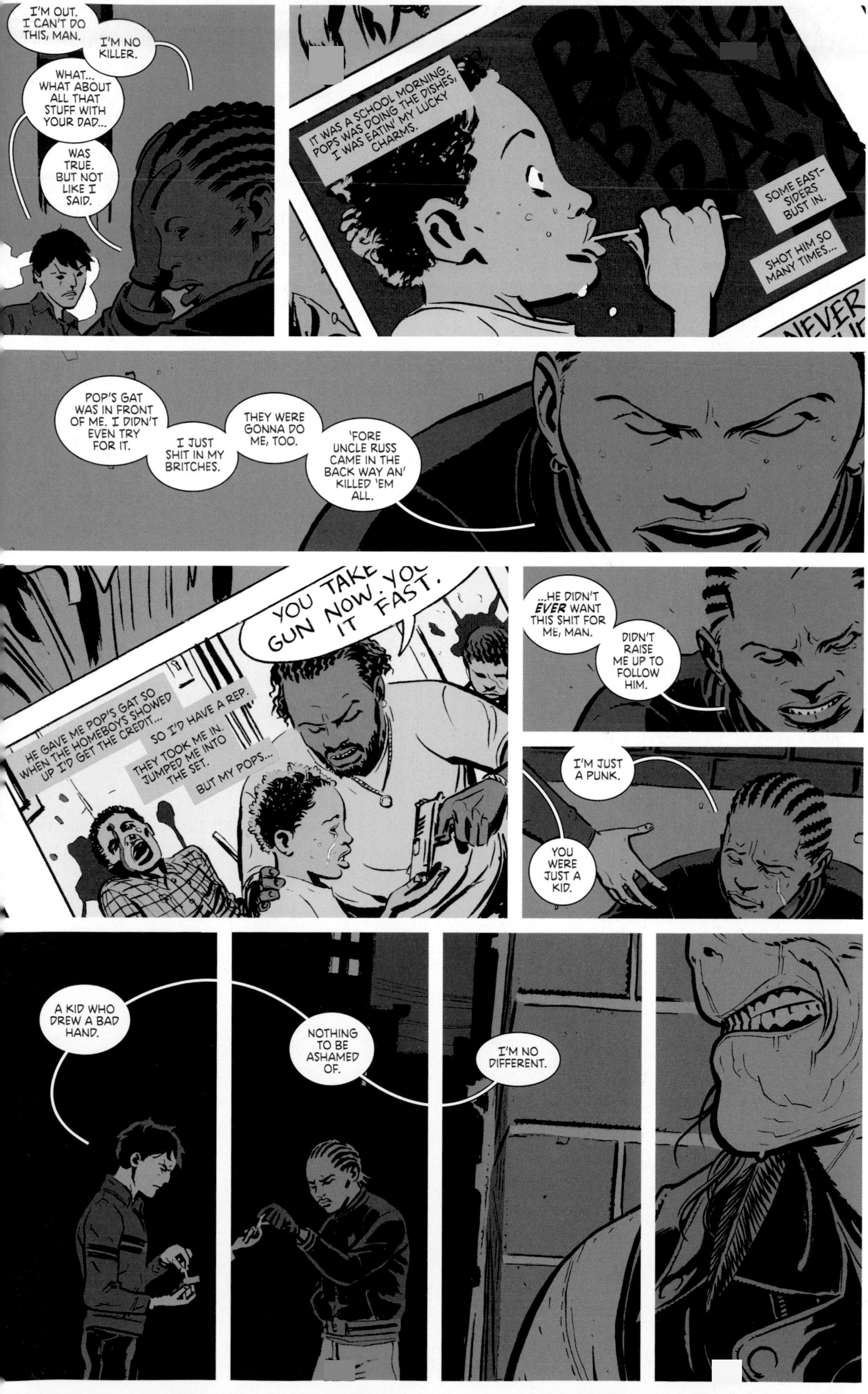

I'M OUT. I CAN'T DO THIS, MAN.
I'M NO KILLER.
WHAT... WHAT ABOUT ALL THAT STUFF WITH YOUR DAD...
WAS TRUE. BUT NOT LIKE I SAID.
IT WAS A SCHOOL MORNING. POPS WAS DOING THE DISHES, I WAS EATIN' MY LUCKY CHARMS.
SOME EAST-SIDERS BUST IN.
SHOT HIM SO MANY TIMES...
NEVER
POP'S GAT WAS IN FRONT OF ME. I DIDN'T EVEN TRY FOR IT.
I JUST SHIT IN MY BRITCHES.
THEY WERE GONNA DO ME, TOO.
'FORE UNCLE RUSS CAME IN THE BACK WAY AN' KILLED 'EM ALL.
YOU TAKE GUN NOW. YOU IT FAST.
HE GAVE ME POP'S GAT SO WHEN THE HOMEBOYS SHOWED UP I'D GET THE CREDIT...
SO I'D HAVE A REP.
THEY TOOK ME IN. JUMPED ME INTO THE SET.
BUT MY POPS...
...HE DIDN'T *EVER* WANT THIS SHIT FOR ME, MAN.
DIDN'T RAISE ME UP TO FOLLOW HIM.
I'M JUST A PUNK.
YOU WERE JUST A KID.
A KID WHO DREW A BAD HAND.
NOTHING TO BE ASHAMED OF.
I'M NO DIFFERENT.

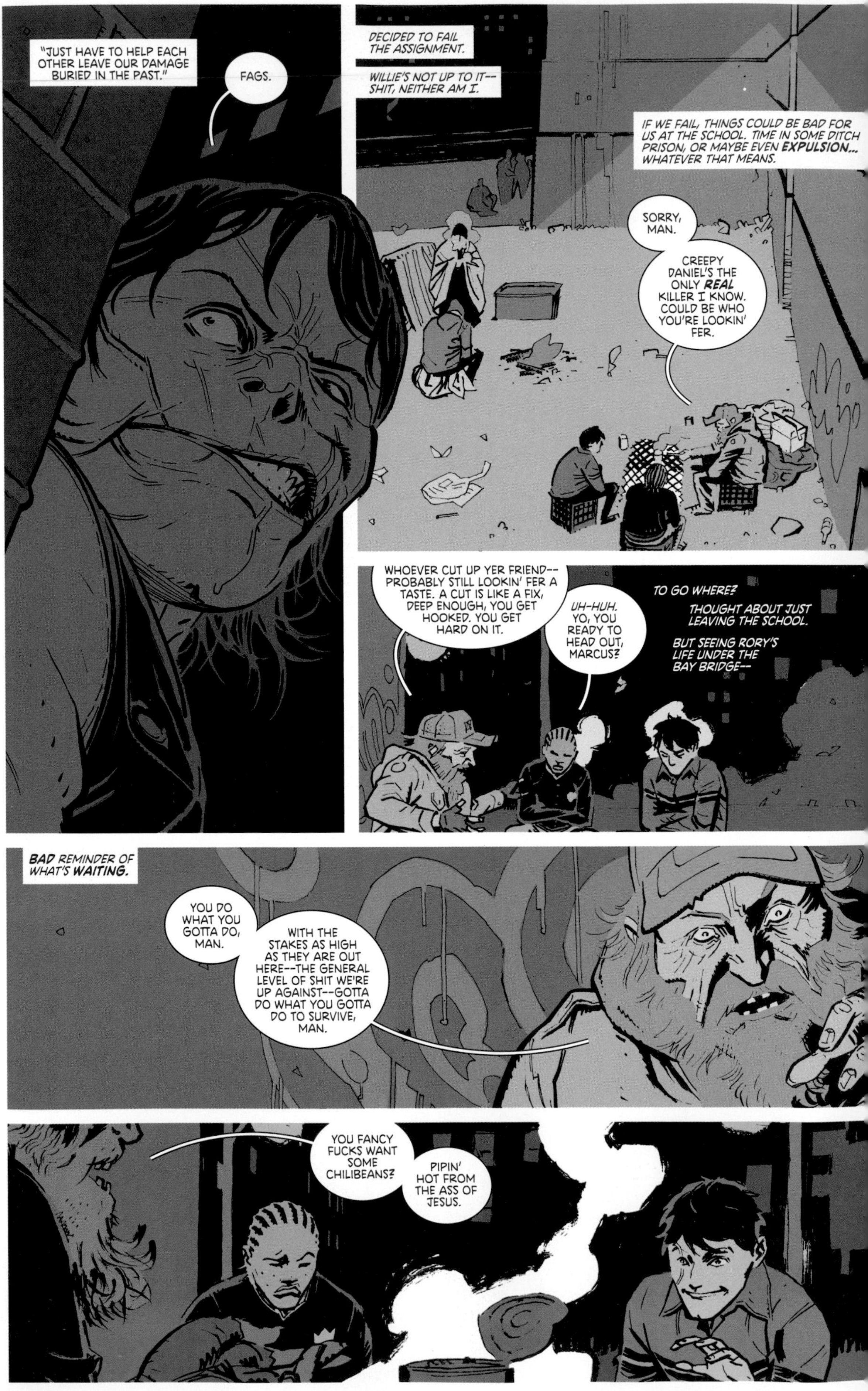

"JUST HAVE TO HELP EACH OTHER LEAVE OUR DAMAGE BURIED IN THE PAST."
FAGS.
DECIDED TO FAIL THE ASSIGNMENT.
WILLIE'S NOT UP TO IT--SHIT, NEITHER AM I.
IF WE FAIL, THINGS COULD BE BAD FOR US AT THE SCHOOL. TIME IN SOME DITCH PRISON, OR MAYBE EVEN EXPULSION... WHATEVER THAT MEANS.
SORRY, MAN.
CREEPY DANIEL'S THE ONLY REAL KILLER I KNOW. COULD BE WHO YOU'RE LOOKIN' FER.
WHOEVER CUT UP YER FRIEND--PROBABLY STILL LOOKIN' FER A TASTE. A CUT IS LIKE A FIX, DEEP ENOUGH, YOU GET HOOKED. YOU GET HARD ON IT.
UH-HUH. YO, YOU READY TO HEAD OUT, MARCUS?
TO GO WHERE?
THOUGHT ABOUT JUST LEAVING THE SCHOOL.
BUT SEEING RORY'S LIFE UNDER THE BAY BRIDGE--
BAD REMINDER OF WHAT'S WAITING.
YOU DO WHAT YOU GOTTA DO, MAN.
WITH THE STAKES AS HIGH AS THEY ARE OUT HERE--THE GENERAL LEVEL OF SHIT WE'RE UP AGAINST--GOTTA DO WHAT YOU GOTTA DO TO SURVIVE, MAN.
YOU FANCY FUCKS WANT SOME CHILIBEANS?
PIPIN' HOT FROM THE ASS OF JESUS.

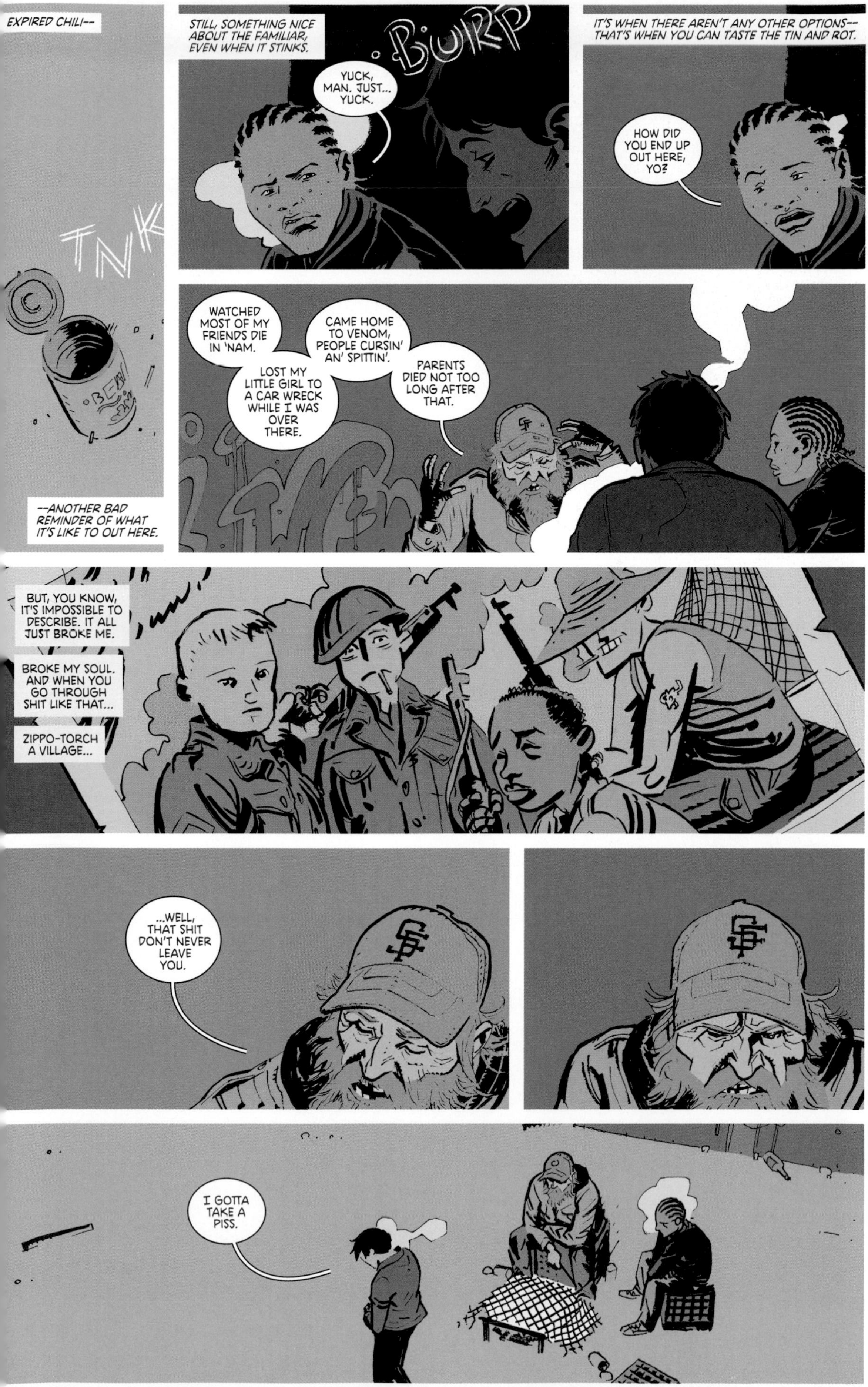
EXPIRED CHILI--
TNK
STILL, SOMETHING NICE ABOUT THE FAMILIAR, EVEN WHEN IT STINKS.
BURP
YUCK, MAN. JUST... YUCK.
IT'S WHEN THERE AREN'T ANY OTHER OPTIONS-- THAT'S WHEN YOU CAN TASTE THE TIN AND ROT.
HOW DID YOU END UP OUT HERE, YO?
WATCHED MOST OF MY FRIENDS DIE IN 'NAM.
LOST MY LITTLE GIRL TO A CAR WRECK WHILE I WAS OVER THERE.
CAME HOME TO VENOM, PEOPLE CURSIN' AN' SPITTIN'.
PARENTS DIED NOT TOO LONG AFTER THAT.
--ANOTHER BAD REMINDER OF WHAT IT'S LIKE TO OUT HERE.
BUT, YOU KNOW, IT'S IMPOSSIBLE TO DESCRIBE. IT ALL JUST BROKE ME.
BROKE MY SOUL. AND WHEN YOU GO THROUGH SHIT LIKE THAT...
ZIPPO-TORCH A VILLAGE...
...WELL, THAT SHIT DON'T NEVER LEAVE YOU.
I GOTTA TAKE A PISS.

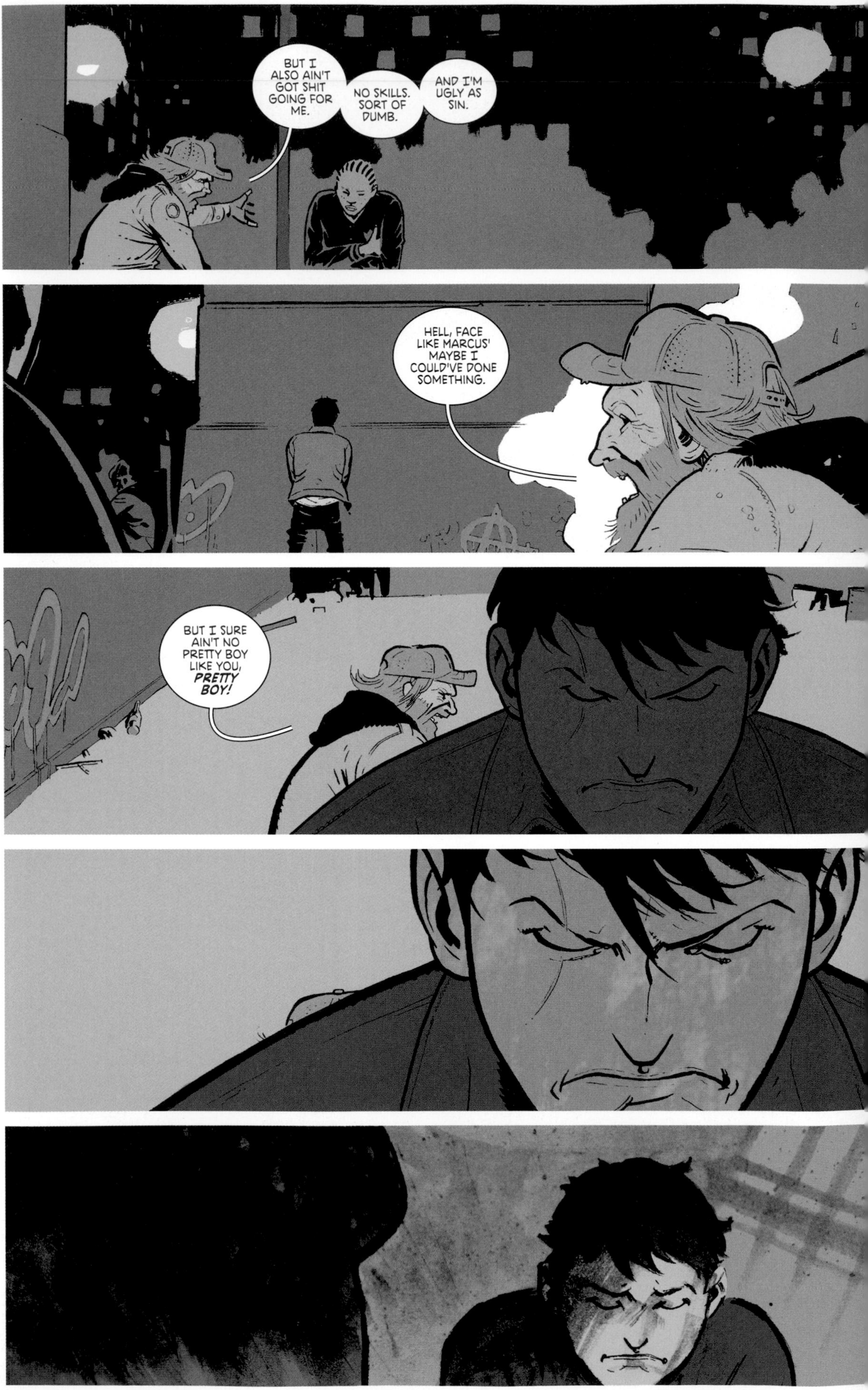
BUT I ALSO AIN'T GOT SHIT GOING FOR ME.
NO SKILLS. SORT OF DUMB.
AND I'M UGLY AS SIN.
HELL, FACE LIKE MARCUS' MAYBE I COULD'VE DONE SOMETHING.
BUT I SURE AIN'T NO PRETTY BOY LIKE YOU, ***PRETTY BOY!***

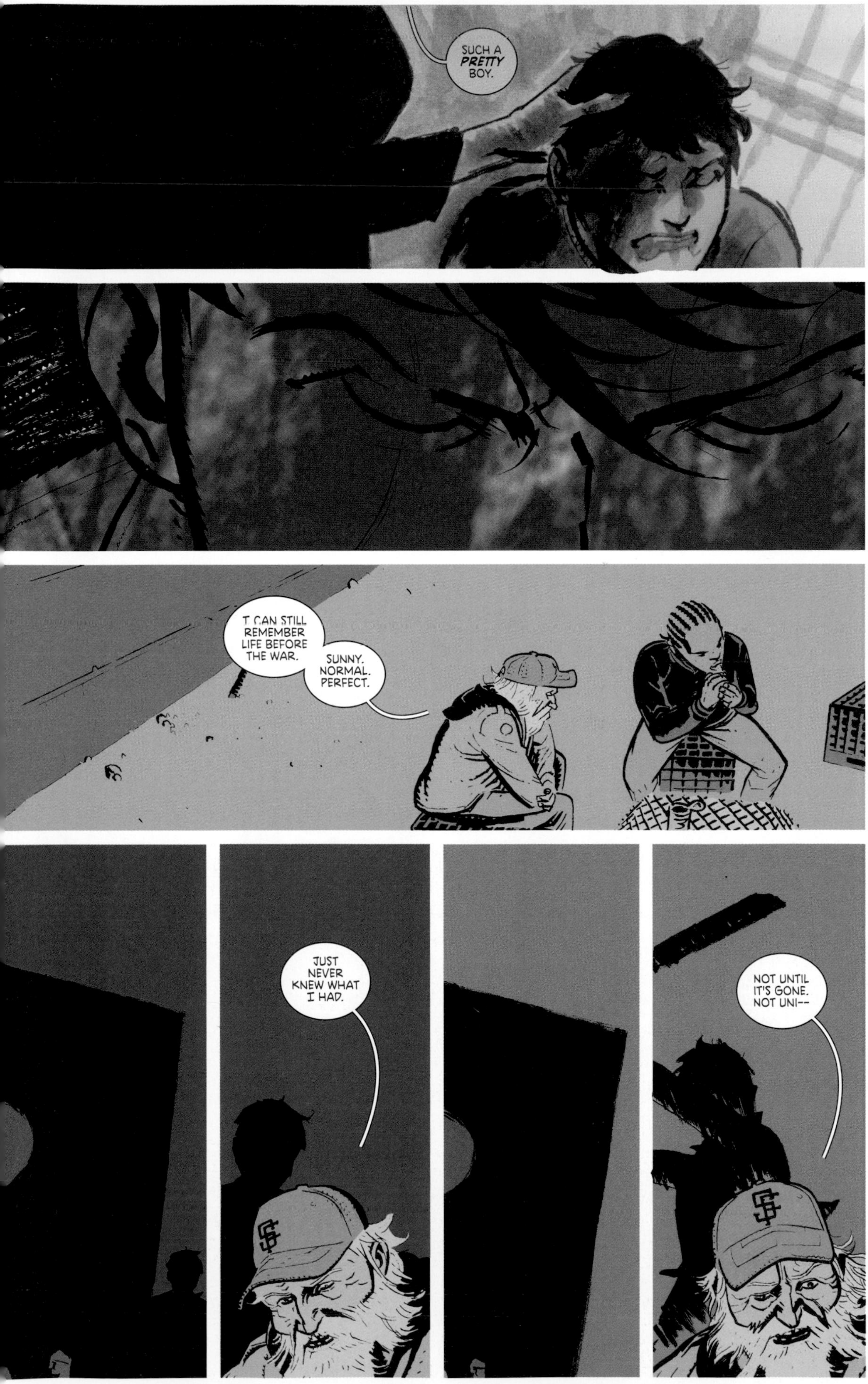
SUCH A *PRETTY* BOY.
I CAN STILL REMEMBER LIFE BEFORE THE WAR.
SUNNY. NORMAL. PERFECT.
JUST NEVER KNEW WHAT I HAD.
NOT UNTIL IT'S GONE. NOT UNI--

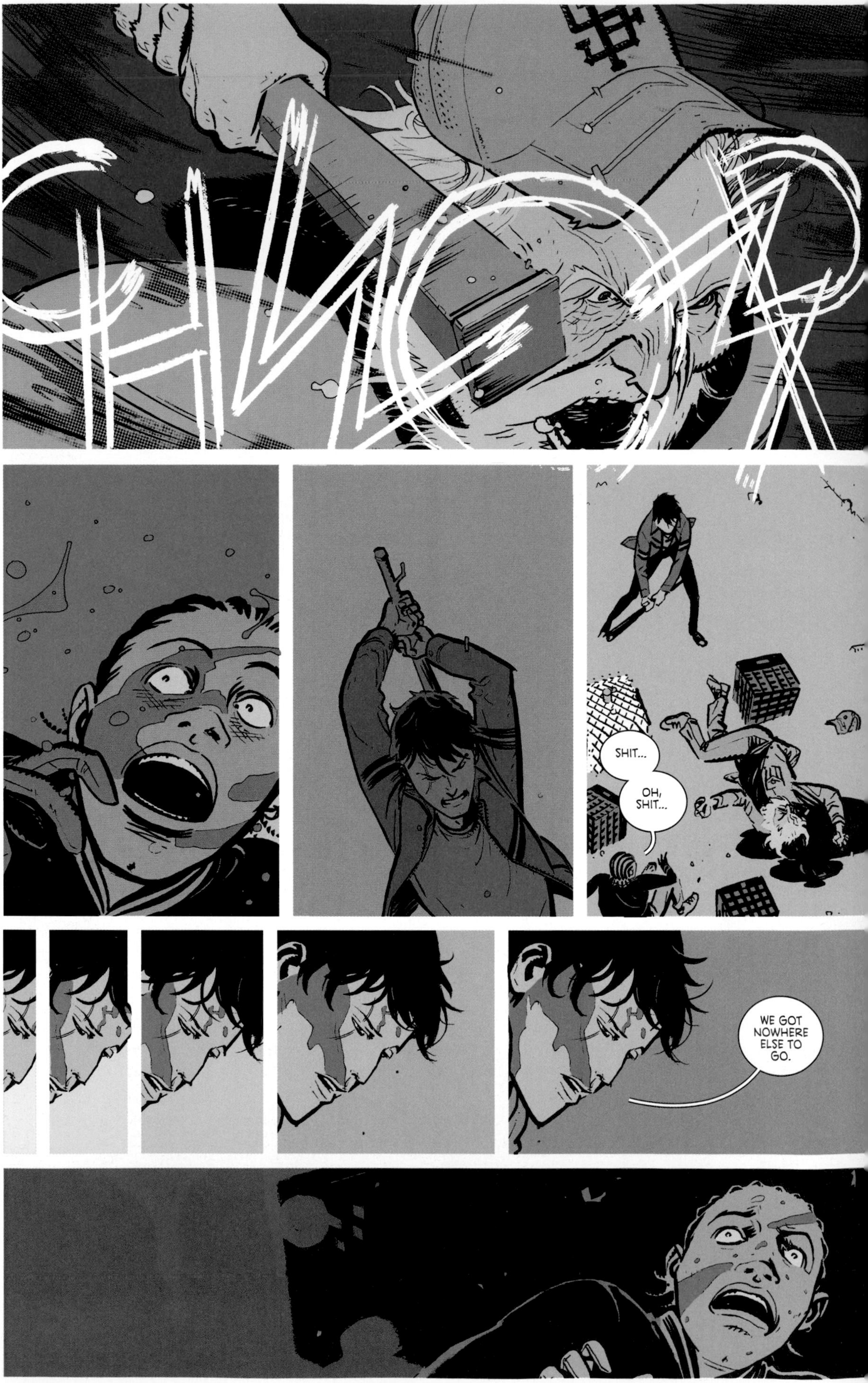
CHUCK
SHIT...
OH, SHIT...
WE GOT NOWHERE ELSE TO GO.

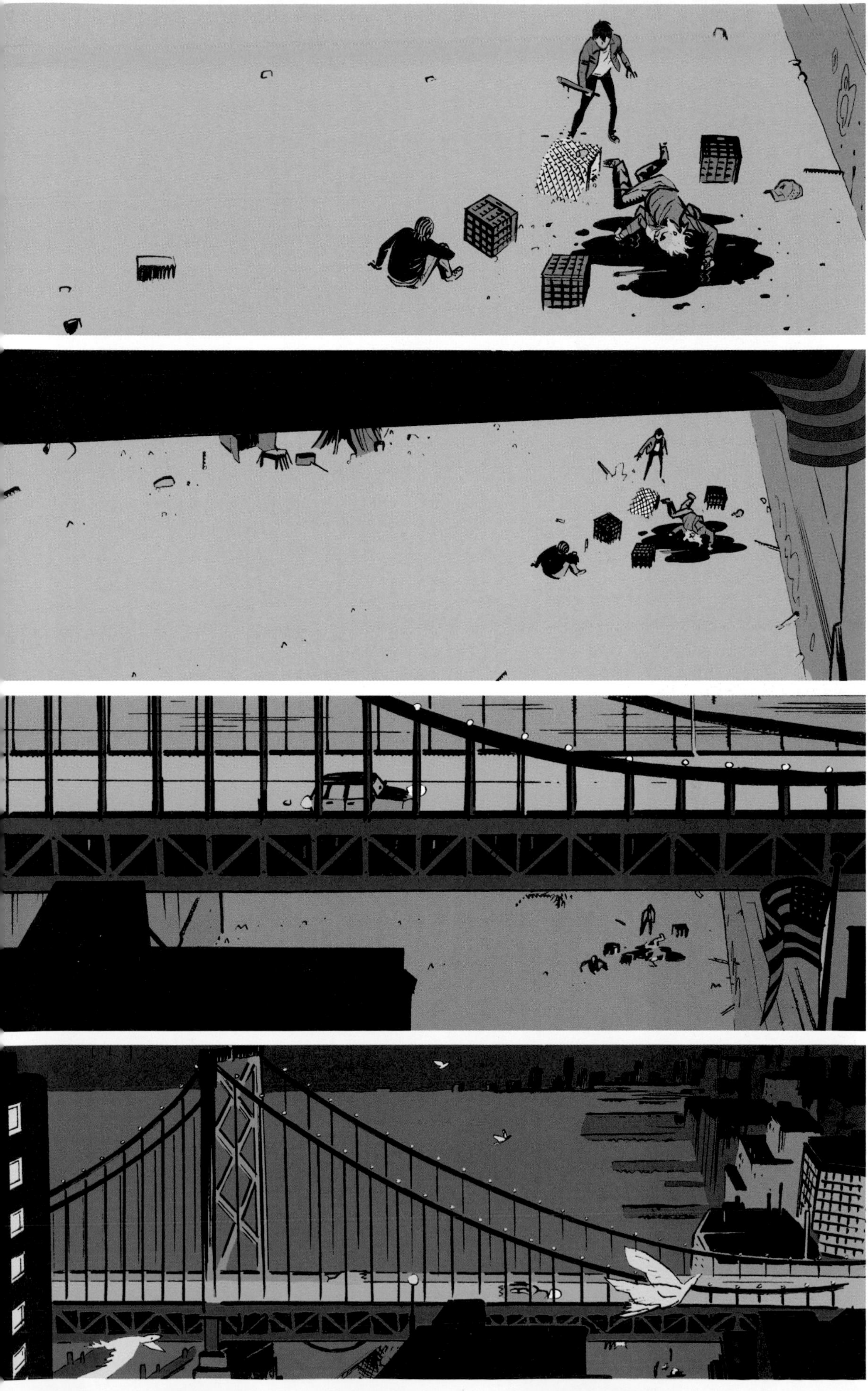

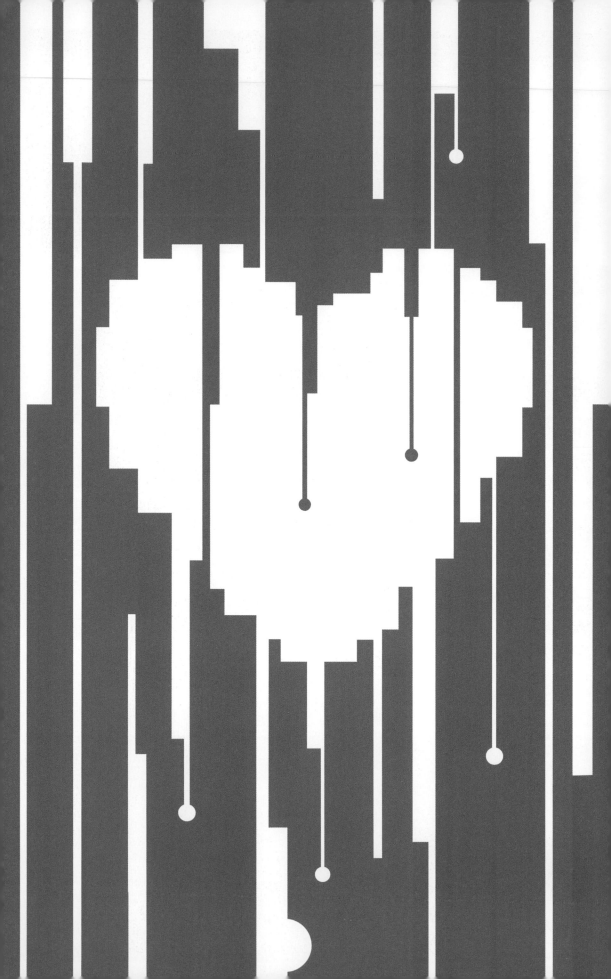

FORGOTTEN ALL
HUMAN ETIQUETTE.

WHAT IS EXPECTED
OF ME HERE?

JUST BE **COOL.**
BE **NORMAL.**

WHAT THE FUCK DO I
DO WITH MY EYES? LOOK
AT HIM? THE FLOOR?

STOP. TRYING TO HIDE
THE TENSION ONLY
MAKES IT **OBVIOUS.**

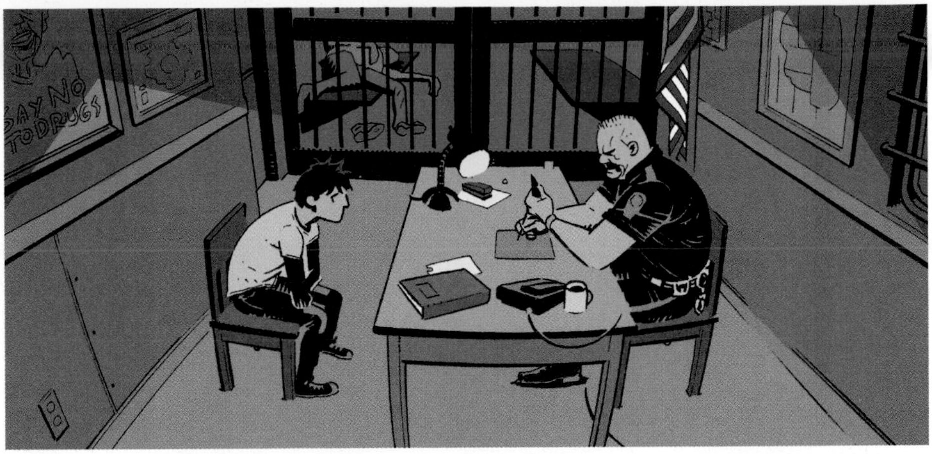
SAY NO
TO DRUGS

WHERE AM I? I **SHOULD** KNOW THAT.

IT STARTED TWO DAYS AGO WITH
POT SNOWCAPPED WITH ANGEL DUST.

IMPORTANT DETAIL NOT OFFERED
UNTIL **AFTER** WE'D SMOKED IT.

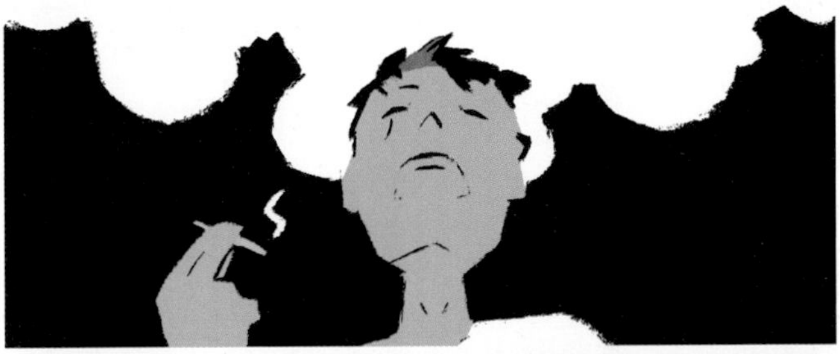

WENT THROUGH TWO OR THREE
EIGHT BALLS OF COCAINE ON
THE DRIVE.

I REMEMBER SPRAYING WATER
THROUGH THE DRIVE-IN WINDOW
AT A JACK IN THE BOX.

I WASN'T WEARING PANTS.

AND IT WASN'T WATER.

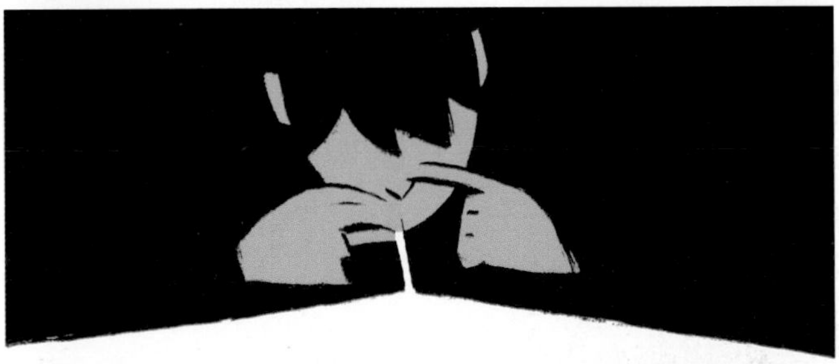

BILLY HAD A BOTTLE OF **ETHER.**

STUFF IS UGLY. ONLY LASTS
A FEW MINUTES, BUT TWISTS
REALITY DOWN HARD.

FLASH FRYING BILLIONS
OF BRAIN CELLS.

IT'S WHERE HUNTER WENT
OFF THE RAILS IN THE BOOK.

BUT **NONE** OF THAT
EVEN MATTERS.

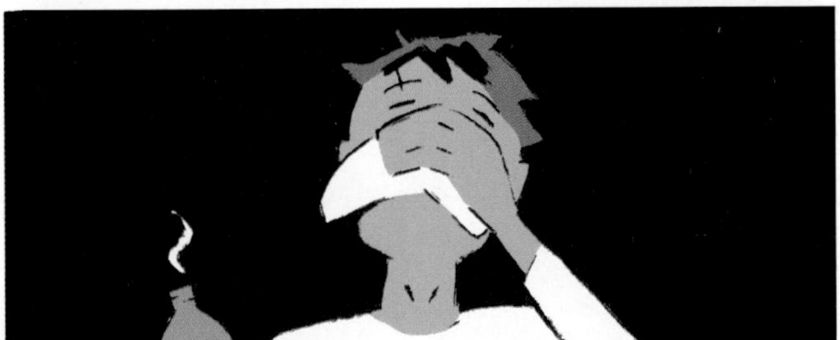

NOTHING BEFORE
THE **ACID** MATTERS.

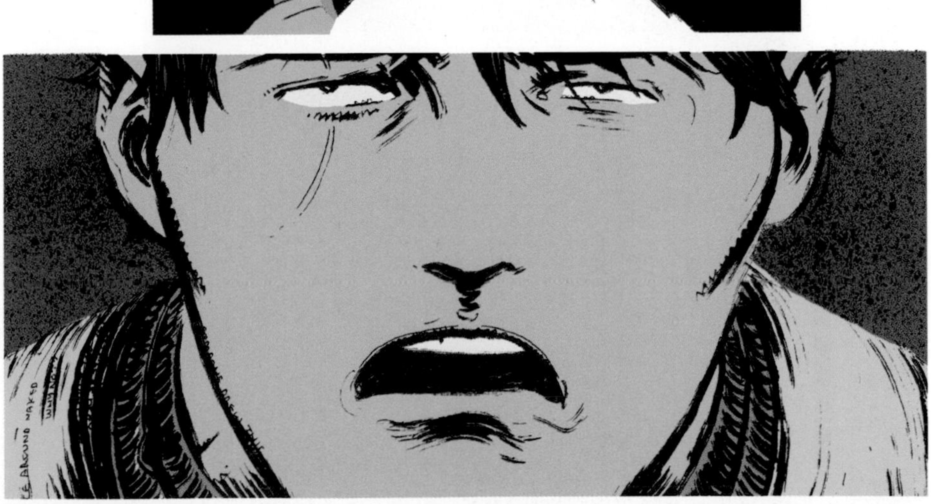

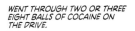

STOMACH LURCHES, COMPRESSING IN ON ITSELF.

HE KNOWS.

BREATHING STUTTERS.

HE KNOWS WHAT YOU'VE DONE.

NUMBNESS IN FACE AND HANDS.

*SOMETHING **BAD.***

TOLD MYSELF TO REMEMBER. BEFORE MR. T SHOWED UP...

*SOMETHING **IMPORTANT...***

*NO, NOT THE SCHOOL. TOO FAR BACK... SOMETHING **ELSE.***

THAT WASN'T IT... JESUS, WHAT'S THE THING?

SOMETHING WORSE THAN THE DRUGS OR THE FAKE I.D....

OH.

FUCK.

THAT'S RIGHT...

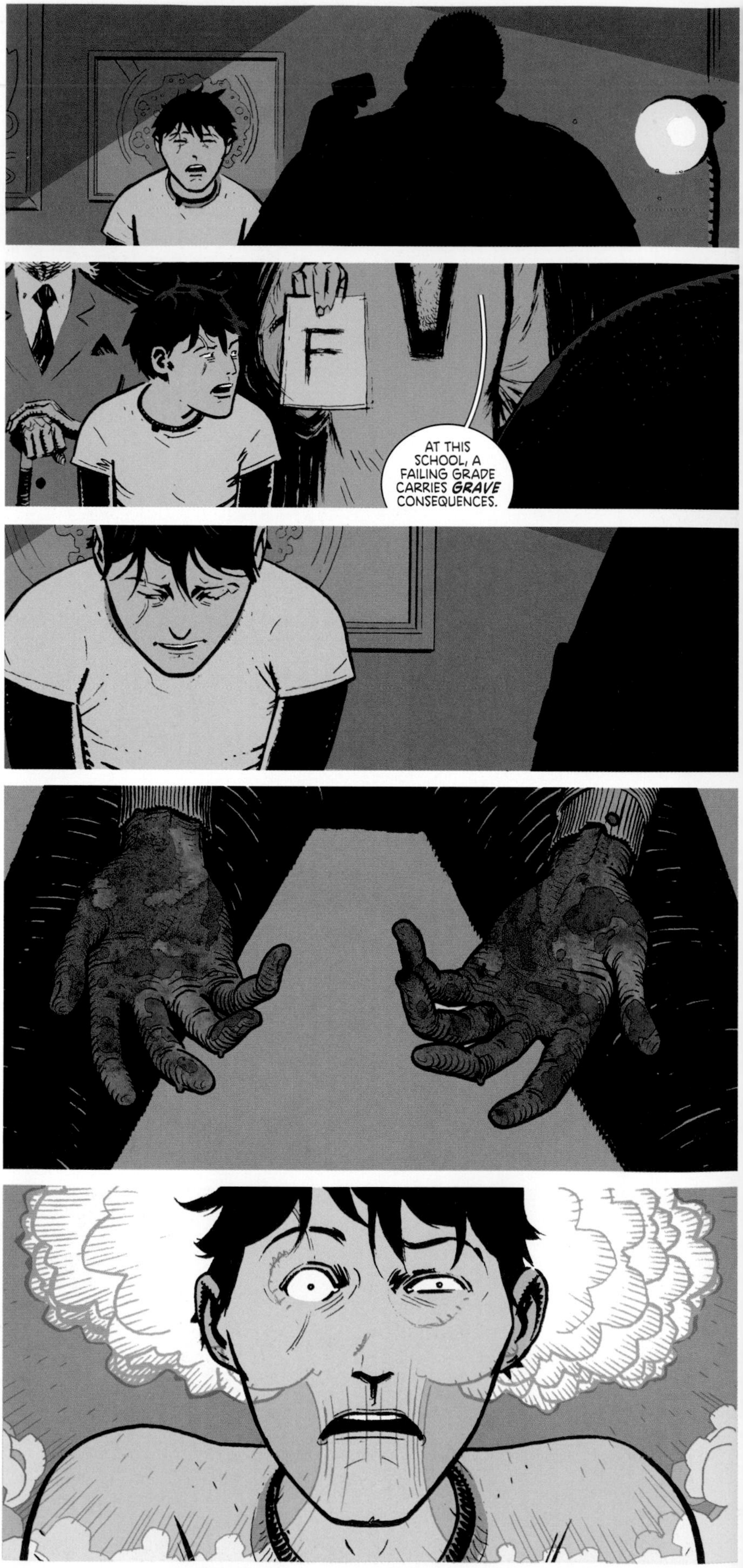
AT THIS SCHOOL, A FAILING GRADE CARRIES GRAVE CONSEQUENCES.

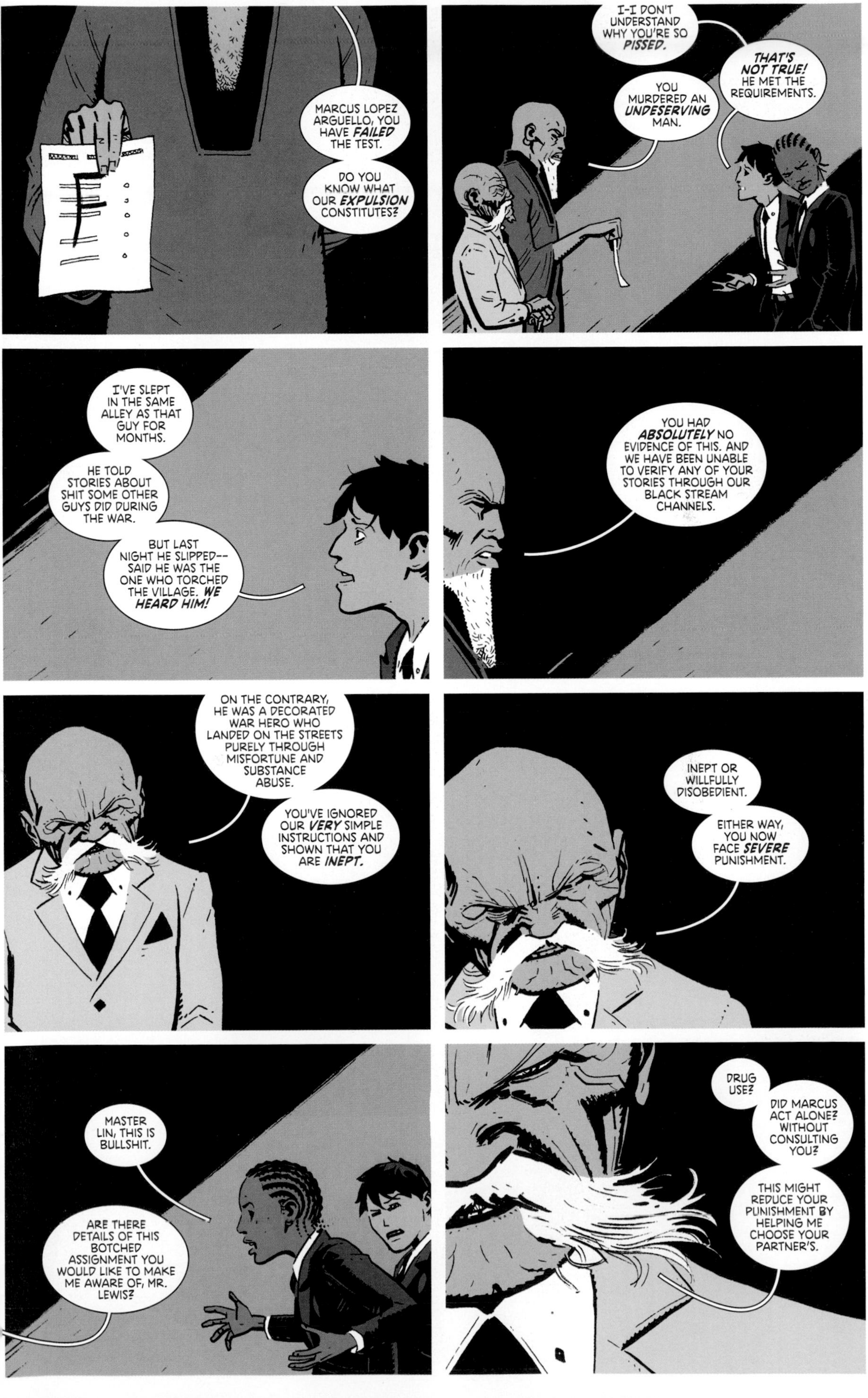
MARCUS LOPEZ ARGUELLO, YOU HAVE FAILED THE TEST.
DO YOU KNOW WHAT OUR EXPULSION CONSTITUTES?
I-I DON'T UNDERSTAND WHY YOU'RE SO PISSED.
YOU MURDERED AN UNDESERVING MAN.
THAT'S NOT TRUE! HE MET THE REQUIREMENTS.
I'VE SLEPT IN THE SAME ALLEY AS THAT GUY FOR MONTHS.
HE TOLD STORIES ABOUT SHIT SOME OTHER GUYS DID DURING THE WAR.
BUT LAST NIGHT HE SLIPPED-- SAID HE WAS THE ONE WHO TORCHED THE VILLAGE. WE HEARD HIM!
YOU HAD ABSOLUTELY NO EVIDENCE OF THIS. AND WE HAVE BEEN UNABLE TO VERIFY ANY OF YOUR STORIES THROUGH OUR BLACK STREAM CHANNELS.
ON THE CONTRARY, HE WAS A DECORATED WAR HERO WHO LANDED ON THE STREETS PURELY THROUGH MISFORTUNE AND SUBSTANCE ABUSE.
YOU'VE IGNORED OUR VERY SIMPLE INSTRUCTIONS AND SHOWN THAT YOU ARE INEPT.
INEPT OR WILLFULLY DISOBEDIENT.
EITHER WAY, YOU NOW FACE SEVERE PUNISHMENT.
MASTER LIN, THIS IS BULLSHIT.
ARE THERE DETAILS OF THIS BOTCHED ASSIGNMENT YOU WOULD LIKE TO MAKE ME AWARE OF, MR. LEWIS?
DRUG USE?
DID MARCUS ACT ALONE? WITHOUT CONSULTING YOU?
THIS MIGHT REDUCE YOUR PUNISHMENT BY HELPING ME CHOOSE YOUR PARTNER'S.

WE DID IT TOGETHER.

YOU ARE FREE TO GO, MR. LEWIS.

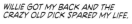

WILLIE GOT MY BACK AND THE CRAZY OLD DICK SPARED MY LIFE.

THREW ME IN "THE DITCH," SOLITARY CONFINEMENT, FOR A WEEK.

*SPENT **DAYS** RELIVING IT.*

DAYS SEEING RORY'S TWITCHING BODY IN THE PUDDLE OF THICK PURPLE GOO THAT CAME OUT OF HIS HEAD.

DID HE SAY HE TORCHED A VILLAGE? WHAT HAVE I DONE?

BASHED A HELPLESS OLD MAN'S HEAD IN.

SAME AS HE TORCHED SOME VILLAGE IN NAM.

*SAME **RATIONALIZATION**...*

...JUST FOLLOWING ORDERS.

HEYA, JAILBIRD.

W-WHAT ARE YOU DOING?

IT'S WHAT **WE** ARE DOING...

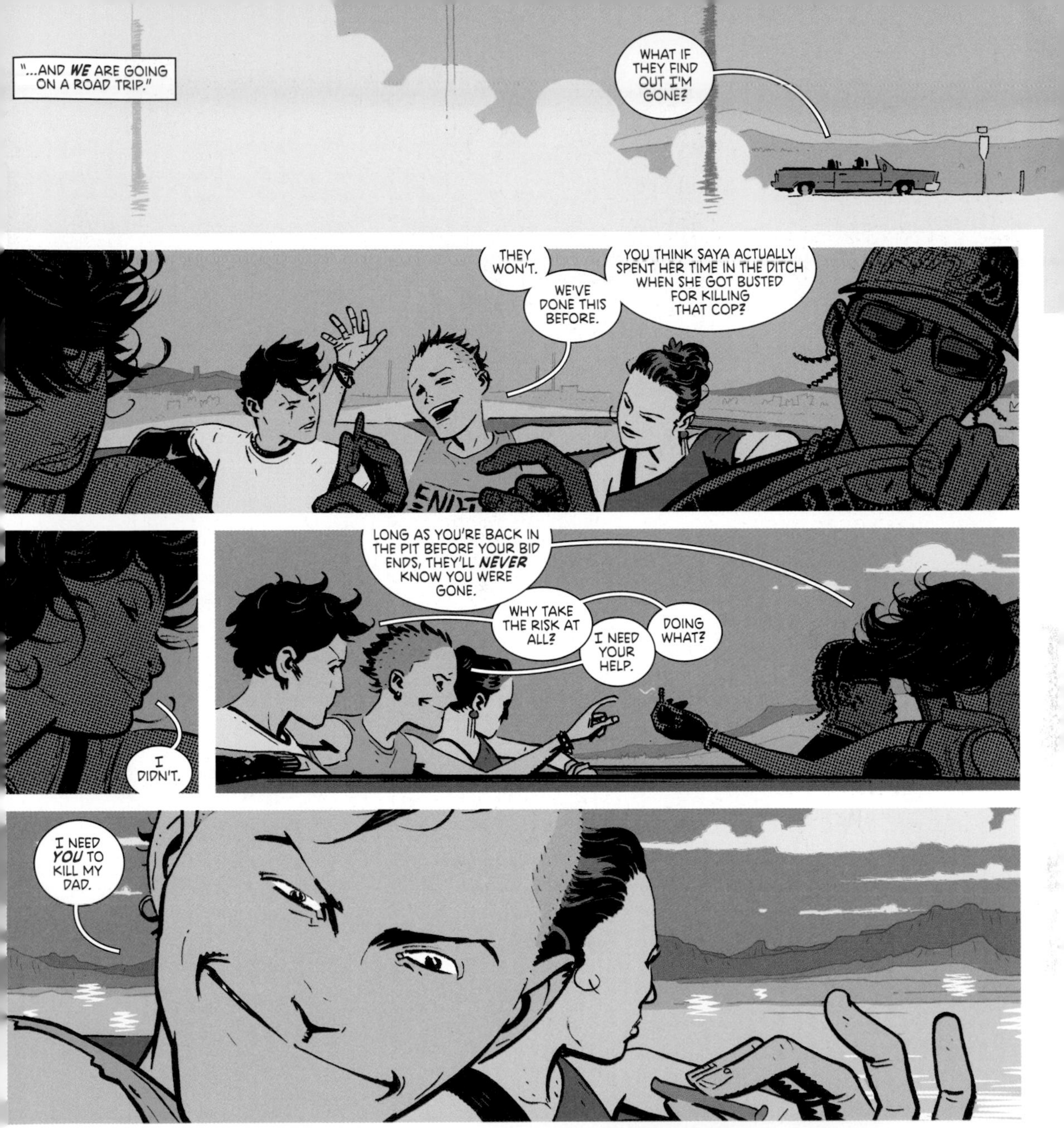
"...AND **WE** ARE GOING ON A ROAD TRIP."
WHAT IF THEY FIND OUT I'M GONE?
THEY WON'T.
WE'VE DONE THIS BEFORE.
YOU THINK SAYA ACTUALLY SPENT HER TIME IN THE DITCH WHEN SHE GOT BUSTED FOR KILLING THAT COP?
I DIDN'T.
LONG AS YOU'RE BACK IN THE PIT BEFORE YOUR BID ENDS, THEY'LL **NEVER** KNOW YOU WERE GONE.
WHY TAKE THE RISK AT ALL?
I NEED YOUR HELP.
DOING WHAT?
I NEED **YOU** TO KILL MY DAD.

BILLY TOLD ME THEY WERE GOING TO LAS VEGAS TO KILL HIS DAD, A DEGENERATE GAMBLER WHO LEFT HIS FAMILY IN THE LURCH, ONLY TO REAPPEAR YEARS LATER TO MAKE THEIR LIVES EVEN WORSE.

HE WAS A SMUGGLER OR SOMETHING, HE'D PUT BILLY IN THE SCHOOL TO TOUGHEN HIM UP, AND IT DID.

TOUGH ENOUGH TO WANT TO SEE HIS DAD KILLED FOR EVERYTHING HE HAD DONE TO HIM GROWING UP. JUST NOT TOUGH ENOUGH TO DO IT HIMSELF.

WORD OF MY KILL HAD SPREAD.

AND IT JUST FELT GOOD TO BE WANTED.

EVEN FOR SOMETHING AS FUCKED AS THIS.

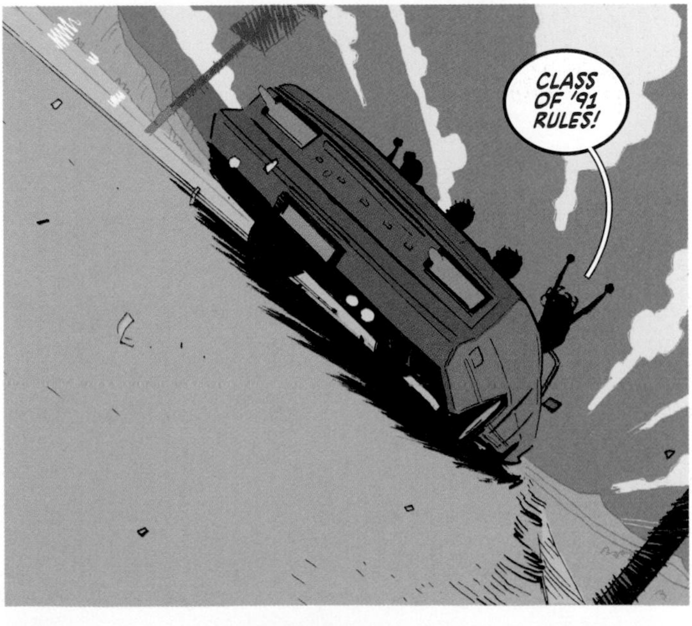
CLASS OF '91 RULES!

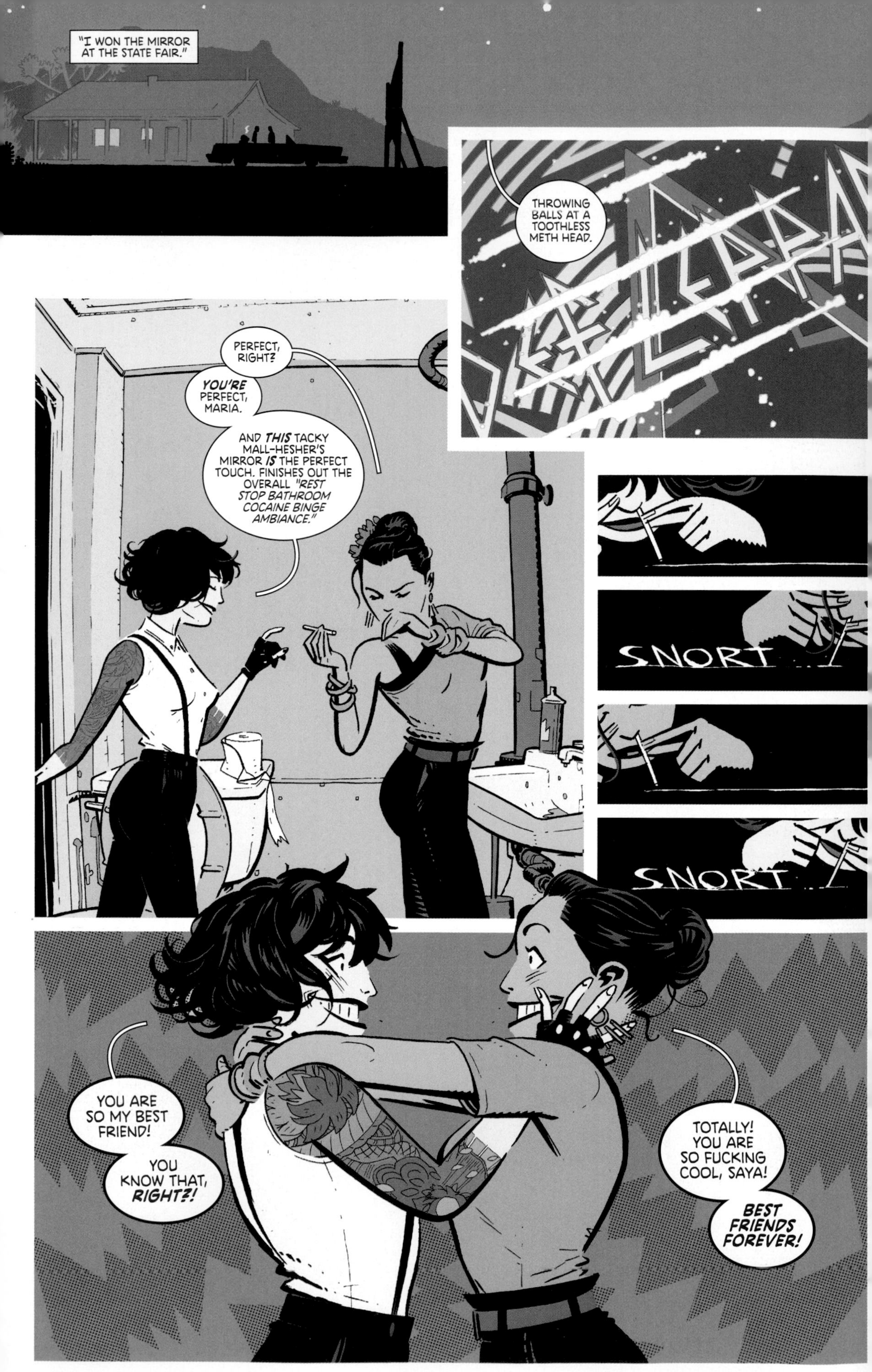
"I WON THE MIRROR AT THE STATE FAIR."
THROWING BALLS AT A TOOTHLESS METH HEAD.
PERFECT, RIGHT?
YOU'RE PERFECT, MARIA.
AND THIS TACKY MALL-HESHER'S MIRROR IS THE PERFECT TOUCH. FINISHES OUT THE OVERALL "REST STOP BATHROOM COCAINE BINGE AMBIANCE."
SNORT
SNORT
YOU ARE SO MY BEST FRIEND!
YOU KNOW THAT, RIGHT?!
TOTALLY! YOU ARE SO FUCKING COOL, SAYA!
BEST FRIENDS FOREVER!

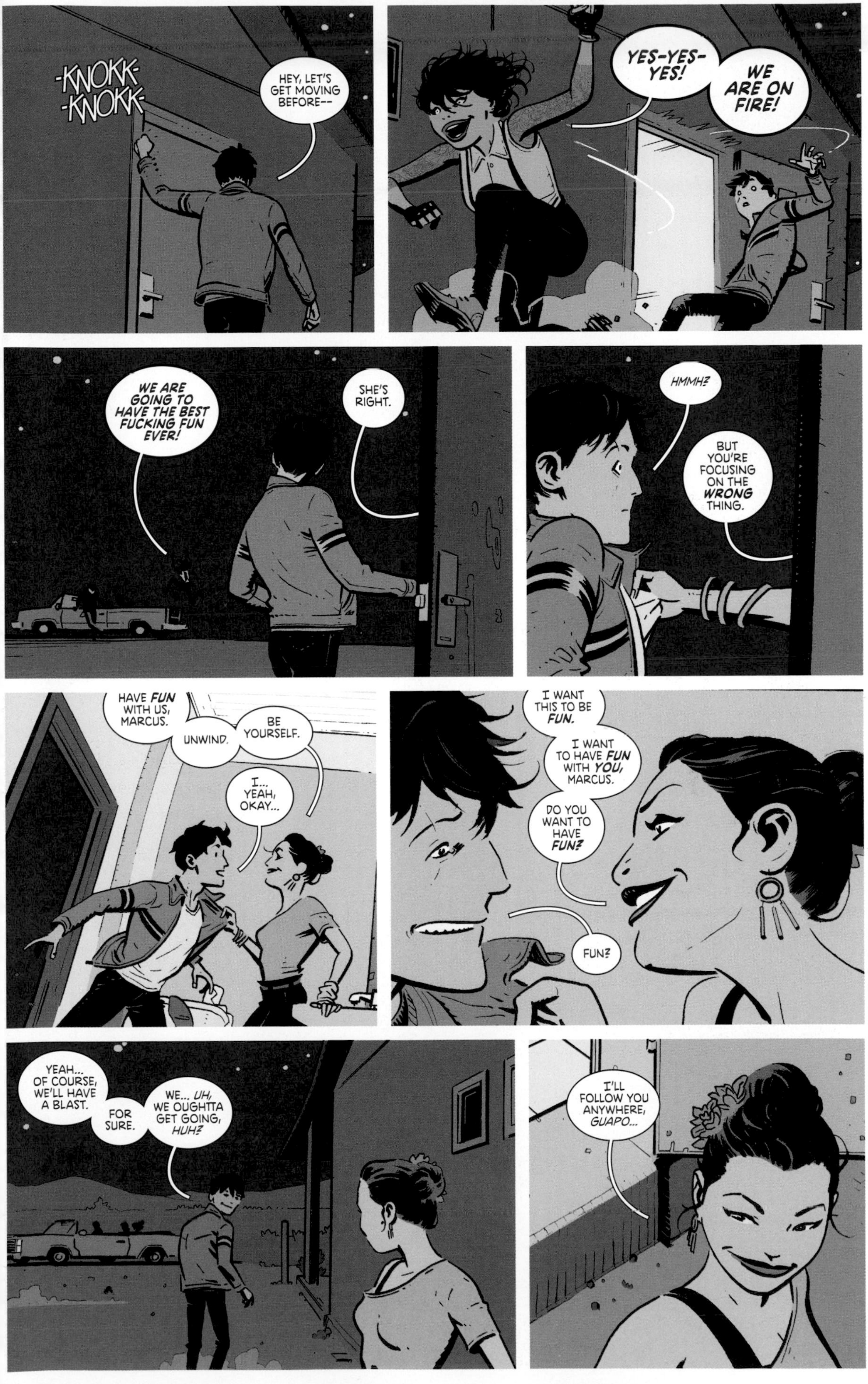
-KNOKK- -KNOKK-
HEY, LET'S GET MOVING BEFORE--
YES-YES-YES!
WE ARE ON FIRE!
WE ARE GOING TO HAVE THE BEST FUCKING FUN EVER!
SHE'S RIGHT.
HMMH?
BUT YOU'RE FOCUSING ON THE WRONG THING.
HAVE FUN WITH US, MARCUS.
UNWIND.
BE YOURSELF.
I... YEAH, OKAY...
I WANT THIS TO BE FUN.
I WANT TO HAVE FUN WITH YOU, MARCUS.
DO YOU WANT TO HAVE FUN?
FUN?
YEAH... OF COURSE, WE'LL HAVE A BLAST.
FOR SURE.
WE... UH, WE OUGHTTA GET GOING, HUH?
I'LL FOLLOW YOU ANYWHERE, GUAPO...

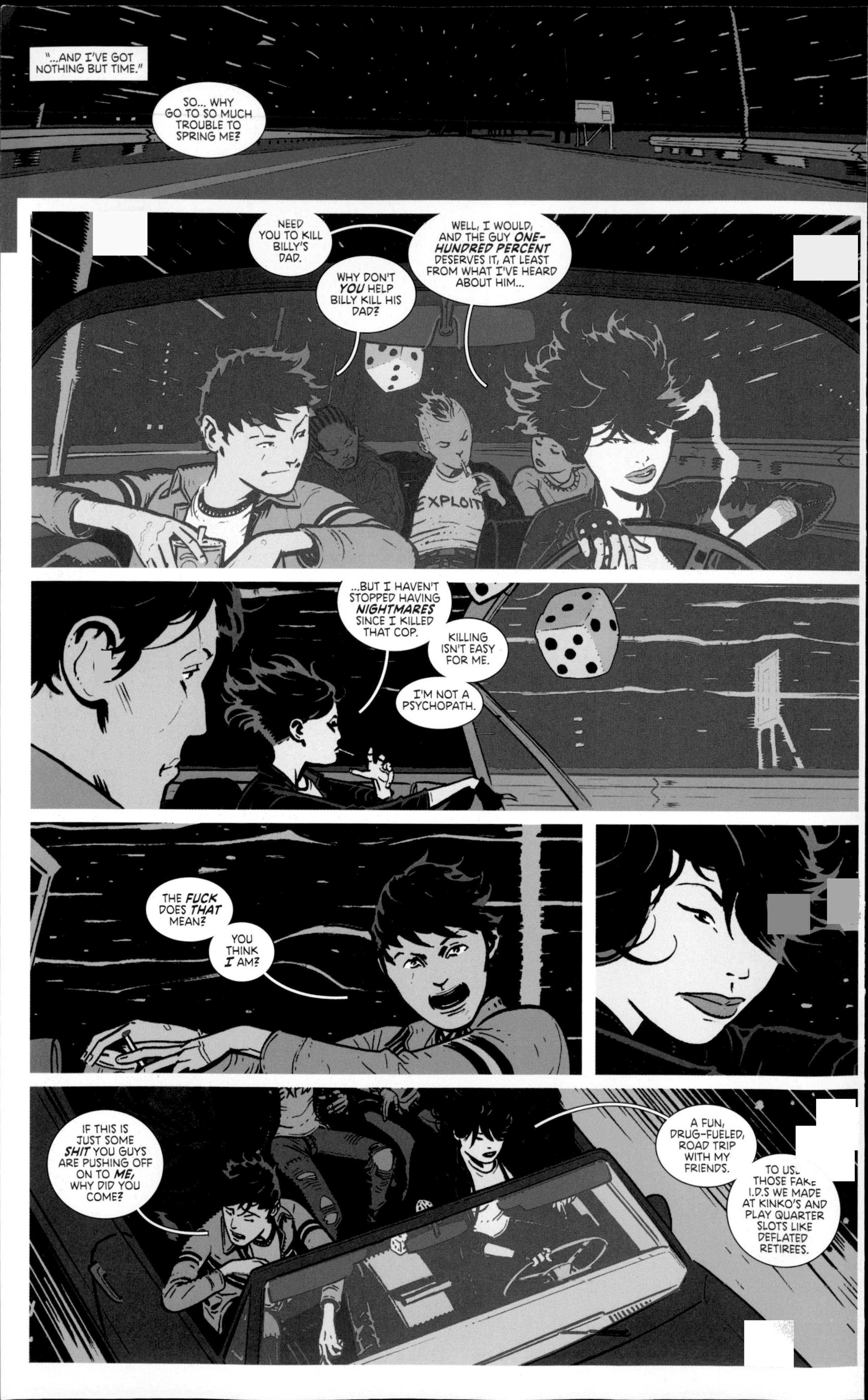
"...AND I'VE GOT NOTHING BUT TIME."
SO... WHY GO TO SO MUCH TROUBLE TO SPRING ME?
NEED YOU TO KILL BILLY'S DAD.
WHY DON'T YOU HELP BILLY KILL HIS DAD?
WELL, I WOULD, AND THE GUY ONE-HUNDRED PERCENT DESERVES IT, AT LEAST FROM WHAT I'VE HEARD ABOUT HIM...
EXPLOIT
...BUT I HAVEN'T STOPPED HAVING NIGHTMARES SINCE I KILLED THAT COP.
KILLING ISN'T EASY FOR ME.
I'M NOT A PSYCHOPATH.
THE FUCK DOES THAT MEAN?
YOU THINK I AM?
IF THIS IS JUST SOME SHIT YOU GUYS ARE PUSHING OFF ON TO ME, WHY DID YOU COME?
A FUN, DRUG-FUELED, ROAD TRIP WITH MY FRIENDS.
TO USE THOSE FAKE I.D.S WE MADE AT KINKO'S AND PLAY QUARTER SLOTS LIKE DEFLATED RETIREES.

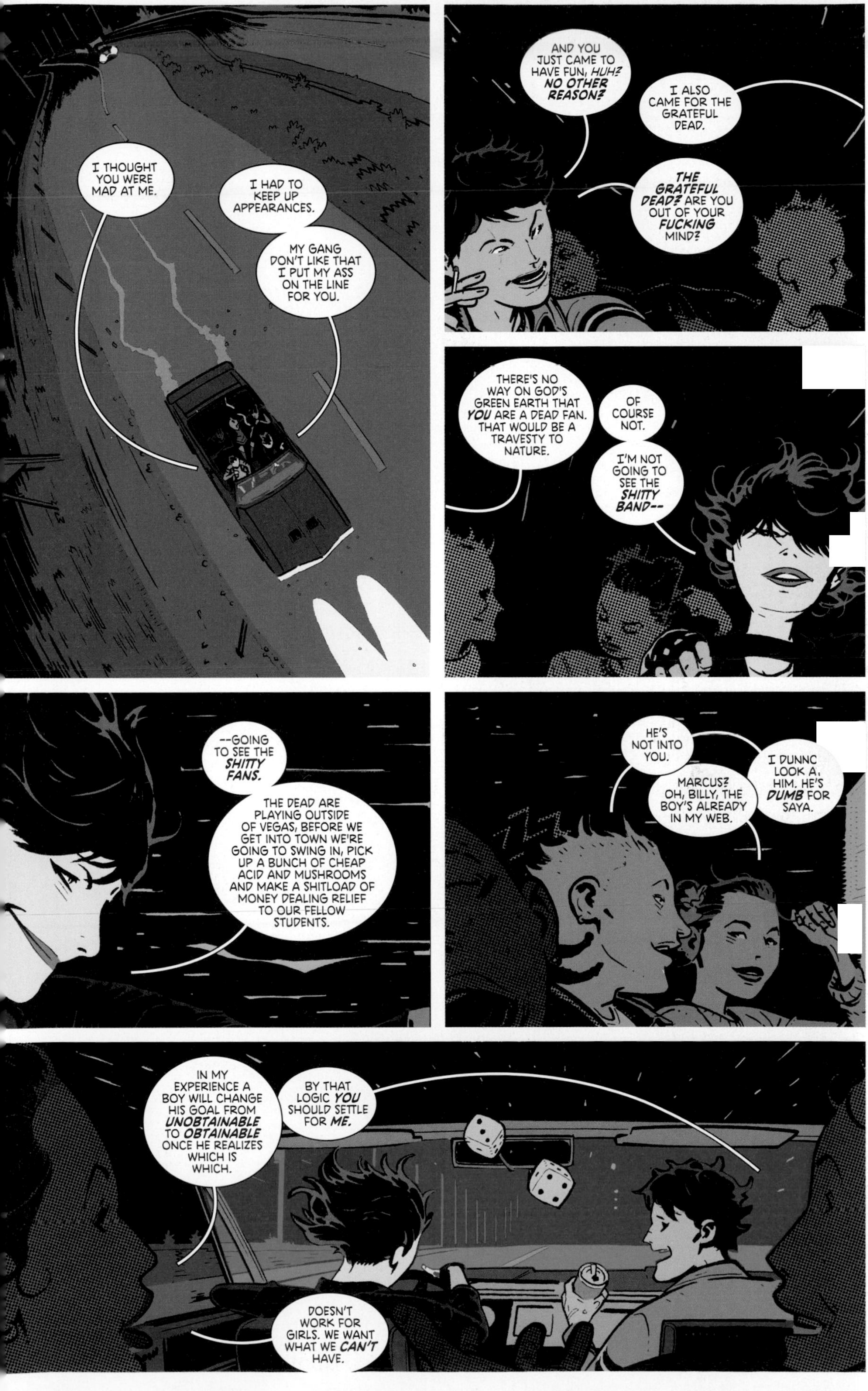
I THOUGHT YOU WERE MAD AT ME.
I HAD TO KEEP UP APPEARANCES.
MY GANG DON'T LIKE THAT I PUT MY ASS ON THE LINE FOR YOU.
AND YOU JUST CAME TO HAVE FUN, HUH? NO OTHER REASON?
I ALSO CAME FOR THE GRATEFUL DEAD.
THE GRATEFUL DEAD? ARE YOU OUT OF YOUR FUCKING MIND?
THERE'S NO WAY ON GOD'S GREEN EARTH THAT YOU ARE A DEAD FAN. THAT WOULD BE A TRAVESTY TO NATURE.
OF COURSE NOT.
I'M NOT GOING TO SEE THE SHITTY BAND--
--GOING TO SEE THE SHITTY FANS.
THE DEAD ARE PLAYING OUTSIDE OF VEGAS, BEFORE WE GET INTO TOWN WE'RE GOING TO SWING IN, PICK UP A BUNCH OF CHEAP ACID AND MUSHROOMS AND MAKE A SHITLOAD OF MONEY DEALING RELIEF TO OUR FELLOW STUDENTS.
HE'S NOT INTO YOU.
MARCUS? OH, BILLY, THE BOY'S ALREADY IN MY WEB.
I DUNNO LOOK A HIM. HE'S DUMB FOR SAYA.
IN MY EXPERIENCE A BOY WILL CHANGE HIS GOAL FROM UNOBTAINABLE TO OBTAINABLE ONCE HE REALIZES WHICH IS WHICH.
BY THAT LOGIC YOU SHOULD SETTLE FOR ME.
DOESN'T WORK FOR GIRLS. WE WANT WHAT WE CAN'T HAVE.

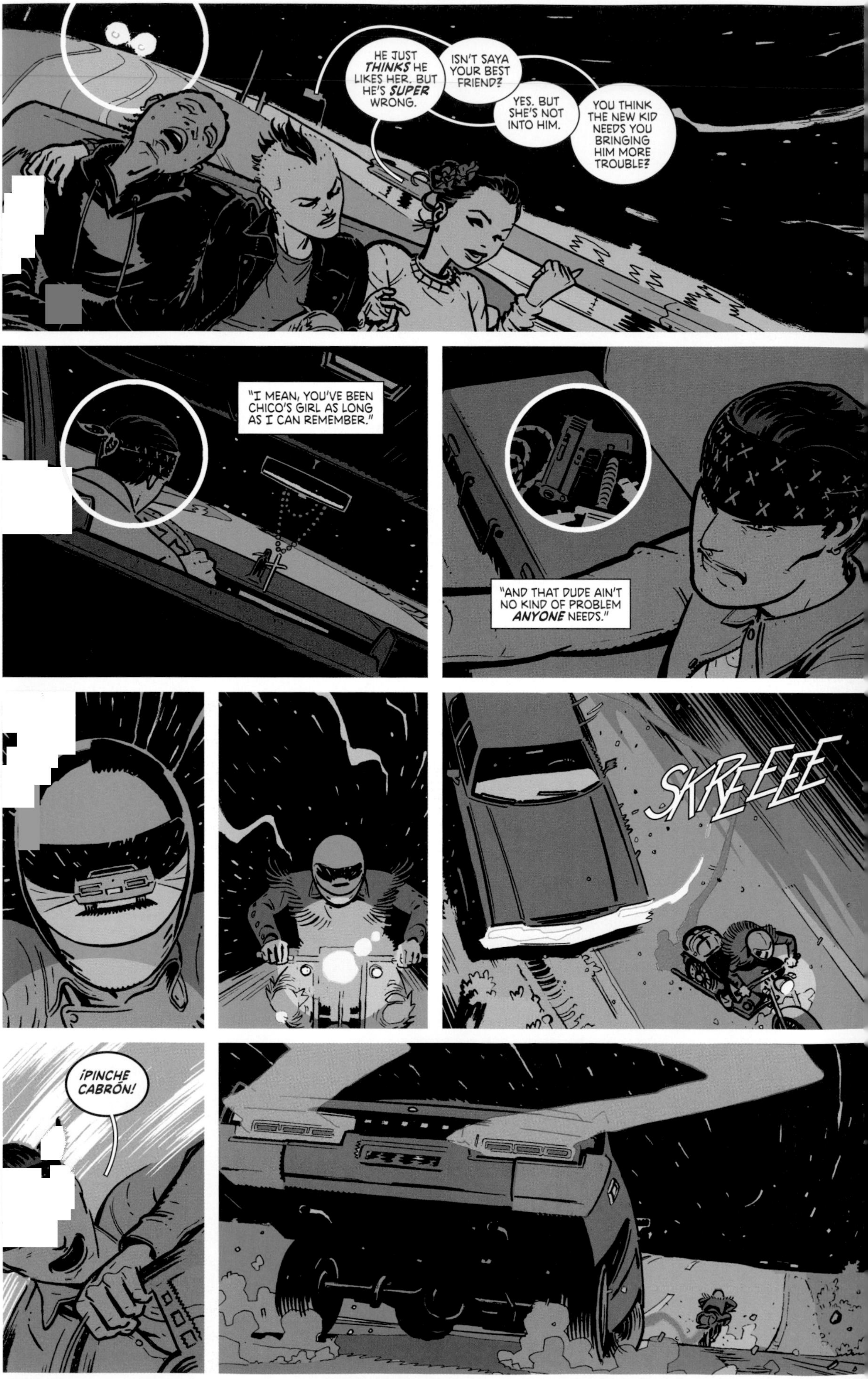
ISN'T SAYA YOUR BEST FRIEND?
HE JUST THINKS HE LIKES HER. BUT HE'S SUPER WRONG.
YES. BUT SHE'S NOT INTO HIM.
YOU THINK THE NEW KID NEEDS YOU BRINGING HIM MORE TROUBLE?
"I MEAN, YOU'VE BEEN CHICO'S GIRL AS LONG AS I CAN REMEMBER."
"AND THAT DUDE AIN'T NO KIND OF PROBLEM ANYONE NEEDS."
SKREEEE
¡PINCHE CABRÓN!

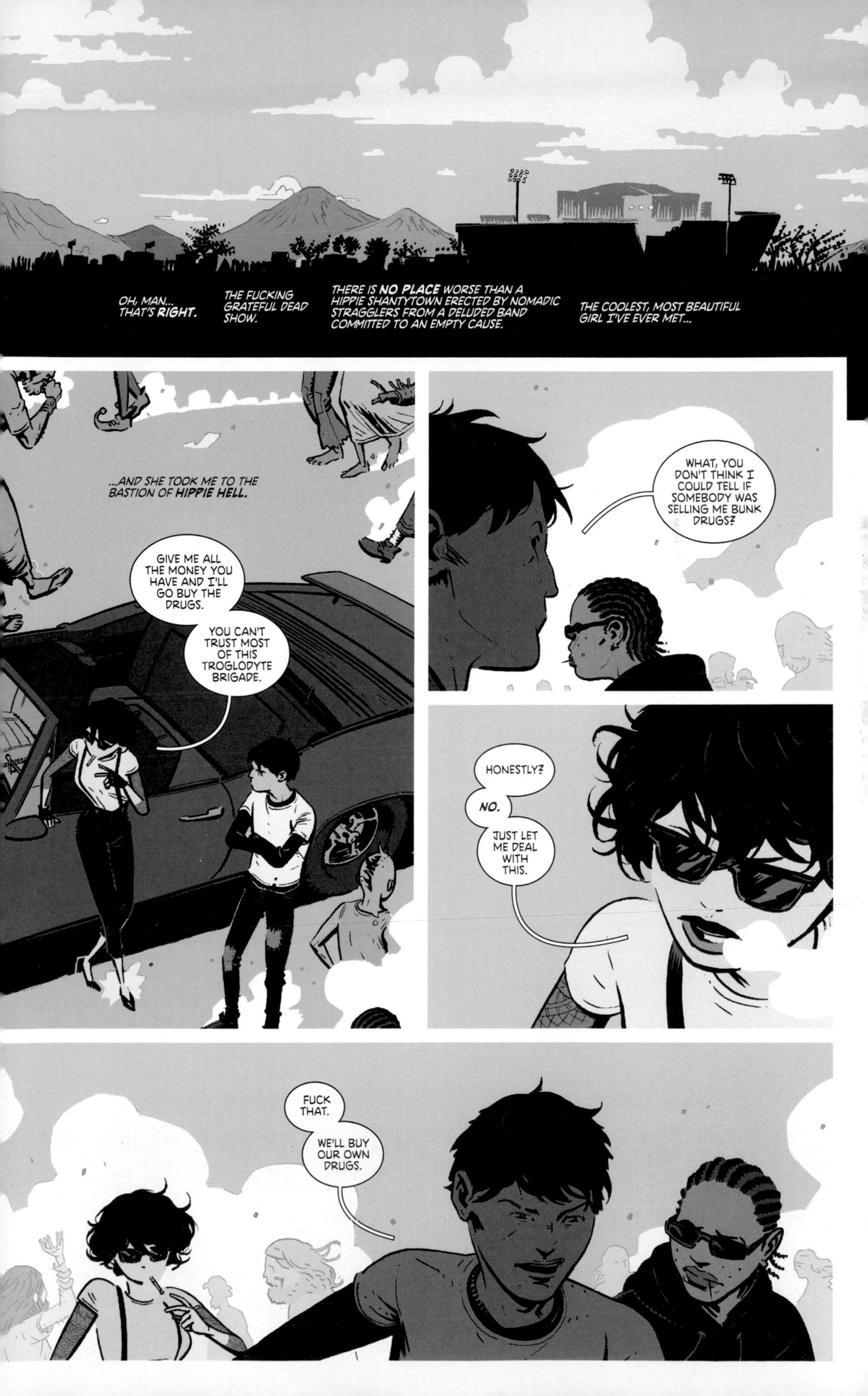
OH, MAN... THAT'S **RIGHT.**
THE FUCKING GRATEFUL DEAD SHOW.
THERE IS **NO PLACE** WORSE THAN A HIPPIE SHANTYTOWN ERECTED BY NOMADIC STRAGGLERS FROM A DELUDED BAND COMMITTED TO AN EMPTY CAUSE.
THE COOLEST, MOST BEAUTIFUL GIRL I'VE EVER MET...
...AND SHE TOOK ME TO THE BASTION OF **HIPPIE HELL.**
GIVE ME ALL THE MONEY YOU HAVE AND I'LL GO BUY THE DRUGS.
YOU CAN'T TRUST MOST OF THIS TROGLODYTE BRIGADE.
WHAT, YOU DON'T THINK I COULD TELL IF SOMEBODY WAS SELLING ME BUNK DRUGS?
HONESTLY?
NO.
JUST LET ME DEAL WITH THIS.
FUCK THAT.
WE'LL BUY OUR OWN DRUGS.

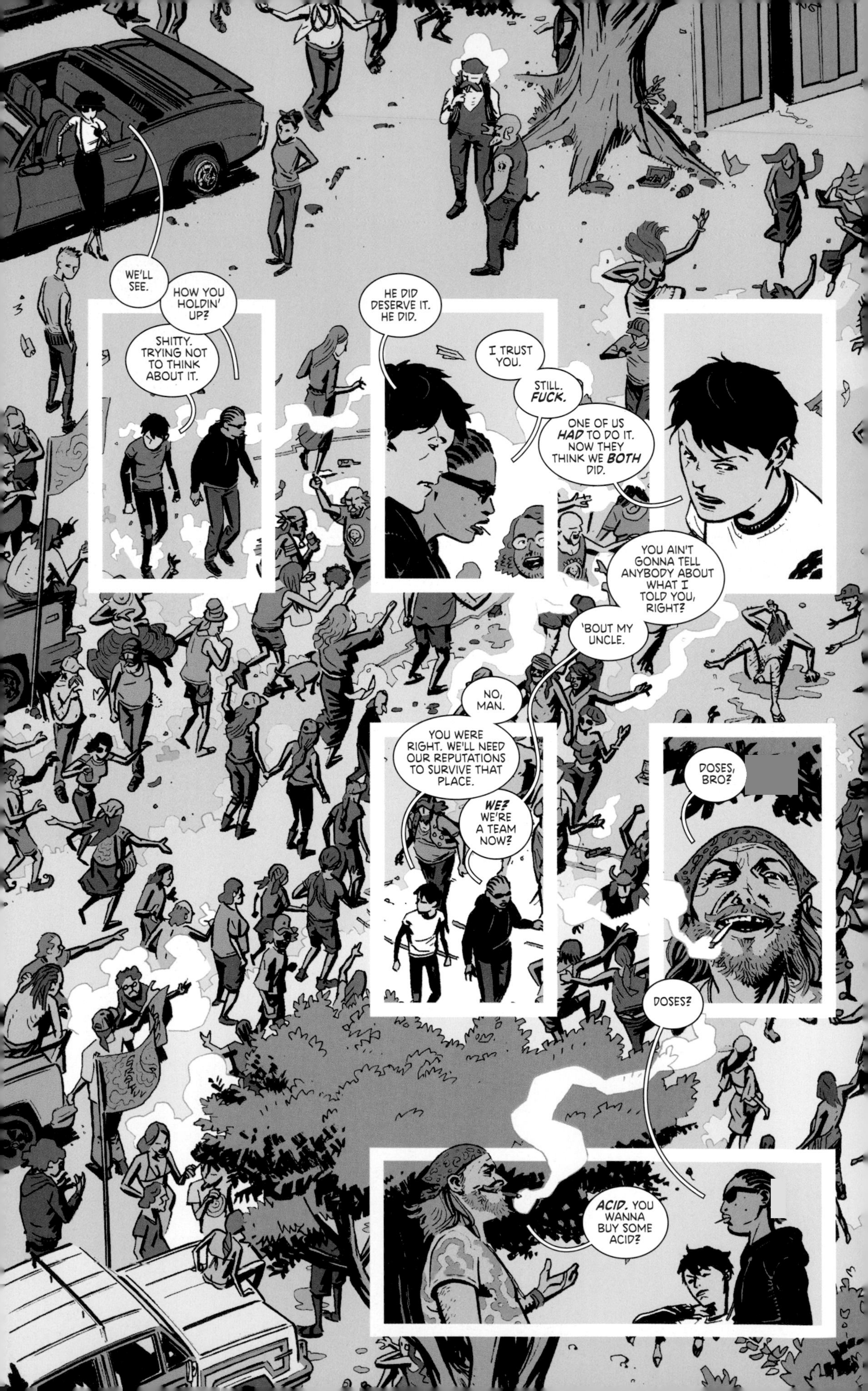
WE'LL SEE.
HOW YOU HOLDIN' UP?
SHITTY. TRYING NOT TO THINK ABOUT IT.
HE DID DESERVE IT. HE DID.
I TRUST YOU.
STILL. *FUCK.*
ONE OF US *HAD* TO DO IT. NOW THEY THINK WE *BOTH* DID.
YOU AIN'T GONNA TELL ANYBODY ABOUT WHAT I TOLD YOU, RIGHT?
'BOUT MY UNCLE.
NO, MAN.
YOU WERE RIGHT. WE'LL NEED OUR REPUTATIONS TO SURVIVE THAT PLACE.
WE? WE'RE A TEAM NOW?
DOSES, BRO?
DOSES?
ACID. YOU WANNA BUY SOME ACID?

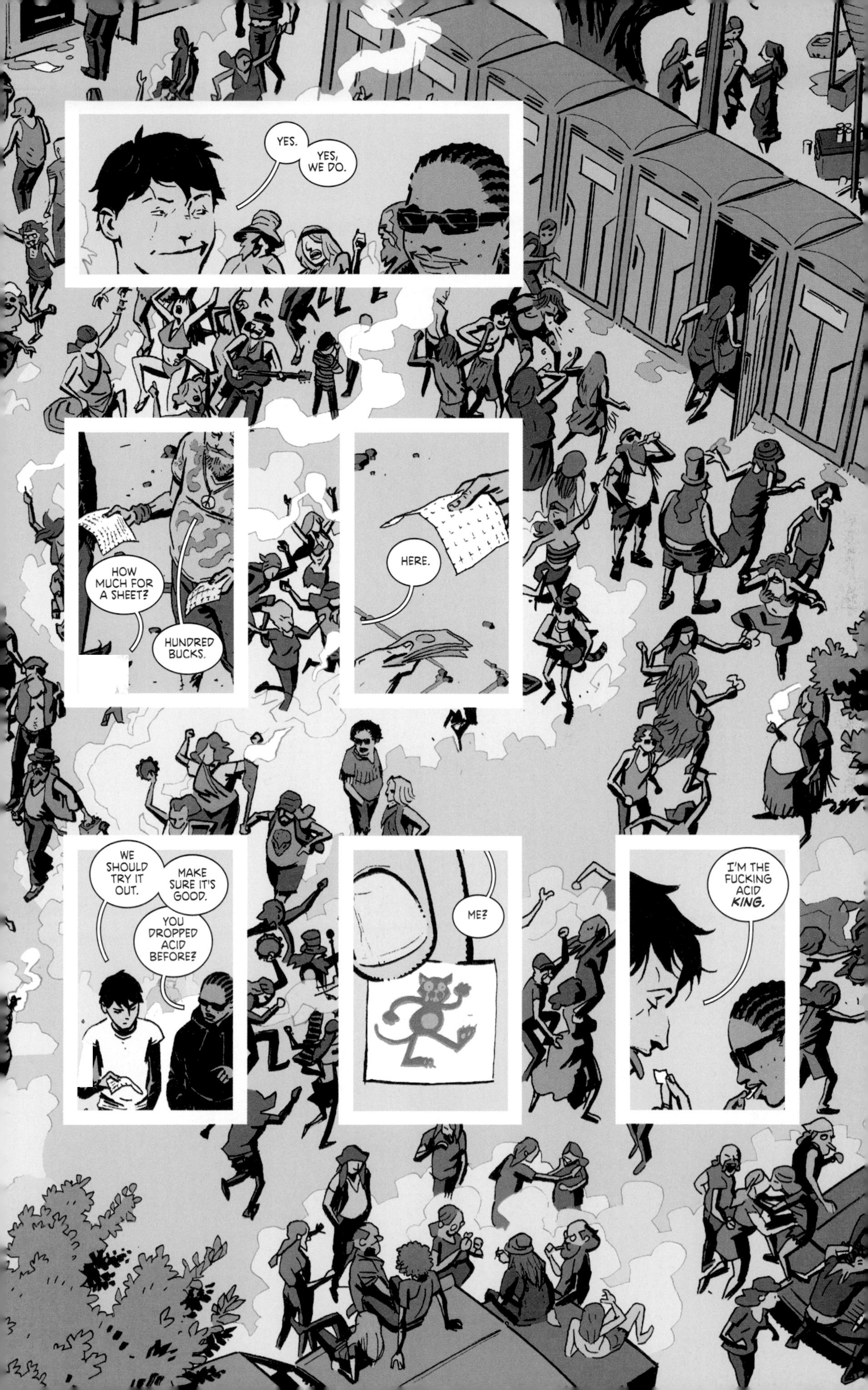
YES.
YES, WE DO.
HOW MUCH FOR A SHEET?
HUNDRED BUCKS.
HERE.
WE SHOULD TRY IT OUT.
MAKE SURE IT'S GOOD.
YOU DROPPED ACID BEFORE?
ME?
I'M THE FUCKING ACID KING.

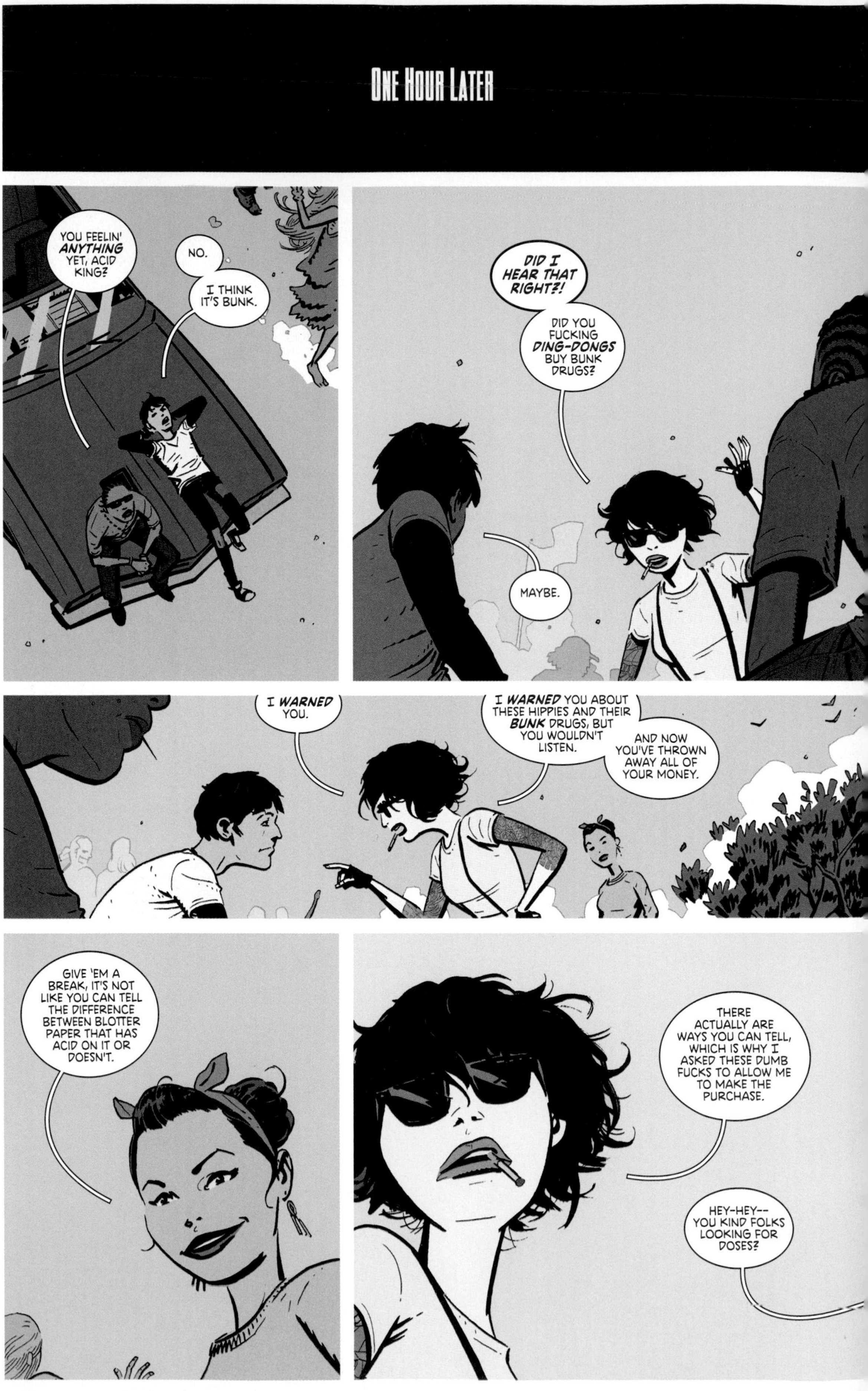
ONE HOUR LATER
YOU FEELIN' ANYTHING YET, ACID KING?
NO.
I THINK IT'S BUNK.
DID I HEAR THAT RIGHT?!
DID YOU FUCKING DING-DONGS BUY BUNK DRUGS?
MAYBE.
I WARNED YOU.
I WARNED YOU ABOUT THESE HIPPIES AND THEIR BUNK DRUGS, BUT YOU WOULDN'T LISTEN.
AND NOW YOU'VE THROWN AWAY ALL OF YOUR MONEY.
GIVE 'EM A BREAK, IT'S NOT LIKE YOU CAN TELL THE DIFFERENCE BETWEEN BLOTTER PAPER THAT HAS ACID ON IT OR DOESN'T.
THERE ACTUALLY ARE WAYS YOU CAN TELL, WHICH IS WHY I ASKED THESE DUMB FUCKS TO ALLOW ME TO MAKE THE PURCHASE.
HEY-HEY-- YOU KIND FOLKS LOOKING FOR DOSES?

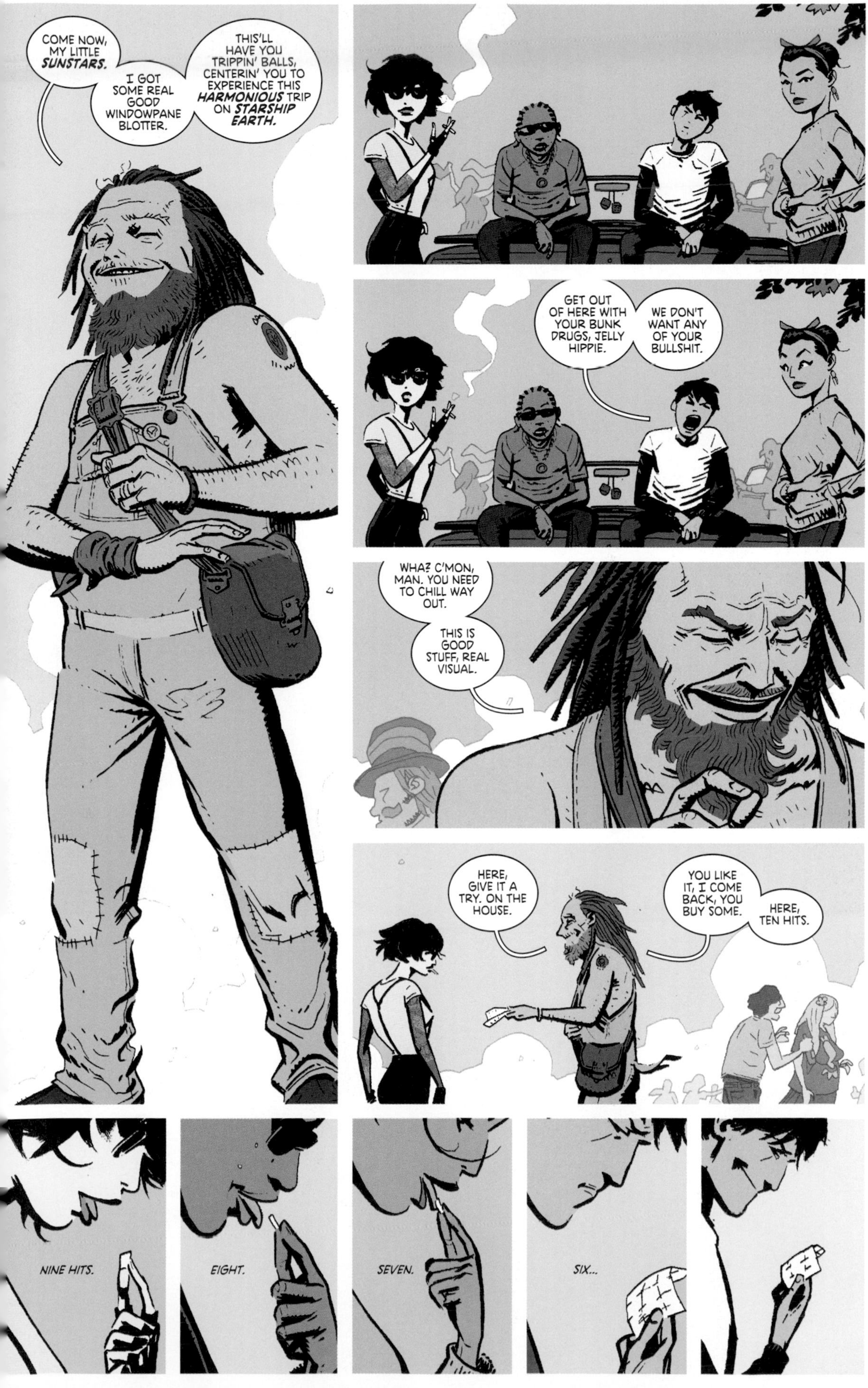
COME NOW, MY LITTLE SUNSTARS.
I GOT SOME REAL GOOD WINDOWPANE BLOTTER.
THIS'LL HAVE YOU TRIPPIN' BALLS, CENTERIN' YOU TO EXPERIENCE THIS HARMONIOUS TRIP ON STARSHIP EARTH.
GET OUT OF HERE WITH YOUR BUNK DRUGS, JELLY HIPPIE.
WE DON'T WANT ANY OF YOUR BULLSHIT.
WHA? C'MON, MAN. YOU NEED TO CHILL WAY OUT.
THIS IS GOOD STUFF, REAL VISUAL.
HERE, GIVE IT A TRY. ON THE HOUSE.
YOU LIKE IT, I COME BACK, YOU BUY SOME.
HERE, TEN HITS.
NINE HITS.
EIGHT.
SEVEN.
SIX...

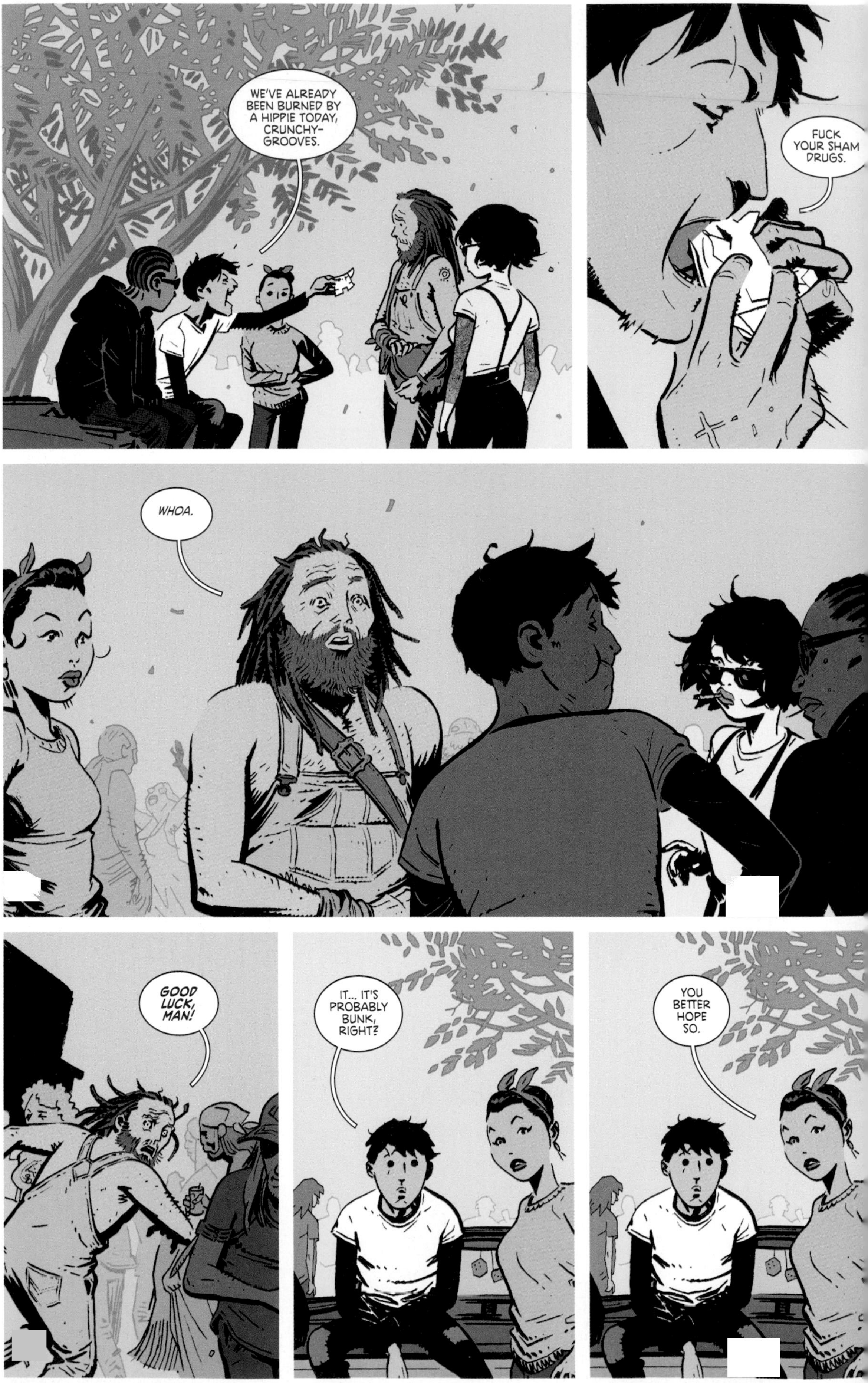
WE'VE ALREADY BEEN BURNED BY A HIPPIE TODAY, CRUNCHY-GROOVES.
FUCK YOUR SHAM DRUGS.
WHOA.
GOOD LUCK, MAN!
IT... IT'S PROBABLY BUNK, RIGHT?
YOU BETTER HOPE SO.

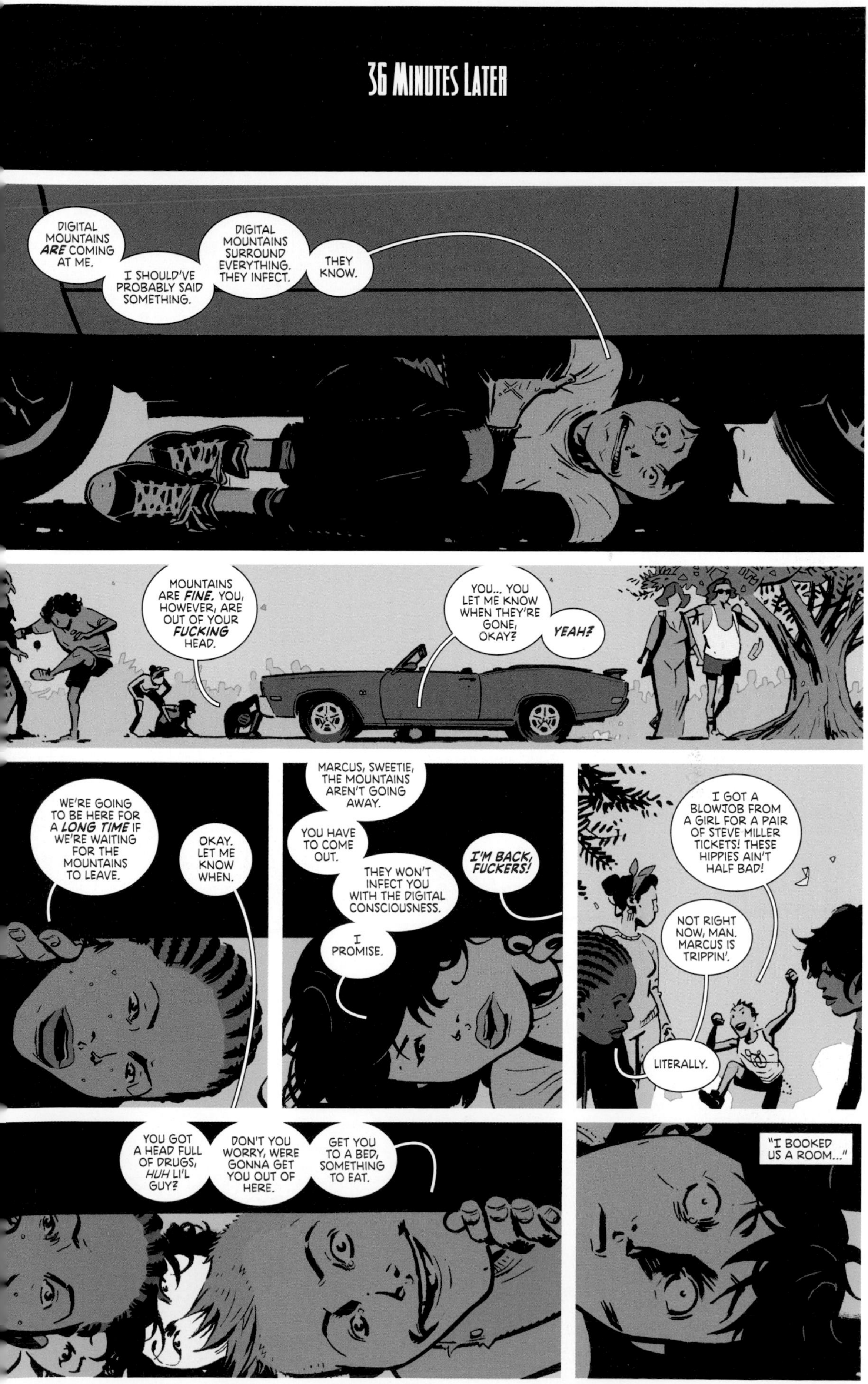
36 MINUTES LATER
DIGITAL MOUNTAINS ARE COMING AT ME.
I SHOULD'VE PROBABLY SAID SOMETHING.
DIGITAL MOUNTAINS SURROUND EVERYTHING. THEY INFECT.
THEY KNOW.
MOUNTAINS ARE FINE. YOU, HOWEVER, ARE OUT OF YOUR FUCKING HEAD.
YOU... YOU LET ME KNOW WHEN THEY'RE GONE, OKAY?
YEAH?
WE'RE GOING TO BE HERE FOR A LONG TIME IF WE'RE WAITING FOR THE MOUNTAINS TO LEAVE.
OKAY. LET ME KNOW WHEN.
MARCUS, SWEETIE, THE MOUNTAINS AREN'T GOING AWAY.
YOU HAVE TO COME OUT.
THEY WON'T INFECT YOU WITH THE DIGITAL CONSCIOUSNESS.
I PROMISE.
I'M BACK, FUCKERS!
I GOT A BLOWJOB FROM A GIRL FOR A PAIR OF STEVE MILLER TICKETS! THESE HIPPIES AIN'T HALF BAD!
NOT RIGHT NOW, MAN. MARCUS IS TRIPPIN'.
LITERALLY.
YOU GOT A HEAD FULL OF DRUGS, HUH LI'L GUY?
DON'T YOU WORRY, WERE GONNA GET YOU OUT OF HERE.
GET YOU TO A BED, SOMETHING TO EAT.
"I BOOKED US A ROOM..."

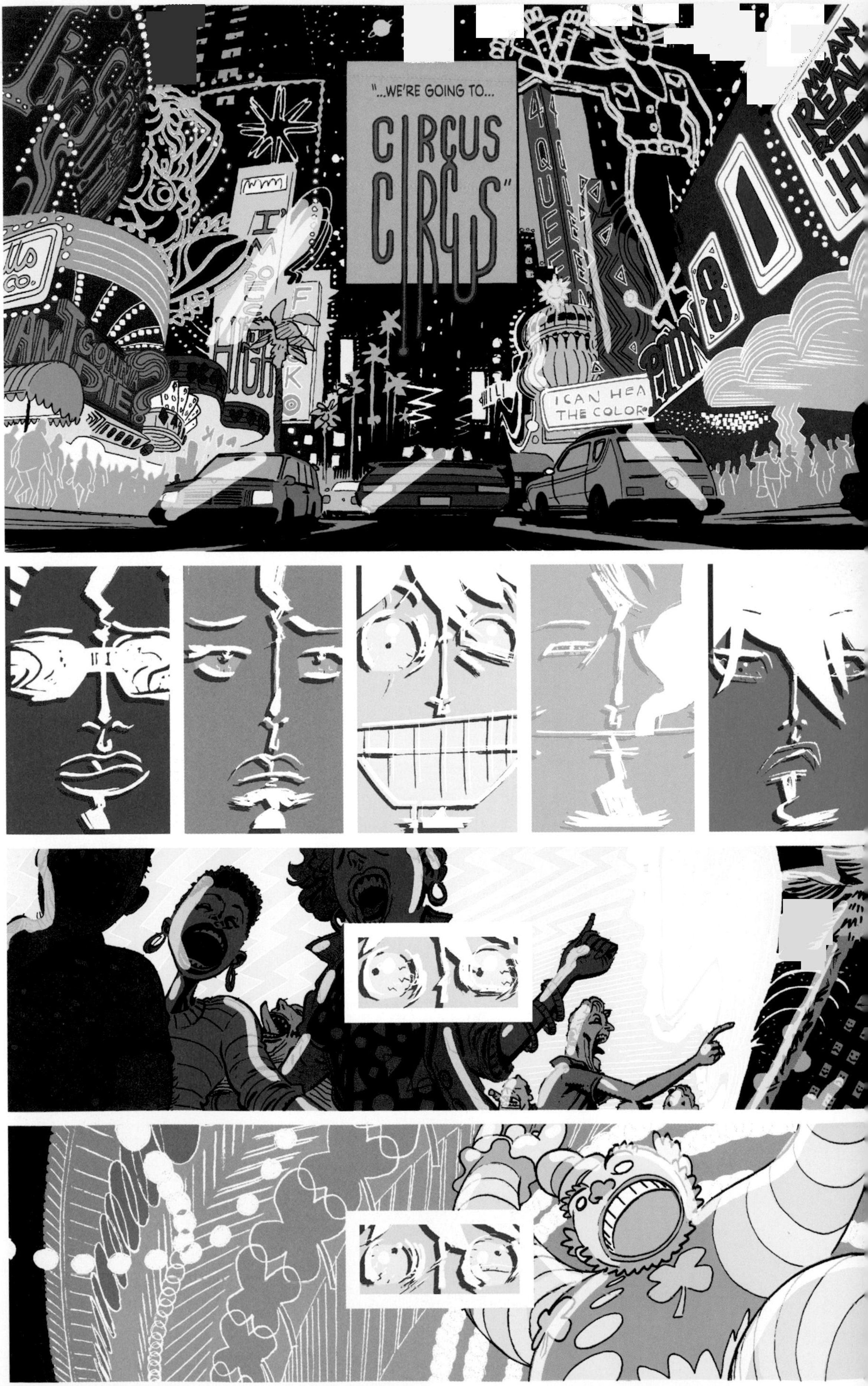
"...WE'RE GOING TO...
CIRCUS CIRCUS"
I CAN HEA THE COLOR

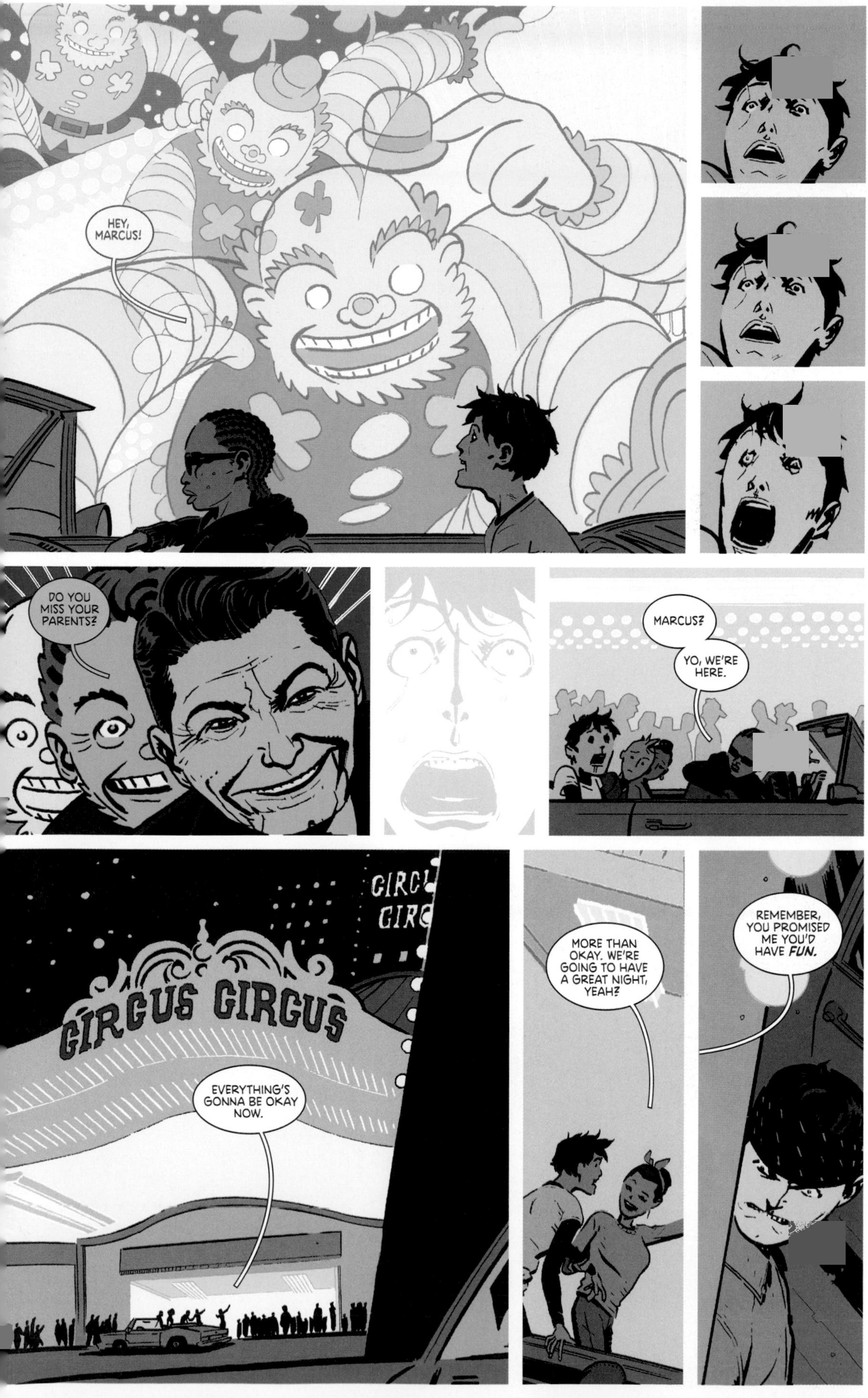
HEY, MARCUS!
DO YOU MISS YOUR PARENTS?
MARCUS?
YO, WE'RE HERE.
CIRCUS CIRCUS
CIRC
CIRC
EVERYTHING'S GONNA BE OKAY NOW.
MORE THAN OKAY. WE'RE GOING TO HAVE A GREAT NIGHT, YEAH?
REMEMBER, YOU PROMISED ME YOU'D HAVE *FUN.*

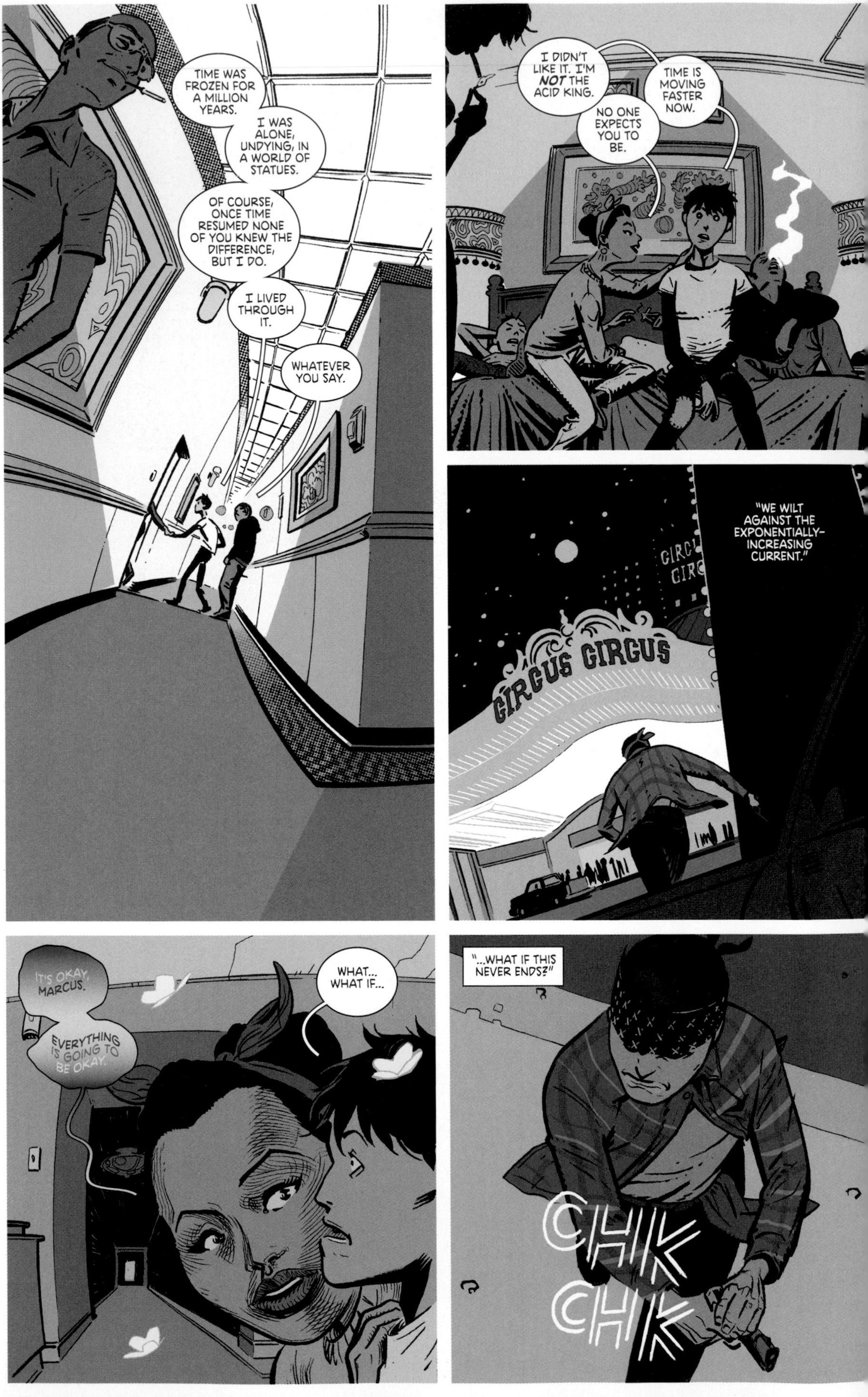
TIME WAS FROZEN FOR A MILLION YEARS.
I WAS ALONE, UNDYING, IN A WORLD OF STATUES.
OF COURSE, ONCE TIME RESUMED NONE OF YOU KNEW THE DIFFERENCE, BUT I DO.
I LIVED THROUGH IT.
WHATEVER YOU SAY.
I DIDN'T LIKE IT. I'M NOT THE ACID KING.
NO ONE EXPECTS YOU TO BE.
TIME IS MOVING FASTER NOW.
"WE WILT AGAINST THE EXPONENTIALLY-INCREASING CURRENT."
CIRCUS CIRCUS
IT'S OKAY, MARCUS.
EVERYTHING IS GOING TO BE OKAY.
WHAT... WHAT IF...
"...WHAT IF THIS NEVER ENDS?"
CHK CHK

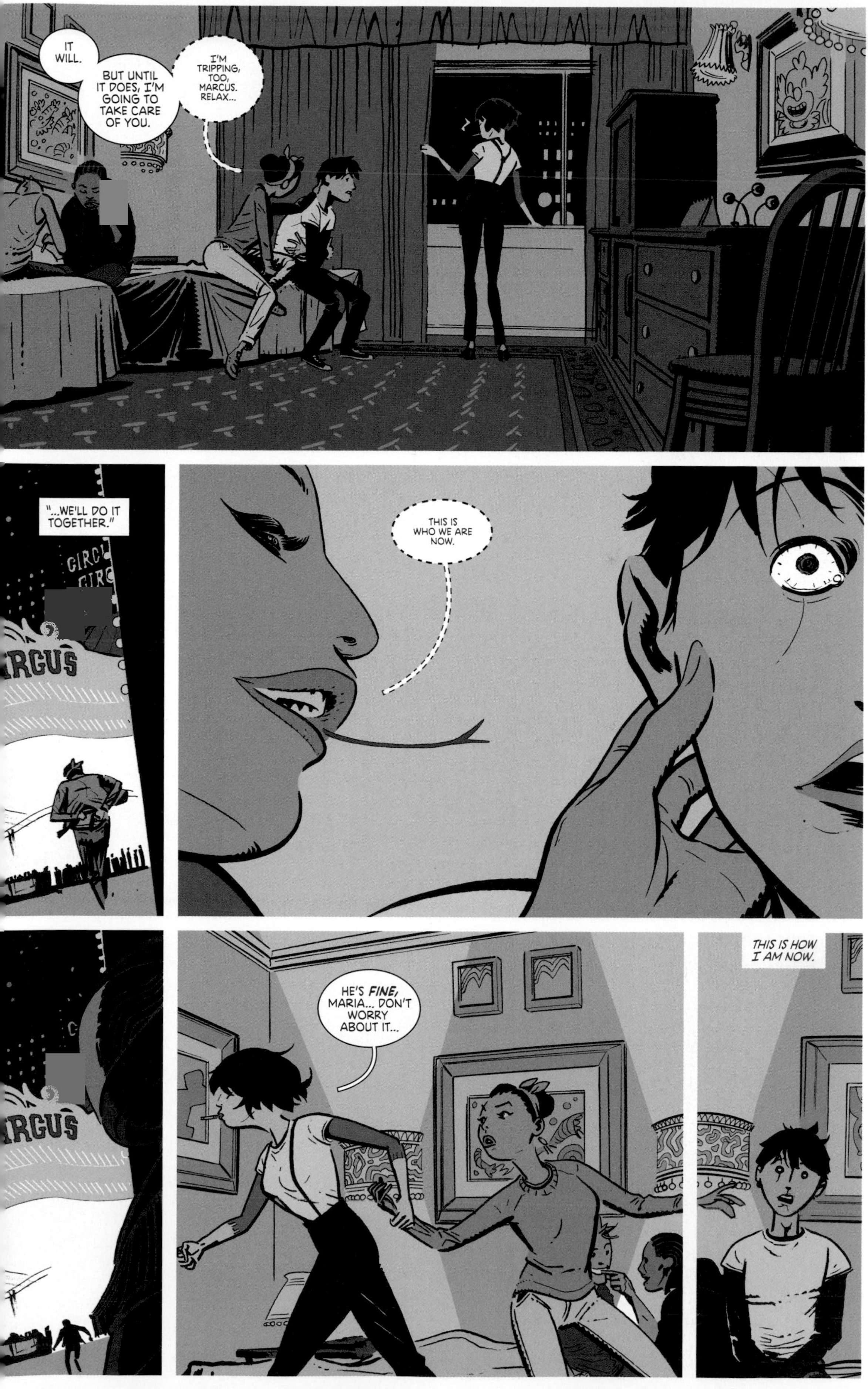
IT WILL.
BUT UNTIL IT DOES, I'M GOING TO TAKE CARE OF YOU.
I'M TRIPPING, TOO, MARCUS. RELAX...
"...WE'LL DO IT TOGETHER."
THIS IS WHO WE ARE NOW.
HE'S *FINE,* MARIA... DON'T WORRY ABOUT IT...
THIS IS HOW I AM NOW.

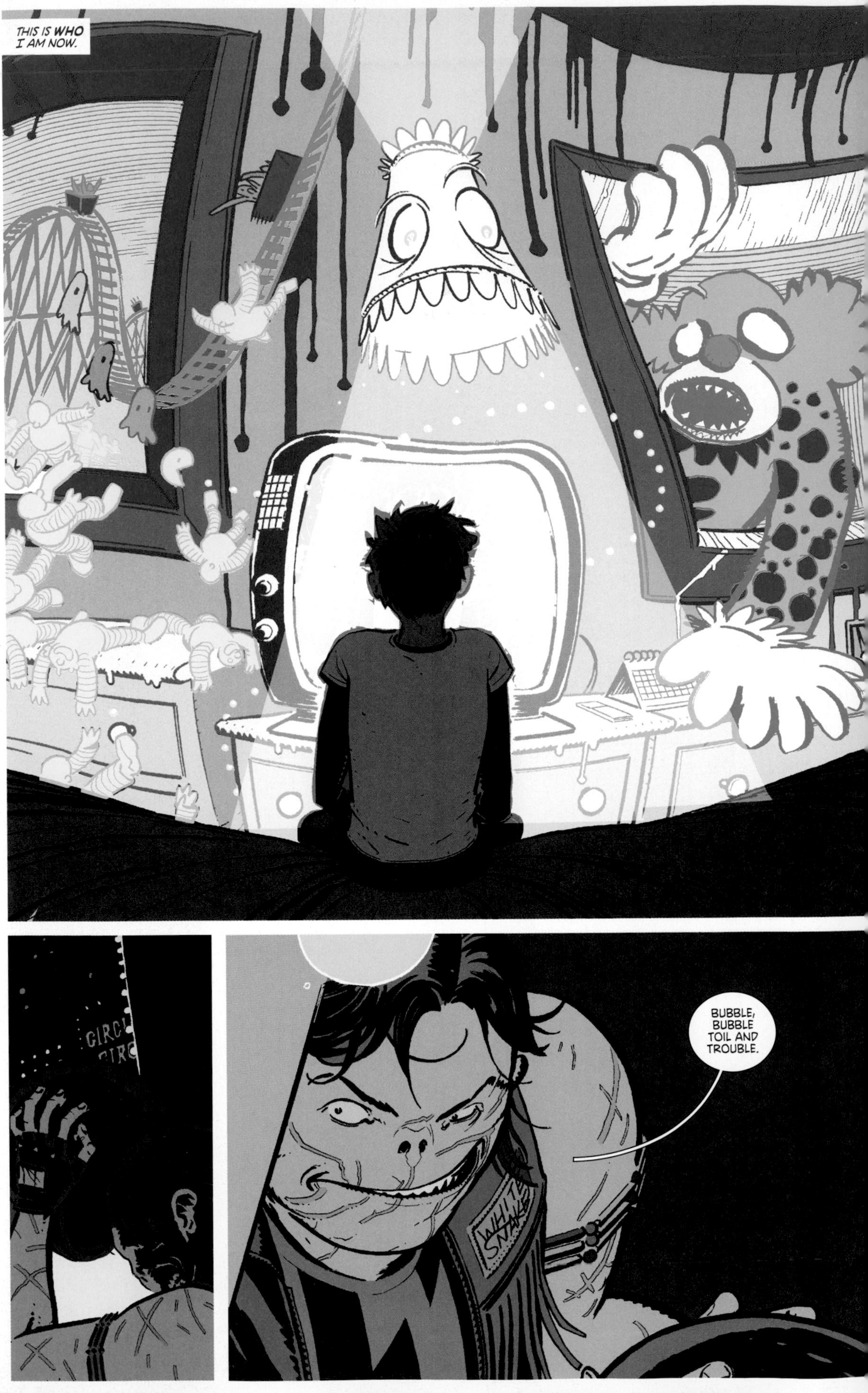
THIS IS WHO I AM NOW.
CIRC
CIRC
WHITE SNAKE
BUBBLE, BUBBLE TOIL AND TROUBLE.

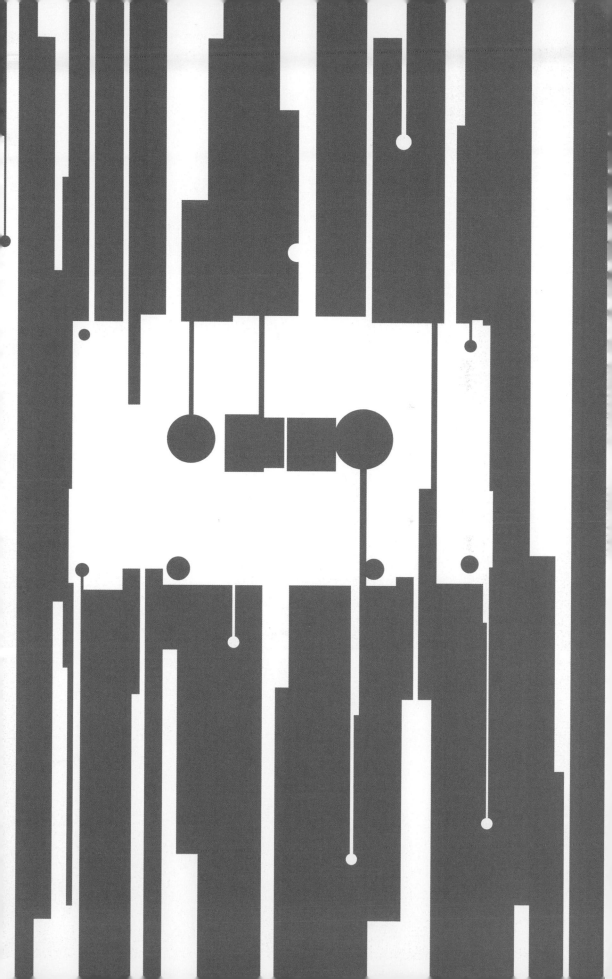

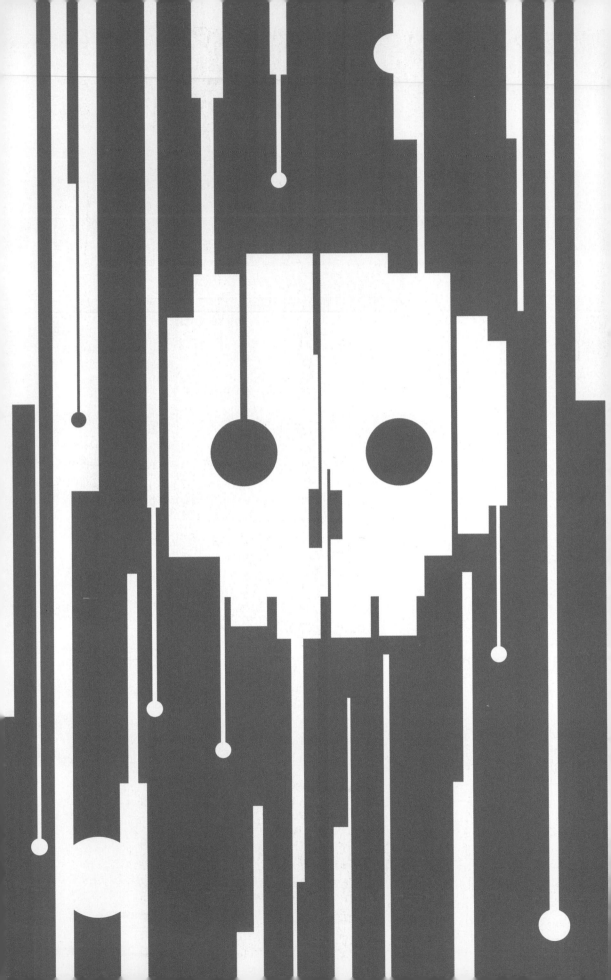

JUST SAY NO
I'VE SEEN SOME SHIT FAKE I.D.S IN MY DAY BUT THIS TAKES THE CAKE, SON.
HOW DID WE GET HERE?
WHERE THE **HELL** ARE WE?
SNORT
WHERE DID EVERYONE GO?
THEY WENT TO THE *ampm* TO GET SMOKES AND SNACKS AND STUFF.
I TOLD YOU THAT LIKE ***SIX*** TIMES, DUDE.
SCHMIT STIX

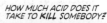

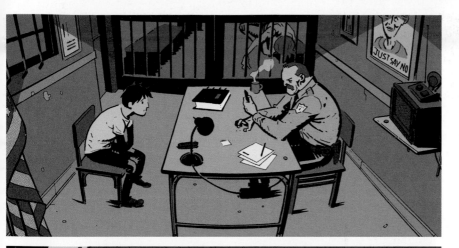

*HOW MUCH ACID DOES IT TAKE TO **KILL** SOMEBODY?*

*I GUESS IT DEPENDS ON HOW STRONG IT WAS. THAT HIPPIE RAN OFF **PRETTY** FAST...*

*GOOD INDICATION I TOOK **TOO MUCH.***

WHY DID I DO IT?

ANSWER MAKES ME NAUSEOUS.

BLOOD-SOAKED, OVERDOSED, NEARING MENTAL AND PHYSICAL COLLAPSE--

*ALL TO **IMPRESS** THEM.*

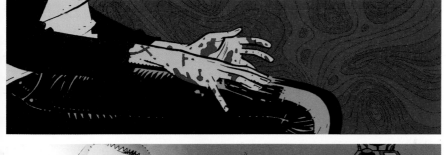

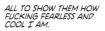

ALL TO SHOW THEM HOW FUCKING FEARLESS AND COOL I AM.

*TO HIDE THE **TRUTH:***

I'M TERRIFIED OF BEING ALONE.

***TERRIFIED** OF ANOTHER YEAR WITHOUT A FRIEND...*

WITHOUT A HOME.

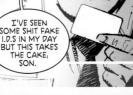

NOW I REMEMBER WHAT I WAS JUST THINKING ABOUT...

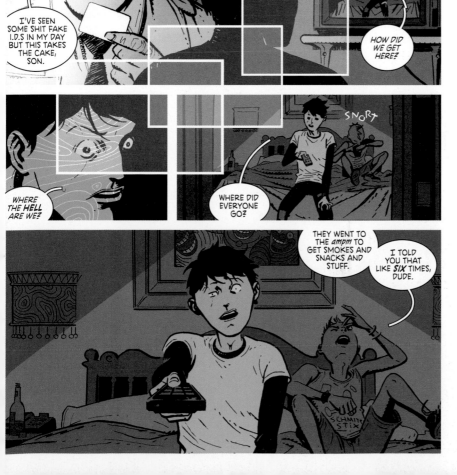

*THEY LEFT ME WATCHING TV FOR **HOURS.***

LEFT ME WITH THAT PUNK ROCK LUNATIC...

*AND THAT'S WHEN THINGS GOT **BAD.***

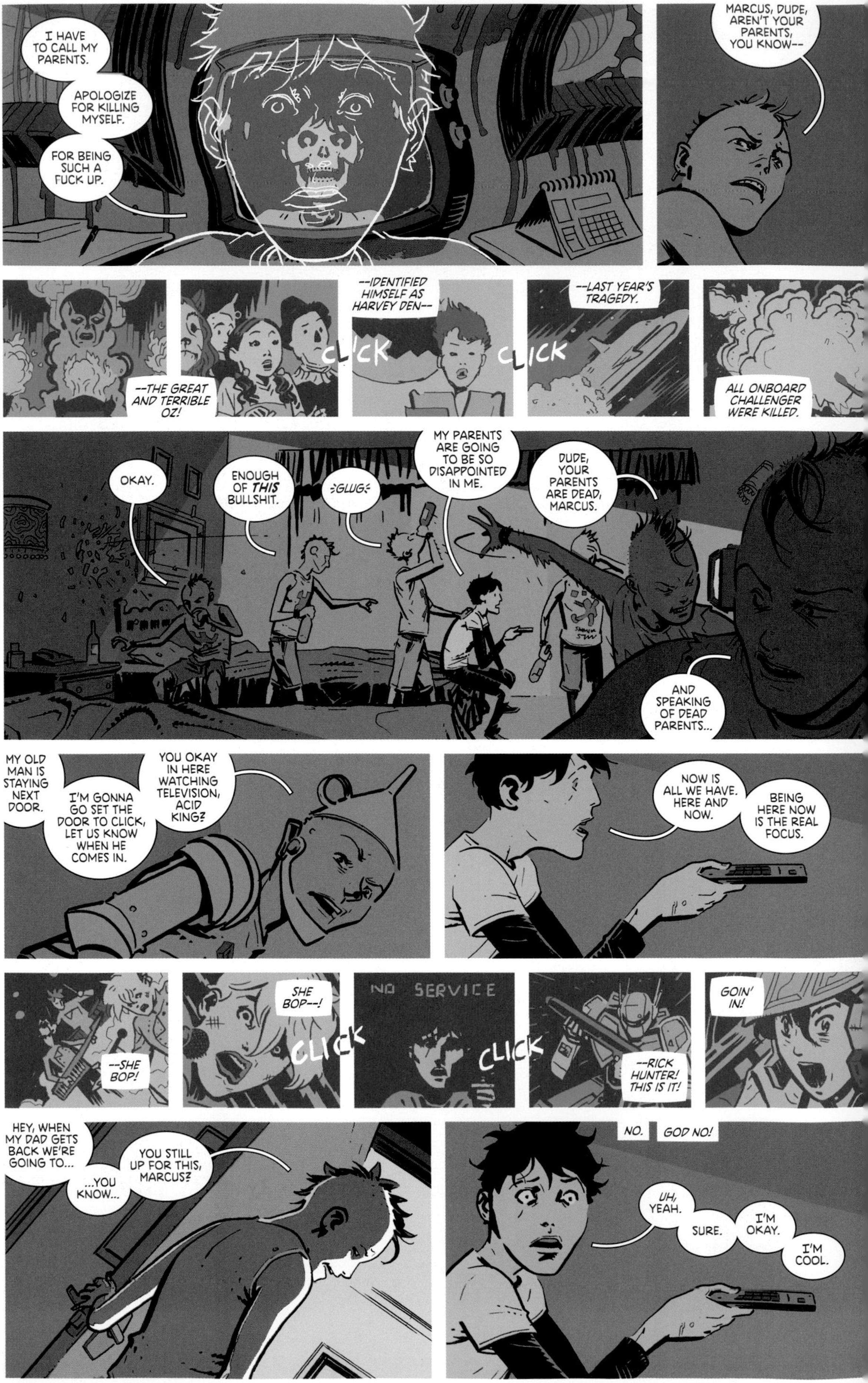
I HAVE TO CALL MY PARENTS.
APOLOGIZE FOR KILLING MYSELF.
FOR BEING SUCH A FUCK UP.
MARCUS, DUDE, AREN'T YOUR PARENTS, YOU KNOW--
--THE GREAT AND TERRIBLE OZ!
--IDENTIFIED HIMSELF AS HARVEY DEN--
CLICK
--LAST YEAR'S TRAGEDY.
CLICK
ALL ONBOARD CHALLENGER WERE KILLED.
OKAY.
ENOUGH OF THIS BULLSHIT.
GLUG
MY PARENTS ARE GOING TO BE SO DISAPPOINTED IN ME.
DUDE, YOUR PARENTS ARE DEAD, MARCUS.
AND SPEAKING OF DEAD PARENTS...
MY OLD MAN IS STAYING NEXT DOOR.
I'M GONNA GO SET THE DOOR TO CLICK, LET US KNOW WHEN HE COMES IN.
YOU OKAY IN HERE WATCHING TELEVISION, ACID KING?
NOW IS ALL WE HAVE. HERE AND NOW.
BEING HERE NOW IS THE REAL FOCUS.
--SHE BOP!
SHE BOP--!
CLICK
NO SERVICE
CLICK
--RICK HUNTER! THIS IS IT!
GOIN' IN!
HEY, WHEN MY DAD GETS BACK WE'RE GOING TO...
...YOU KNOW...
YOU STILL UP FOR THIS, MARCUS?
NO.
GOD NO!
UH, YEAH.
SURE.
I'M OKAY.
I'M COOL.

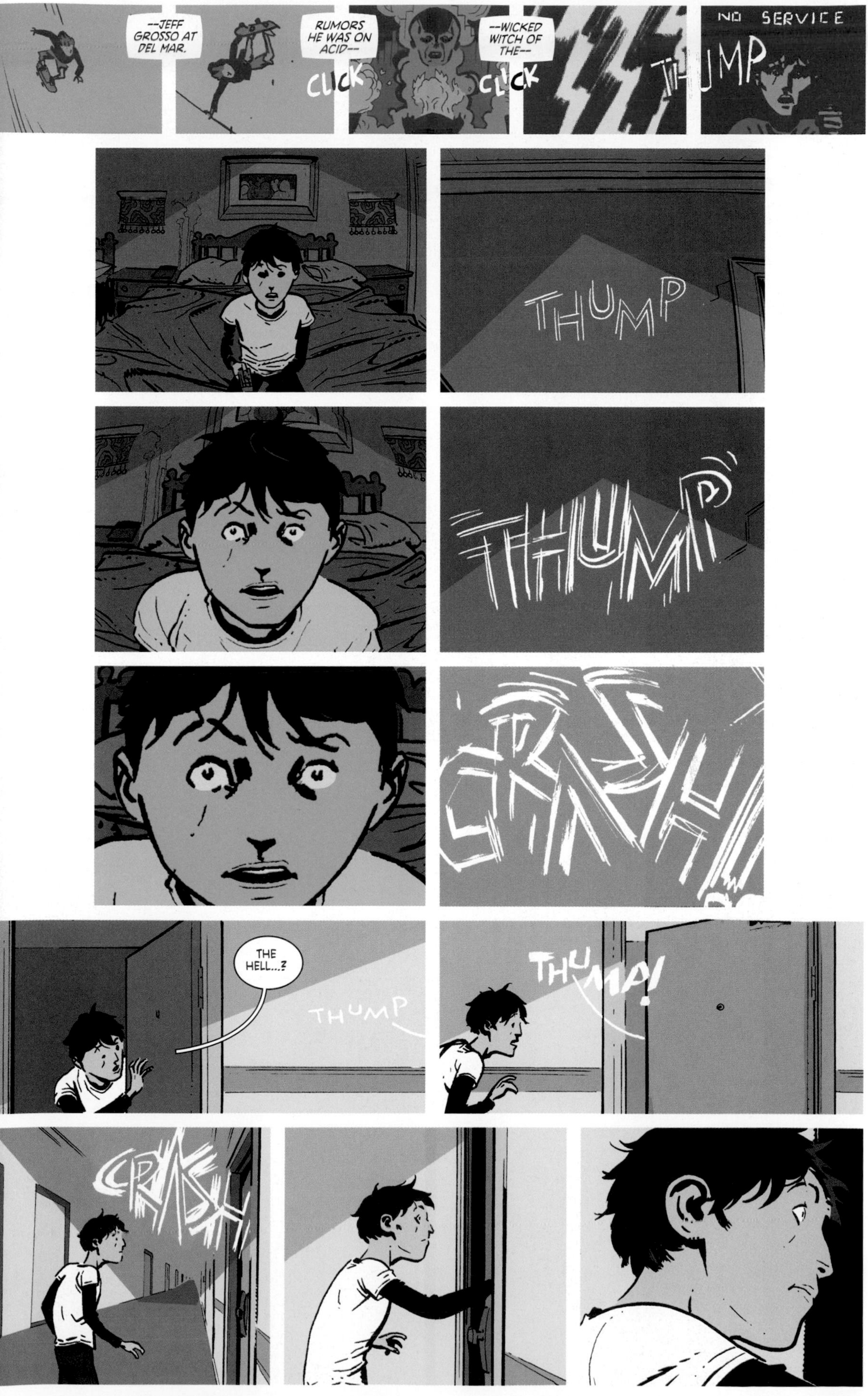
--JEFF GROSSO AT DEL MAR.
RUMORS HE WAS ON ACID--
CLICK
--WICKED WITCH OF THE--
CLICK
NO SERVICE
THUMP
THUMP
THUMP
CRASH
THE HELL...?
THUMP
THUMP!
CRASH

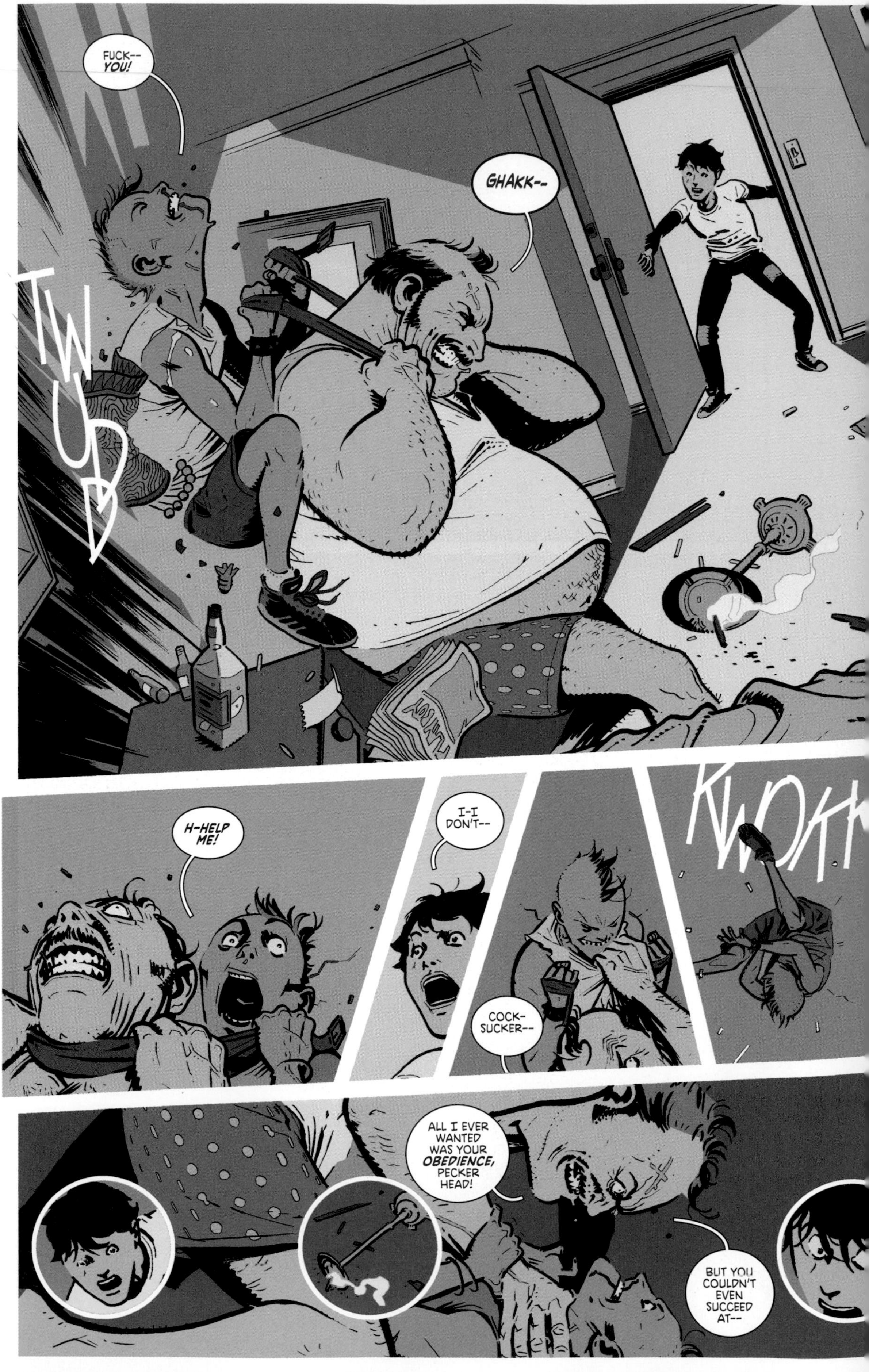
FUCK-- *YOU!*
TWUDD
GHAKK--
H-HELP ME!
I-I DON'T--
COCK-SUCKER--
KWOKK
ALL I EVER WANTED WAS YOUR *OBEDIENCE,* PECKER HEAD!
BUT YOU COULDN'T EVEN SUCCEED AT--

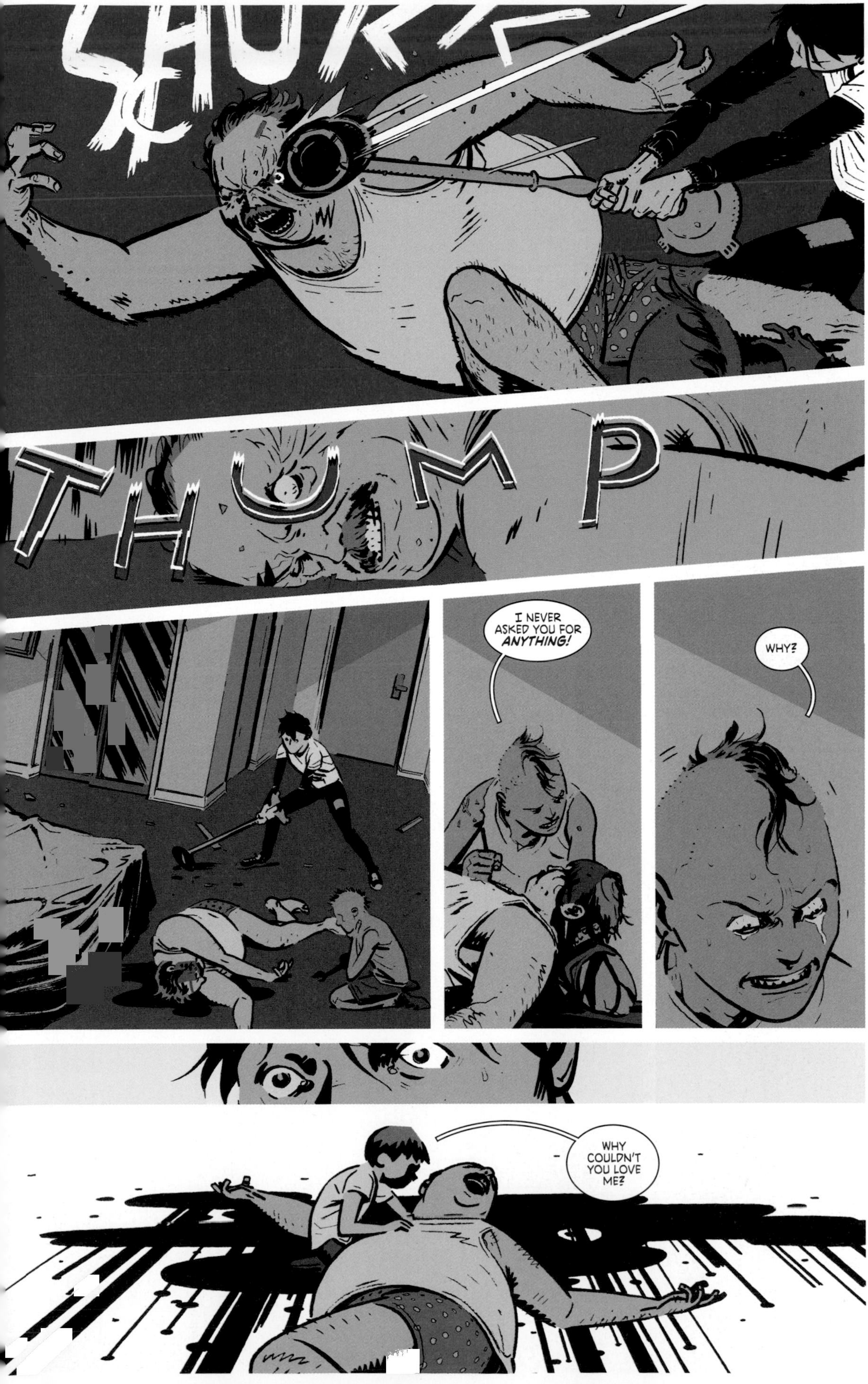
SHUK
THUMP
I NEVER ASKED YOU FOR ANYTHING!
WHY?
WHY COULDN'T YOU LOVE ME?

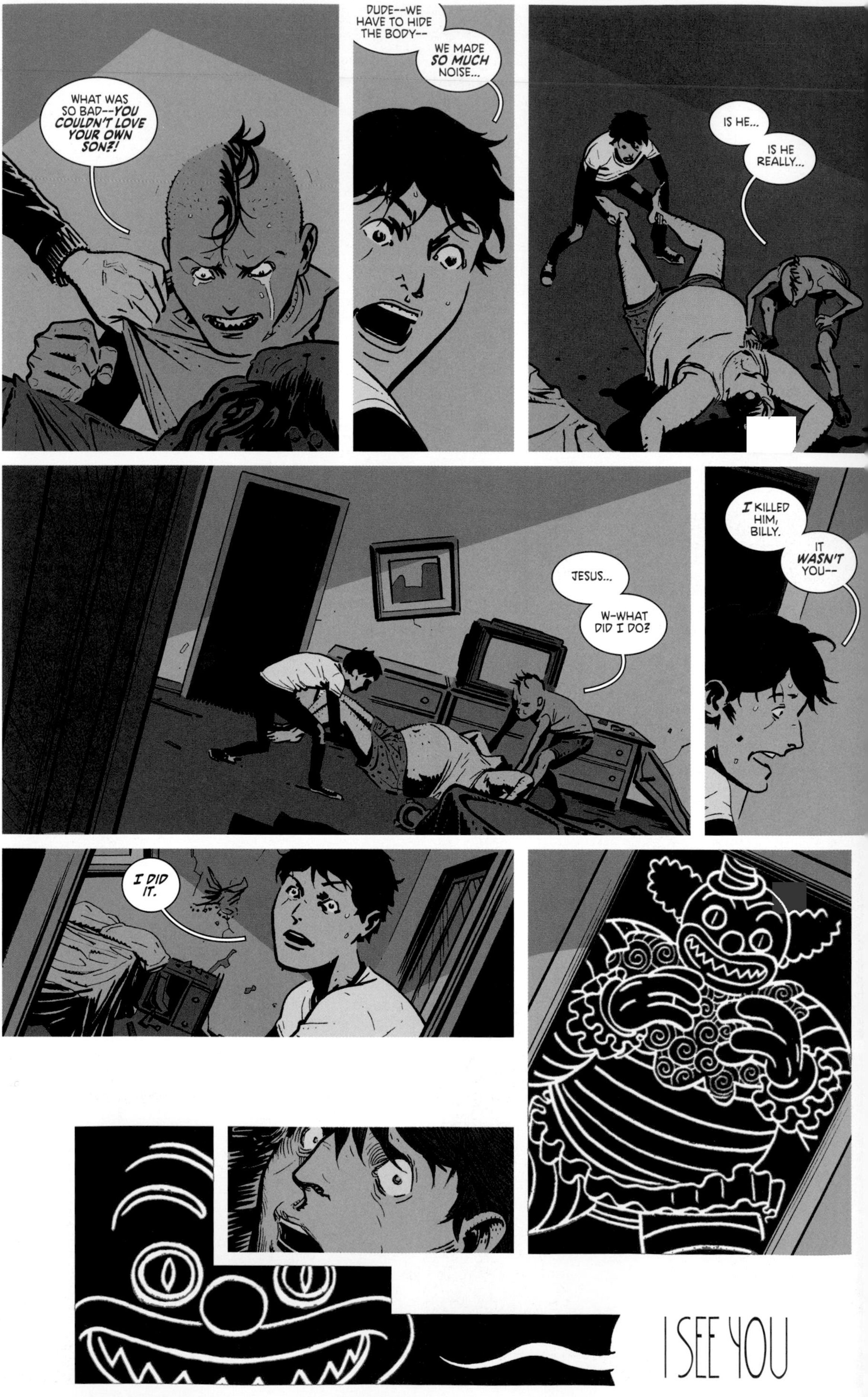

WHAT WAS SO BAD--YOU COULDN'T LOVE YOUR OWN SON?!
DUDE--WE HAVE TO HIDE THE BODY--
WE MADE SO MUCH NOISE...
IS HE...
IS HE REALLY...
JESUS...
W-WHAT DID I DO?
I KILLED HIM, BILLY.
IT WASN'T YOU--
I DID IT.
I SEE YOU

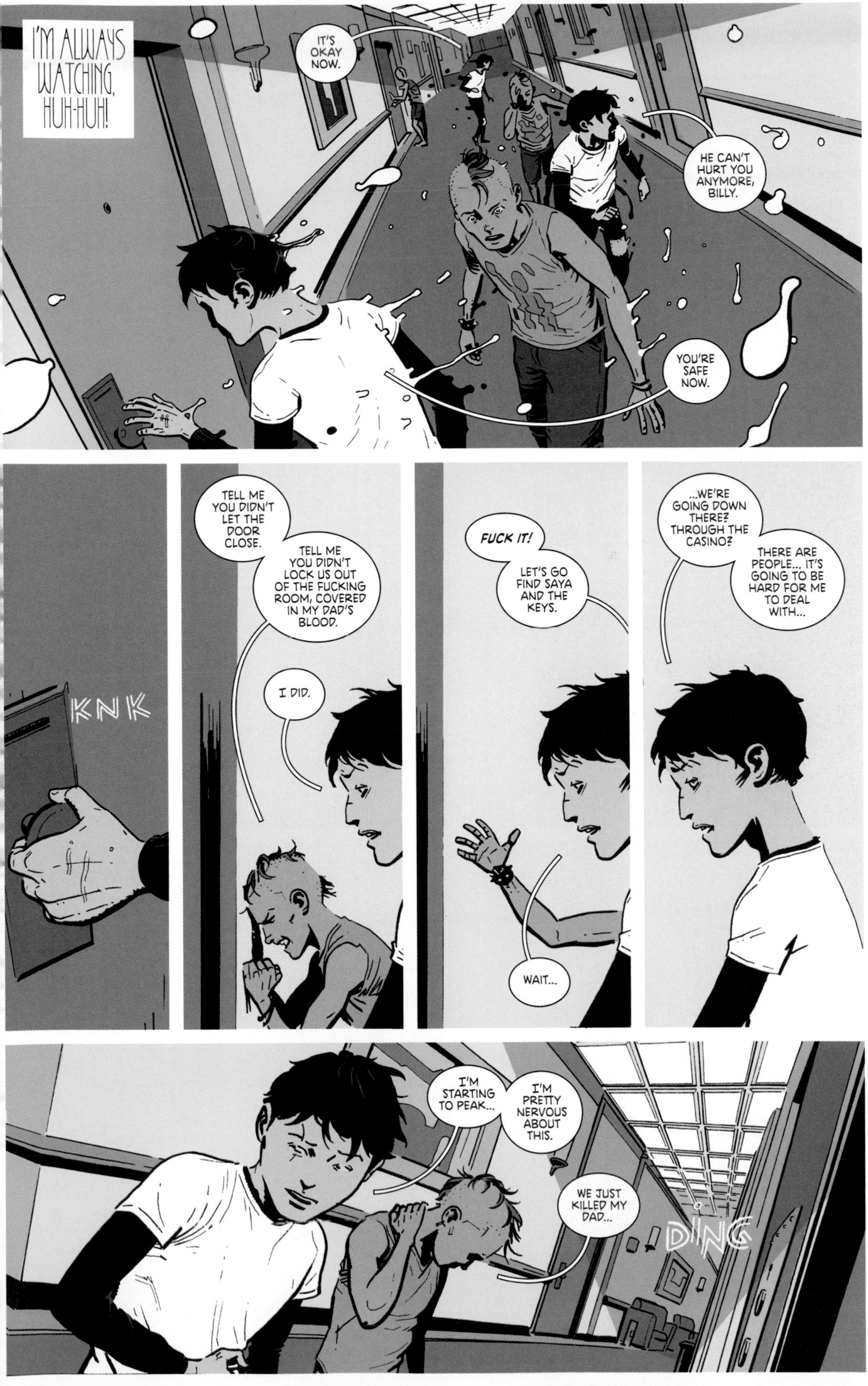
I'M ALWAYS WATCHING, HUH-HUH!
IT'S OKAY NOW.
HE CAN'T HURT YOU ANYMORE, BILLY.
YOU'RE SAFE NOW.
KNK
TELL ME YOU DIDN'T LET THE DOOR CLOSE.
TELL ME YOU DIDN'T LOCK US OUT OF THE FUCKING ROOM, COVERED IN MY DAD'S BLOOD.
I DID.
FUCK IT!
LET'S GO FIND SAYA AND THE KEYS.
WAIT...
...WE'RE GOING DOWN THERE? THROUGH THE CASINO?
THERE ARE PEOPLE... IT'S GOING TO BE HARD FOR ME TO DEAL WITH...
I'M STARTING TO PEAK...
I'M PRETTY NERVOUS ABOUT THIS.
WE JUST KILLED MY DAD...
DING

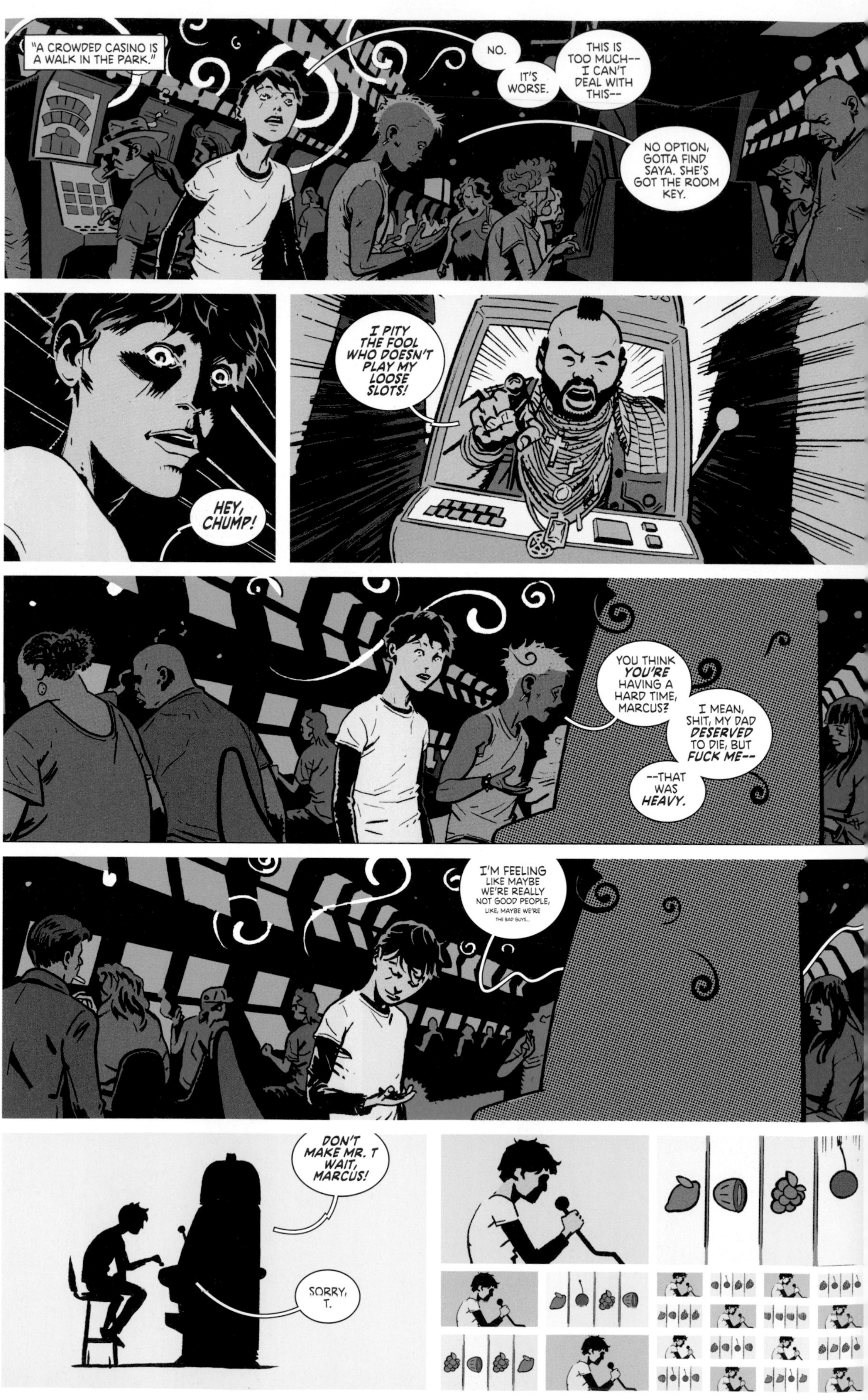
"A CROWDED CASINO IS A WALK IN THE PARK."
NO.
IT'S WORSE.
THIS IS TOO MUCH-- I CAN'T DEAL WITH THIS--
NO OPTION, GOTTA FIND SAYA. SHE'S GOT THE ROOM KEY.
I PITY THE FOOL WHO DOESN'T PLAY MY LOOSE SLOTS!
HEY, CHUMP!
YOU THINK YOU'RE HAVING A HARD TIME, MARCUS?
I MEAN, SHIT, MY DAD DESERVED TO DIE, BUT FUCK ME--
--THAT WAS HEAVY.
I'M FEELING LIKE MAYBE WE'RE REALLY NOT GOOD PEOPLE, LIKE, MAYBE WE'RE THE BAD GUYS...
DON'T MAKE MR. T WAIT, MARCUS!
SORRY, T.

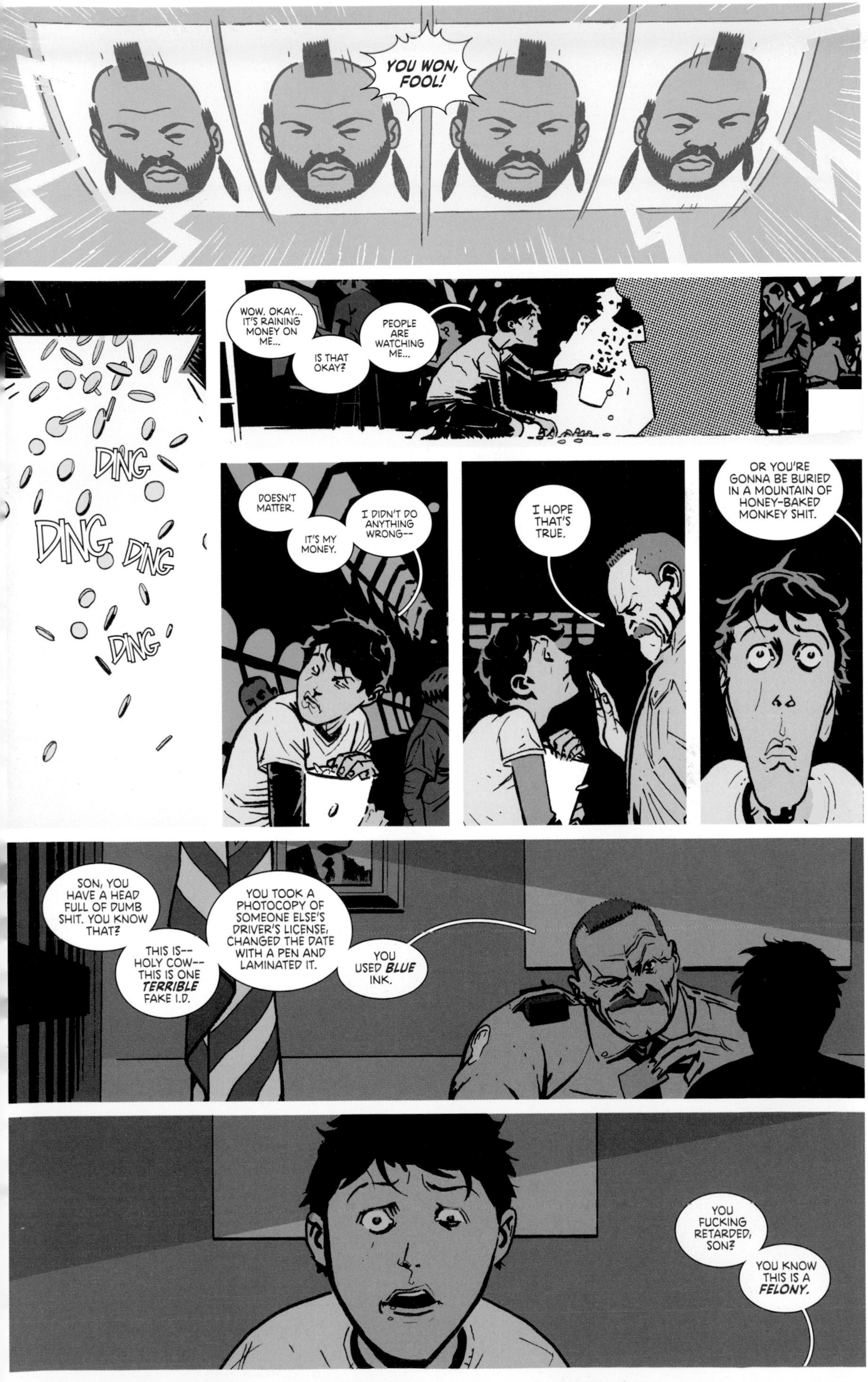
YOU WON, FOOL!
DING
DING
DING
DING
WOW. OKAY... IT'S RAINING MONEY ON ME...
IS THAT OKAY?
PEOPLE ARE WATCHING ME...
DOESN'T MATTER.
IT'S MY MONEY.
I DIDN'T DO ANYTHING WRONG--
I HOPE THAT'S TRUE.
OR YOU'RE GONNA BE BURIED IN A MOUNTAIN OF HONEY-BAKED MONKEY SHIT.
SON, YOU HAVE A HEAD FULL OF DUMB SHIT. YOU KNOW THAT?
THIS IS-- HOLY COW-- THIS IS ONE TERRIBLE FAKE I.D.
YOU TOOK A PHOTOCOPY OF SOMEONE ELSE'S DRIVER'S LICENSE, CHANGED THE DATE WITH A PEN AND LAMINATED IT.
YOU USED BLUE INK.
YOU FUCKING RETARDED, SON?
YOU KNOW THIS IS A FELONY.

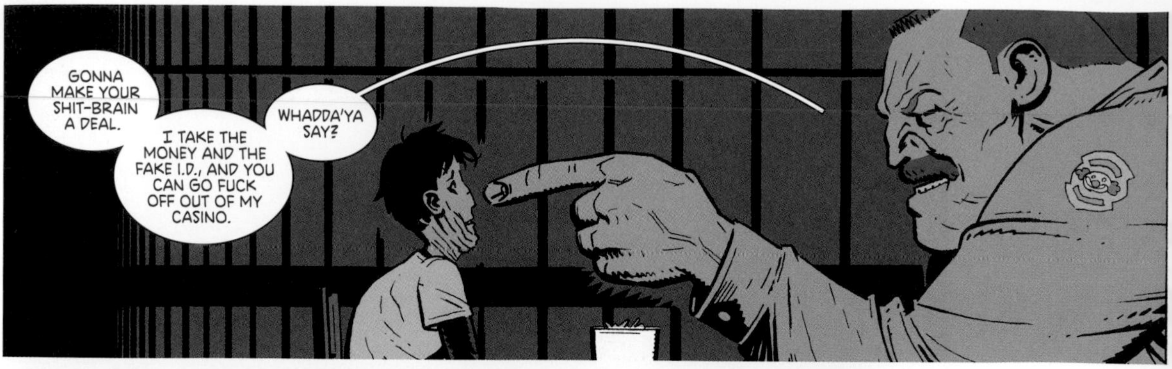
GONNA MAKE YOUR SHIT-BRAIN A DEAL.
I TAKE THE MONEY AND THE FAKE I.D., AND YOU CAN GO FUCK OFF OUT OF MY CASINO.
WHADDA'YA SAY?

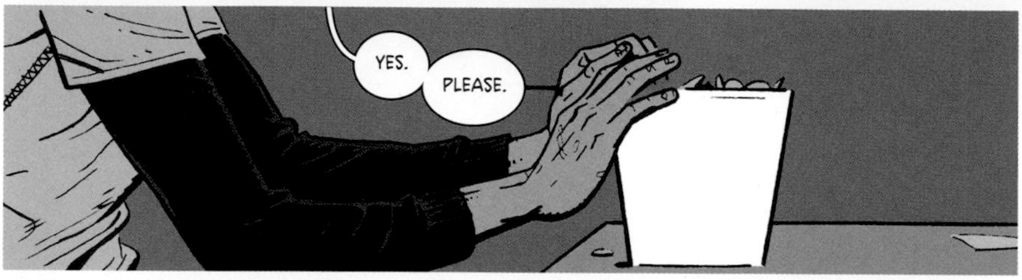
YES.
PLEASE.

GET READY FOR HIM TO SEE MY HANDS. TO SEE MY BLOOD SOAKED HANDS. TO KNOW WHAT I DID.

HOLY SHIT!

MY HANDS...

HANDS ARE CLEAN.

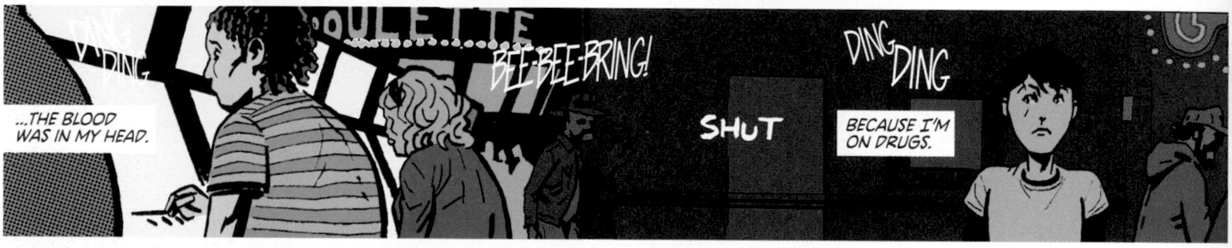
DING DING
...THE BLOOD WAS IN MY HEAD.
BEE-BEE-BRING!
SHUT
DING DING
BECAUSE I'M ON DRUGS.

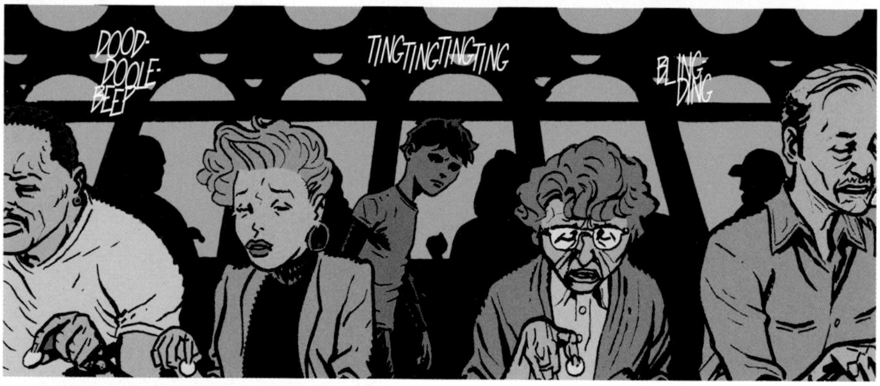
DOOD-DOOLE-BEEP
TINGTINGTINGTING
BLING DING

KEEP HAVING AN URGE TO CALL MY MOM.

TO APOLOGIZE FOR WHAT I BECAME. TO TELL HER IT WASN'T HER FAULT.

SHE USED TO TELL ME THAT WHAT YOU DON'T FOCUS ON WOULD COME TRUE.

TRY NOT TO FOCUS ON HOW BAD I WANT FOR THIS TO BE OVER.

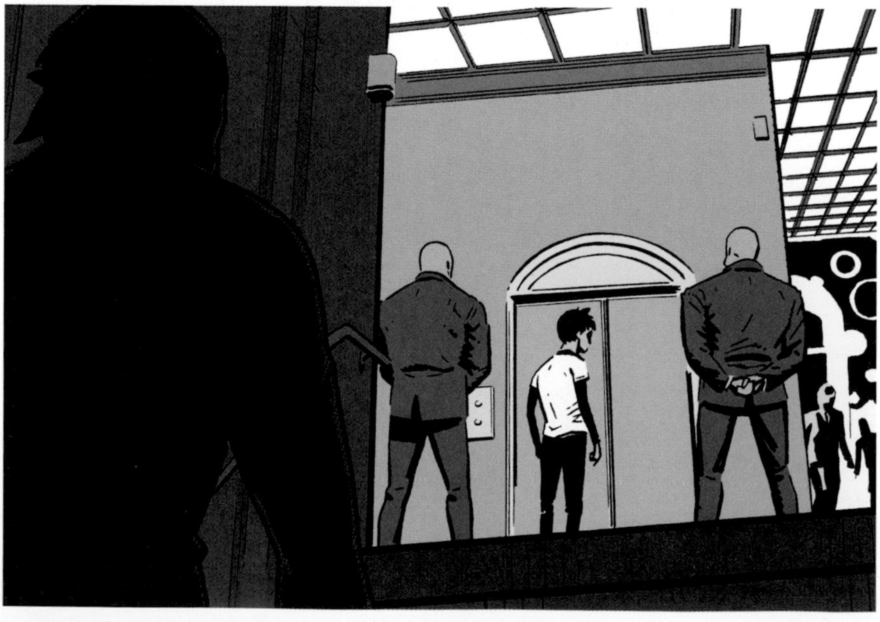

TRY NOT TO FOCUS ON HOW BAD I WANT TO BE BACK HOME WITH THEM.

HOW BAD I MISS THEM.

HOW BAD I WANT TO BE HER INNOCENT LITTLE BOY AGAIN.

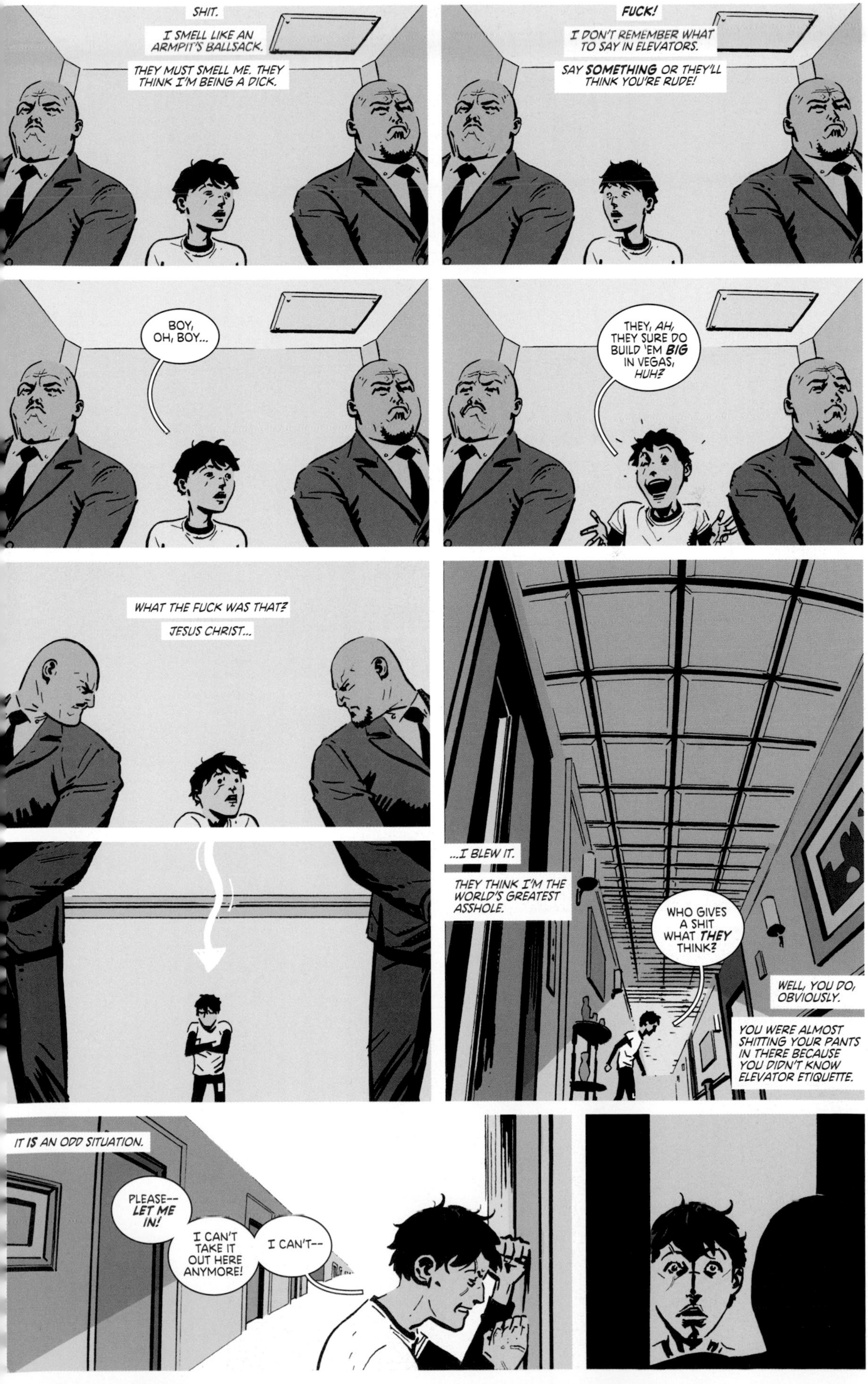
SHIT.
I SMELL LIKE AN ARMPIT'S BALLSACK.
THEY MUST SMELL ME. THEY THINK I'M BEING A DICK.
FUCK!
I DON'T REMEMBER WHAT TO SAY IN ELEVATORS.
SAY SOMETHING OR THEY'LL THINK YOU'RE RUDE!
BOY, OH, BOY...
THEY, AH, THEY SURE DO BUILD 'EM BIG IN VEGAS, HUH?
WHAT THE FUCK WAS THAT?
JESUS CHRIST...
...I BLEW IT.
THEY THINK I'M THE WORLD'S GREATEST ASSHOLE.
WHO GIVES A SHIT WHAT THEY THINK?
WELL, YOU DO, OBVIOUSLY.
YOU WERE ALMOST SHITTING YOUR PANTS IN THERE BECAUSE YOU DIDN'T KNOW ELEVATOR ETIQUETTE.
IT IS AN ODD SITUATION.
PLEASE-- LET ME IN!
I CAN'T TAKE IT OUT HERE ANYMORE!
I CAN'T--

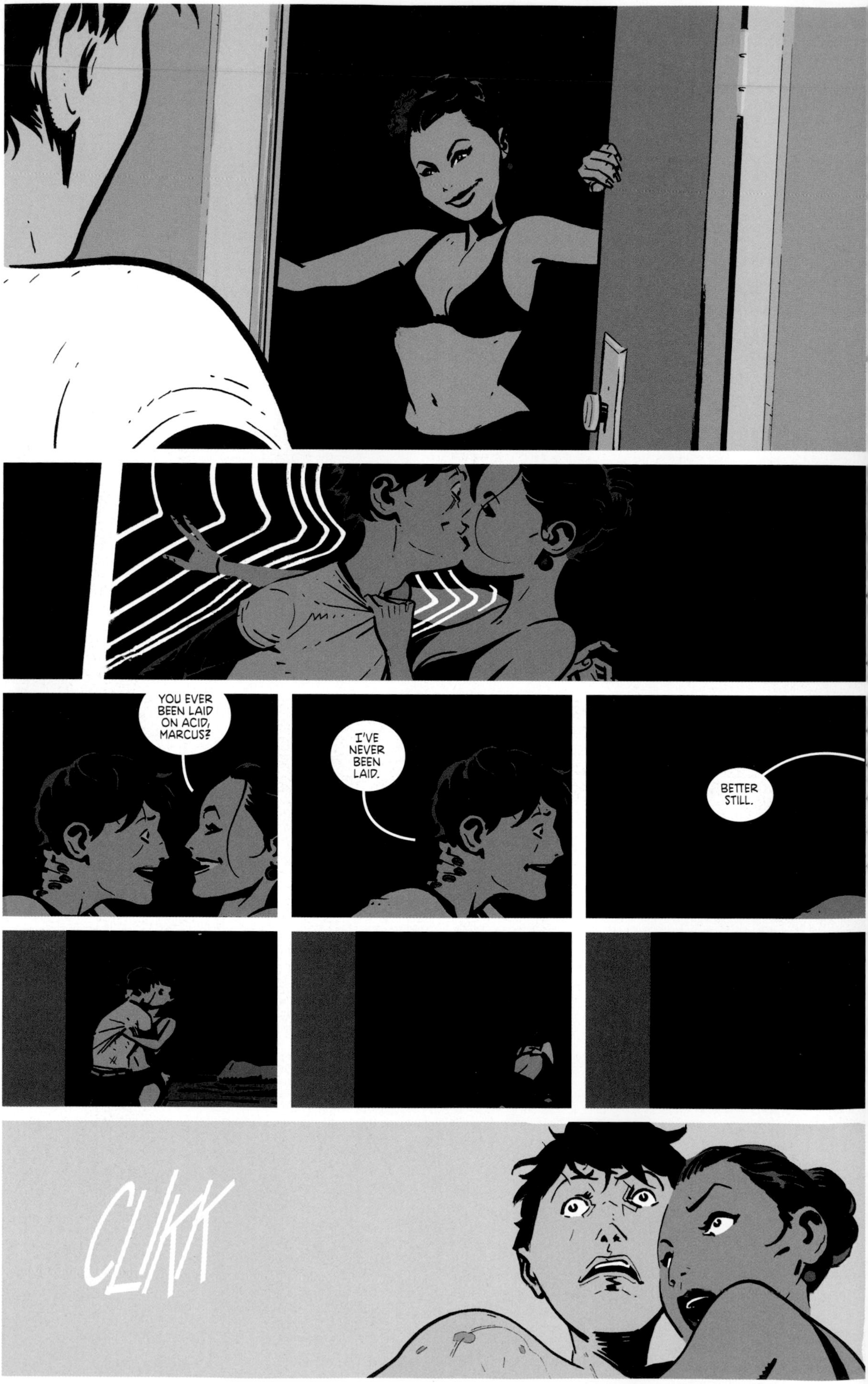

YOU EVER BEEN LAID ON ACID, MARCUS?
I'VE NEVER BEEN LAID.
BETTER STILL.
CLIKK

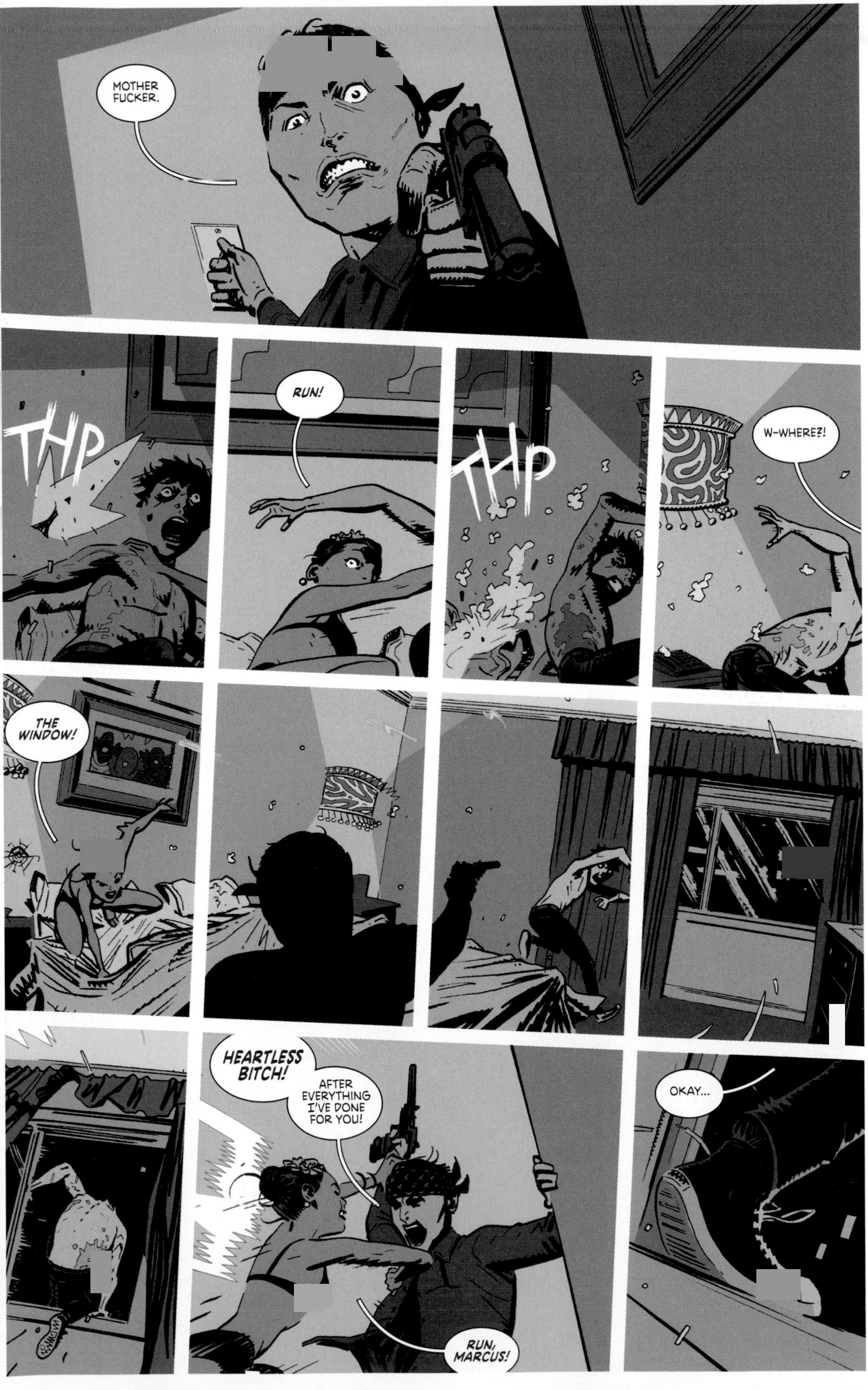
MOTHER FUCKER.
THP
RUN!
THP
W-WHERE?!
THE WINDOW!
HEARTLESS BITCH!
AFTER EVERYTHING I'VE DONE FOR YOU!
RUN, MARCUS!
OKAY...

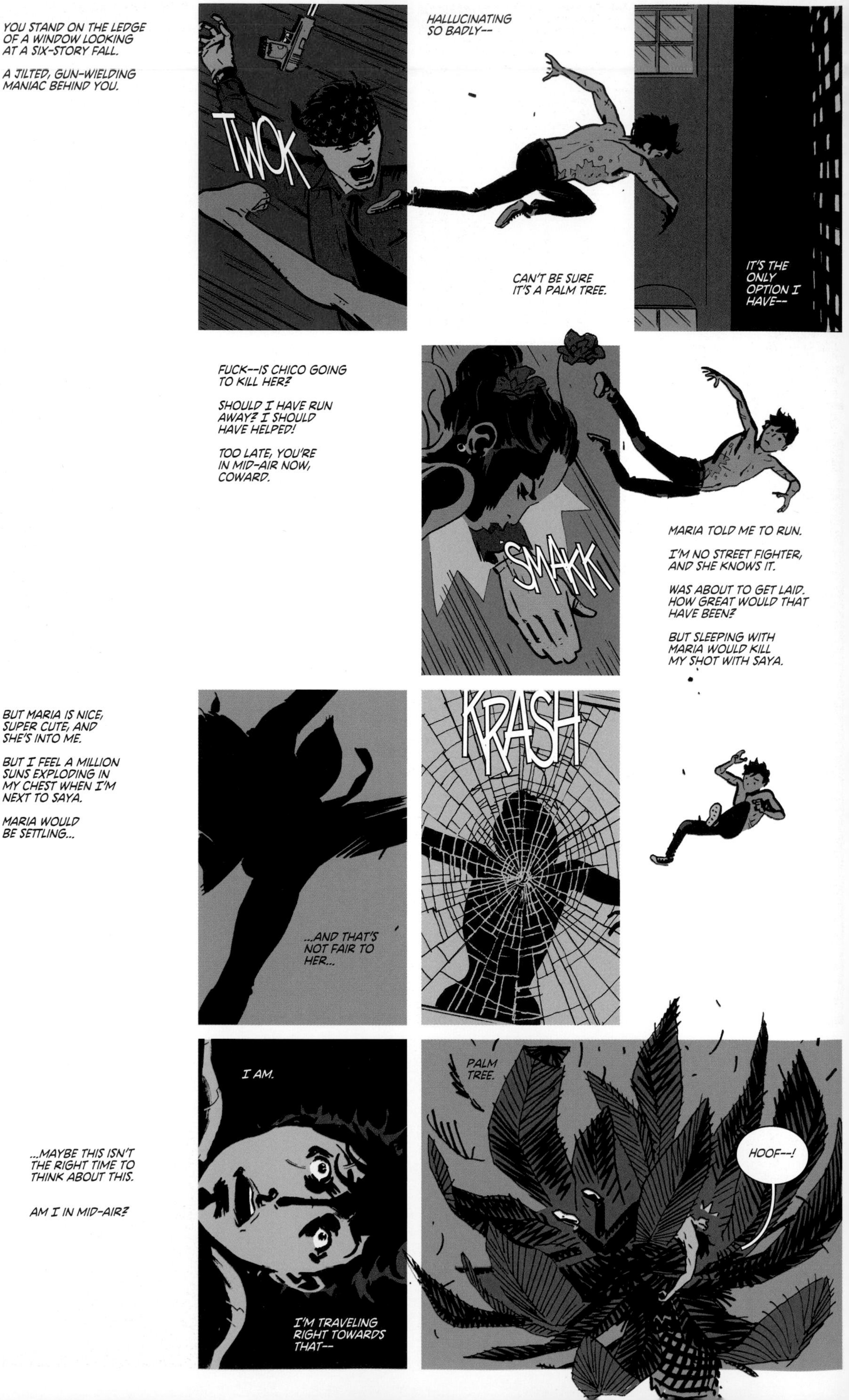
YOU STAND ON THE LEDGE OF A WINDOW LOOKING AT A SIX-STORY FALL.
A JILTED, GUN-WIELDING MANIAC BEHIND YOU.
TWOK
HALLUCINATING SO BADLY--
CAN'T BE SURE IT'S A PALM TREE.
IT'S THE ONLY OPTION I HAVE--
FUCK--IS CHICO GOING TO KILL HER?
SHOULD I HAVE RUN AWAY? I SHOULD HAVE HELPED!
TOO LATE, YOU'RE IN MID-AIR NOW, COWARD.
SMAKK
MARIA TOLD ME TO RUN.
I'M NO STREET FIGHTER, AND SHE KNOWS IT.
WAS ABOUT TO GET LAID. HOW GREAT WOULD THAT HAVE BEEN?
BUT SLEEPING WITH MARIA WOULD KILL MY SHOT WITH SAYA.
BUT MARIA IS NICE, SUPER CUTE, AND SHE'S INTO ME.
BUT I FEEL A MILLION SUNS EXPLODING IN MY CHEST WHEN I'M NEXT TO SAYA.
MARIA WOULD BE SETTLING...
...AND THAT'S NOT FAIR TO HER...
KRASH
...MAYBE THIS ISN'T THE RIGHT TIME TO THINK ABOUT THIS.
AM I IN MID-AIR?
I AM.
I'M TRAVELING RIGHT TOWARDS THAT--
PALM TREE.
HOOF--!

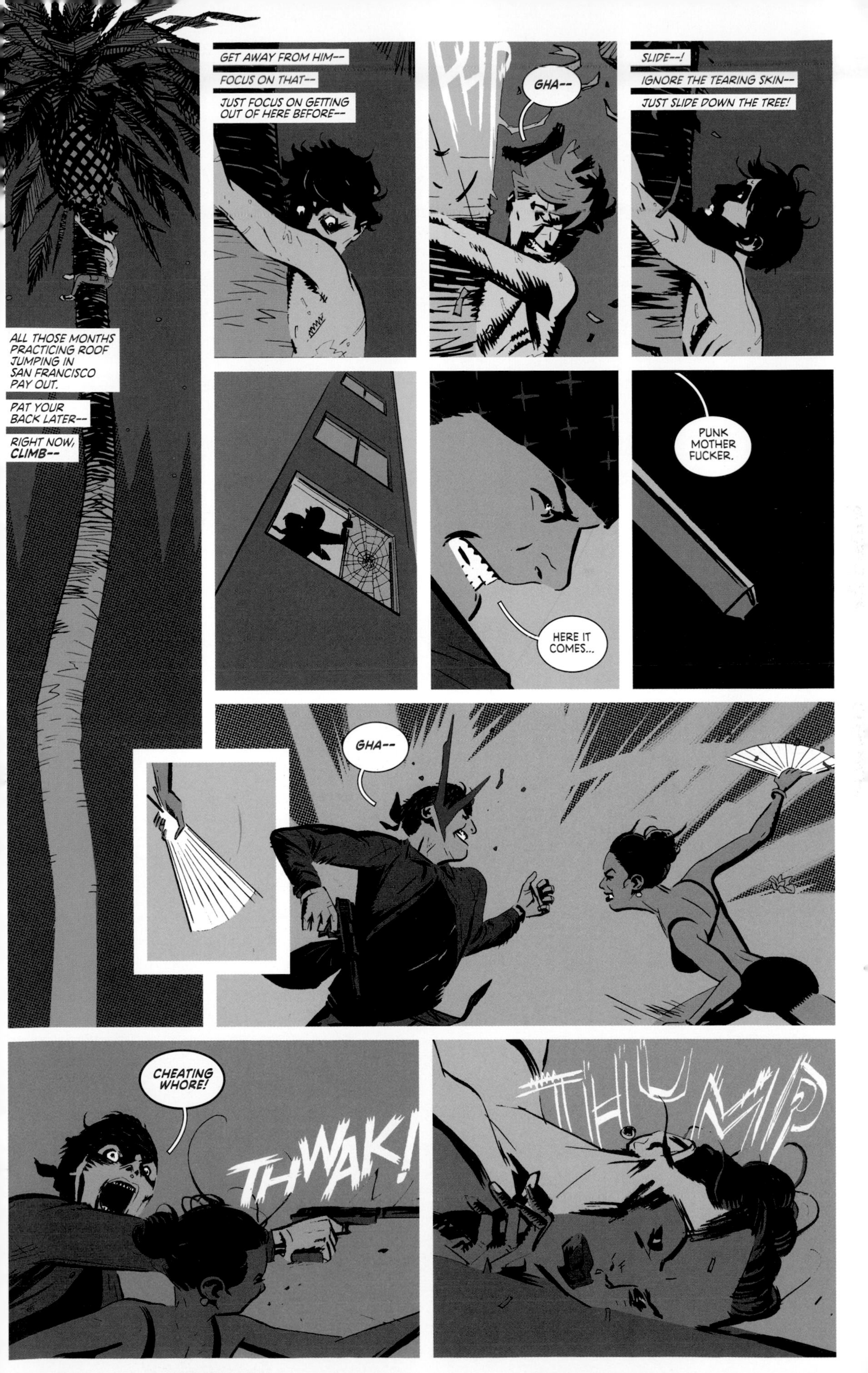
GET AWAY FROM HIM--
FOCUS ON THAT--
JUST FOCUS ON GETTING OUT OF HERE BEFORE--
GHA--
SLIDE--!
IGNORE THE TEARING SKIN--
JUST SLIDE DOWN THE TREE!
ALL THOSE MONTHS PRACTICING ROOF JUMPING IN SAN FRANCISCO PAY OUT.
PAT YOUR BACK LATER--
RIGHT NOW, CLIMB--
HERE IT COMES...
PUNK MOTHER FUCKER.
GHA--
CHEATING WHORE!
THWAK!
THUMP

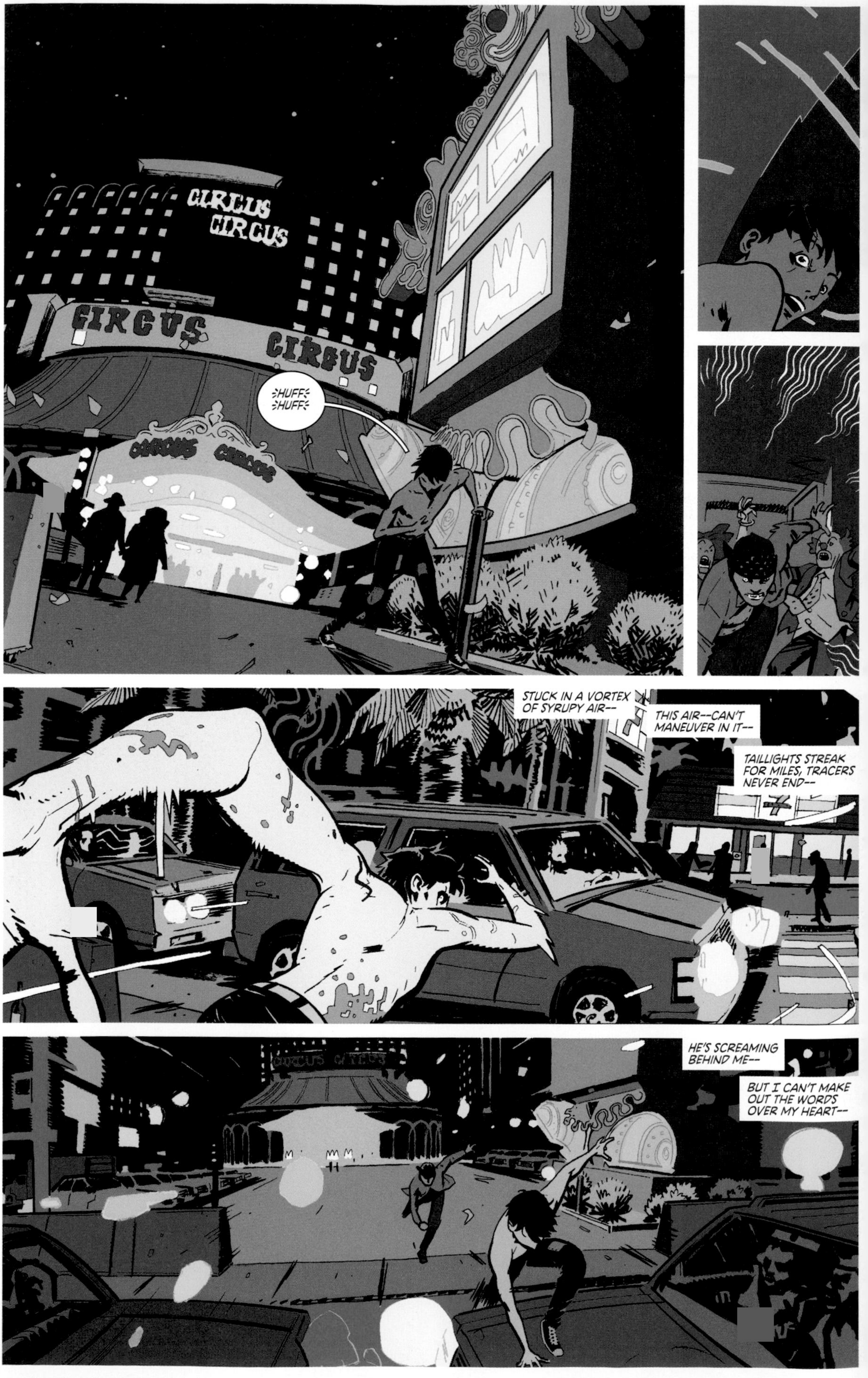
CIRCUS
CIRCUS
HUFF HUFF
STUCK IN A VORTEX OF SYRUPY AIR--
THIS AIR--CAN'T MANEUVER IN IT--
TAILLIGHTS STREAK FOR MILES, TRACERS NEVER END--
HE'S SCREAMING BEHIND ME--
BUT I CAN'T MAKE OUT THE WORDS OVER MY HEART--

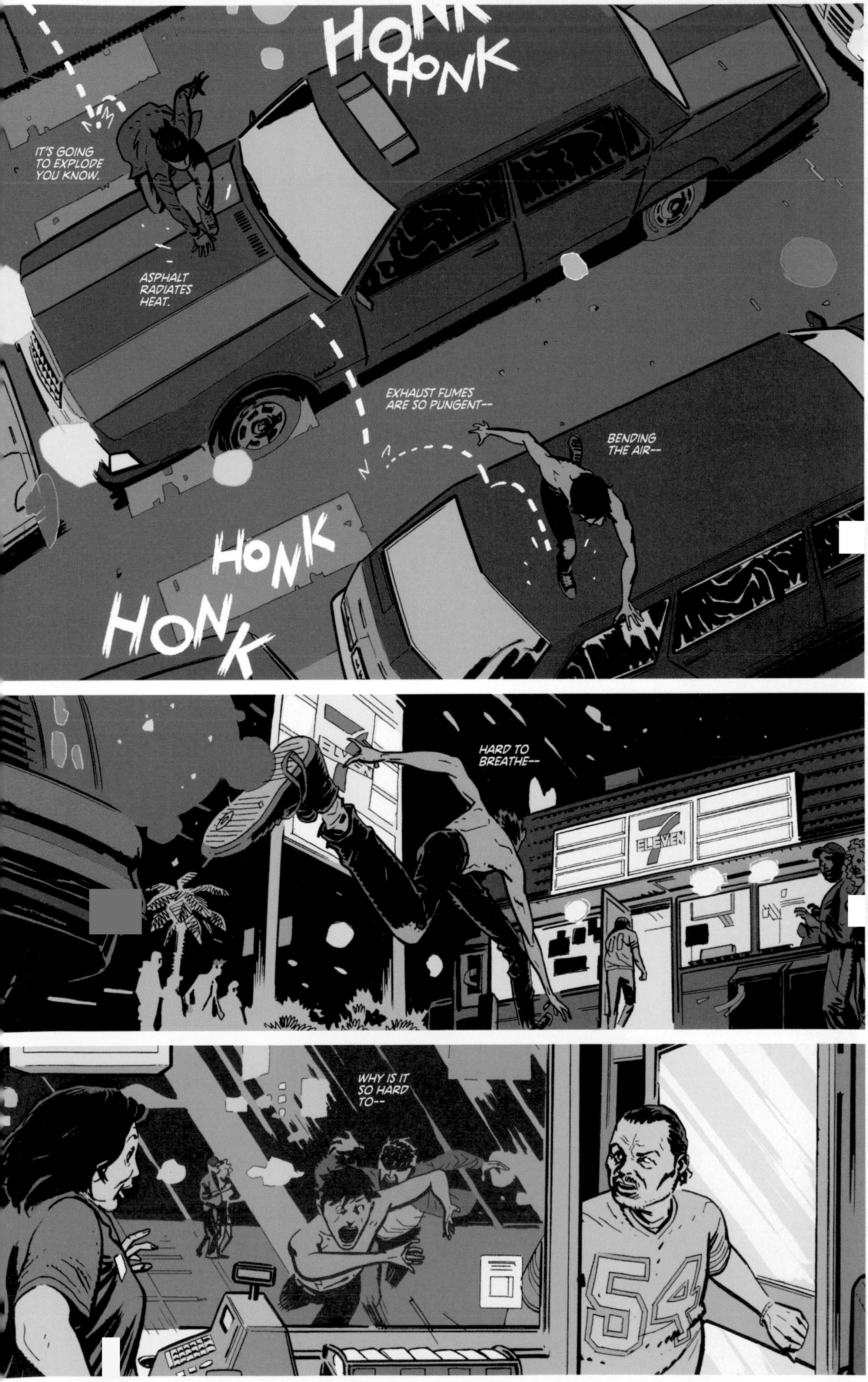
HONK
HONK
IT'S GOING TO EXPLODE YOU KNOW.
ASPHALT RADIATES HEAT.
EXHAUST FUMES ARE SO PUNGENT--
BENDING THE AIR--
HONK
HONK
HARD TO BREATHE--
7 ELEVEN
WHY IS IT SO HARD TO--

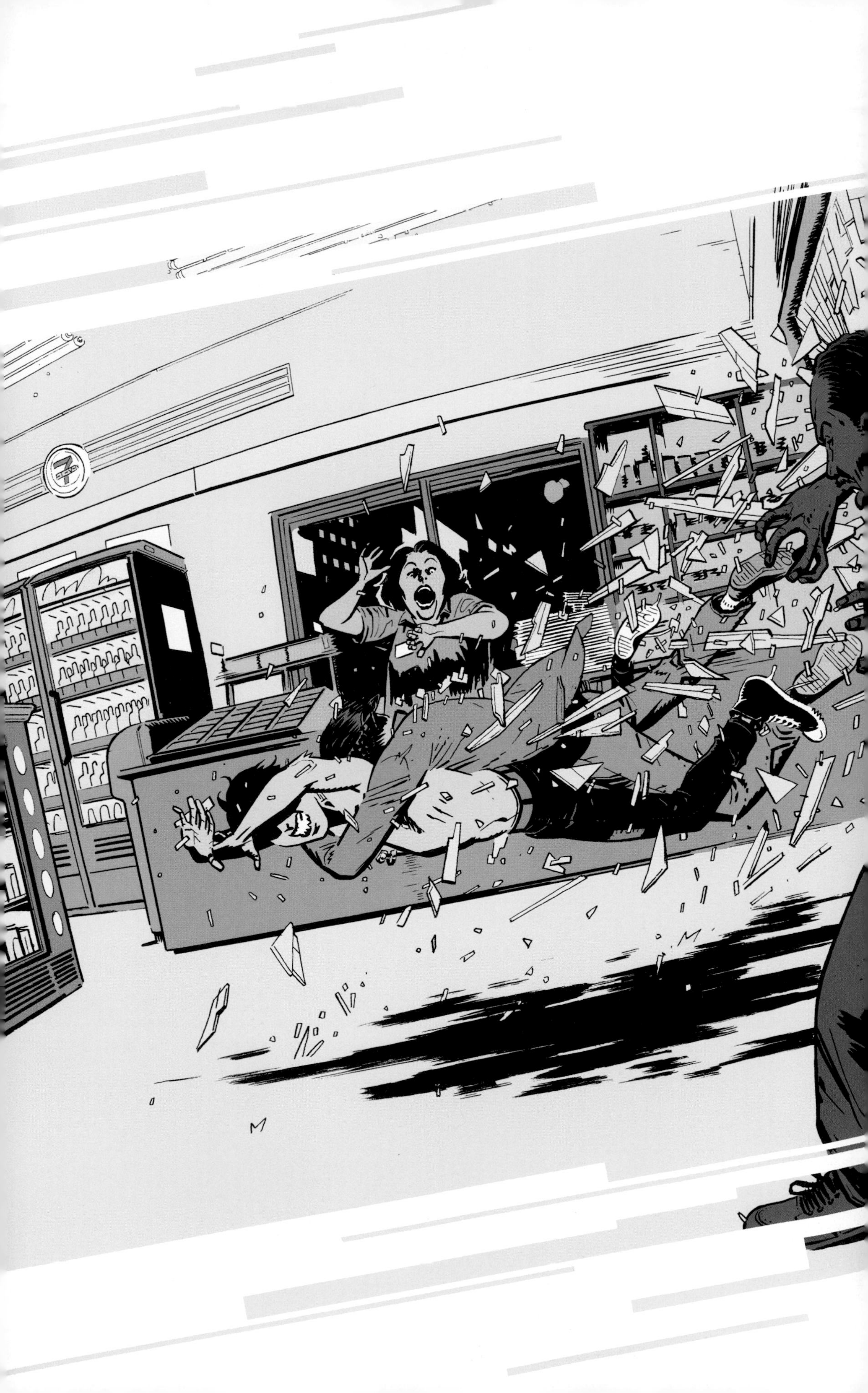

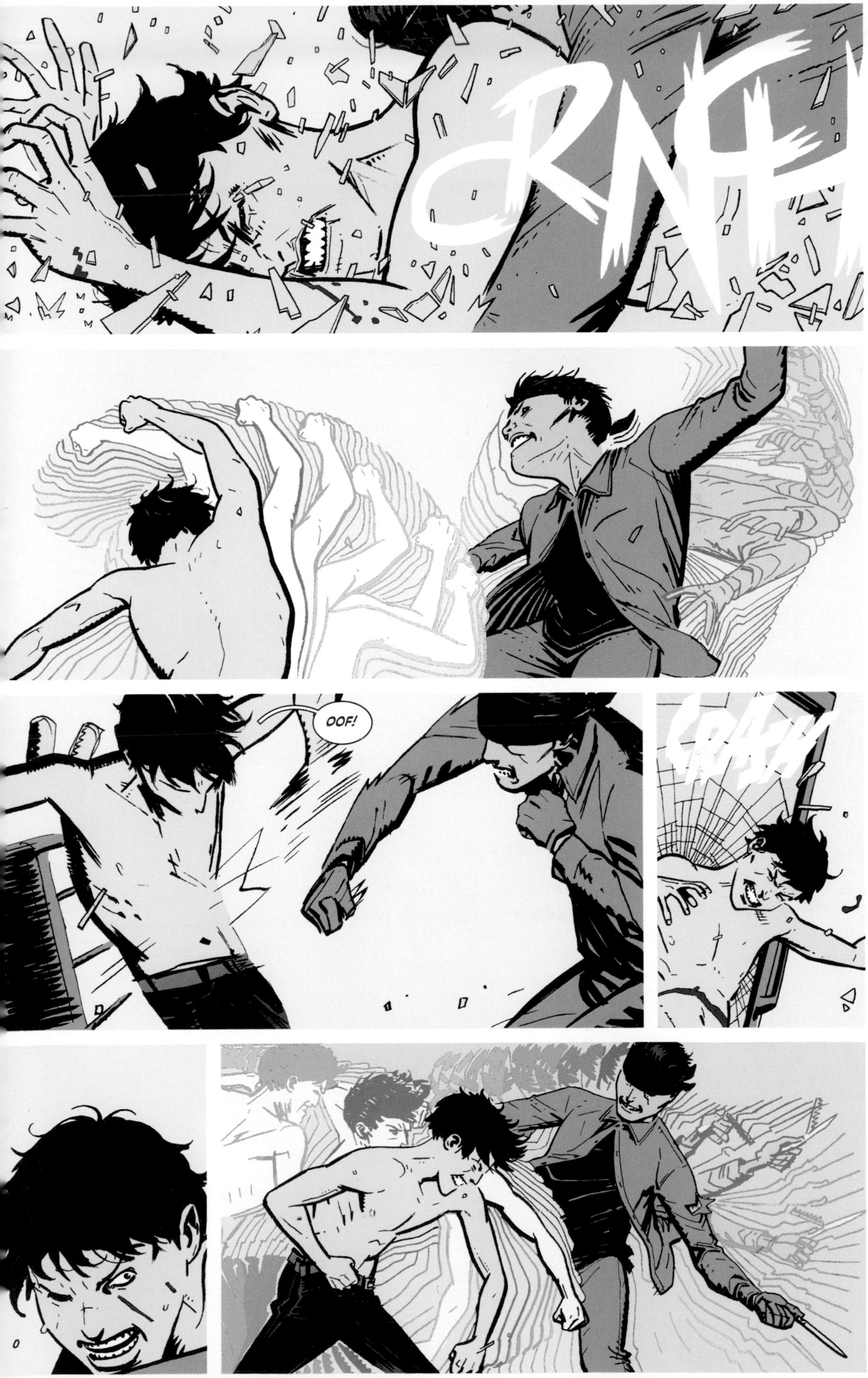
CRASH
OOF!
CRASH

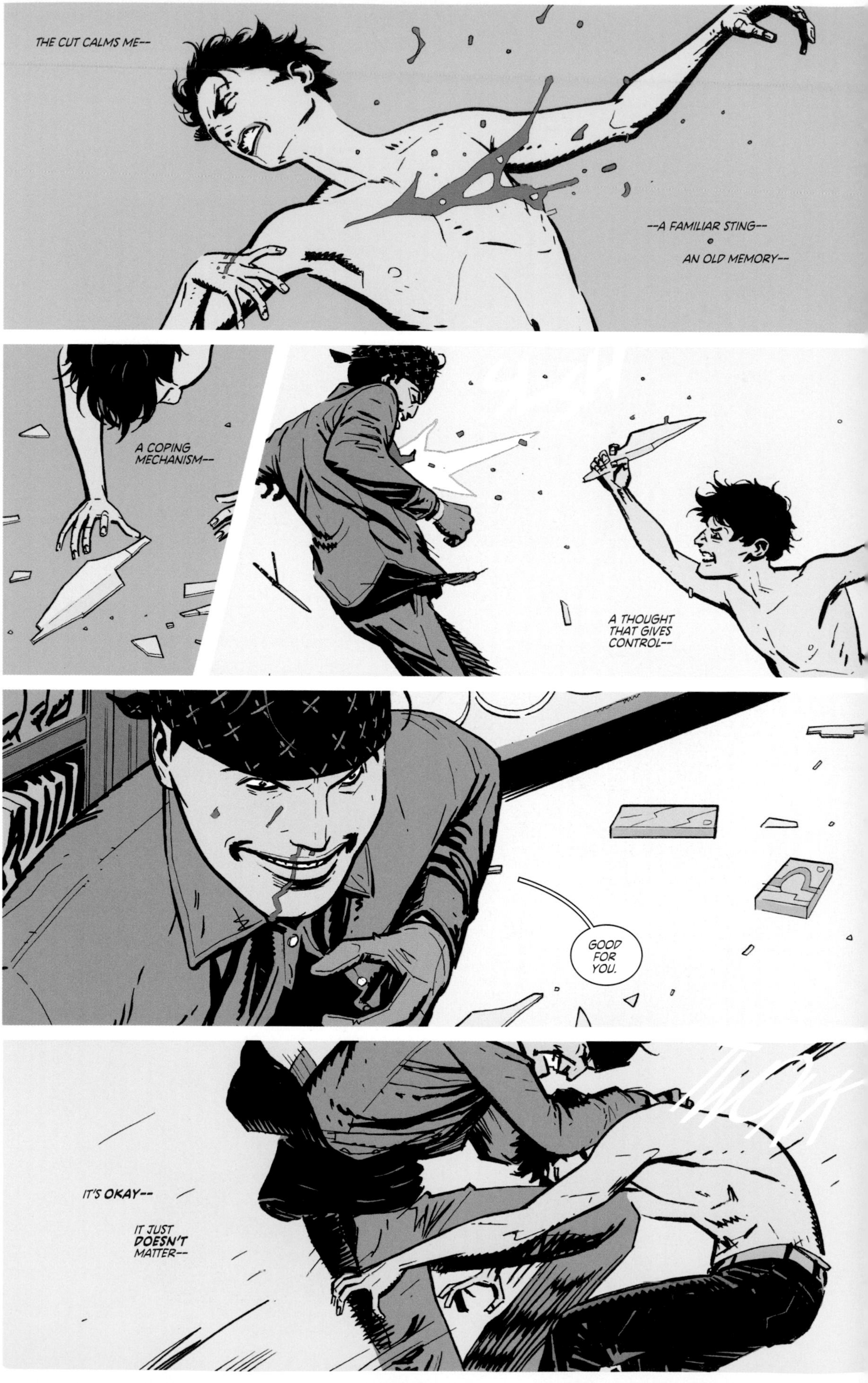
THE CUT CALMS ME--
--A FAMILIAR STING--
AN OLD MEMORY--
A COPING MECHANISM--
A THOUGHT THAT GIVES CONTROL--
GOOD FOR YOU.
IT'S **OKAY**--
IT JUST **DOESN'T** MATTER--

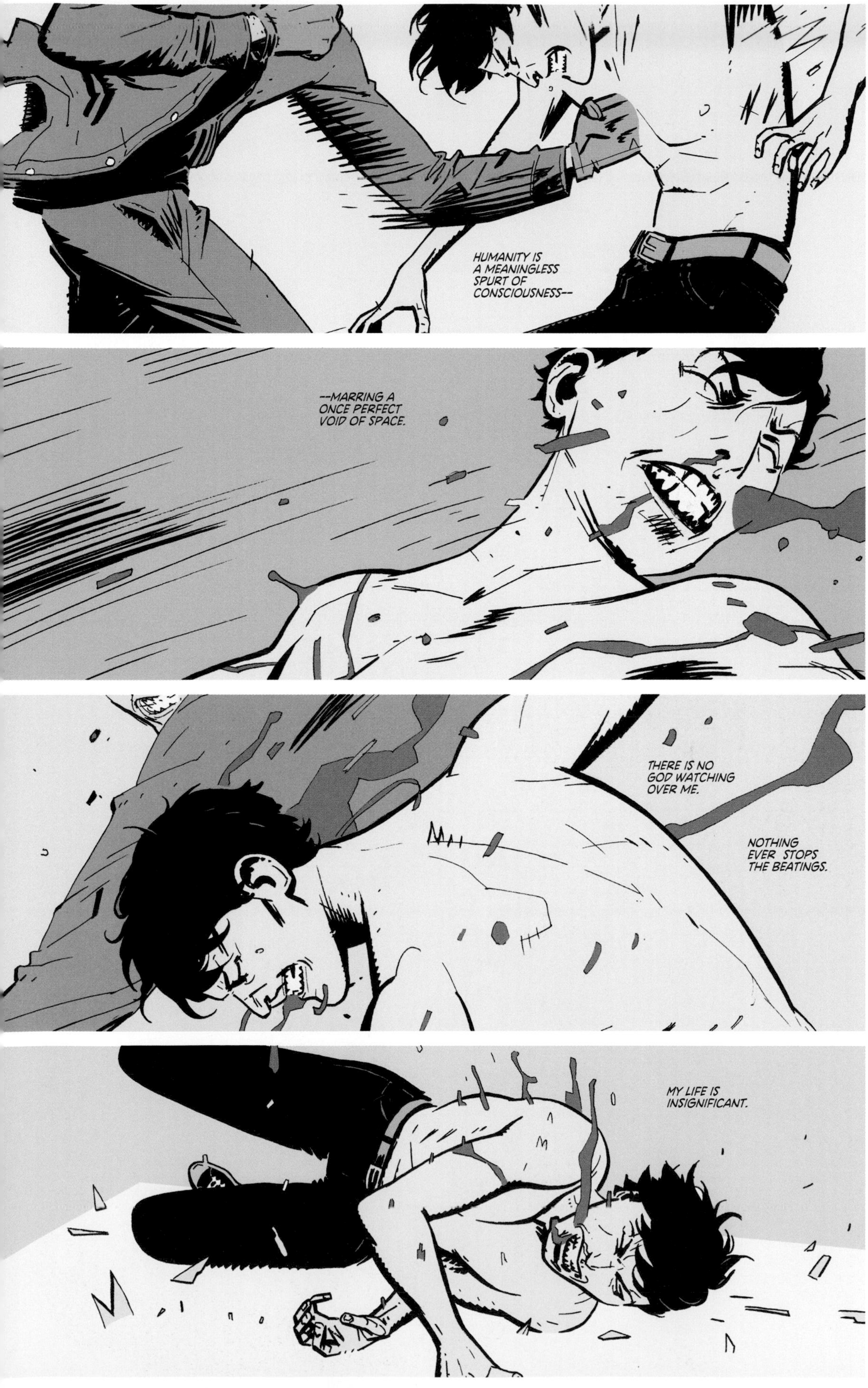
HUMANITY IS A MEANINGLESS SPURT OF CONSCIOUSNESS--
--MARRING A ONCE PERFECT VOID OF SPACE.
THERE IS NO GOD WATCHING OVER ME.
NOTHING EVER STOPS THE BEATINGS.
MY LIFE IS INSIGNIFICANT.

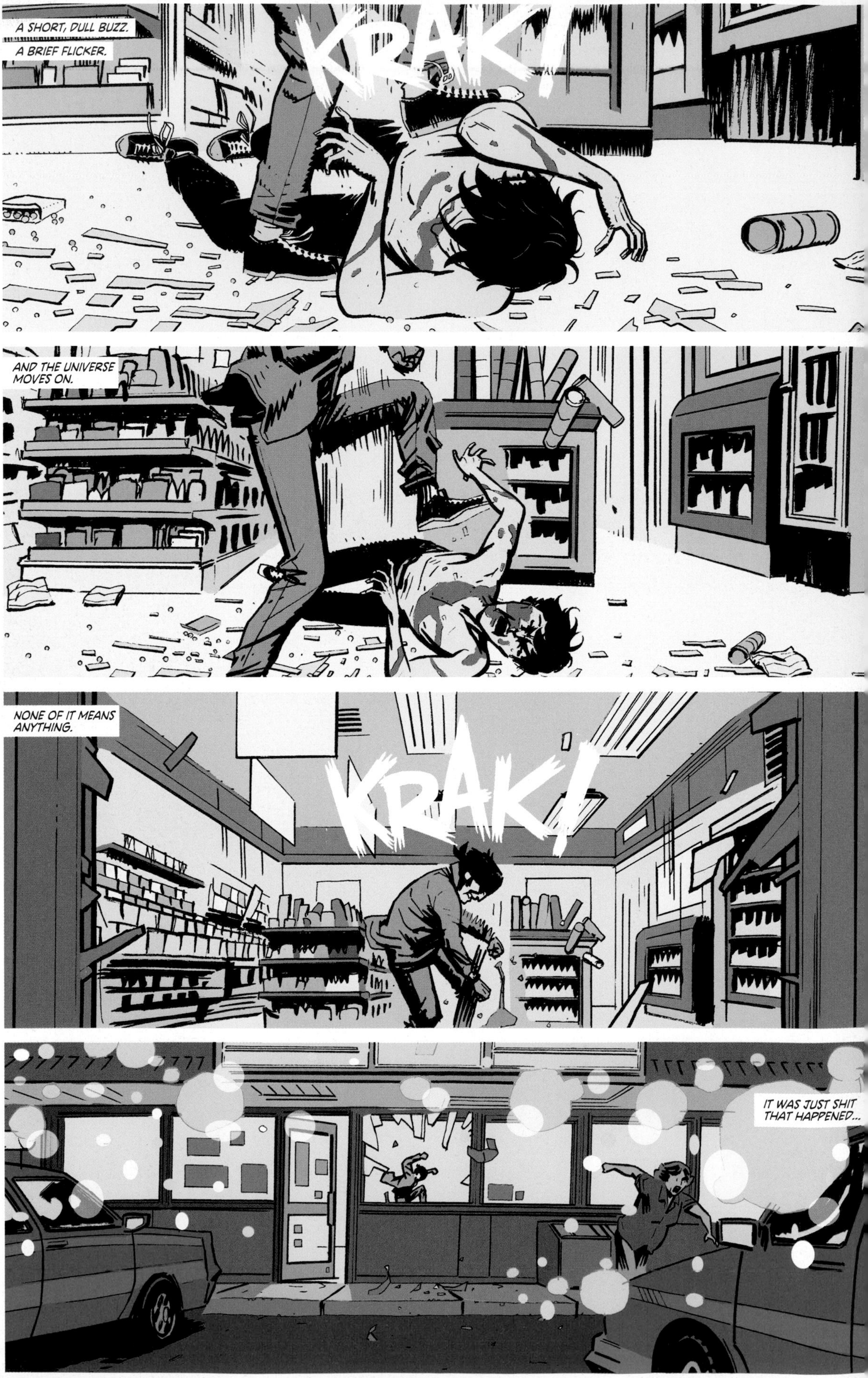
A SHORT, DULL BUZZ.
A BRIEF FLICKER.
KRAK!
AND THE UNIVERSE MOVES ON.
NONE OF IT MEANS ANYTHING.
KRAK!
IT WAS JUST SHIT THAT HAPPENED...

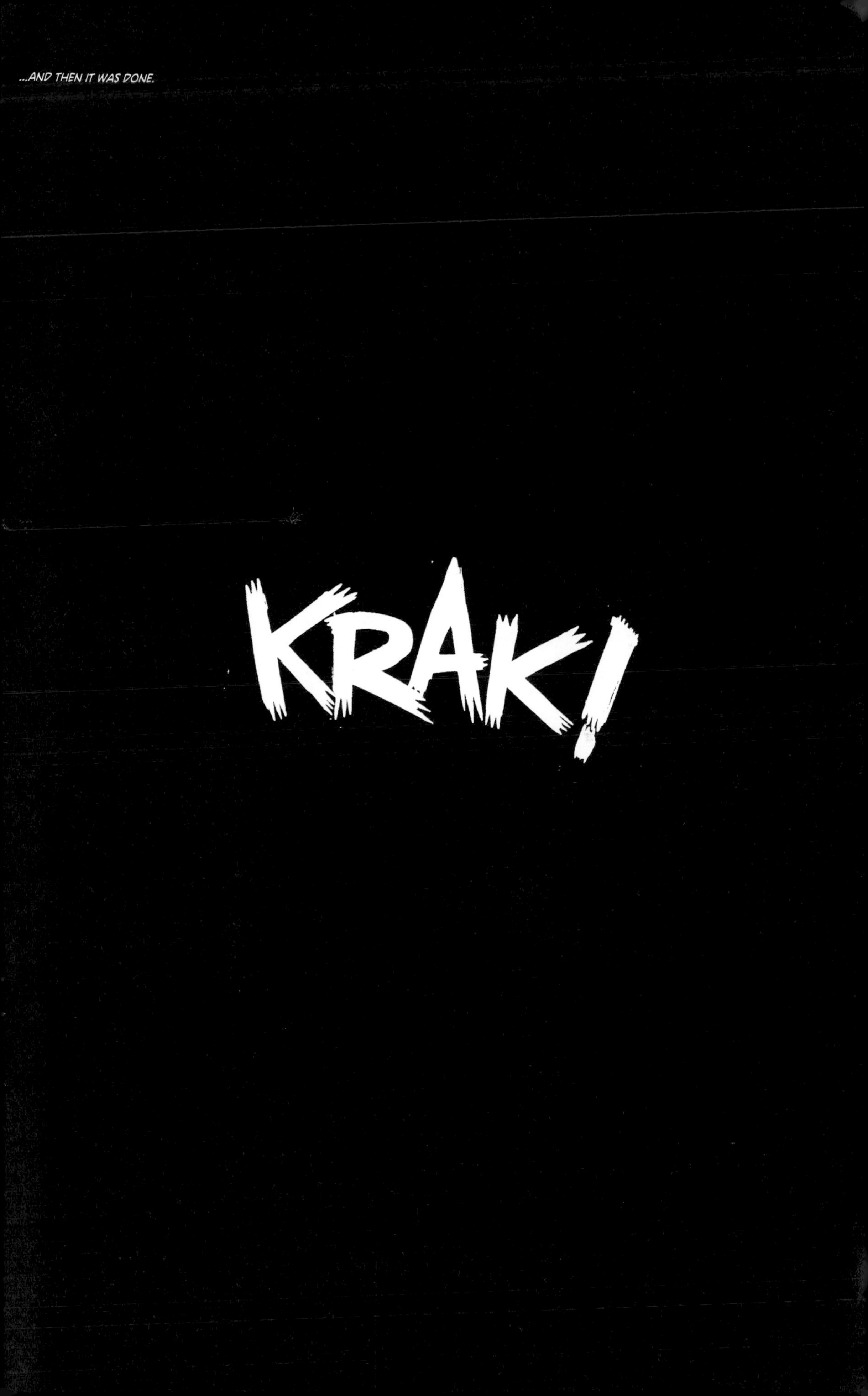
...AND THEN IT WAS DONE.
KRAK!

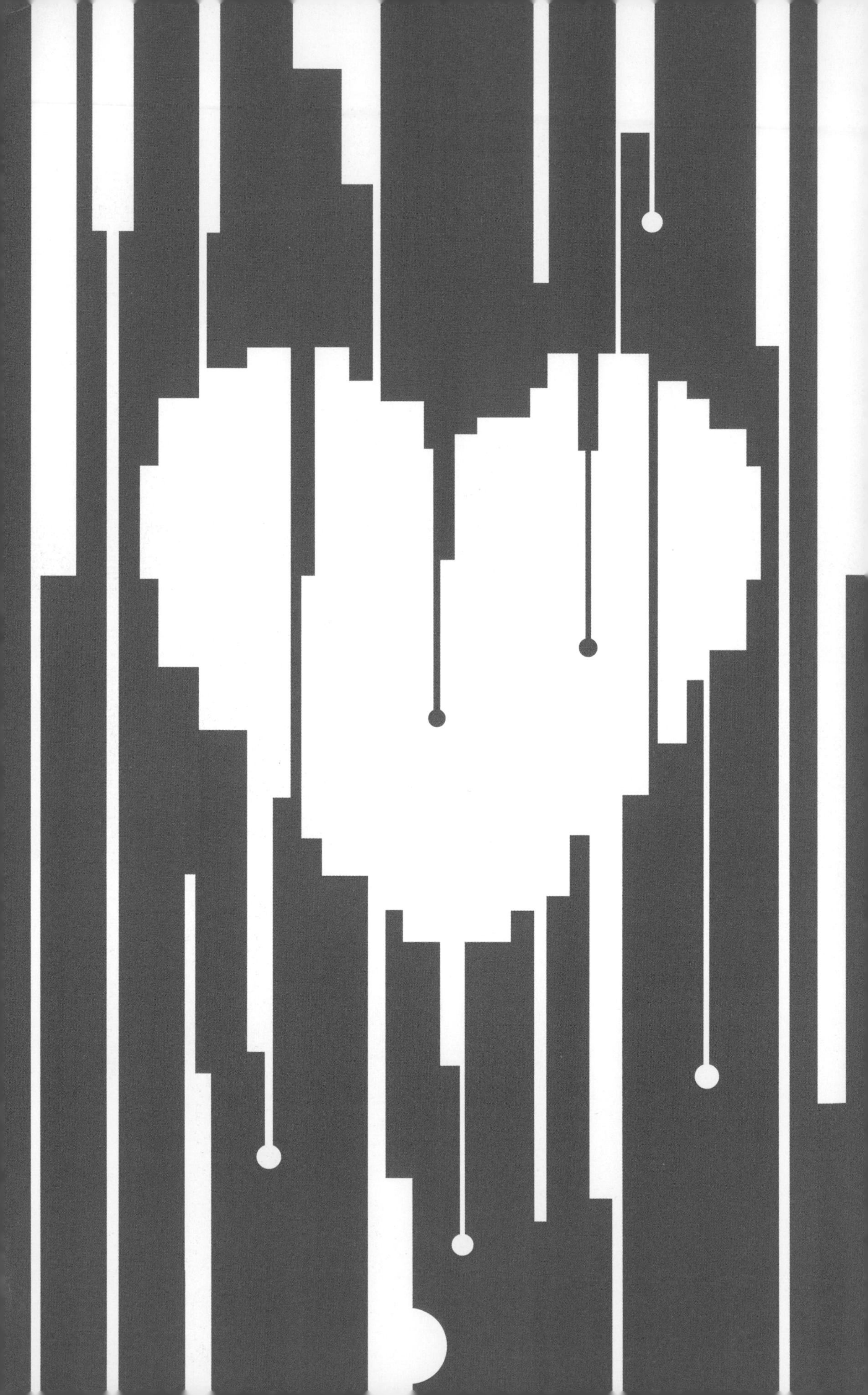

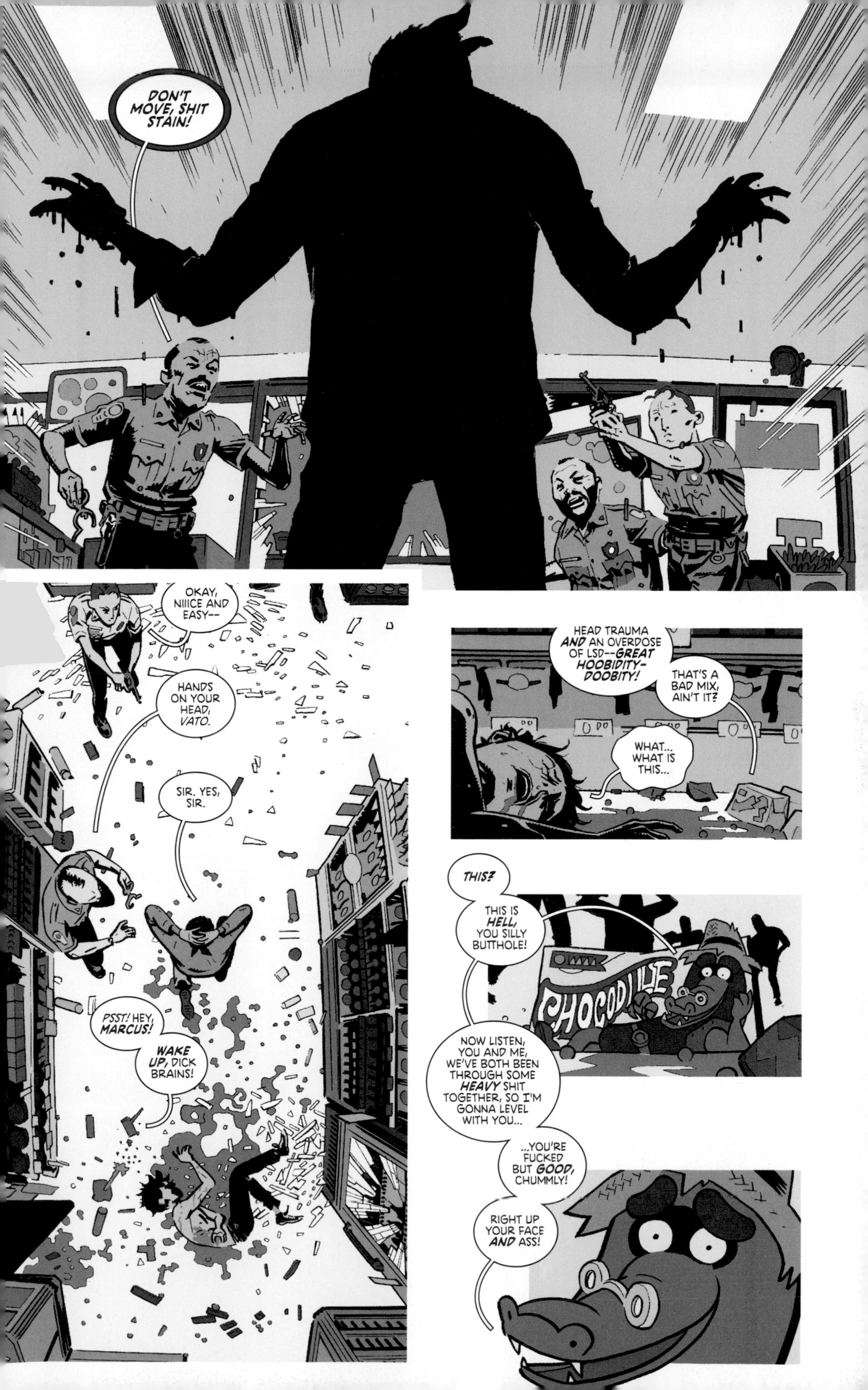
DON'T MOVE, SHIT STAIN!
OKAY, NIIICE AND EASY--
HANDS ON YOUR HEAD, VATO.
SIR. YES, SIR.
PSST! HEY, MARCUS!
WAKE UP, DICK BRAINS!
HEAD TRAUMA AND AN OVERDOSE OF LSD--GREAT HOOBIDITY-DOOBITY!
THAT'S A BAD MIX, AIN'T IT?
WHAT... WHAT IS THIS...
THIS?
THIS IS HELL, YOU SILLY BUTTHOLE!
CHOCODILE
NOW LISTEN, YOU AND ME, WE'VE BOTH BEEN THROUGH SOME HEAVY SHIT TOGETHER, SO I'M GONNA LEVEL WITH YOU...
...YOU'RE FUCKED BUT GOOD, CHUMMLY!
RIGHT UP YOUR FACE AND ASS!

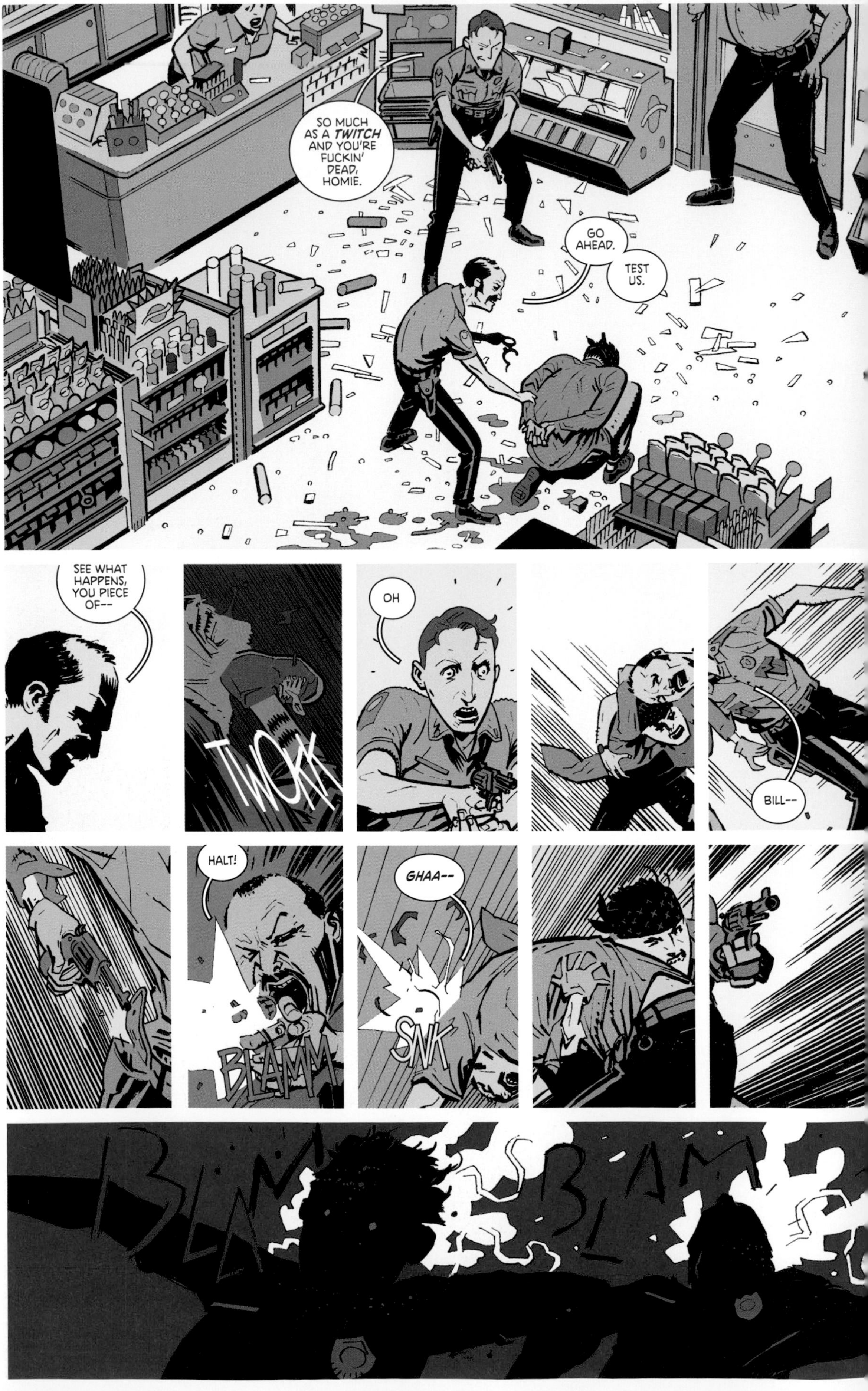
SO MUCH AS A TWITCH AND YOU'RE FUCKIN' DEAD, HOMIE.
GO AHEAD.
TEST US.
SEE WHAT HAPPENS, YOU PIECE OF--
TWOKK
OH
BILL--
HALT!
BLAMM
GHAA--
SNK
BLAM BLAM BLAM BLAM

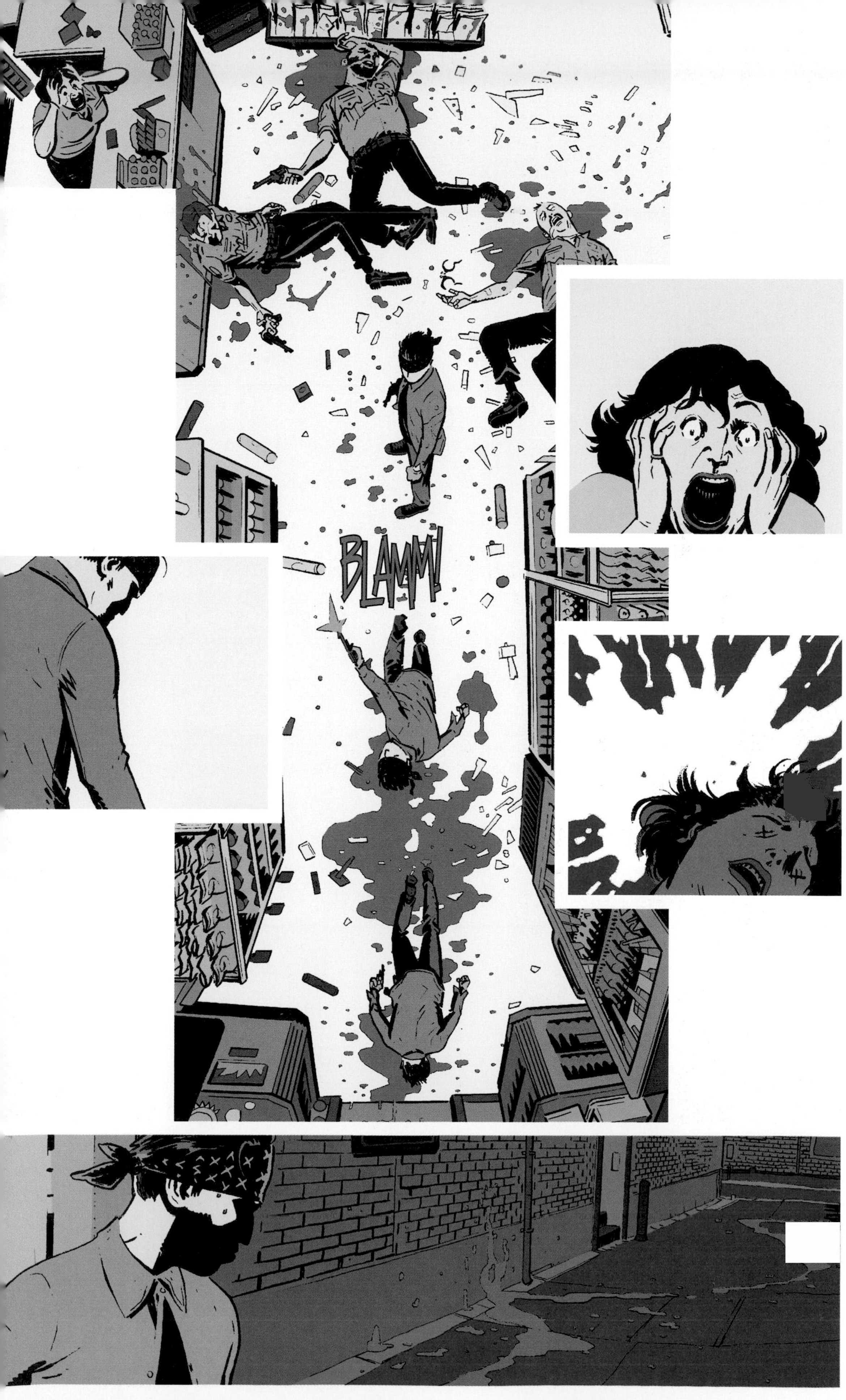
BLAMM!

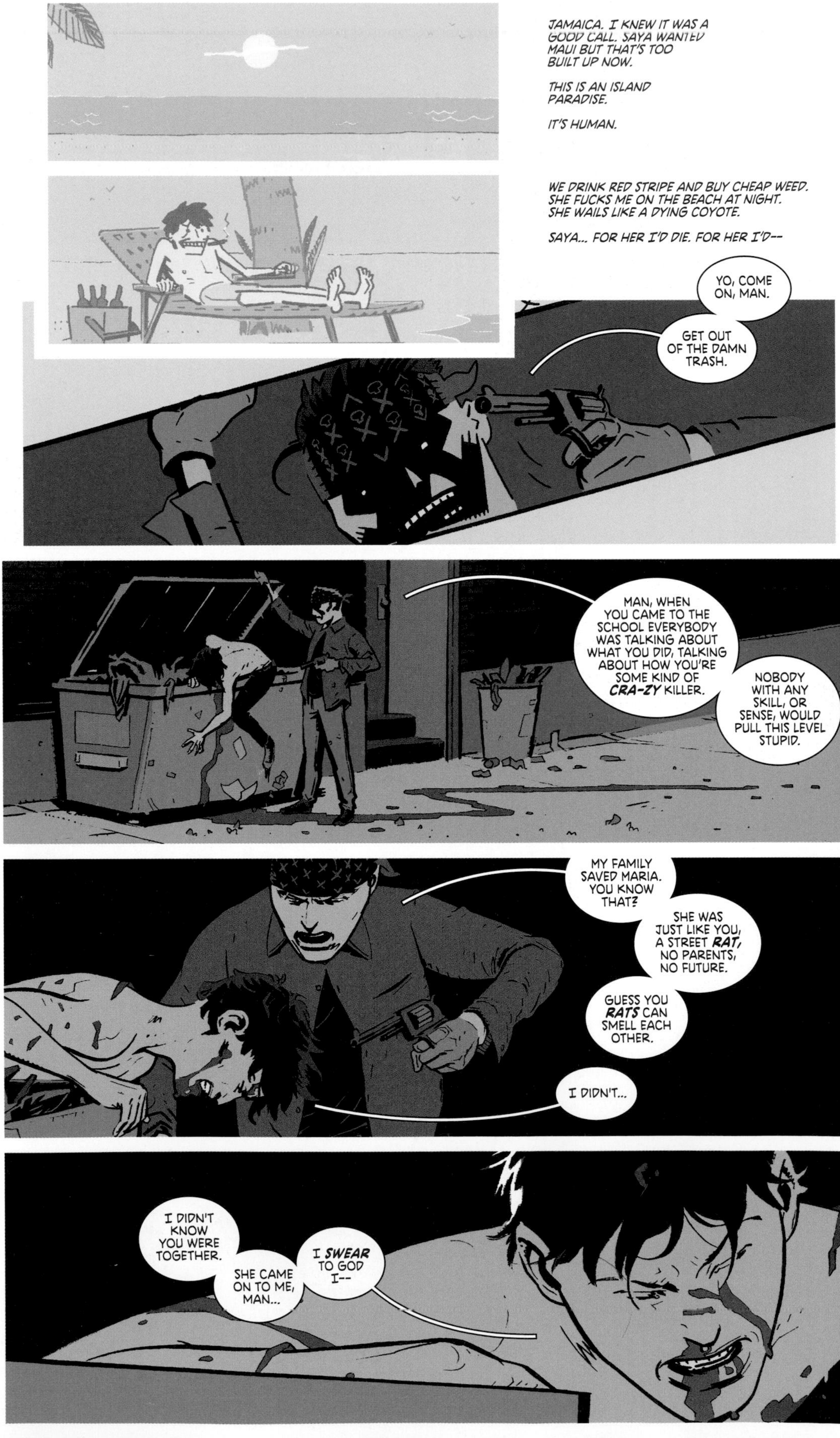
JAMAICA. I KNEW IT WAS A GOOD CALL. SAYA WANTED MAUI BUT THAT'S TOO BUILT UP NOW.
THIS IS AN ISLAND PARADISE.
IT'S HUMAN.
WE DRINK RED STRIPE AND BUY CHEAP WEED. SHE FUCKS ME ON THE BEACH AT NIGHT. SHE WAILS LIKE A DYING COYOTE.
SAYA... FOR HER I'D DIE. FOR HER I'D--
YO, COME ON, MAN.
GET OUT OF THE DAMN TRASH.
MAN, WHEN YOU CAME TO THE SCHOOL EVERYBODY WAS TALKING ABOUT WHAT YOU DID, TALKING ABOUT HOW YOU'RE SOME KIND OF CRA-ZY KILLER.
NOBODY WITH ANY SKILL, OR SENSE, WOULD PULL THIS LEVEL STUPID.
MY FAMILY SAVED MARIA. YOU KNOW THAT?
SHE WAS JUST LIKE YOU, A STREET RAT, NO PARENTS, NO FUTURE.
GUESS YOU RATS CAN SMELL EACH OTHER.
I DIDN'T...
I DIDN'T KNOW YOU WERE TOGETHER.
SHE CAME ON TO ME, MAN...
I SWEAR TO GOD I--

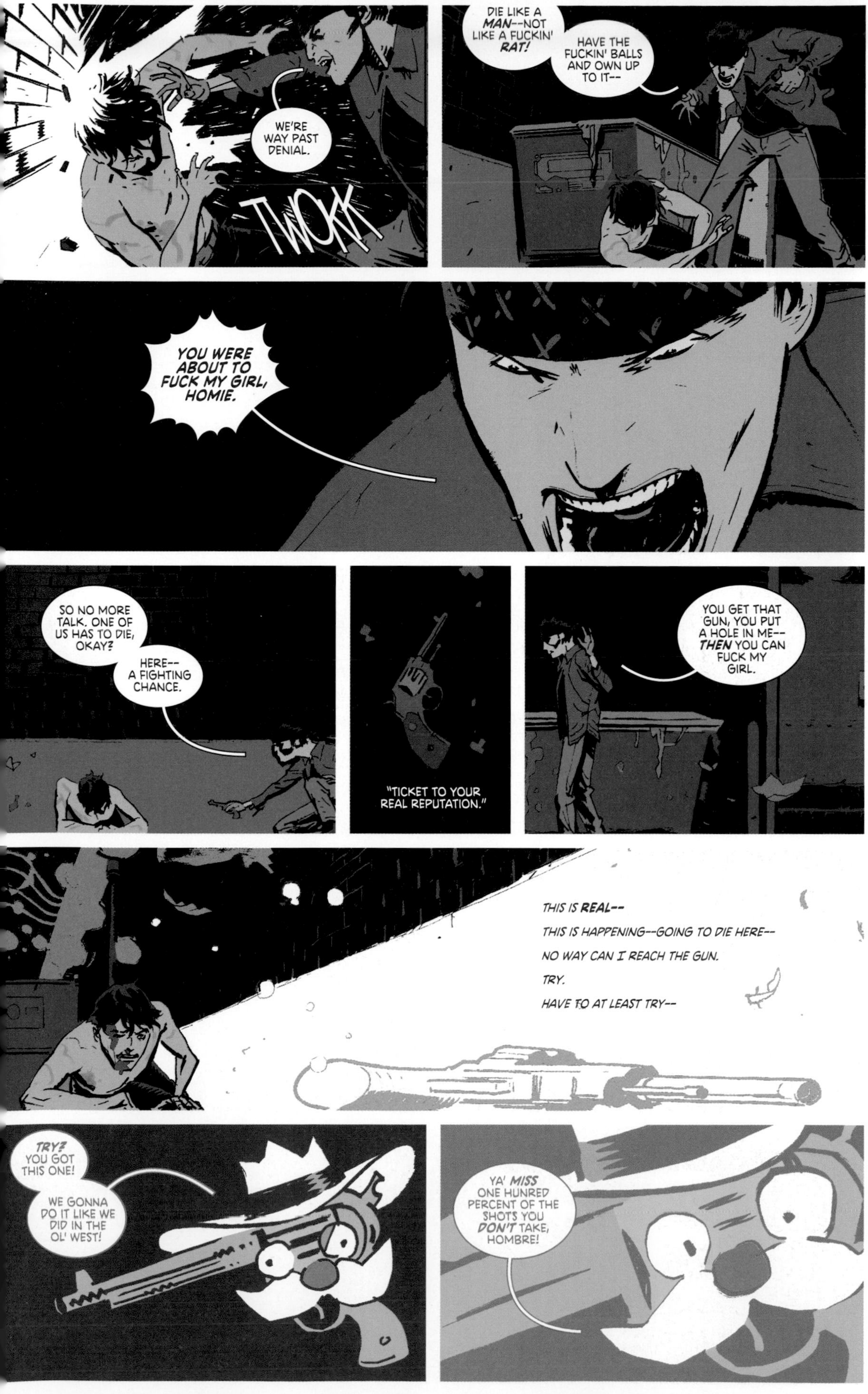

WE'RE WAY PAST DENIAL.
TWOKK
DIE LIKE A MAN--NOT LIKE A FUCKIN' RAT!
HAVE THE FUCKIN' BALLS AND OWN UP TO IT--
YOU WERE ABOUT TO FUCK MY GIRL, HOMIE.
SO NO MORE TALK. ONE OF US HAS TO DIE, OKAY?
HERE-- A FIGHTING CHANCE.
"TICKET TO YOUR REAL REPUTATION."
YOU GET THAT GUN, YOU PUT A HOLE IN ME-- THEN YOU CAN FUCK MY GIRL.
THIS IS REAL--
THIS IS HAPPENING--GOING TO DIE HERE--
NO WAY CAN I REACH THE GUN.
TRY.
HAVE TO AT LEAST TRY--
TRY? YOU GOT THIS ONE!
WE GONNA DO IT LIKE WE DID IN THE OL' WEST!
YA' MISS ONE HUNRED PERCENT OF THE SHOTS YOU DON'T TAKE, HOMBRE!

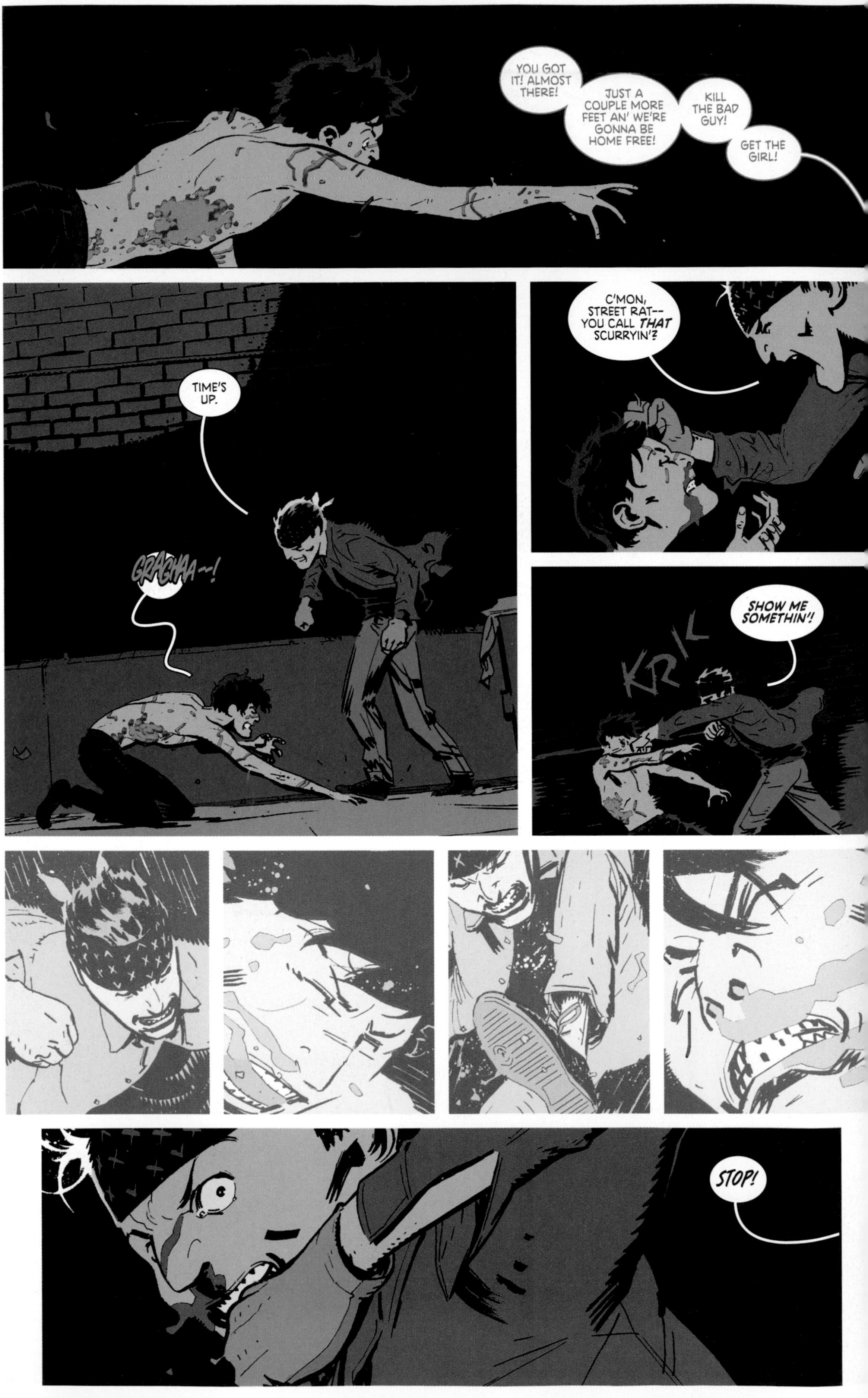
YOU GOT IT! ALMOST THERE!
JUST A COUPLE MORE FEET AN' WE'RE GONNA BE HOME FREE!
KILL THE BAD GUY!
GET THE GIRL!
TIME'S UP.
GRAGHAA--!
C'MON, STREET RAT-- YOU CALL *THAT* SCURRYIN'?
KRIK
SHOW ME SOMETHIN'!
STOP!

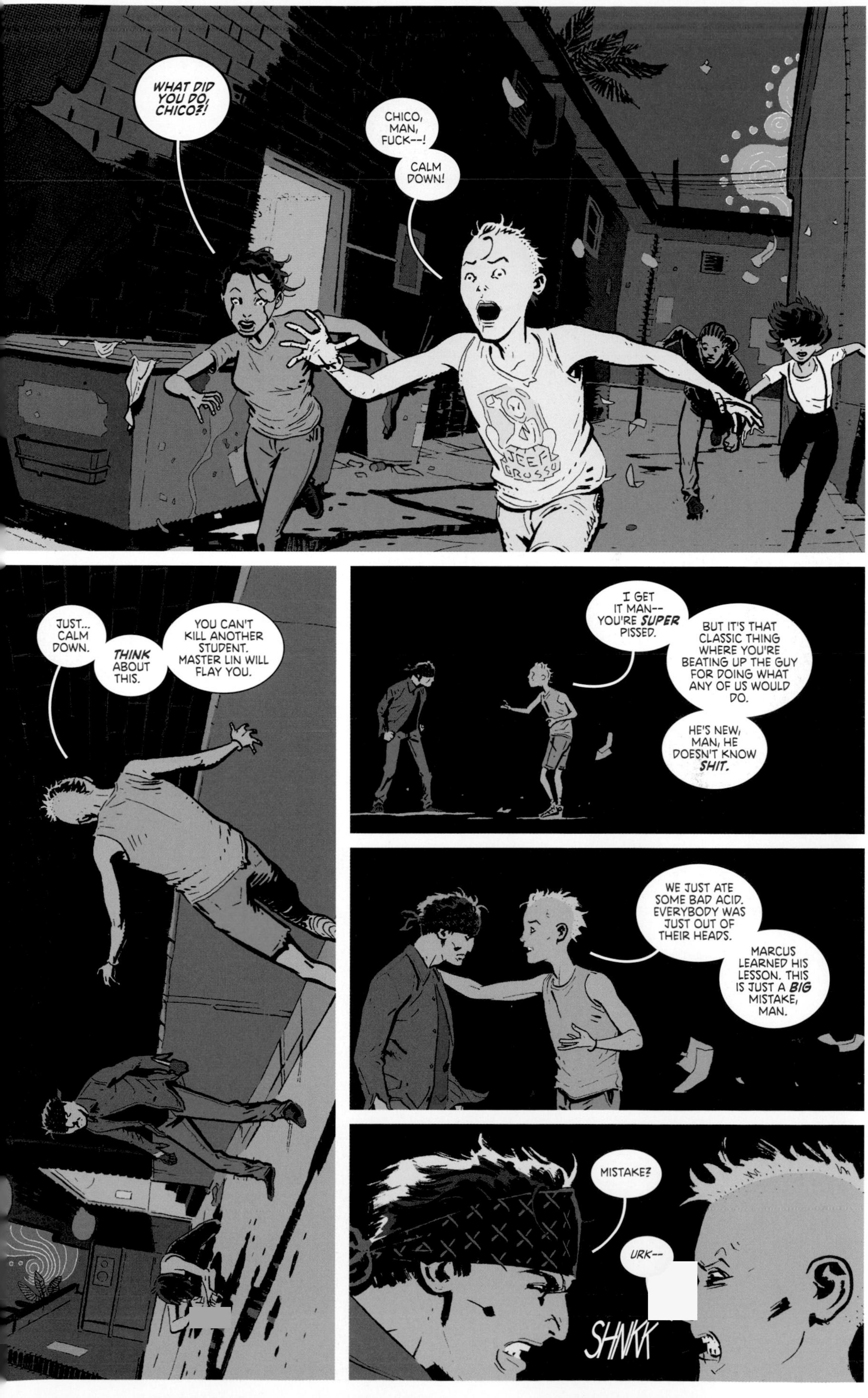
WHAT DID YOU DO, CHICO?!
CHICO, MAN, FUCK--!
CALM DOWN!
JUST... CALM DOWN.
THINK ABOUT THIS.
YOU CAN'T KILL ANOTHER STUDENT. MASTER LIN WILL FLAY YOU.
I GET IT MAN-- YOU'RE SUPER PISSED.
BUT IT'S THAT CLASSIC THING WHERE YOU'RE BEATING UP THE GUY FOR DOING WHAT ANY OF US WOULD DO.
HE'S NEW, MAN, HE DOESN'T KNOW SHIT.
WE JUST ATE SOME BAD ACID. EVERYBODY WAS JUST OUT OF THEIR HEADS.
MARCUS LEARNED HIS LESSON. THIS IS JUST A BIG MISTAKE, MAN.
MISTAKE?
URK--
SHNKK

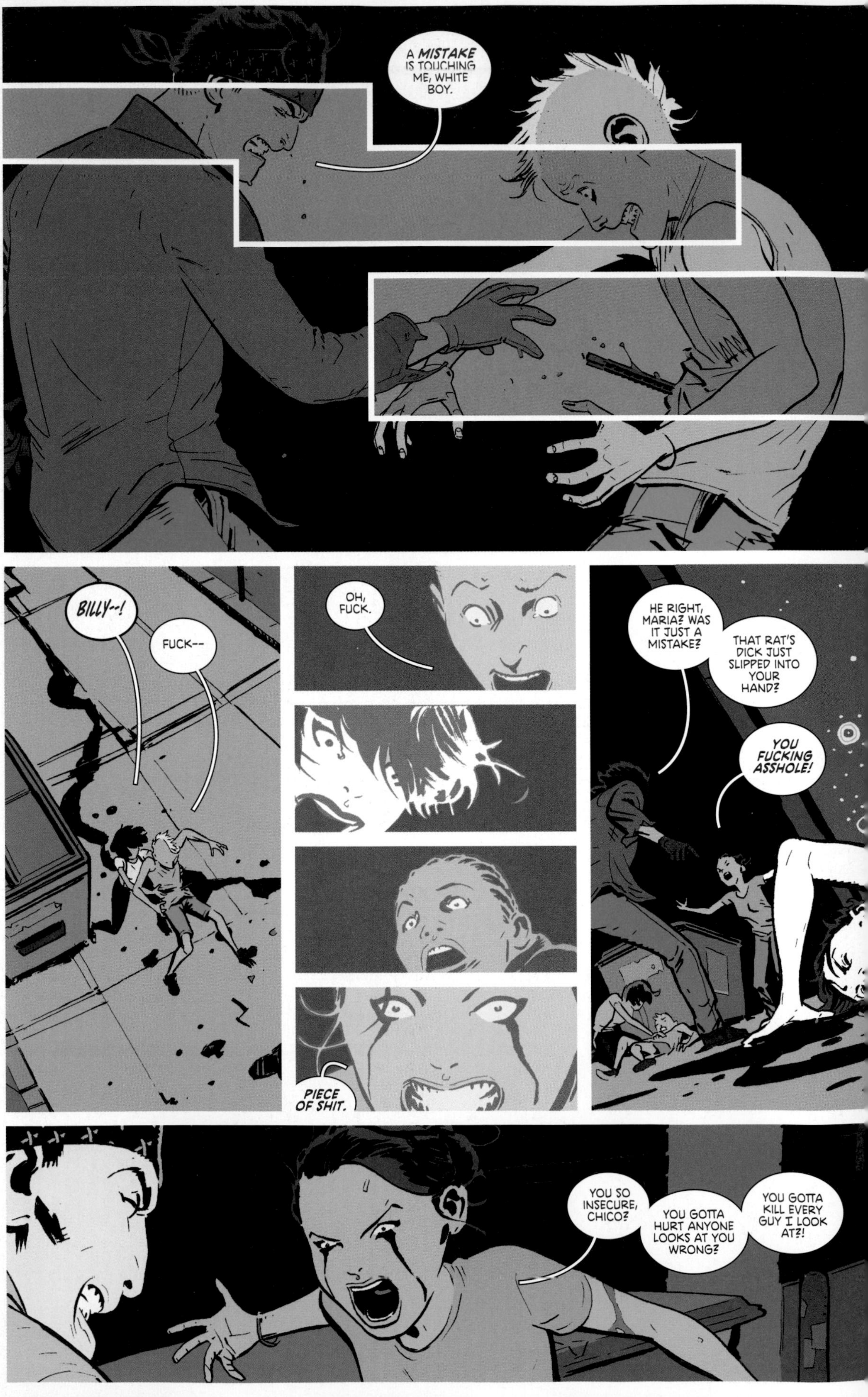
A MISTAKE IS TOUCHING ME, WHITE BOY.
BILLY--!
FUCK--
OH, FUCK.
PIECE OF SHIT.
HE RIGHT, MARIA? WAS IT JUST A MISTAKE?
THAT RAT'S DICK JUST SLIPPED INTO YOUR HAND?
YOU FUCKING ASSHOLE!
YOU SO INSECURE, CHICO?
YOU GOTTA HURT ANYONE LOOKS AT YOU WRONG?
YOU GOTTA KILL EVERY GUY I LOOK AT?!

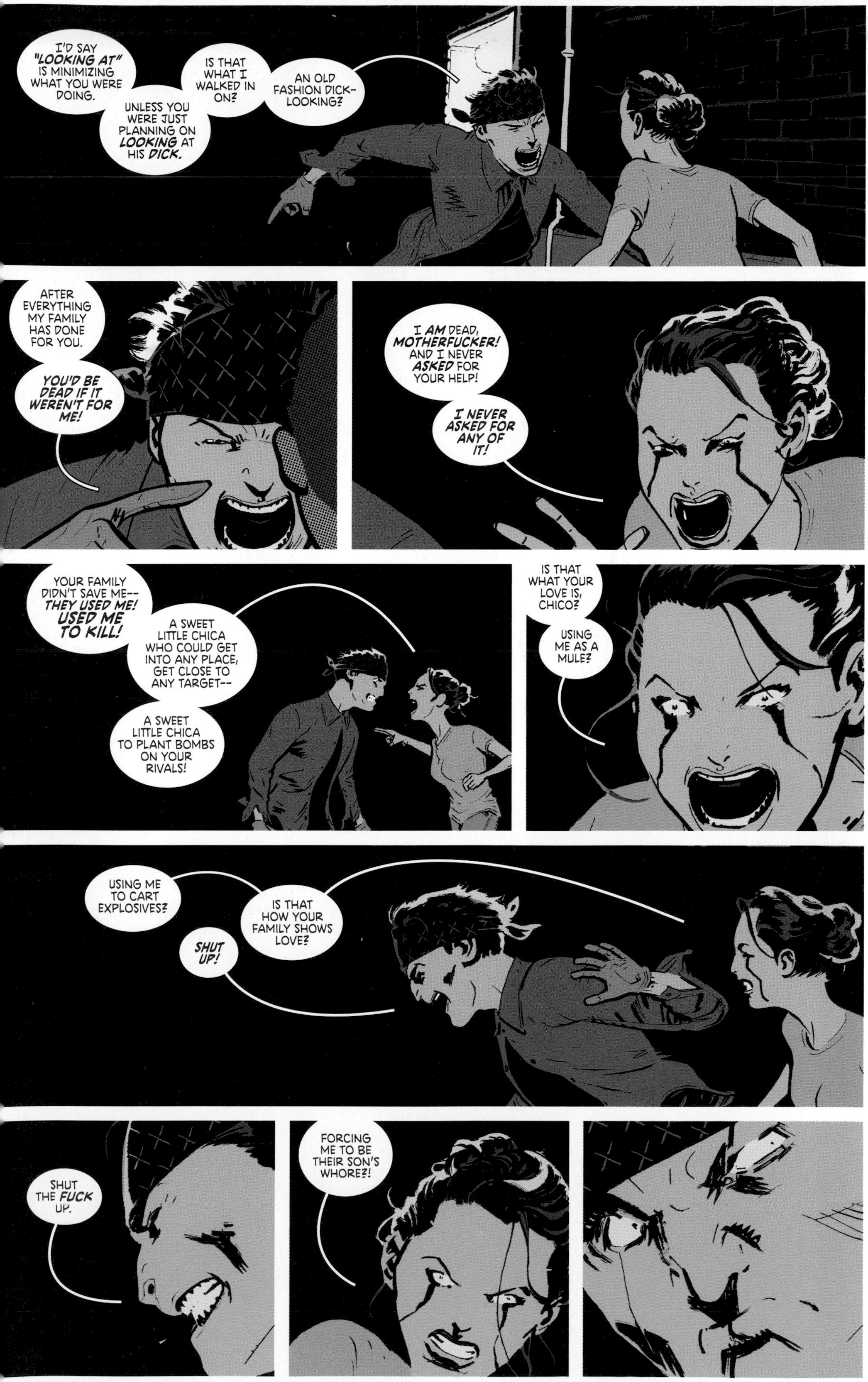
I'D SAY "*LOOKING AT*" IS MINIMIZING WHAT YOU WERE DOING.
UNLESS YOU WERE JUST PLANNING ON *LOOKING* AT HIS *DICK.*
IS THAT WHAT I WALKED IN ON?
AN OLD FASHION DICK-LOOKING?
AFTER EVERYTHING MY FAMILY HAS DONE FOR YOU.
YOU'D BE DEAD IF IT WEREN'T FOR ME!
I *AM* DEAD, *MOTHERFUCKER!* AND I NEVER *ASKED* FOR YOUR HELP!
I NEVER ASKED FOR ANY OF IT!
YOUR FAMILY DIDN'T SAVE ME-- *THEY USED ME! USED ME TO KILL!*
A SWEET LITTLE CHICA WHO COULD GET INTO ANY PLACE, GET CLOSE TO ANY TARGET--
A SWEET LITTLE CHICA TO PLANT BOMBS ON YOUR RIVALS!
IS THAT WHAT YOUR LOVE IS, CHICO?
USING ME AS A MULE?
USING ME TO CART EXPLOSIVES?
IS THAT HOW YOUR FAMILY SHOWS LOVE?
SHUT UP!
SHUT THE *FUCK* UP.
FORCING ME TO BE THEIR SON'S WHORE?!

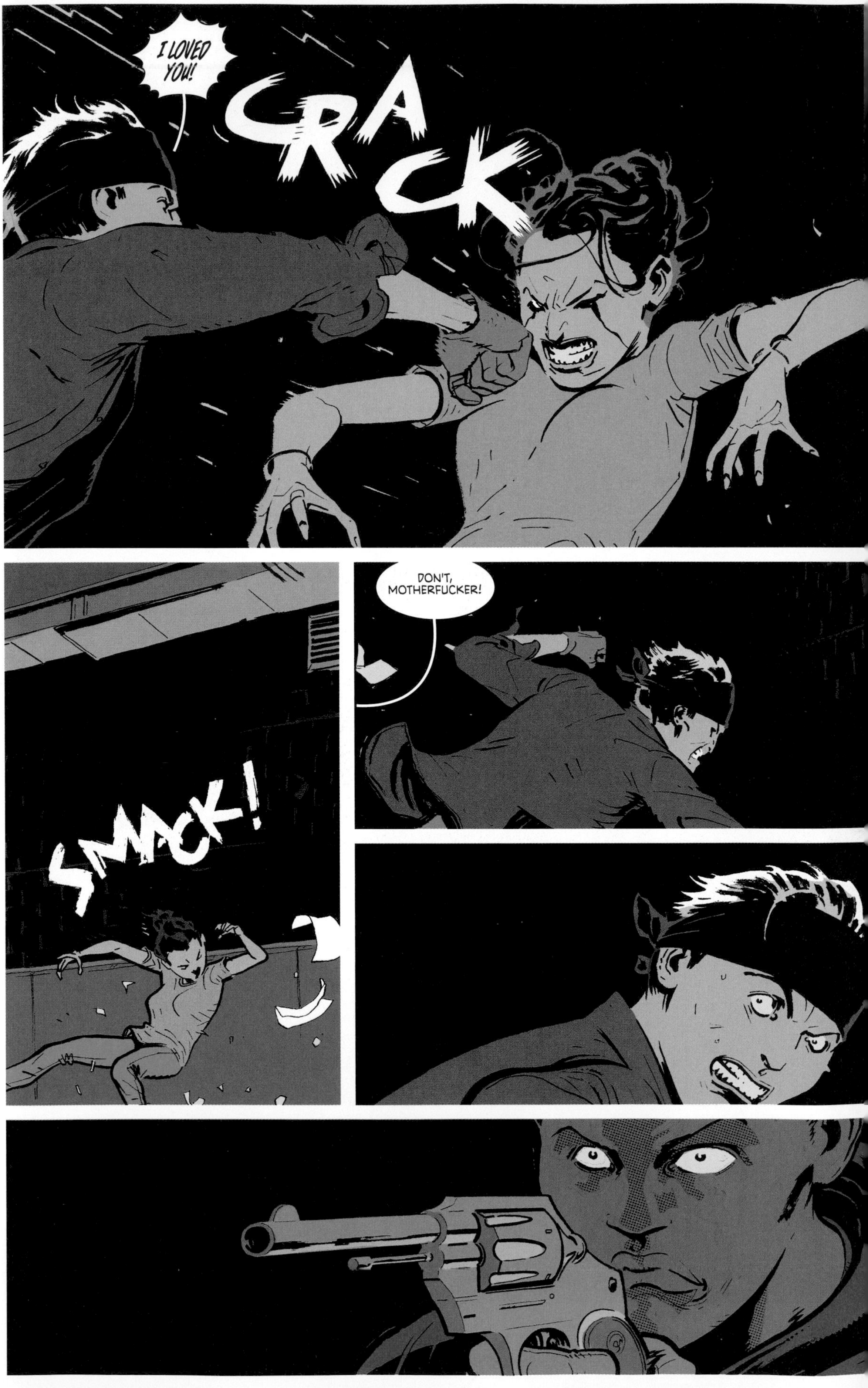
I LOVED YOU!
CRACK
SMACK!
DON'T, MOTHERFUCKER!

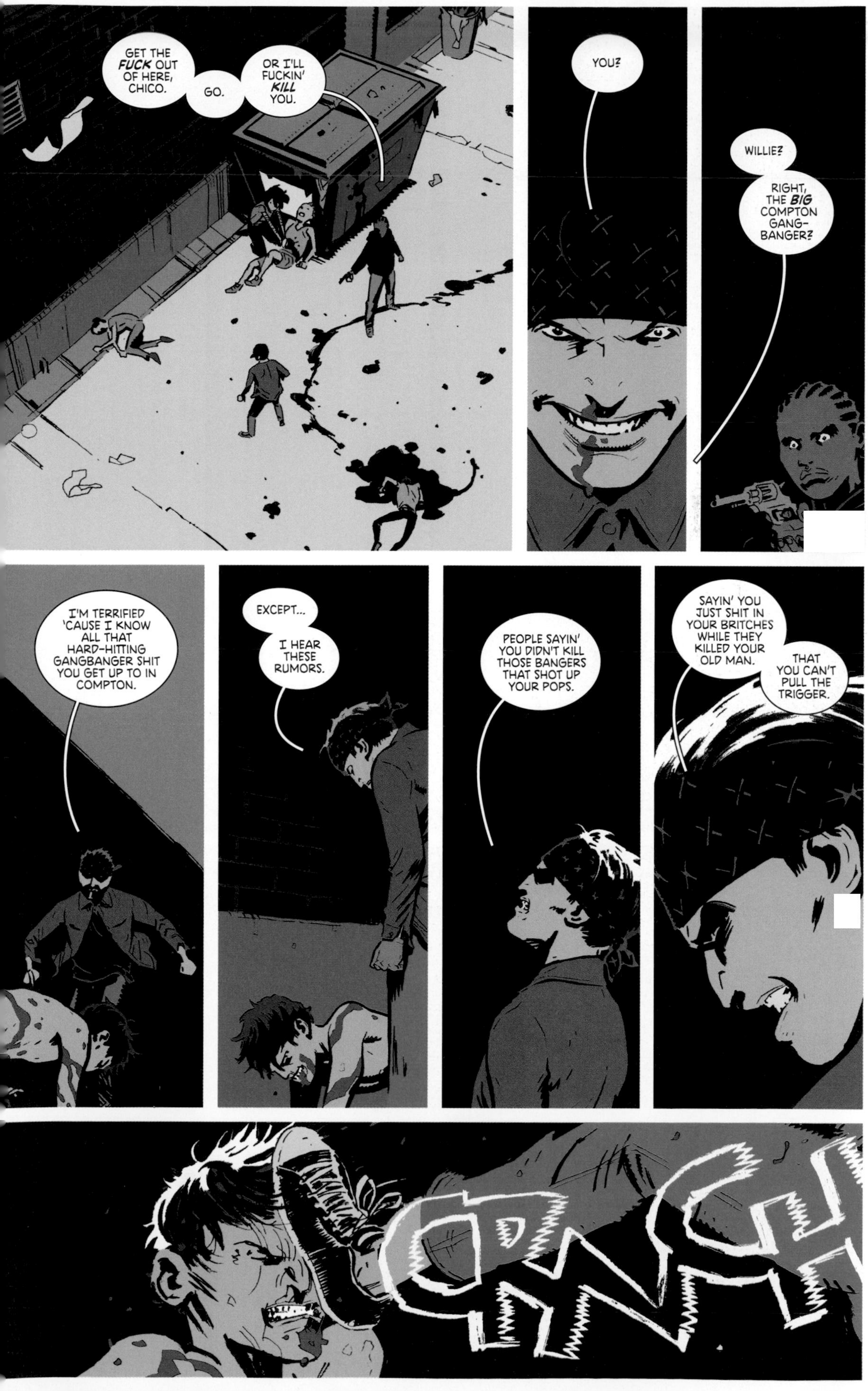
GET THE FUCK OUT OF HERE, CHICO.
GO.
OR I'LL FUCKIN' KILL YOU.
YOU?
WILLIE?
RIGHT, THE BIG COMPTON GANG-BANGER?
I'M TERRIFIED 'CAUSE I KNOW ALL THAT HARD-HITTING GANGBANGER SHIT YOU GET UP TO IN COMPTON.
EXCEPT...
I HEAR THESE RUMORS.
PEOPLE SAYIN' YOU DIDN'T KILL THOSE BANGERS THAT SHOT UP YOUR POPS.
SAYIN' YOU JUST SHIT IN YOUR BRITCHES WHILE THEY KILLED YOUR OLD MAN.
THAT YOU CAN'T PULL THE TRIGGER.

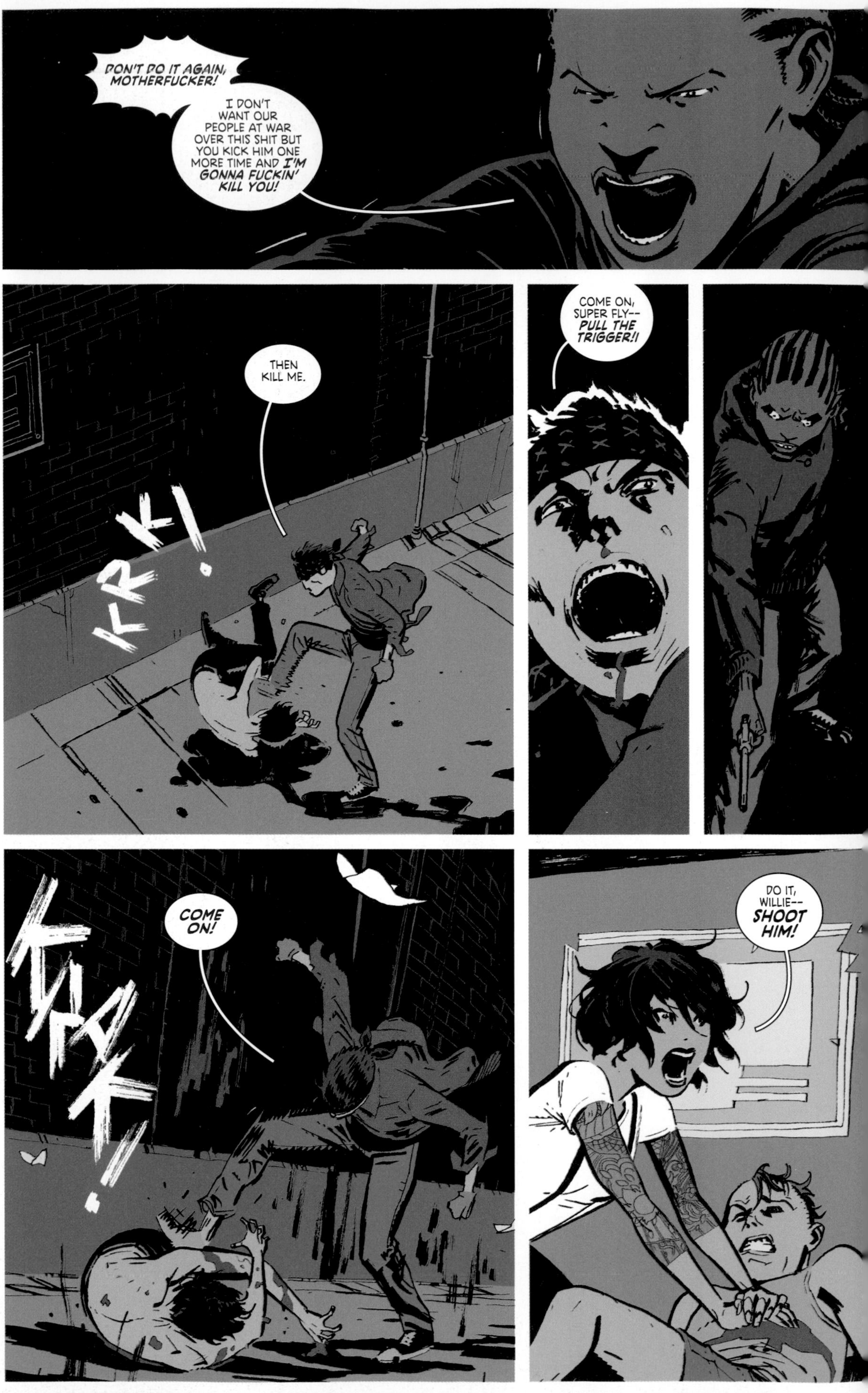
DON'T DO IT AGAIN, MOTHERFUCKER!
I DON'T WANT OUR PEOPLE AT WAR OVER THIS SHIT BUT YOU KICK HIM ONE MORE TIME AND I'M GONNA FUCKIN' KILL YOU!
THEN KILL ME.
KRRK!
COME ON, SUPER FLY-- PULL THE TRIGGER!!
KUDAK!
COME ON!
DO IT, WILLIE-- SHOOT HIM!

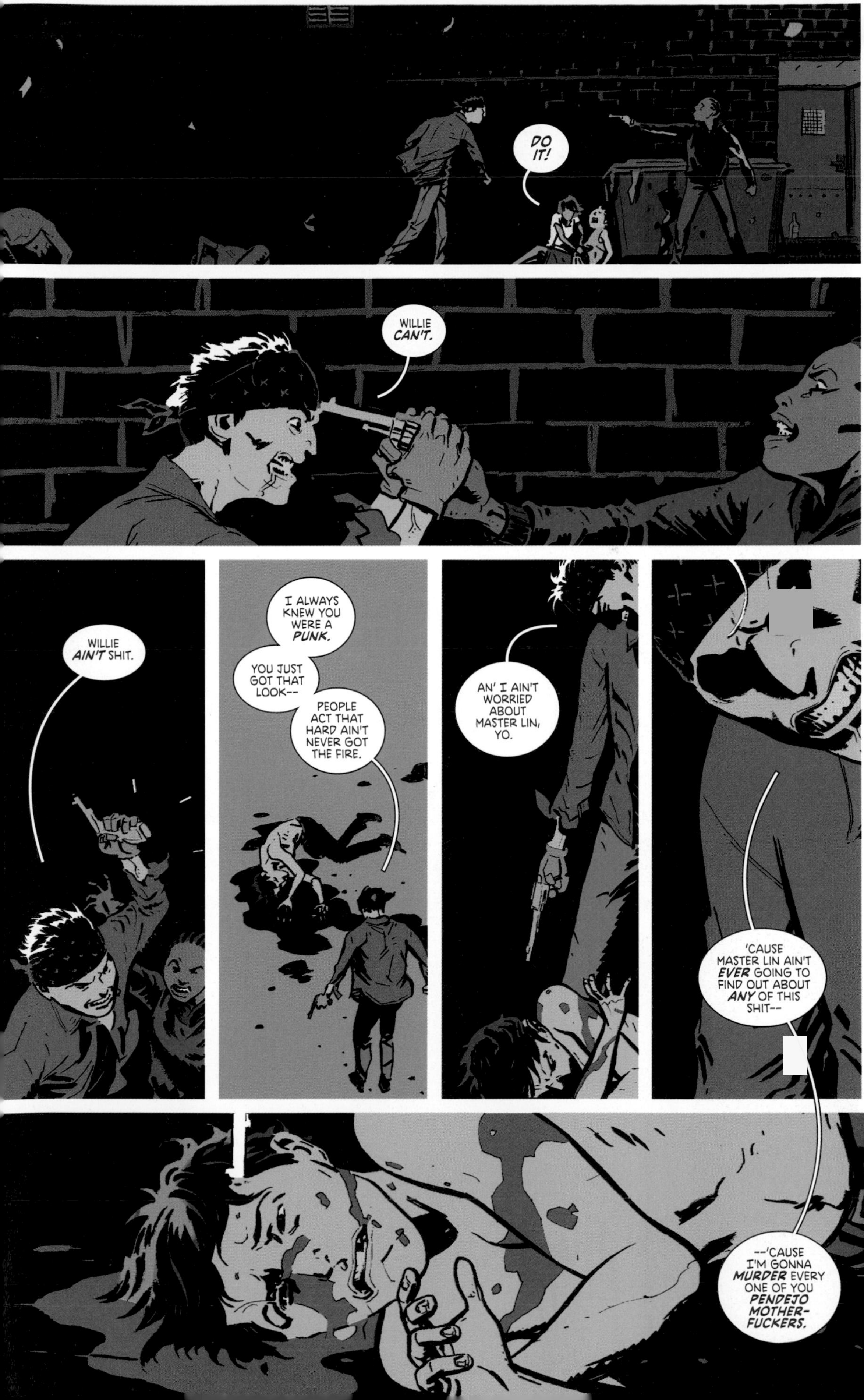
DO IT!
WILLIE CAN'T.
WILLIE AIN'T SHIT.
I ALWAYS KNEW YOU WERE A PUNK.
YOU JUST GOT THAT LOOK--
PEOPLE ACT THAT HARD AIN'T NEVER GOT THE FIRE.
AN' I AIN'T WORRIED ABOUT MASTER LIN, YO.
'CAUSE MASTER LIN AIN'T EVER GOING TO FIND OUT ABOUT ANY OF THIS SHIT--
--'CAUSE I'M GONNA MURDER EVERY ONE OF YOU PENDEJO MOTHER-FUCKERS.

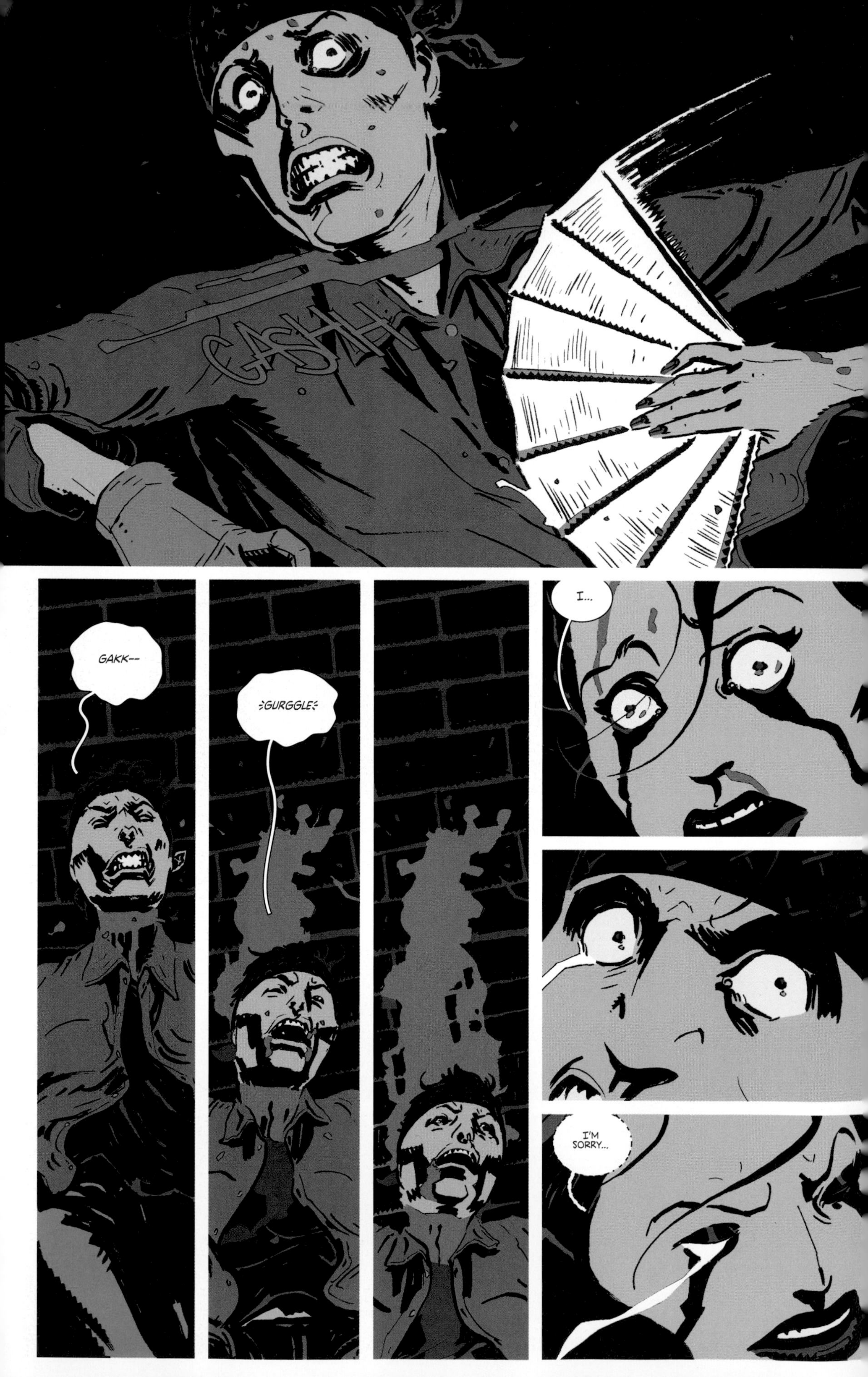
GAKK--
GURGGLE
I...
I'M SORRY...

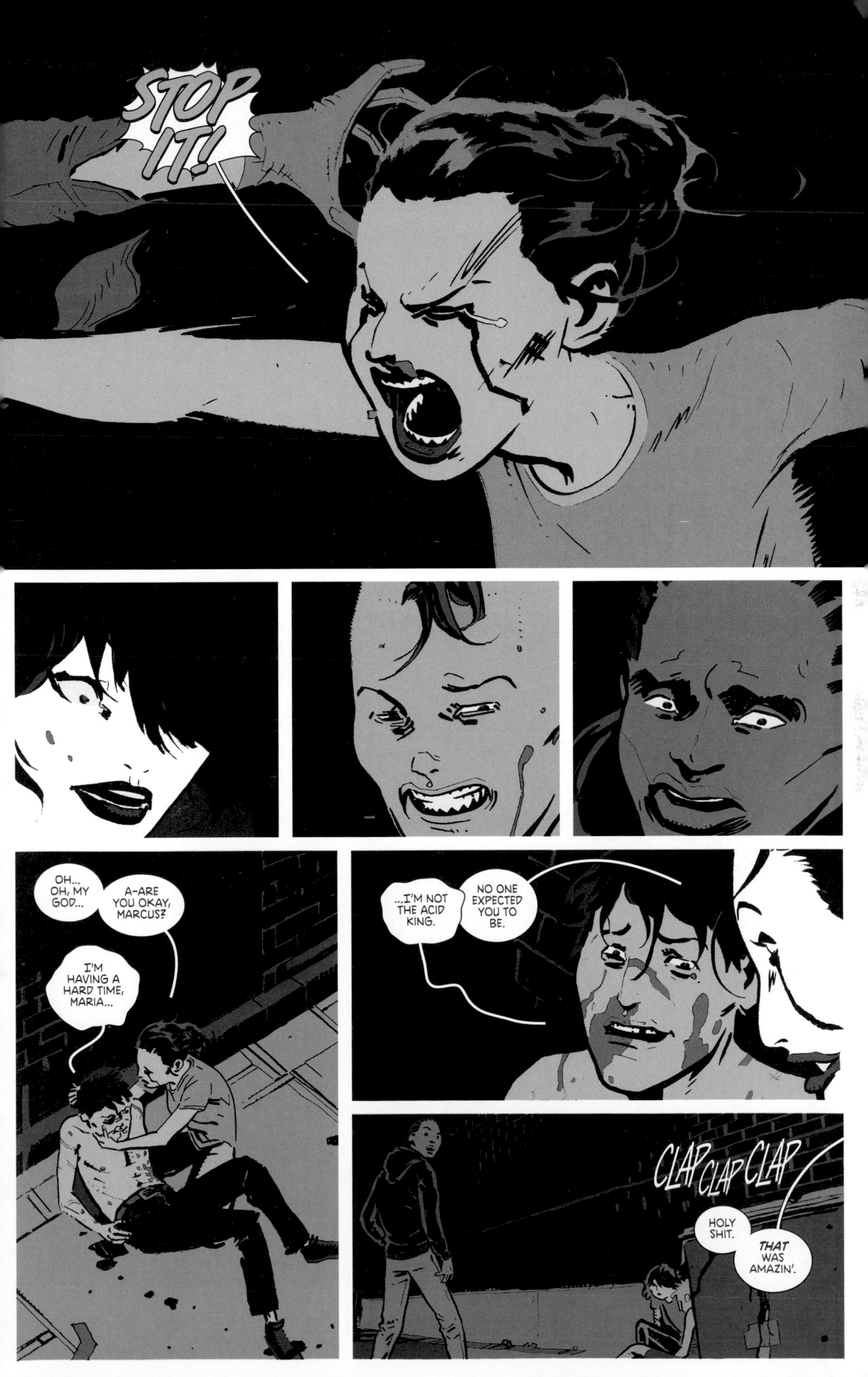
STOP IT!
OH... OH, MY GOD...
A-ARE YOU OKAY, MARCUS?
I'M HAVING A HARD TIME, MARIA...
...I'M NOT THE ACID KING.
NO ONE EXPECTED YOU TO BE.
CLAP CLAP CLAP
HOLY SHIT.
THAT WAS AMAZIN'.

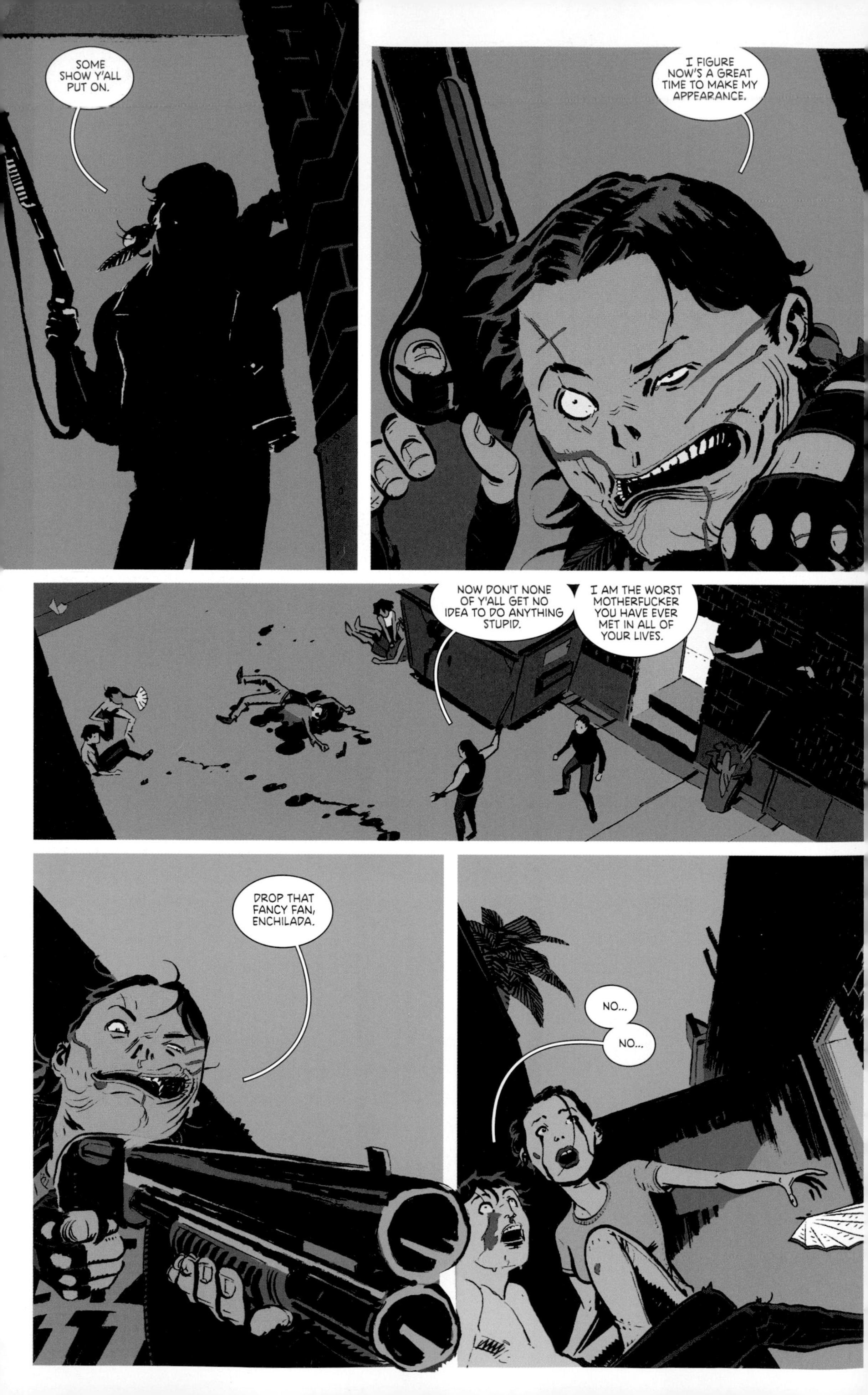
SOME SHOW Y'ALL PUT ON.
I FIGURE NOW'S A GREAT TIME TO MAKE MY APPEARANCE.
NOW DON'T NONE OF Y'ALL GET NO IDEA TO DO ANYTHING STUPID.
I AM THE WORST MOTHERFUCKER YOU HAVE EVER MET IN ALL OF YOUR LIVES.
DROP THAT FANCY FAN, ENCHILADA.
NO...
NO...

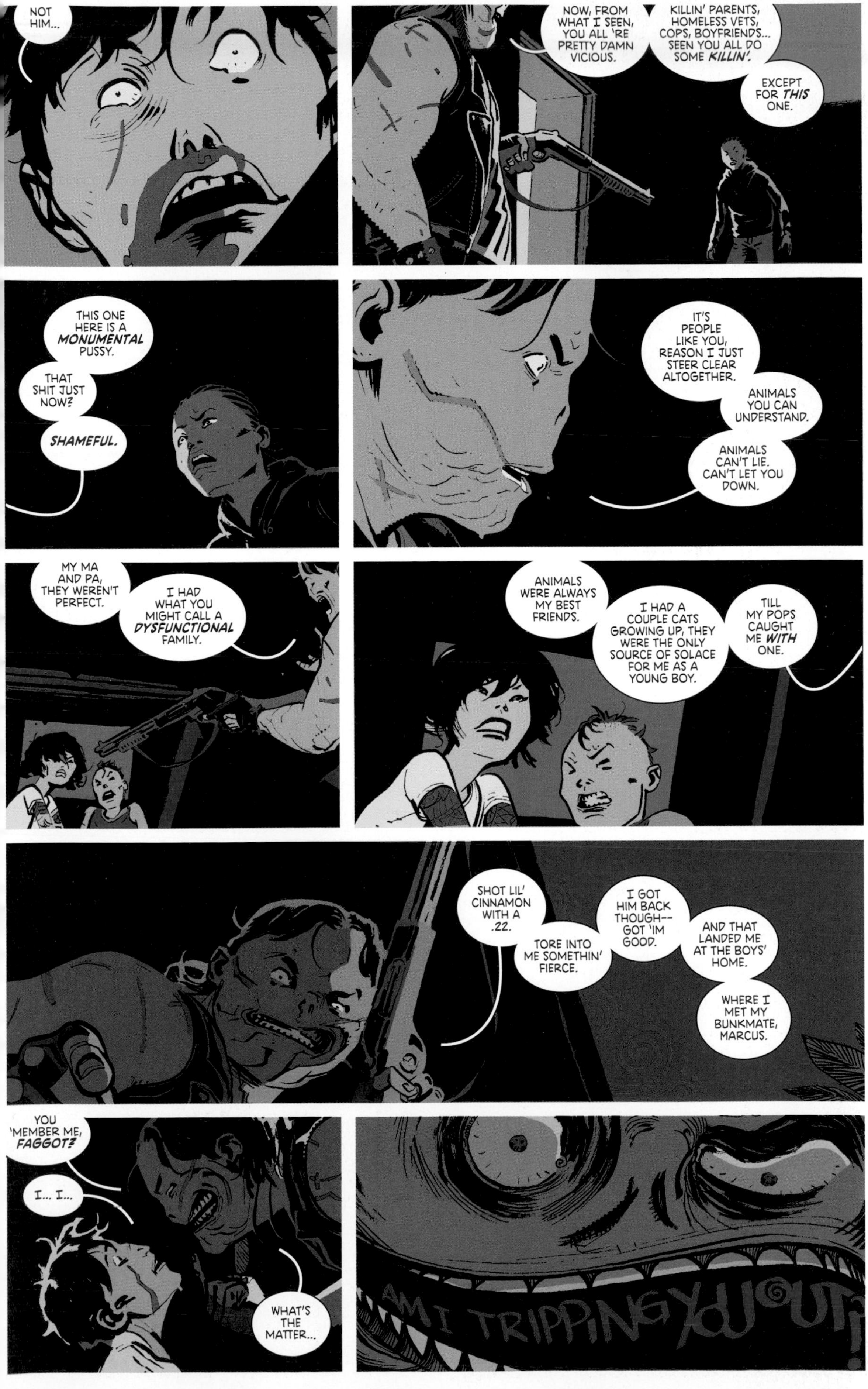
NOT HIM...
NOW, FROM WHAT I SEEN, YOU ALL 'RE PRETTY DAMN VICIOUS.
KILLIN' PARENTS, HOMELESS VETS, COPS, BOYFRIENDS... SEEN YOU ALL DO SOME KILLIN'.
EXCEPT FOR THIS ONE.
THIS ONE HERE IS A MONUMENTAL PUSSY.
THAT SHIT JUST NOW?
SHAMEFUL.
IT'S PEOPLE LIKE YOU, REASON I JUST STEER CLEAR ALTOGETHER.
ANIMALS YOU CAN UNDERSTAND.
ANIMALS CAN'T LIE. CAN'T LET YOU DOWN.
MY MA AND PA, THEY WEREN'T PERFECT.
I HAD WHAT YOU MIGHT CALL A DYSFUNCTIONAL FAMILY.
ANIMALS WERE ALWAYS MY BEST FRIENDS.
I HAD A COUPLE CATS GROWING UP, THEY WERE THE ONLY SOURCE OF SOLACE FOR ME AS A YOUNG BOY.
TILL MY POPS CAUGHT ME WITH ONE.
SHOT LIL' CINNAMON WITH A .22.
TORE INTO ME SOMETHIN' FIERCE.
I GOT HIM BACK THOUGH-- GOT 'IM GOOD.
AND THAT LANDED ME AT THE BOYS' HOME.
WHERE I MET MY BUNKMATE, MARCUS.
YOU 'MEMBER ME, FAGGOT?
I... I...
WHAT'S THE MATTER...
AM I TRIPPING YOU OUT

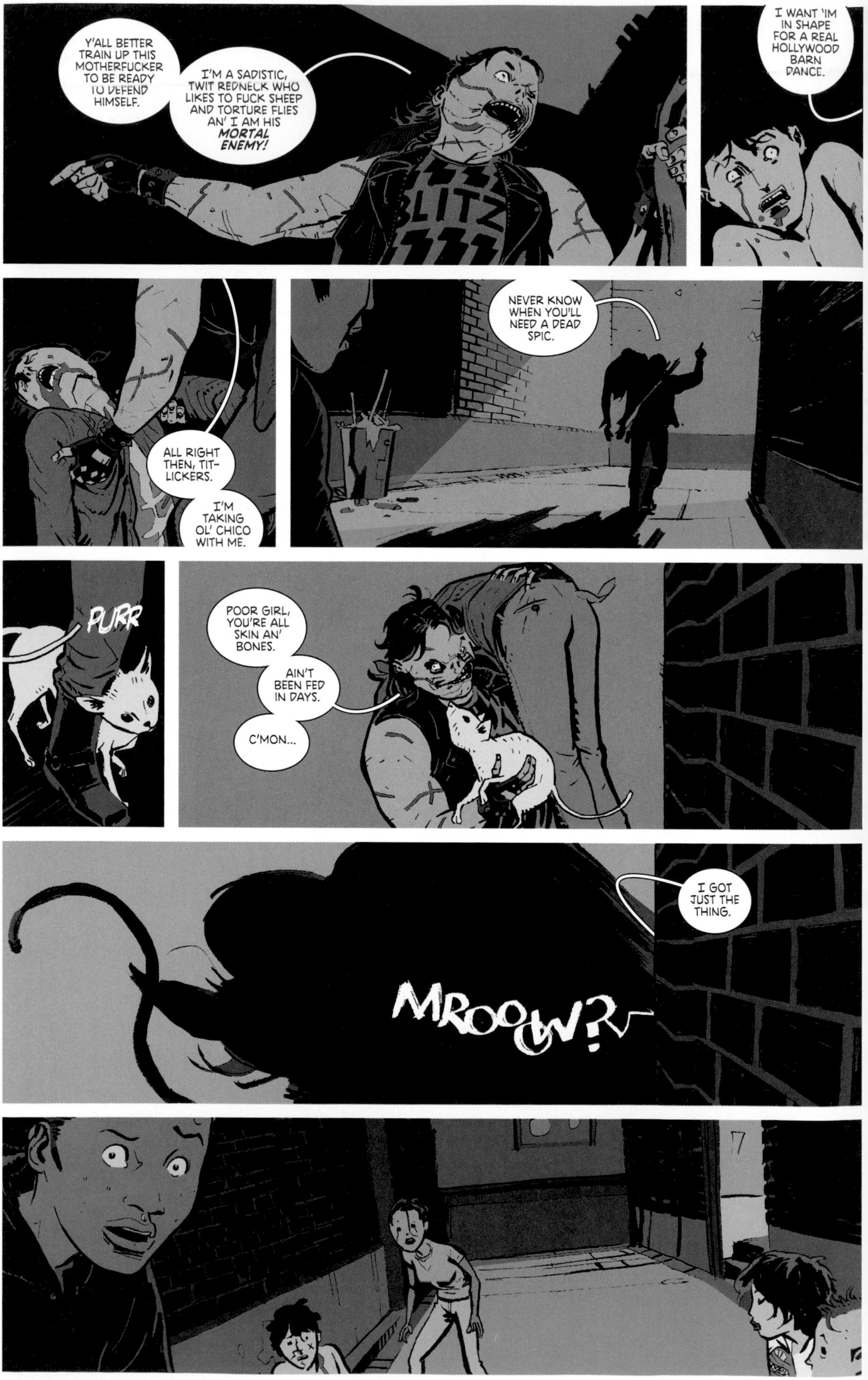
Y'ALL BETTER TRAIN UP THIS MOTHERFUCKER TO BE READY TO DEFEND HIMSELF.
I'M A SADISTIC, TWIT REDNECK WHO LIKES TO FUCK SHEEP AND TORTURE FLIES AN' I AM HIS MORTAL ENEMY!
BLITZ
I WANT 'IM IN SHAPE FOR A REAL HOLLYWOOD BARN DANCE.
ALL RIGHT THEN, TIT-LICKERS.
I'M TAKING OL' CHICO WITH ME.
NEVER KNOW WHEN YOU'LL NEED A DEAD SPIC.
PURR
POOR GIRL, YOU'RE ALL SKIN AN' BONES.
AIN'T BEEN FED IN DAYS.
C'MON...
I GOT JUST THE THING.
MROOOW?

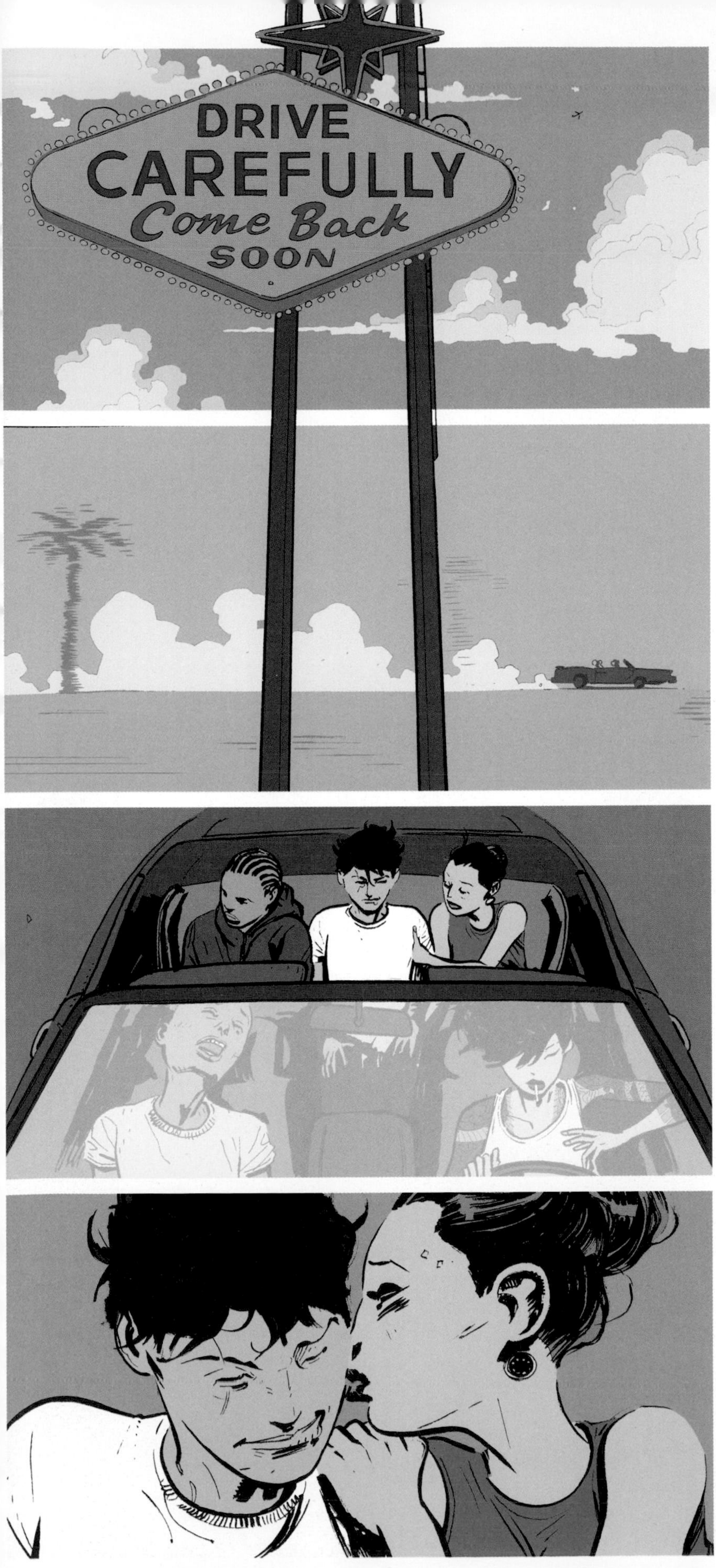
DRIVE
CAREFULLY
Come Back
SOON

WE BURIED BILLY'S DAD DEEP IN THE MOHAVE DESERT. NO ONE SAID A WORD.

WE GOT STITCHED UP AT ONE OF THE SECRET BACK DOOR MEDICAL CLINICS LISTED IN OUR GUILD HANDBOOK. THE ACID HAD WORN OFF, BUT THE ADRENALINE FRIED OUR NERVES. THE DOC GAVE US ENOUGH VALIUM TO KEEP MOVING, TO FIGHT THE PARALYSIS.

AT SOME POINT ON THE WAY I DOZED OFF FOR THE FIRST TIME IN DAYS. WOKE UP BACK ON THE STREETS, FALLING INTO THAT DARK HOLE.

UNTIL EVENTUALLY I JUST ACCEPTED IT.

ACCEPTED MY DESCENT. ACCEPTED EACH DAY WOULD BE WORSE THAN THE ONE BEFORE IT.

A HORRIBLE TATTOO HAD SPREAD ALL OVER MY ARM UP TO MY FACE. THE LADY WHO GAVE IT TO ME WAS THERE, IN THE SHADOWS, WHERE I USED TO LIVE. SHE TOOK MY HAND AND LED ME TO THE BAY, BY THE WATER.

SHE KISSED ME AND WHISPERED, "LIFE TATTOOS US WITH DAMAGE AS A REMINDER. IT'S INKED ONTO YOUR FACE AND BODY NOW."

"IT WON'T BE VISIBLE WHEN YOU AWAKEN, BUT PEOPLE WHO KNOW WHAT TO LOOK FOR WILL SEE IT, OTHER VICTIMS OF THE SAME NEEDLE."

"IT TAKES TIME TO SEE THEM. IT TAKES TIME TO SEE ANYONE'S REAL DAMAGE."

"BUT YOUR PEOPLE WILL SEE THE COLORS--LIKE A FLAG--AND THEY WILL CALL YOU HOME TO THEM."

I WOKE UP WITH A PROFOUND AND INDESCRIBABLE FEELING.

A SPECIFIC SENSATION I HAVEN'T HAD SINCE I WAS A KID, SINCE MY PARENTS WERE ALIVE.

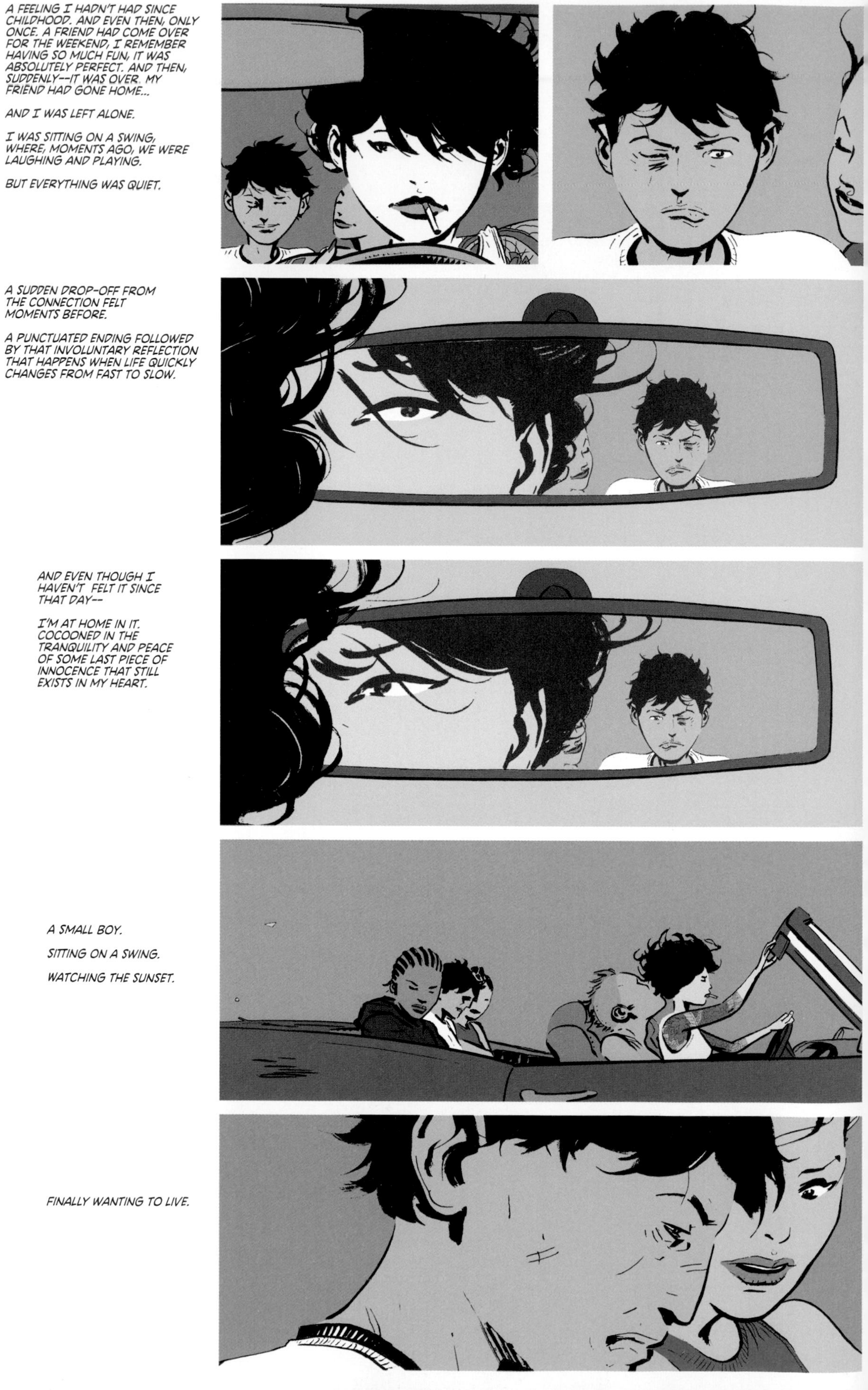
A FEELING I HADN'T HAD SINCE CHILDHOOD. AND EVEN THEN, ONLY ONCE. A FRIEND HAD COME OVER FOR THE WEEKEND, I REMEMBER HAVING SO MUCH FUN, IT WAS ABSOLUTELY PERFECT. AND THEN, SUDDENLY--IT WAS OVER. MY FRIEND HAD GONE HOME...
AND I WAS LEFT ALONE.
I WAS SITTING ON A SWING, WHERE, MOMENTS AGO, WE WERE LAUGHING AND PLAYING.
BUT EVERYTHING WAS QUIET.
A SUDDEN DROP-OFF FROM THE CONNECTION FELT MOMENTS BEFORE.
A PUNCTUATED ENDING FOLLOWED BY THAT INVOLUNTARY REFLECTION THAT HAPPENS WHEN LIFE QUICKLY CHANGES FROM FAST TO SLOW.
AND EVEN THOUGH I HAVEN'T FELT IT SINCE THAT DAY--
I'M AT HOME IN IT. COCOONED IN THE TRANQUILITY AND PEACE OF SOME LAST PIECE OF INNOCENCE THAT STILL EXISTS IN MY HEART.
A SMALL BOY.
SITTING ON A SWING.
WATCHING THE SUNSET.
FINALLY WANTING TO LIVE.

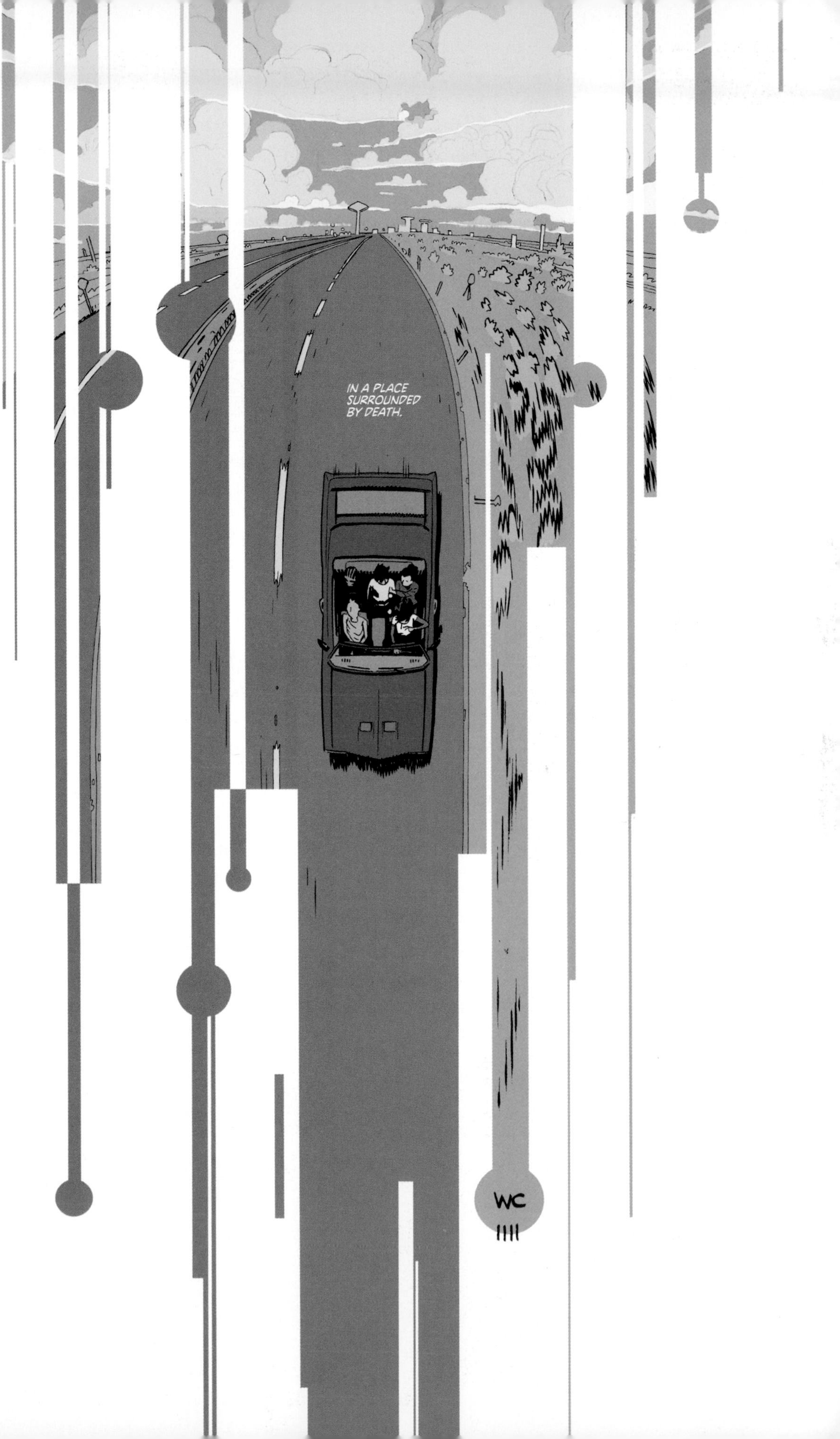
IN A PLACE SURROUNDED BY DEATH.
WC

A F T E R W ● R D

rowing up, my family moved about every two or three years to a new neighborhood, meaning I had to start over and make new friends every couple of years. Always the new kid, always the kid nobody knew anything about. It was difficult. Kids are vicious.

By the time I was in 8th grade, I had been living in the same area for a couple of years and had made a good group of friends. I was living in downtown Phoenix and the Los Angeles punk/skate scene had sort of blended into the subculture there. So we spent most of our time skateboarding, listening to punk rock and, in my case, reading comic books and drawing.

That was 1987, the year that cooked me into the person I am today. So, it's probably no coincidence that it's also the year that Marcus entered the strange and frightening Kings Dominion School for the Deadly Arts.

One week before high school, my family moved again, this time to a small town an hour south of Phoenix, right in the middle of the desert, where, as a punker kid, I did not exactly fit in. So the first couple of years of high school for me were spent being endlessly fucked with by rednecks, jocks, and hillbillies in a foreign place far from home. Basically until I turned 16 when I got my drivers license and left home.

High School was always a perfect magnification of my lifelong feeling that I don't belong anywhere. Over time, after I got back to Phoenix, I reconnected with a group of friends that felt like home. We were the kids out behind the gym, being disenfranchised, and smoking weed between class (remember when high schools had a smoking area?). We were the outcasts and freaks, the punkers, the goths, skaters, hip-hop kids, dropouts, gearheads, all the colors of the freak rainbow.

Phoenix was a violent place in the late 80s early 90s, and standing out in a city like that led to numerous beatings, stabbings and shootings amongst my friends. I've seen a man shot in the head, I had a friend shot in the back while trying to flee a gunfight, had a friend overdose on heroin before he shot himself in the head, another was stabbed, and I was personally jumped and brutally beaten by gangbangers twice.

Violence was just something you got used to being around.

So, I wanted to explore that time in my life and the impressions high school, coupled with that violence, left on me. I wanted to explore the idea of that meanness and that drama and that feeling of being ostracized and disconnected with some real-life danger, a magnification of what it was for me growing up.

Deadly Class is a pure collaboration, so there's also a lot of my co-creator Wes Craig and editor Sebastian Girner in there as well. We spent countless hours on the phone beating this thing in shape and cooking up new characters before Wes realized them in his own visual language while making them all entirely authentic to the era.

When you see Wes draw skate rats bombing the streets of San Francisco, they look like the skate rats you knew in the mid-80s. When you see a Goth girl or a Straightedge kid, or Stoners, or a Metal-head or a Rockabilly kid... they are authentic. And those pages, my lord, Wes is a superstar of art jive and disco dreams.

Lee Loughridge and I spent an entire night drinking scotch, talking over how he was going to approach the colors. It's really the fun of making creator-owned books, sitting around with a friend, working together to make something new.

Then we all worked with Rus Wooton who cooked up our very striking and distinct logo and lettering style and--presto. The comic you now hold in your hands.

This story takes place in a recognizable world. There's no magic. No spaceships. No one can fly or shoot eye beams. It's a coming of age story about broken kids expected to deal with a violent world. It's the 80s. No cell phones or email. And many of these stories are based on true events.

I've never tried anything quite like this before.

And I've never had so much fun making a comic.

Hard to believe 1987 was 27 years ago. It's a good thing for me I never grew up, or that might make me feel old.

Rick Remender

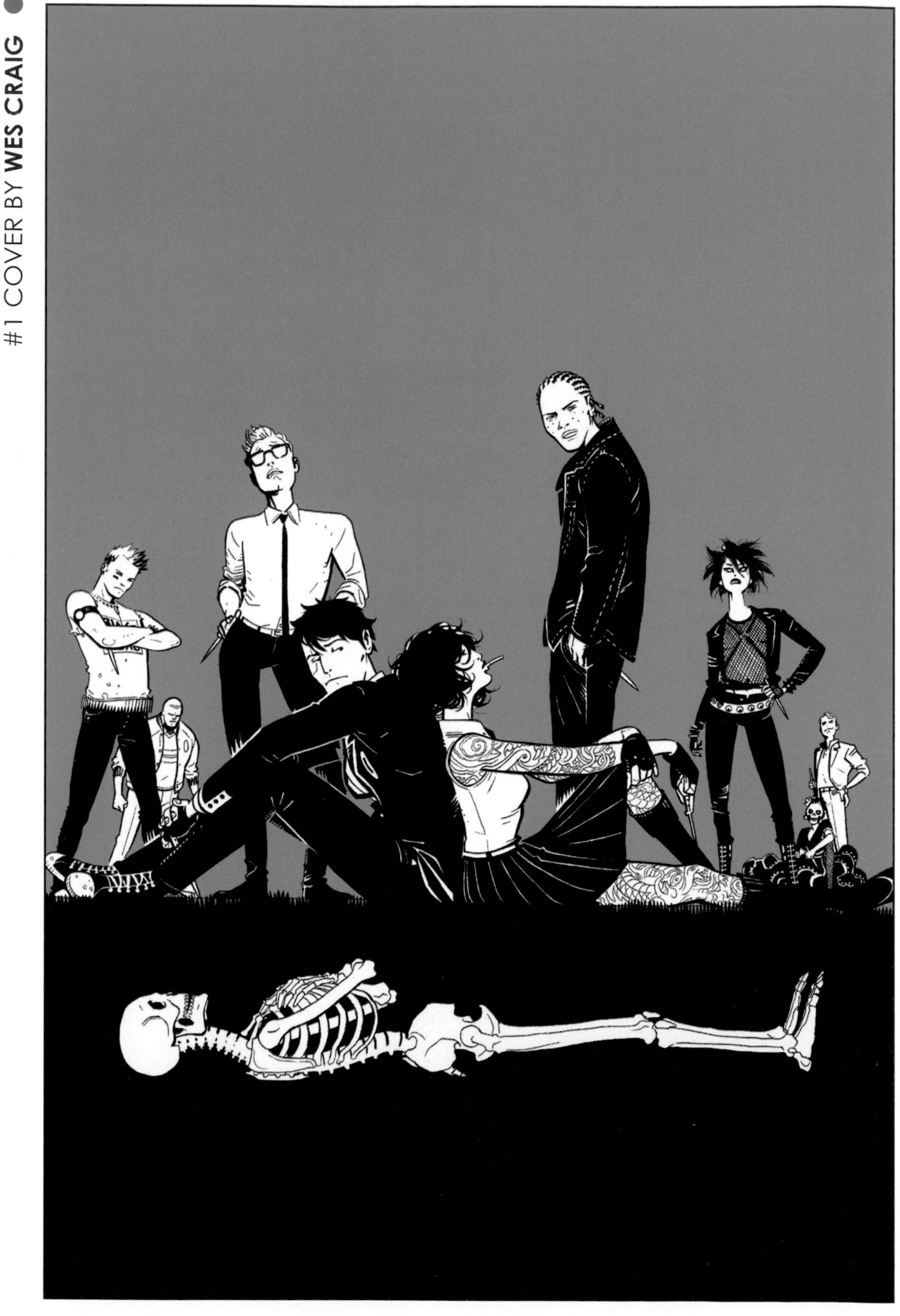

#1 COVER BY **WES CRAIG**

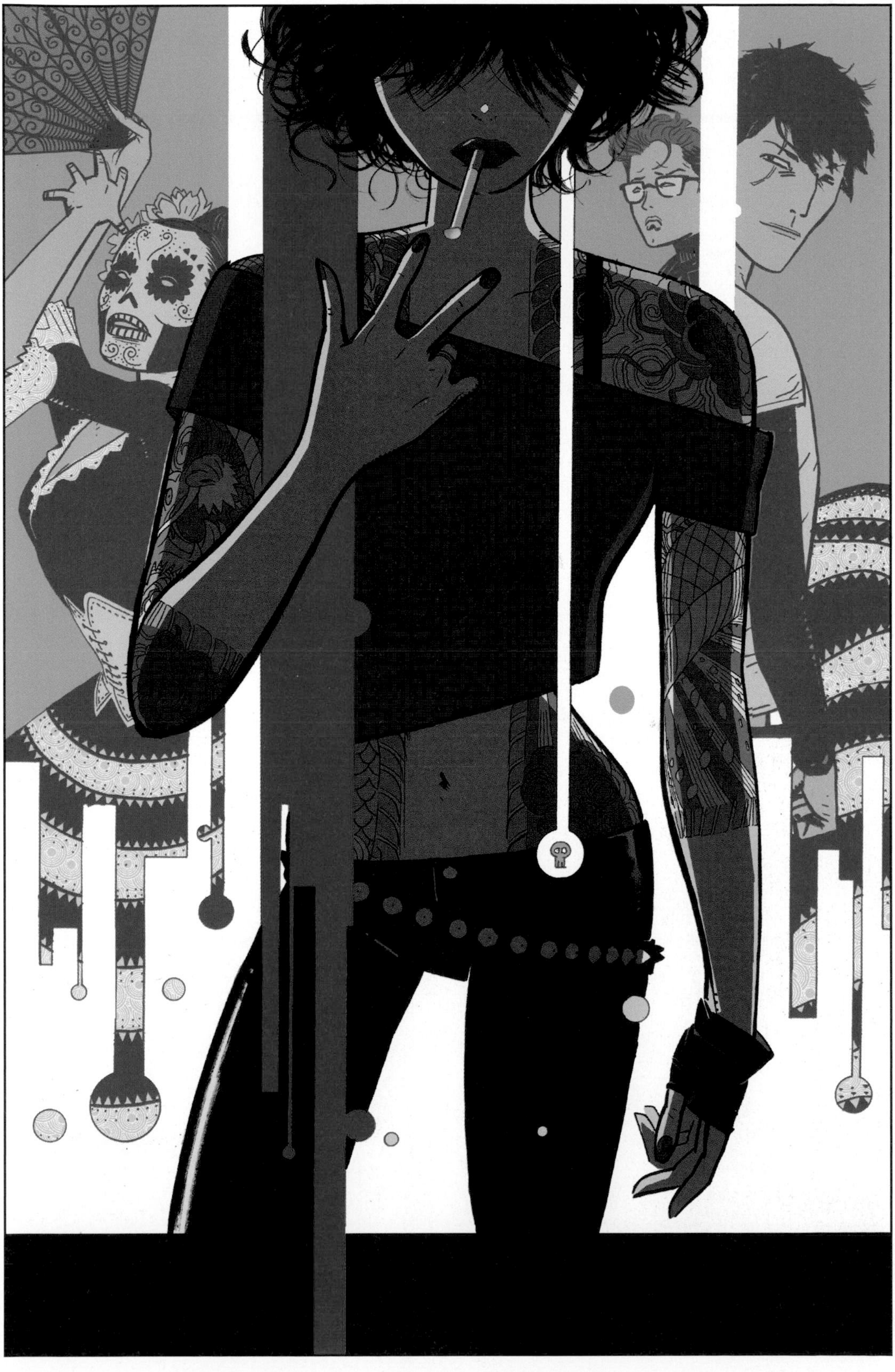

SDCC 2013 EXCLUSIVE POSTER / #1 VARIANT COVER BY **WES CRAIG**

#1 BEACH BALL COMICS VARIANT BY **ERIC CANETE & DEAN WHITE**

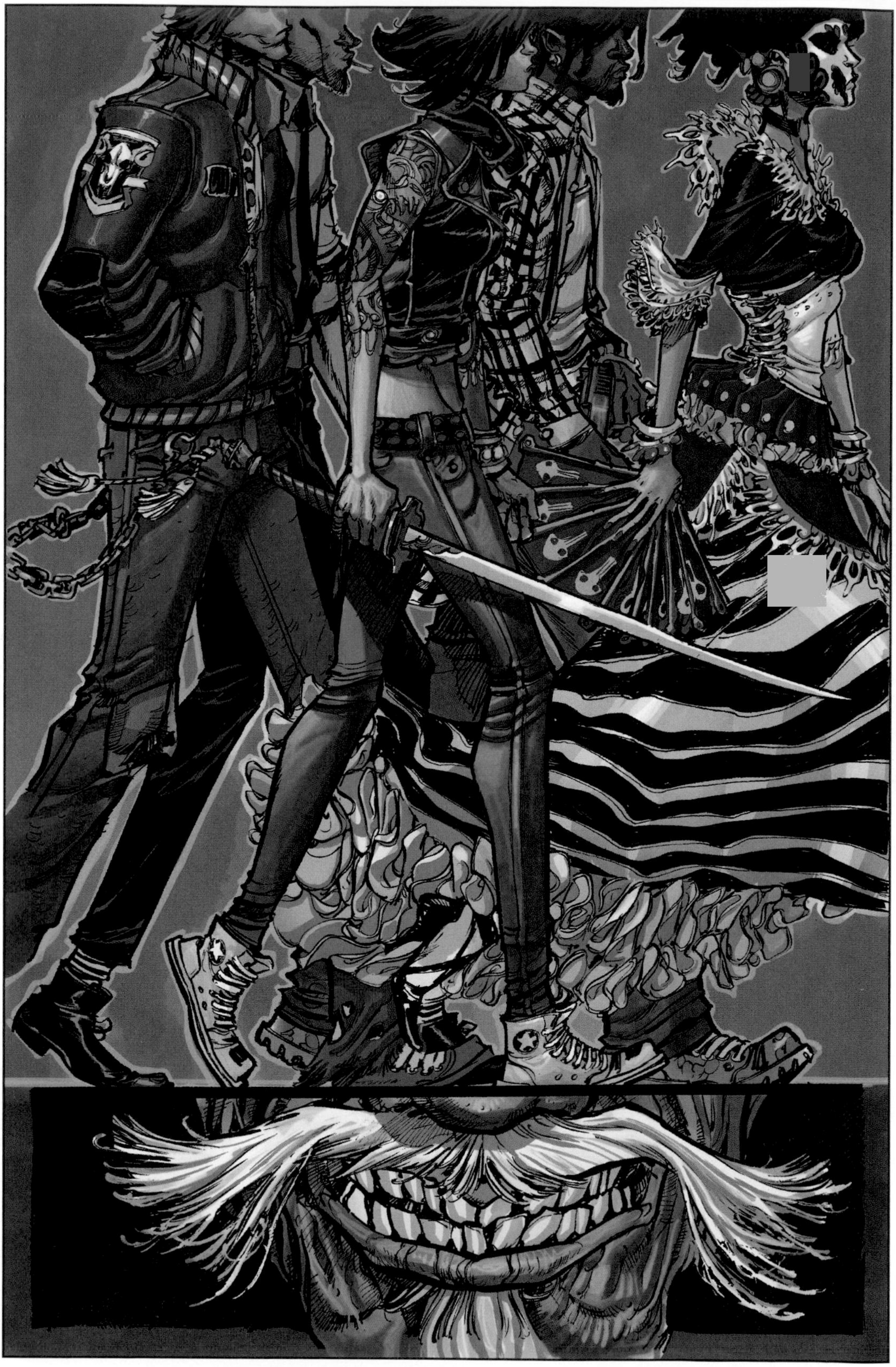

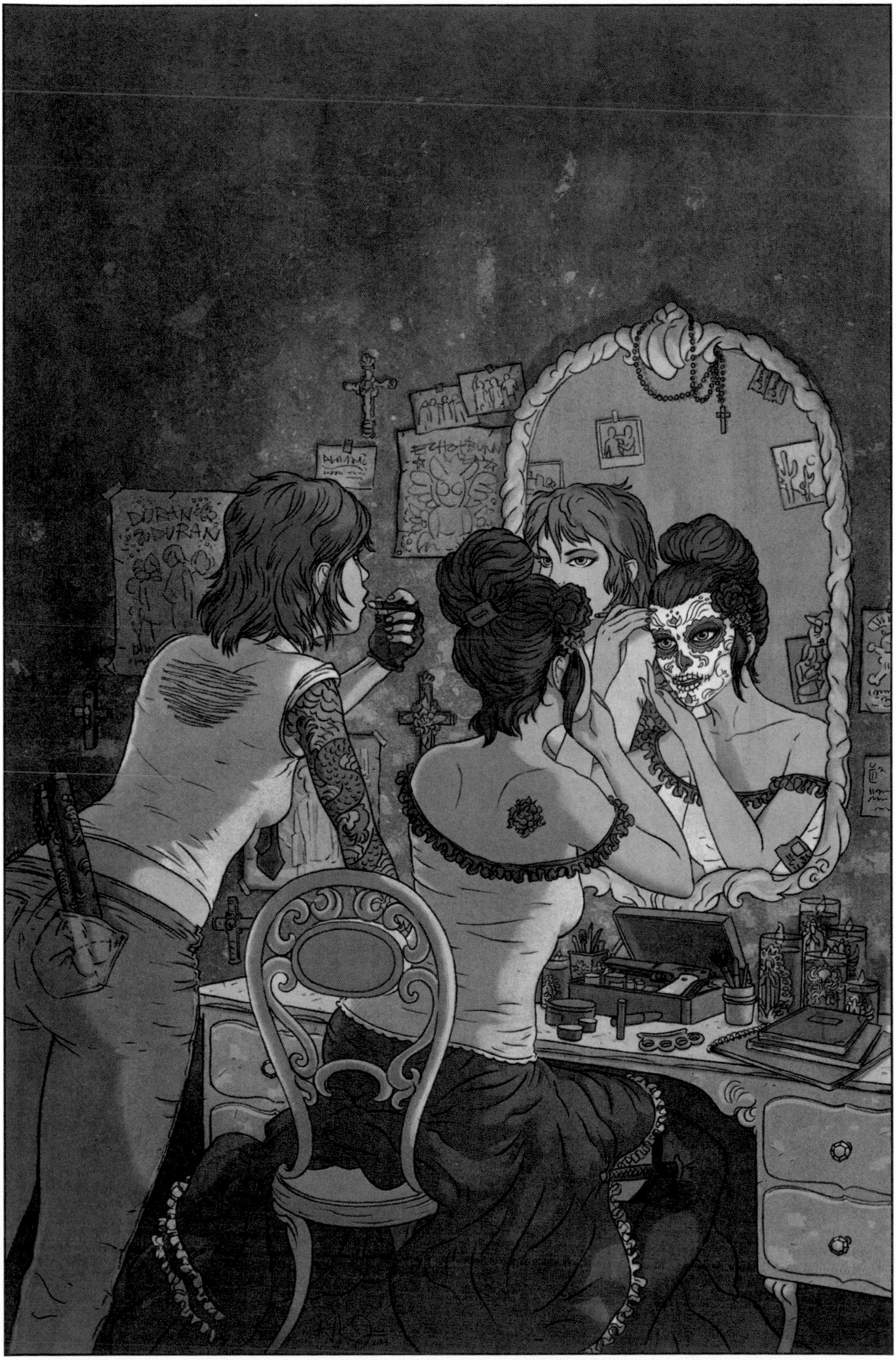
DURAN
DURAN

#1 THIRD EYE COMICS VARIANT BY **HARPER JATEN**

#1 EH! VARIANT BY **FAREL DALRYMPLE**

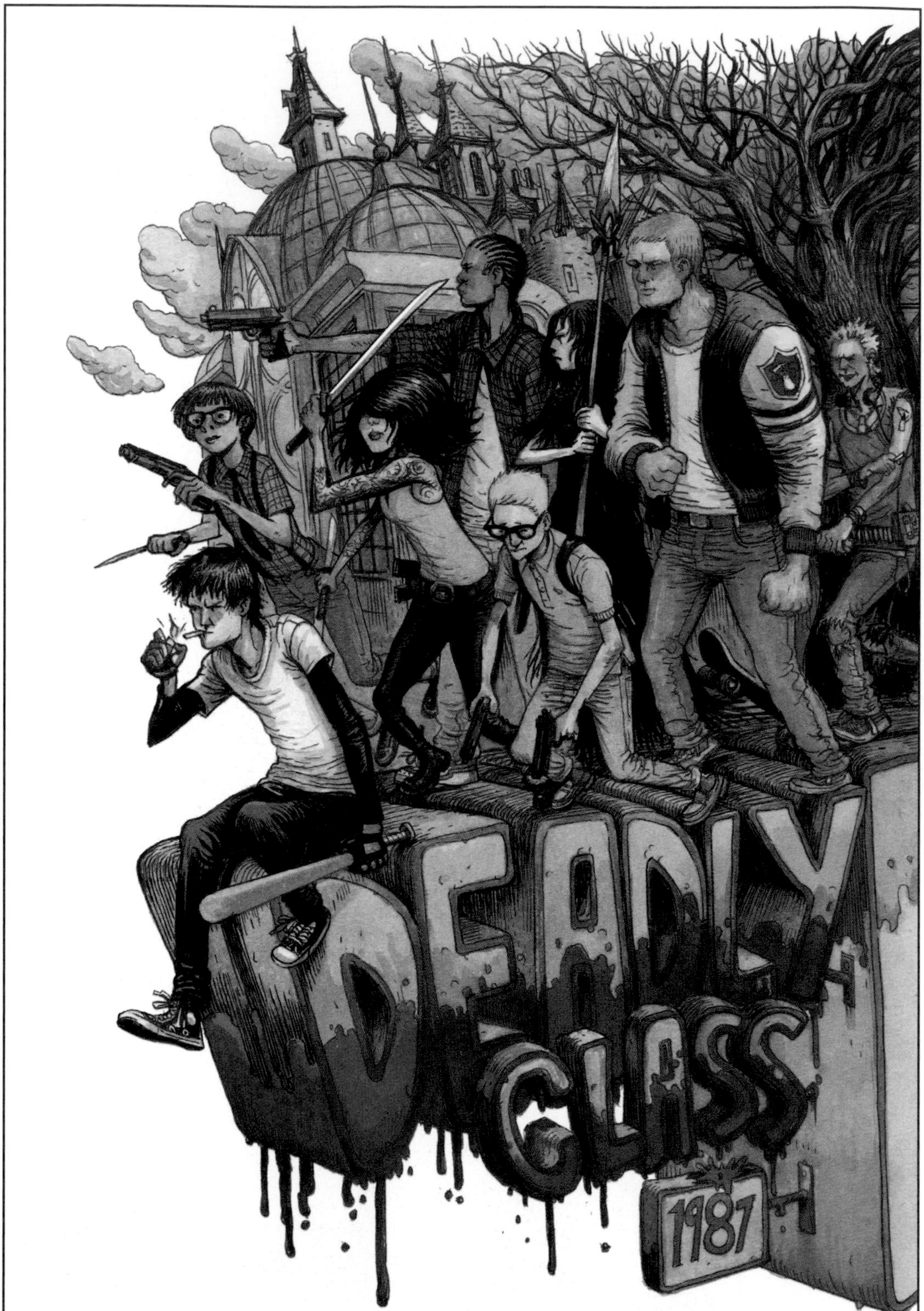
DEADLY
CLASS
1987

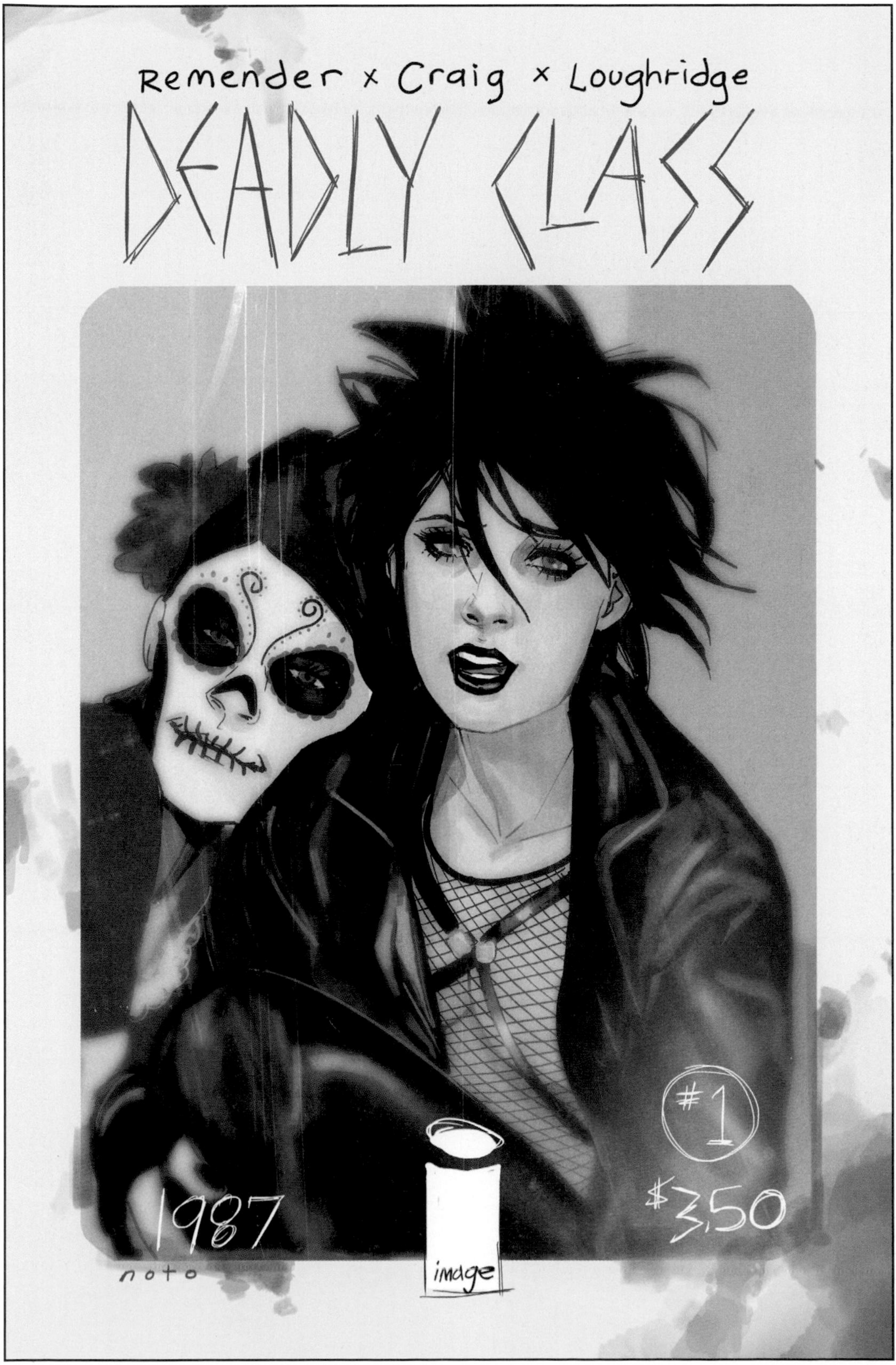
Remender x Craig x Loughridge
DEADLY CLASS
#1
$3,50
1987
noto
image

#1 FORBIDDEN PLANET VARIANT BY **PHIL NOTO**

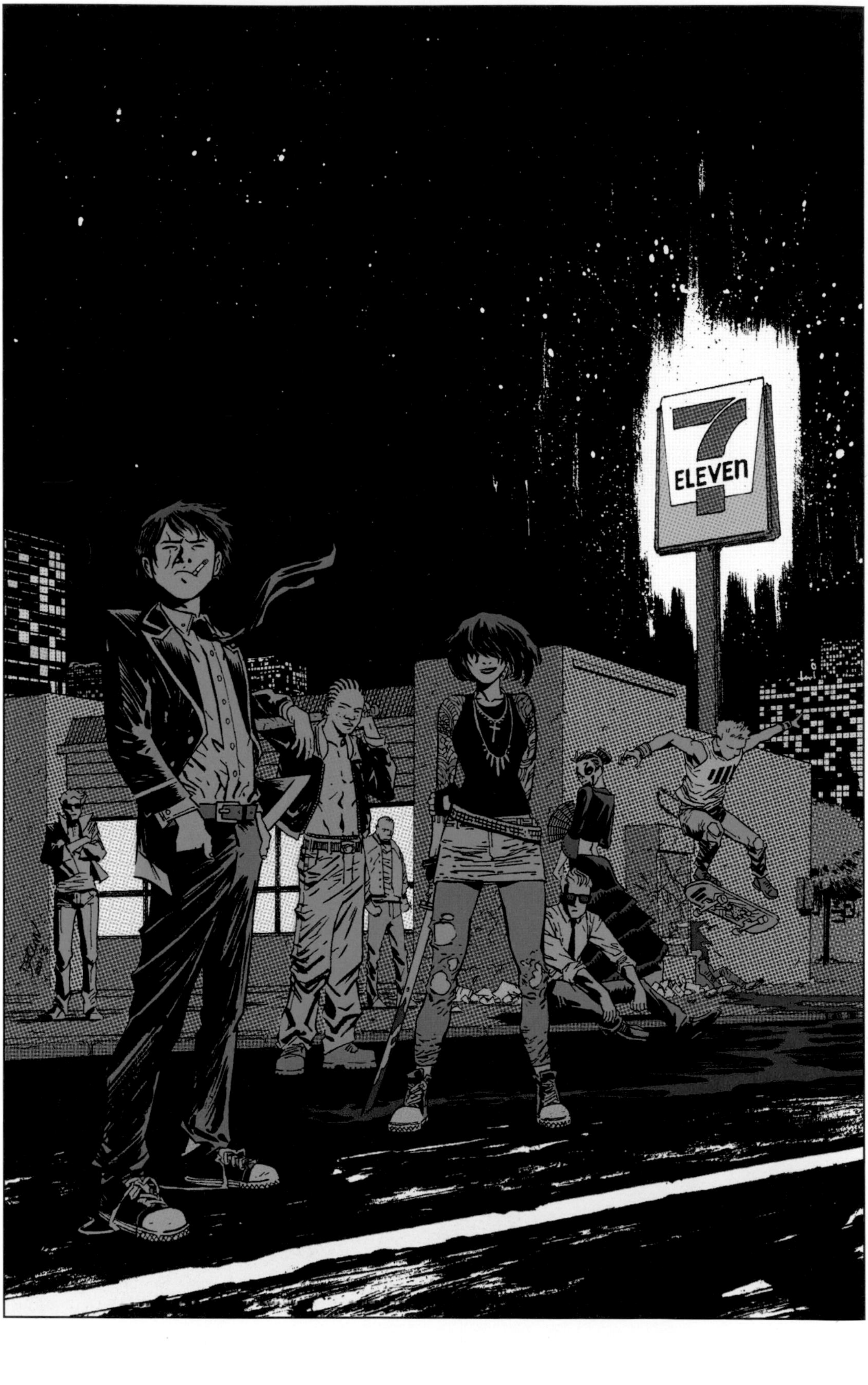
7
ELEVEN

#1 DCBS VARIANT BY **DECLAN SHALVEY & JORDIE BELLAIRE**

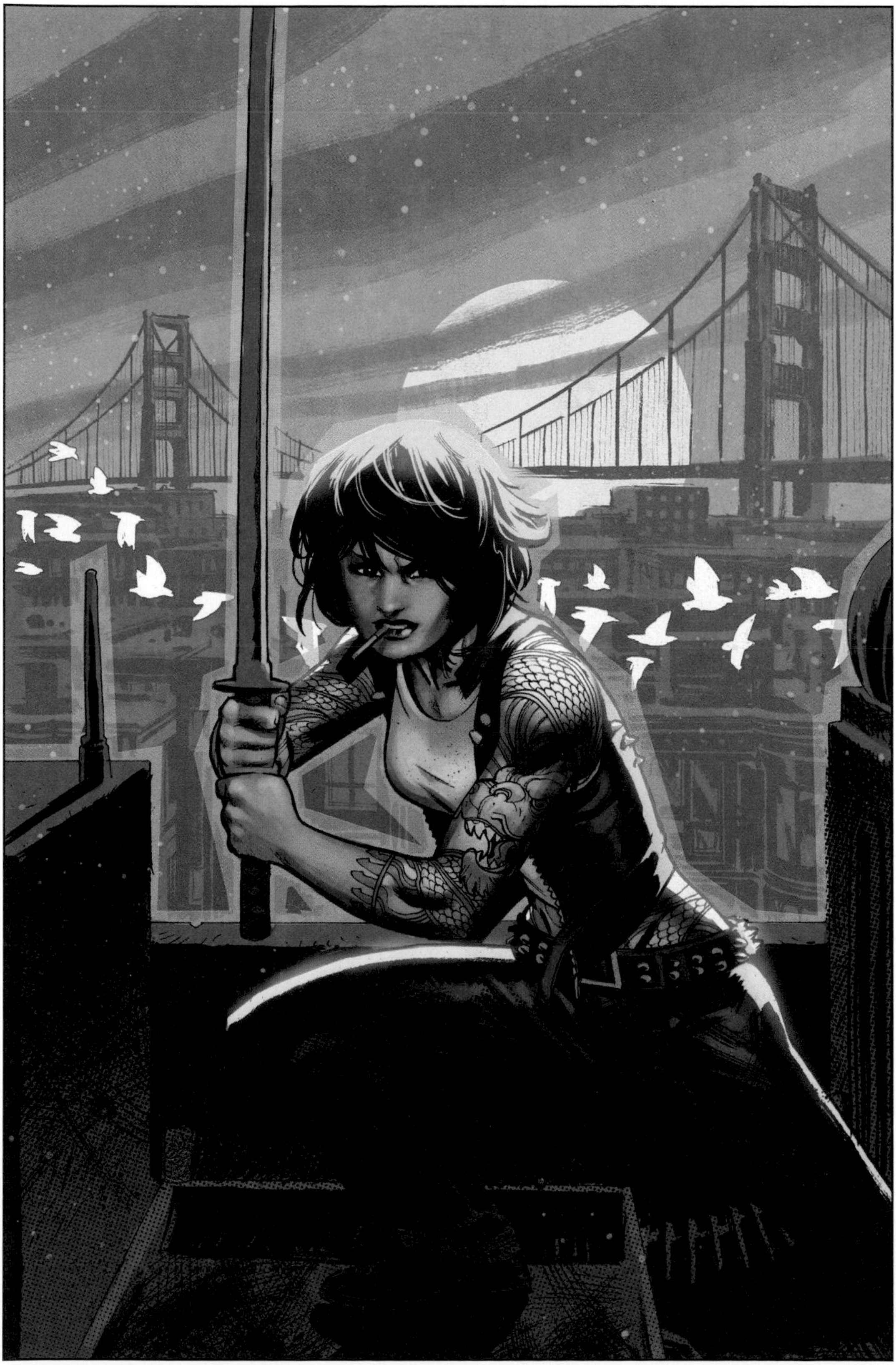

#1 CBLDF VARIANT BY **NIC KLEIN**

#2 COVER BY **WES CRAIG**

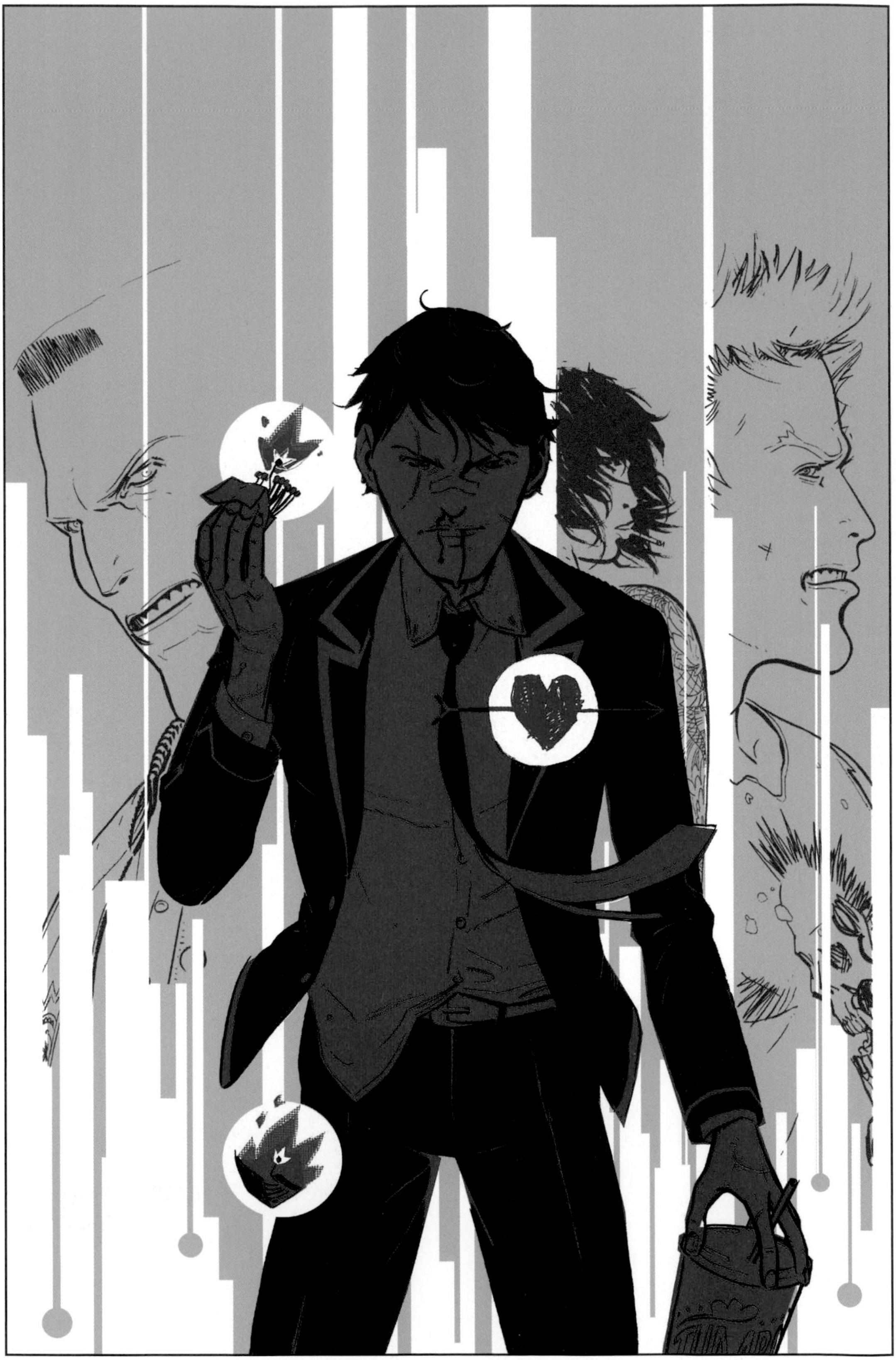

#3 COVER BY **WES CRAIG**

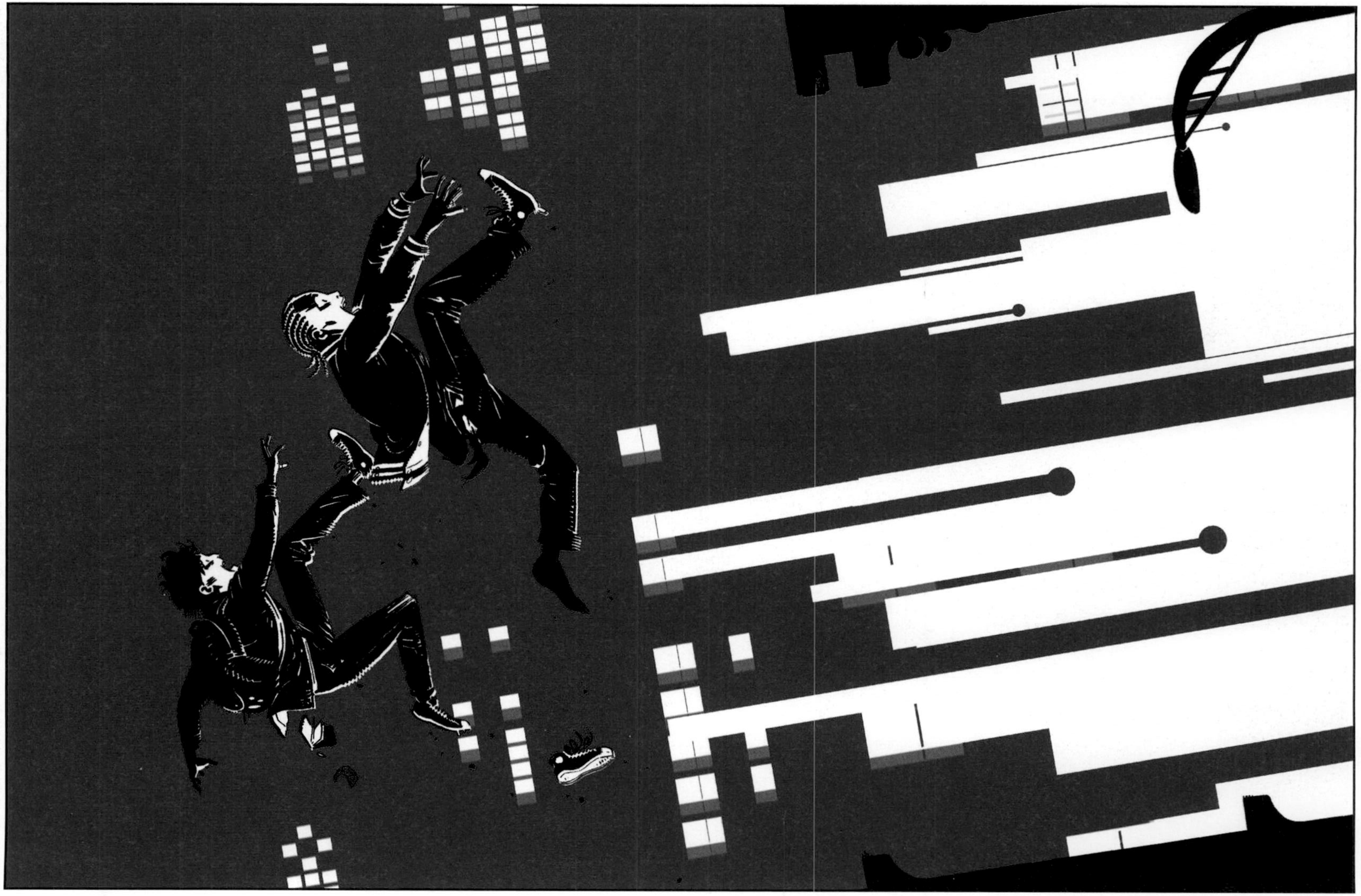

#3 SECOND PRINTING VARIANT BY **WES CRAIG**

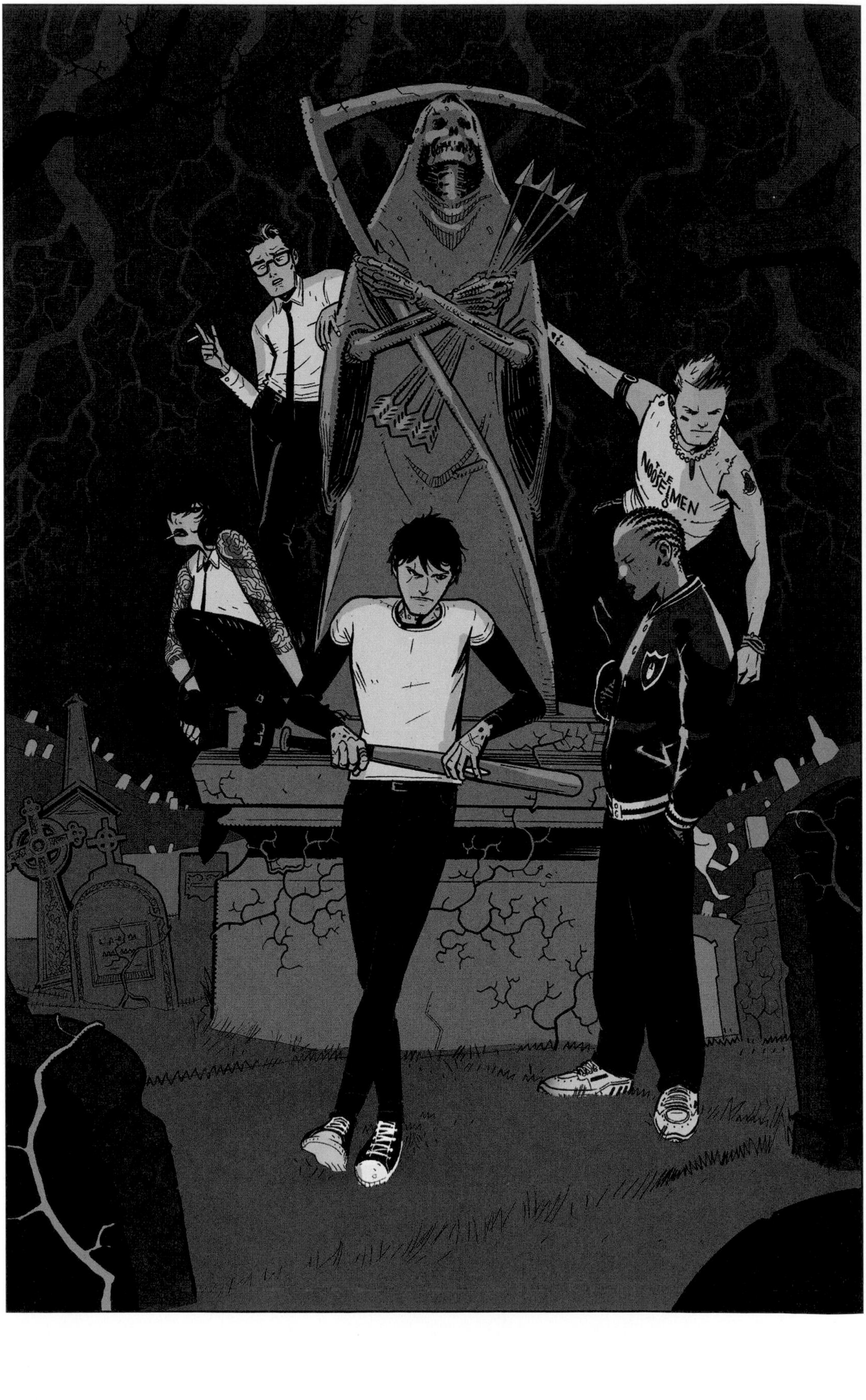
THE NOOSEMEN

#4 COVER BY **WES CRAIG**

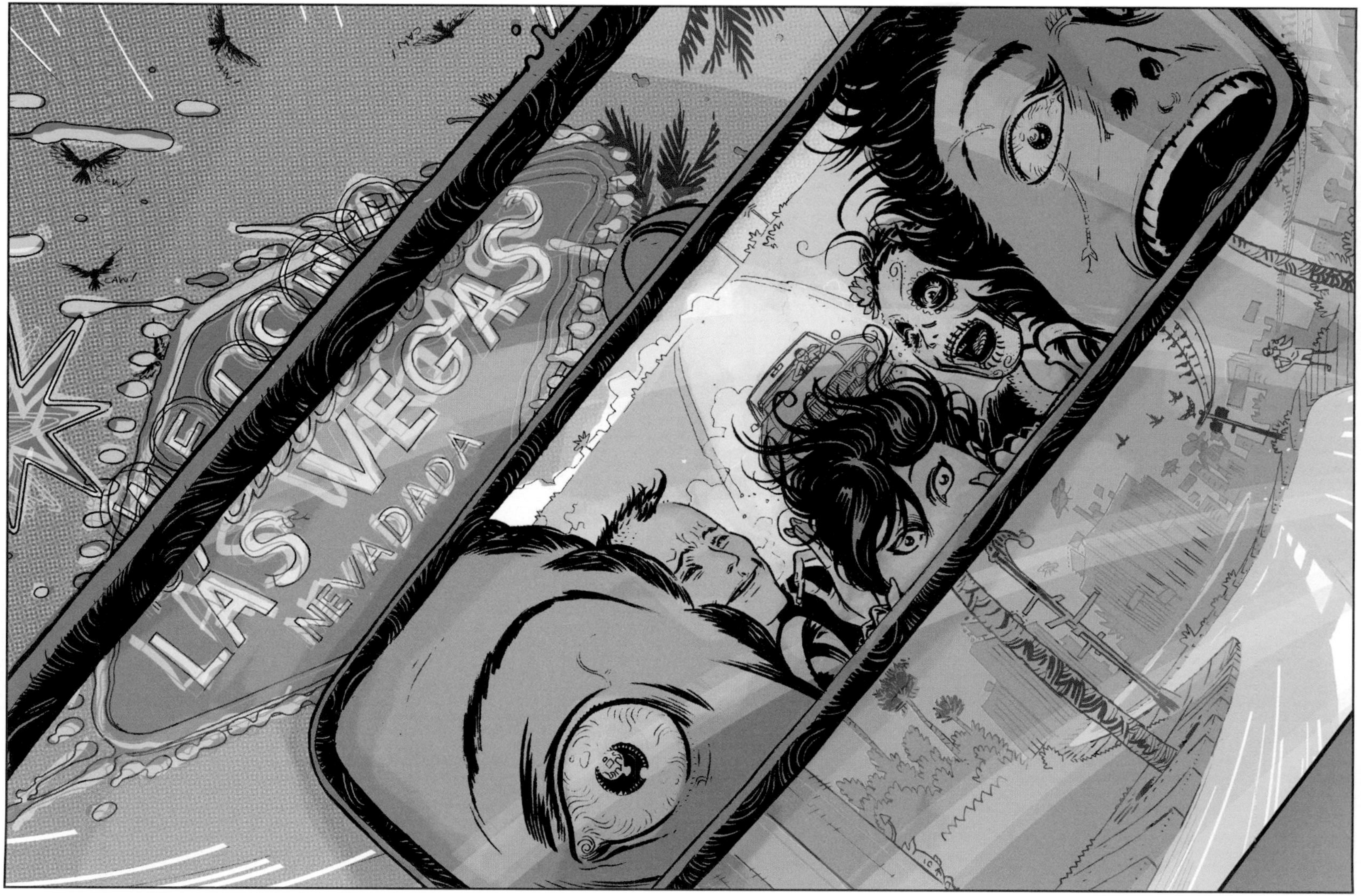
LAS VEGAS
NEVADADA
CAW!
CAW!

#5 COVER BY **WES CRAIG**

HEEHE
HEE HEE HEE
OW
QUACK

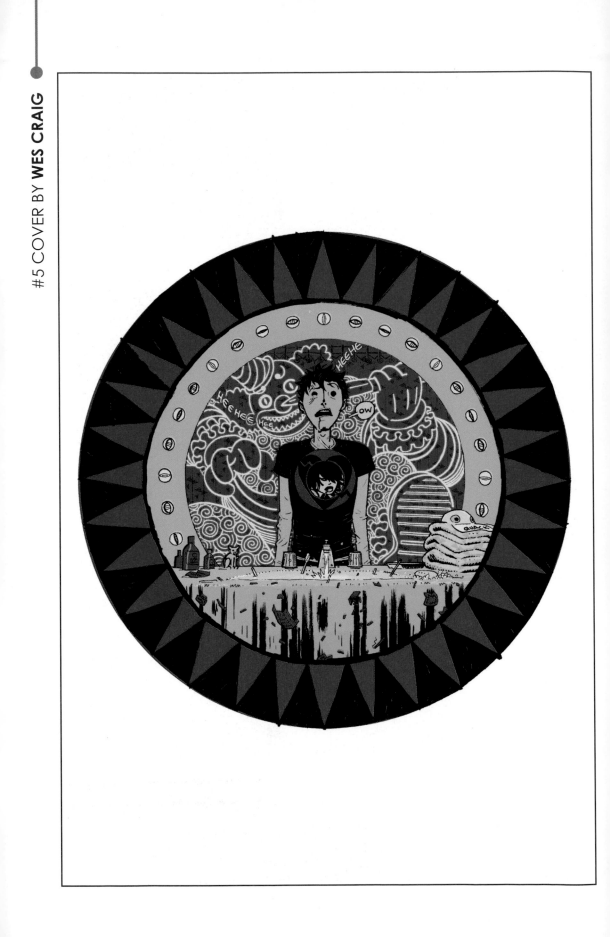

#6 COVER BY **WES CRAIG**

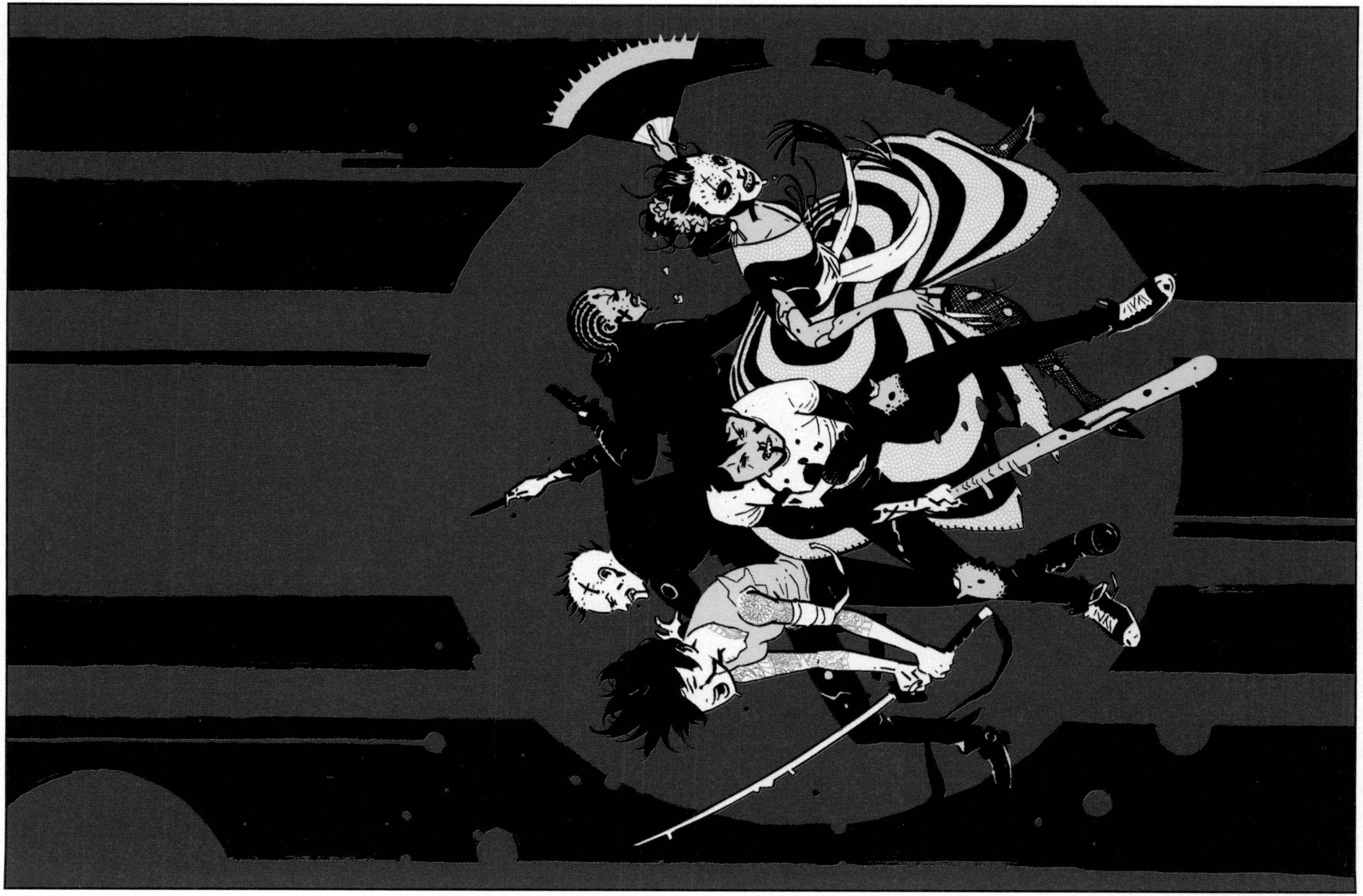

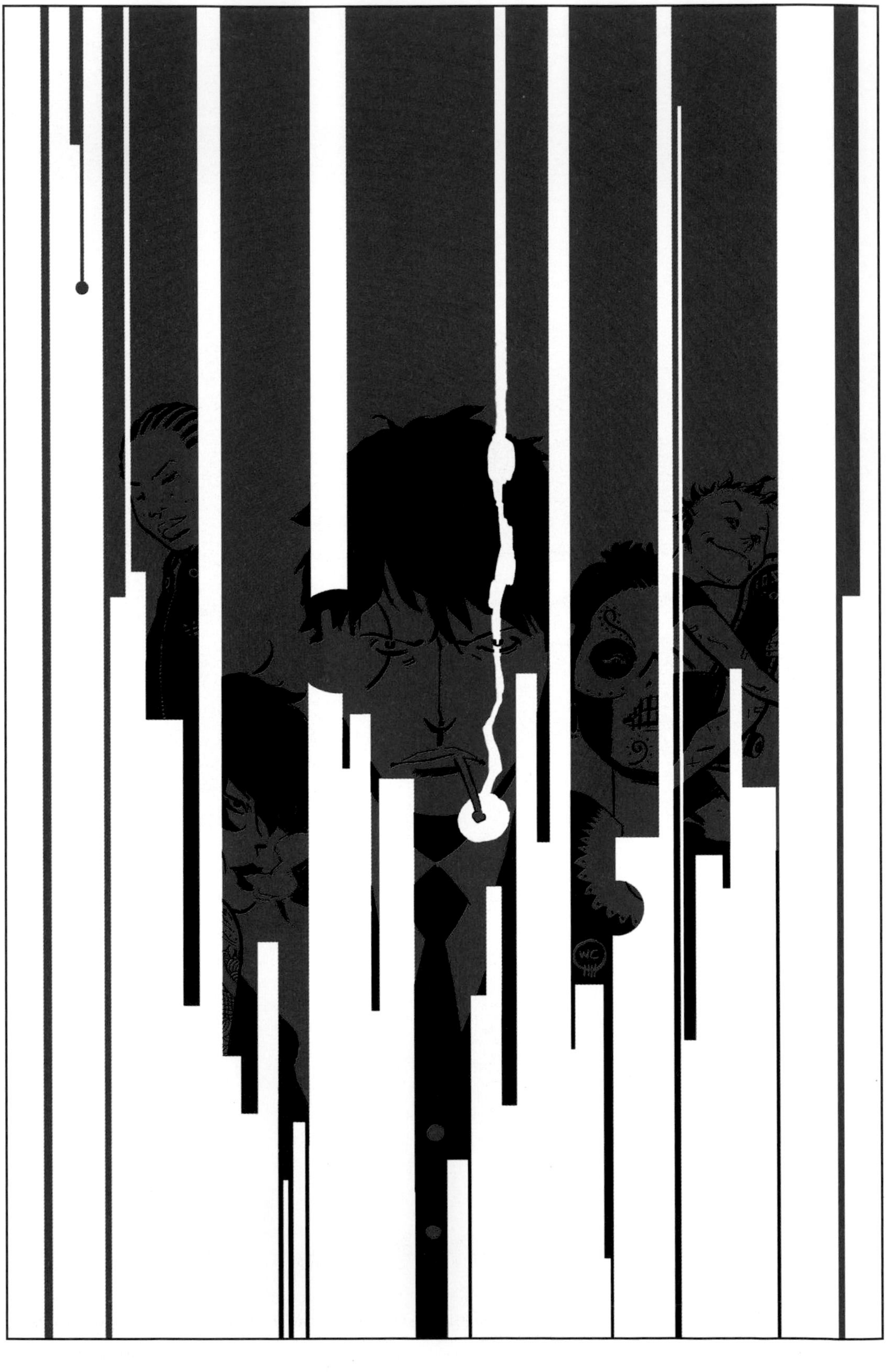

SDCC 2014 EXCLUSIVE HARDCOVER ART BY **WES CRAIG**

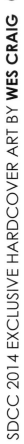

IMAGE COMICS, INC.

Robert Kirkman • Chief Operating Officer
Erik Larsen • Chief Financial Officer
Todd McFarlane • President
Marc Silvestri • Chief Executive Officer
Jim Valentino • Vice-President
Eric Stephenson • Publisher
Corey Murphy • Director of Sales
Jeremy Sullivan • Director of Digital Sales
Kat Salazar • Director of PR & Marketing
Emily Miller • Director of Operations
Branwyn Bigglestone • Senior Accounts Manager
Sarah Mello • Accounts Manager
Drew Gill • Art Director
Jonathan Chan • Production Manager
Meredith Wallace • Print Manager
Randy Okamura • Marketing Production Designer
David Brothers • Content Manager
Addison Duke • Production Artist
Vincent Kukua • Production Artist
Sasha Head • Production Artist
Tricia Ramos • Production Artist
Emilio Bautista • Sales Assistant
Jessica Ambriz • Administrative Assistant

imagecomics.com

3 2121 00072 6451

JEFF POWELL
collection design

DEADLY CLASS VOLUME 1: REAGAN YOUTH. Third Printing. July 2015. Published by Image Comics, Inc. Office of publication: 2001 Center Street, 6th Floor, Berkeley, CA 94704. Copyright © 2015 Rick Remender. All rights reserved. Originally published in single magazine form as DEADLY CLASS #1-6. DEADLY CLASS™ (including all prominent characters featured herein), its logo and all character likenesses are trademarks of Rick Remender, unless otherwise noted. Image Comics® and its logos are registered trademarks of Image Comics, Inc. No part of this publication may be reproduced or transmitted, in any form or by any means (except for short excerpts for review purposes) without the express written permission of Image Comics, Inc. All names, characters, events and locales in this publication are entirely fictional. Any resemblance to actual persons (living or dead), events or places, without satiric intent, is coincidental. **PRINTED IN THE U.S.A.** For information regarding the CPSIA on this printed material call: 203-595-3636 and provide reference # RICH – 628492. For international rights inquiries, contact: foreignlicensing@imagecomics.com. ISBN 978-1-63215-003-5

EST 1637

IN VITAM MORTEM

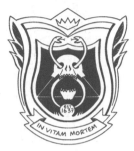